Praise for C. Hope Clark

C. Hope Clark's books have been honored as winners of the Epic Award, Silver Falchion Award, and the Daphne du Maurier Award.

Murder on Edisto selected as a Route 1 Read by the South Carolina Center for the Book!

"Carolina Slade is a smart, fun character. . . ."
—Lynn Simmons, NetGalley Reviewer on *Lowcountry Bribe*

"Award-winning writer C. Hope Clark delivers another one-two punch of intrigue with *Edisto Stranger*. . . . Clark really knows how to hook her readers with a fantastic story and characters that jump off the page with abandon. Un-put-downable from the get-go."
—Rachel Gladston, All Booked Up Reviews

"Her beloved protagonist, Callie, continues to delight readers as a strong, savvy, and a wee-bit-snarky police chief."
—Julie Cantrell, *New York Times* and *USA Today* bestselling author on *Dying on Edisto*

The Novels of C. Hope Clark

The Carolina Slade Mysteries

Lowcountry Bribe

Tidewater Murder

Palmetto Poison

Newberry Sin

Salkehatchie Secret

The Edisto Island Mysteries

Murder on Edisto

Edisto Jinx

Echoes of Edisto

Edisto Stranger

Dying on Edisto

Edisto Tidings

Reunion on Edisto

Murdered in Craven

Book 1 of The Craven County Mysteries

by

C. Hope Clark

[signature: C. Hope Clark]

Bell Bridge Books

Bell Bridge Books
PO BOX 300921
Memphis, TN 38130
Print ISBN: 978-1-61026-169-2

Bell Bridge Books is an Imprint of BelleBooks, Inc.

We at BelleBooks enjoy hearing from readers.
Visit our websites
BelleBooks.com
BellBridgeBooks.com
ImaJinnBooks.com

10 9 8 7 6 5 4 3 2 1

Cover design: Debra Dixon
Interior design: Hank Smith
Photo/Art credits: C. Hope Clark

:Lmsw:01:

Dedication

To Ron Whitten, who I believe loves my characters almost as much as I do, and taught me how much audio books matter.

Chapter 1

LATE. SHE NEVER did late.

Quinn slammed her truck door and trotted across the gravel lot, the condition of her work boots forgotten until she reached the entrance and noticed the crap. Brown clumps of it, too, peeking out around the edges of her soles.

Rubbing her feet across pine straw beside the cement landing of the bar, she gave up after scraping off most of it. She ran hands over the red mess of hair she hadn't had time to tame back at the farm. Taking two clips out that she had shoved into her pocket from the Ford's cup holder, she blew the hay dust off them and did a second once-over of the parking lot as she laid her hair flat and out of her face.

Parked two widths away from the nearest vehicle, a champagne-colored BMW shouted its presence, as did the mid-to-late-forties man waiting behind the steering wheel. No doubt her client's driver, because nobody in her county had money to flaunt like that.

She took a breath and put on her interview face.

Once inside, her eyes had to adjust from the blue-sky sun to the dark-paneled interior of Jackson Hole. The bar functioned as a hometown diner midday, when the owner's infamous cayenne fried chicken aroma filled the air. Ringing an order, Lenore Jackson looked up from her prepping behind the counter and snapped a tiny nod to her right, to the back corner where the kitchen door opened and closed, hiding the last booth. Quinn's table of choice.

The meet was for eleven thirty. It was ten past that. Quinn usually arrived early to watch her clients come in. One could tell a lot about a person by how they approached a private investigator, usually crossing into a world they had no clue about . . . were scared to death of . . . or more rarely, felt they could leverage for their own personal gain.

She'd had one of the latter types in her early days, and it was the only one she ever intended to have. The guy she'd been hired to run down got pummeled by her client over a girl. Left the poor guy looking nothing like his driver's license picture . . . permanently.

The current potential client presented as the age noted in Quinn's research—thirty. Birthday last month. Tinted glasses, slacks, and sharp-as-hell boots. Leather jacket. Blond hair with a cut that appeared just unruly enough to seem natural and probably cost a hundred dollars paid to a fancy stylist. She was nursing a coffee.

A jet-black German shepherd lay at her feet, head up, blending into the dark floor and shadows. Lenore didn't let animals in her place. Service dog? Guard dog? None of that had come out in the background check.

As Quinn approached, the lady half rose, held out her hand, and smiled. "Hey, Catherine Renault. You must be Quinn Sterling."

Quinn took the offered hand. A moderate shake, neither inhibited nor assertive. "Yes. Sorry I'm late. Emergency."

With sufficient dismay, Catherine sat. "Gracious, I hope nothing serious."

The dog watched. Eighty-five pounds of patience, especially with food pouring out of the kitchen.

Quinn turned her full attention from the dog to the woman. "A scare, but all's fine. Thanks for the concern." She chose not to explain the details of a llama's difficult birth and the reason for the small blood spatter she just noticed on her right jean leg.

Most folks envisioned a PI as only a PI, like on TV. When not on cases, they holed up drinking in a seedy apartment on the sleazy side of town or wore out the same stool in their friend's bar, commiserating over a dark discretion. Paying penance for the rest of their lives. Living for investigations because they had nothing else to live for. Or every-thing to atone for.

But with twenty-seven hundred acres to her name on the south end of Craven County, Quinn was happy to miss the stereotype by a mile. She was, to quote the bio last reported by a local paper, "a thirty-four-year-old heiress of a working pecan farm dating back to a 1709 British land grant to her ancestors." In other words, she was the last heir of the oldest family in the oldest county in the state of South Carolina. The Sterling Banks Plantation was bordered by the Edisto River on one side and the Ashepoo River to the southwest.

Definitely not the stereotypical PI.

Not to say she didn't have a past with assorted regrets.

Quinn began the meet. Breaking bread usually made people relax and show more of their hand. "You want something to eat? I'm sure you caught a whiff of Ms. Lenore's chicken. My regular is a double side of the okra and a piece of cornbread." She waved at Lenore who held up a finger that she'd be there in a moment.

"Um, no thanks." Catherine gripped her cup. "Coffee's fine."

Hmm, no more smile. Her problem apparently back to the front of her mind.

Lenore appeared, placed iced tea in front of Quinn then wiped her hands on a deep-red apron. "Okra?"

"See?" Quinn said, tipping her chin at their waitress. "Yes'm. Just one helping."

"You been working outside?" Lenore asked.

Quinn touched her hair, then her t-shirt, and pulled her denim jacket closer in front to cover any stains. "Why?"

"Just means you need two helpings, is all," she said. "It's spring. Guessing you're dropping babies on Sterling Banks."

"You talked me into it."

The client's interest piqued. "Babies?"

"The family farm." Quinn hesitated letting folks know she owned a plantation. Like being born into a legacy made her less of an investigator because she wasn't broke and desperate for money.

Lenore left with her all-knowing grin and hollered hello at two middle-aged guys in work khakis who'd just come in. She motioned them to sit at a table conveniently distant from the booth. Lenore was Quinn's unofficial personal assistant and had known her from the time she'd skinned her first knee.

Relaxing in hopes of Catherine doing the same, Quinn took out a small notepad already with two pages of scribble. Recorders came later, when a case was in full throttle. Right now, this was about Miss Renault proving herself to the PI as much as the PI proving herself to the client.

"Is your daddy Ronald Renault, stockbroker with an office on Broad Street in Charleston?" The family had multi-generational roots in the Holy City.

A big sigh. "Yes. That's me."

Daddy's address said enough, but Quinn knew of him. He was loaded.

A glass fell, and Catherine turned, light catching the tanzanite necklace that, along with the three rings on her hands, could cost as much as the Beemer outside. Not wise to flaunt such wealth, but then she came with a driver/bodyguard and a beast of a dog.

Since Daddy could afford the biggest, baddest investigative firm in the state, baby girl wanted to keep something on the down low coming to Quinn. And Catherine'd had to ask around to find Quinn, because she didn't advertise.

The dog had lowered his head. Only his eyes moved, working the room.

"Now," Quinn said, moving her tea aside. "What's this all about?"

Catherine's eyes fell. Some embarrassment, maybe. "My partner is missing."

Quinn waited. Silence worked wonders with people afraid to talk. They filled in the emptiness with words . . . and more information than they originally planned to give.

Catherine took little time to spill more. "We entered into this . . . business arrangement."

Quinn waited.

"He was to meet potential investors in Savannah."

Here we go.

"And he's missing," she said, strong emphasis on the last word. "I need you to find him. And I know how it sounds," she threw in.

Quinn tried to make eye contact again. "What do you mean when you say *missing?*"

Catherine looked up, but Quinn saw no tears. "It means he hasn't

4

returned my calls for three weeks, and I haven't seen him in a month. He never came home from Savannah."

Home. "Are you living together?"

A tiny flinch. "Yes. He moved into my place two months ago. He's quite intelligent and has an idea for a series of phone apps that's brilliant. He wanted to speak to Daddy about the concept, but I told him no. My father would steal an idea like that."

Looked funny for a rich woman to snap fingers.

"Did you have him checked out before you . . . got involved?" Rich people did that.

"Of course." She pushed her hair back, and life returned to her voice. "He established two other apps on his own and did well. Just didn't have the financial backing to take him where he could be."

Quinn pretended to scribble. "How did you meet him?"

"We ran into each other in Marion Square. Downtown Charleston?"

"I'm familiar," Quinn said. "You frequently stroll alone like that?"

"I had Nero," she said, lowering a hand to touch the dog's head that had risen at the sound of his name. "And my driver, of course. I'm sure you saw him in the car."

Quinn nodded. "What's your boyfriend's name?"

The girl sat back. "I'd rather not say yet. Just call him Mitchell for now."

Quinn sat back as well. "Why are you here then if not for me to find *Mitchell?*"

"I'm checking you out."

"You did that before you came here. I might be somewhat of a recluse, but I'm not a secret. Like you, I can't hide from my name either."

"I'm *feeling* you out, then."

"Likewise, Miss Renault. We have to trust each other for this to work."

Catherine's hand still lay on the dog, rubbing as if for reassurance.

Quinn closed her notepad and tucked it away. "Sounds like a situation for the police anyway. I don't take every case, and you don't trust easily. Doesn't feel like a fit."

Lenore surely read the body language, because she tactfully appeared with the okra, piled hot and crispy in a big soup bowl. She reached over Quinn, snared the hot sauce from a caddie, and set it next to the bowl. "Made that new batch just for you, honey." She turned to the guest. "Now, sure I can't get you something?"

Catherine shook her head, giving a tight smile in afterthought. Lenore robotically refilled the coffee before leaving, Catherine's hands backing away suddenly from the cup.

Popping an okra morsel in her mouth, Quinn watched the mental tug-of-war playing out across the table. She ate another morsel. Then another. She'd let this play out until the okra was gone, then she was done. Jule needed her back at the farm.

Quinn wiped her mouth. "You're avoiding your daddy, aren't sure of Mitchell, and seem quite reluctant to talk. This guy screwed you over, and you don't know how to face it. Cut your losses and move on, I say. He take much money?"

"Yes," she said. "But I've already changed my bank accounts, stopped the two credit cards, and cut off funds, because I was worried someone had taken advantage of *him*."

In love with serious blinders on.

Nope. This was not a case to accept.

"He loves me for who I am," Catherine said, pleading. "That's why I'm sure he's hurt, kidnapped, maybe even dead. He wouldn't take advantage. That's not who Mickey is."

Quinn caught the slip into the familiar. "Sounds like you really trust the guy."

Her okra was half gone.

Catherine's chest pressed against the table. "I do. To the core of my being, Ms. Sterling."

Silence drifted into a sniffle from across the table. Might be real.

Jackson Hole was almost full, lunch at its peak, when a uniform walked in. "Hey, Ty," echoed across the room from assorted tables.

Sheriff's deputies wore khakis in Craven County. Too hot to wear black, navy, or dark brown in the muggy South Carolina Lowcountry, with Jacksonboro only forty-five minutes from Edisto Beach by road, twenty by boat on the Edisto River, with decent horsepower. Being April, the department had already shifted to short sleeves.

Quinn nodded at the tall, dark-skinned, broad-shouldered uniform. He tipped his head in return and bellied up to the bar. Unasked, Lenore poured him a Coke and disappeared into the kitchen but not before drawing his head down and kissing her son on the brow. Quinn smiled warmly at what was Lenore's standard greeting for Tyson Jackson and recalled how the gesture used to humiliate the hell out of him.

Now the humiliation was countywide. Jackson Hole sat a half-mile off the main highway, but close enough for every kind of person to make the drive. Lenore had quite the blended crowd in both occupation, social standing, and racial mix.

Quinn popped another okra in her mouth. Only five bites to go.

"Catherine," she finally said, aiming to wrap up this meeting. "What's your gut telling you? Not your heart . . . your gut. Did Mitchell scam you, or is something really wrong? If you think he's been hurt, then why? Someone have a grudge with him? With you? I take it there's been no ransom demand."

"No, nobody's called, emailed, nothing." Catherine seemed to ponder for a second. "And nobody's mad at either of us that I'm aware of. I mean . . . it's phone apps."

Money was money, whether phone apps or gold ingots. It turned some people ugly. Quinn studied her for a long second, seeing this chat as anything but transparent. "Would your dad take steps against your choice of beau?"

A lot of head shaking. "No, no, no. Daddy doesn't even know about Mitchell."

"Or that's what he wants you to think."

More head shaking. "Nope. Don't believe Daddy's involved. He has too much going on in his own life."

All the answers too cut and dried.

"You've cut Mitchell totally off?"

"Yes," she said, appearing to hang on to what Quinn might say next.

"Let's say he did scam you."

Catherine wasn't happy with that. "I don't think—"

"Just a sec." Quinn held up a palm. "Let's just pretend he did. What're you wanting to do about it?"

The *what-if* drew Catherine up short but not for long. "If he did, I don't care. I'm more concerned about his health . . . his life. I just need to know."

"This might not be what you want to hear," Quinn said, "but it might be best to just cut this puppy loose and see if he comes home when he gets hungry."

"Wait." Catherine reached out then returned to her arms crossed. "I already hired one PI. He disappeared, too."

Now Quinn drew up short. "A private investigator?"

"Yes, he took five thousand dollars with him."

Not common, but she guessed it could happen. "Well, he's easy enough to find if he's licensed. You saw his license, right?"

"No!" Holding her hands up, movements clipped and flustered, Catherine's suave facade melted. And Nero came out from under the table. "I never considered myself that poor of a judge of character before, but I'm floundering here. I don't seem to be making the right decisions or thinking clearly. I can't tell who to trust. Do you blame me for second-guessing you?"

Quinn watched the dog, who had his big black eyes trained on her. "Your pup seems a little disturbed," she said.

Catherine touched the animal, cooed to him once, and he eased back into place, his ears still piqued. "Sorry," she said and took a breath.

The PI had probably bailed, no doubt for many of the reasons Quinn could relate to now, assuming he was even a PI. Assuming he even put in an hour's work before cashing the check.

And the boyfriend had probably taken advantage of her, one of the oldest stories in history.

Quinn eased out of the booth and reached into her back pocket. "There's my card."

The girl dropped hands to the table and felt, sliding both hands until one fumbled across the card.

Chagrined, Quinn sat back down. "I'm sorry. I wasn't certain you were blind."

"Wow," Catherine said, a twinge of anger deepening itself in her cheeks. "You must be an amazing investigator. Shouldn't the dog have been a giveaway?"

"I'm saying that you behave like a sighted person," Quinn said. "Damn, take the compliment. But you hid it, girlfriend. You offered to shake my hand first so I'd find you. Came in early, I bet, so you'd be seated before I arrived. Didn't eat. Tried to look intently at me when I spoke. And you trusted someone else to see if your PI guy was licensed. I found nothing saying you were blind. When did it happen?"

Catherine's voice lowered. "It was gradual, so it's not common knowledge," she said. "I still see shadows as long as there's light. Not like in here. Once it worsened, Mitchell was the first person who didn't treat me like I had a handicap."

Which made him an even lower-life con than before.

"Listen," Quinn said, rising for good this time. "Report the PI to SLED, the State Law Enforcement Division. They hold his license. The boyfriend will show up eventually. That or you don't need him. That's my best advice. No charge."

Catherine pulled out her phone and texted by feel, Quinn dying to peer over. She probably could sneak a peek, but suddenly, in that way of hers that made her appear fully sighted, Catherine looked up at Quinn, making the PI glad she hadn't sneaked that peek. "You won't take the case? It's not a matter of money."

"No, it's not," Quinn said. "I don't do this work for money . . . nor pity for you. I take a case only on its merits. Keep my card. Let me dwell on it." Her pat reply when a client couldn't take no for an answer.

Catherine ended their chat with a quiet, "Okay."

The driver entered the door. Quinn waved him over, shook his hand, and wished them a safe drive home. They left with only Nero's eyes looking back over his shoulder.

Catherine's trust had been hammered, but this sort of client could have you chasing your tail. Quinn wasn't up for the game.

She moved to a stool next to the uniform and snagged a french fry off his plate. "Got the county all safe and sound today, Deputy?"

"As always," Ty said. "Catch a case?"

"Nah," she said. "Simple boyfriend issue. Not my style."

Quinn aimed at another fry.

Lenore popped her on the sleeve in rebuke. "Girl," Lenore said, letting the word drag out. "Let that boy eat. How you stay skinny as a bean pole eating like you do?"

Ty answered for her. "Good, clean, God-fearing living, Momma." Then he sank teeth into a cheeseburger, the sandwich dwarfed in his big hands. "Isn't that right, Q?" he managed around that mouthful.

She laughed easily with him, their history going back to when they toddled around the Sterling barn, his daddy working for hers. When she'd lost her own mother as a child of eight, Quinn slid into Lenore's consoling arms easily. They were family.

She glanced back at the exit, as if still seeing Catherine. "You recognize Catherine Renault?"

"Heard of her," he mumbled, then swallowed. "Imagine Craven isn't her stomping ground much."

"Exactly. So why'd she hunt me down?"

His radio went off, and quickly he turned down the volume, holding still in order to hear. Then he threw down his napkin. "Damn. We got a suspicious death at the motel."

Quinn's pulse kicked in. "You serious?" Nothing like that happened in their county.

Ty leaped up, his mother swiftly shifting uneaten food into a go-box. "I'm assuming you're coming with, Q?" he asked, loud enough to turn heads.

"My truck'll be right behind you."

Boots skittering on parking lot gravel as she hauled herself to a stop, she hoisted herself into the pickup. That feeling . . . the fervent enthusiasm to play. Someone usually paid a dire price for such moments but damn if she didn't love them. Analyzing a scene, solving a puzzle, putting a wrong to right. Especially the latter. Nobody hated an unsolved case more than Quinn.

Ty's blue lights lit the way, spiking her adrenaline. It had been so damn long.

Murder didn't happen here, so likely natural causes. Sheriff Larry Sterling didn't allow such crime, or so her uncle proclaimed to anyone who'd listen about how well he did his job—the big-mouth son of a bitch. When you're the sheriff and can't solve your own brother's death, what damn good are you?

Fired from the FBI and unable to stomach working for her uncle, private investigations did little to satisfy Quinn's urges, but it was all she had. Some said she couldn't let loose of it.

One of those Sterling things.

Only those closest to her knew how broken she pretended not to be.

Chapter 2

QUINN RODE TY'S tail, his blue LEDs flashing, but she stopped before he did, going only as far as the front of the parking lot. She wasn't getting hemmed in. This type of thing could take hours, and while she'd stay as long as she could, she'd been shooed off enough times to know the drill.

She might not be official law enforcement, but she was a major employer in the county and had inherited generations of concern for the county's people. She had to know who the body was, assuming they weren't dealing with an outsider passing through.

Ty exited his vehicle and strode to the open door of room twelve, on the bottom floor where three other uniforms milled about outside awaiting the coroner and sheriff.

Craven County's population of nine thousand could support only one motel. The Jacksonian. Half the enterprises in the county had one of two names on them: Sterling or Jackson. People didn't stay at the motel unless Walterboro was filled up, twenty-five miles away.

There were forty rooms total on two floors. Half on one side and half on the other of a long red-brick retro building built in the sixties, when the interstate highway system was all the rage. With I-26 going all the way to Charleston, and I-95 down to Savannah, carrying families and business people smoother and faster, the landowner at the time had dreams of folks using SC Highway 17 to cut through from one to the other. Problem was folks *chose* one or the other, having little need to navigate between. Craven County, situated in a distant rural pocket of the state, went stagnant by the mid-seventies. Agriculture continued as its biggest economy, to include the Sterling Banks pecan orchard operation. That and a mattress plant near Parkers Ferry.

In a town too small to have its own police department, Jacksonboro relied upon Sheriff Larry Sterling and his staff of twenty-four deputies for law enforcement. Quinn stayed on his heels when she had half a chance. She'd call the first murder in three years one of those chances.

She didn't trust Uncle Larry.

Every four years since he'd been Quinn's age nobody dared run against him; therefore, he freelanced the law, with the only serious oversight of his performance having been loosely provided by his niece. Nobody whistle blew in this county.

Quinn moved slowly toward the scene, studying the area outside leading to the room first, a site already trampled on.

"Hey, Steve," she said to a deputy. Nodded at another named Harrison, the guy she'd shared drinks with one lonely evening after she'd not long returned to Craven. They met at Lenore's and took their private party to the farm, to the manor that had suddenly become way too big for just her. She thought they hit it off pretty well, until he got married the following weekend.

"How you boys doing?" she said.

Various greetings returned with nobody stopping her approach . . . especially Harrison.

She reached the threshold and peered in, hand instinctively over the bottom half of her face, the odor having commandeered the room. Based on the green-tinged complexions of one deputy inside, he fought to hold it together. The other held the curtain over his nose.

"Mike? If you're even thinking about puking, take it across the parking lot," she scolded. "Randy, how do you know those curtains don't hold forensic evidence?" Both men welcomed the opportunity to leave.

Accustomed to Quinn scolding deputies, Ty ignored them, oblivious to anything but the crime scene.

The entire force on duty had clustered here, but heaven help the poor soul who tried to take advantage of Sheriff Sterling's distraction and commit a crime elsewhere. They wouldn't get away with it long and would pay a higher price for the attempt.

Some of these deputies she'd drunk with since high school. Others

13

came to Craven because they needed a place to start ... or weren't qualified enough to clinch positions in bigger cities like Charleston where college degrees had become the norm. Most of the department was younger than her thirty-four years.

Start with the body and move out, Quinn told herself as she took in the room, putting on the gloves that Ty handed her.

Flat on his back, feet toward the door, the victim was tall. Over six foot. Forties, she guessed. Vaguely familiar but not in a local resident sort of way. No, more than vaguely. She knew him ... from where?

Dark beard. Thicker than the norm, in stark contrast to his bald head—as in completely shaved to either finish what genetics had already started or an attempt to play badass.

Her gut wrenched. *Jesus. Couldn't be.*

Pulling out her phone, she went to her voice mails. Victor Whitmarsh. He had left her a message day before yesterday in that smooth, self-assured tone of his she hadn't heard for, what ... three years? *Want to run something by you. Call me.* A pause, then ... *Would love to see you again.*

Familiar enough to have his name pop up when he called, but she hadn't gotten around to calling back. Hadn't been sure she wanted to revive that night of endless margaritas and slick sheets.

His death made her ponder the purpose of the call, though. In hindsight, couldn't have been purely social. Not after all this time.

A couple quarts of dark blood soaked the dated, paisley design in the carpet. The stain had dried but still looked spongy in spots. He wore an undershirt under an unbuttoned short-sleeved shirt, both now red, but she predicted his back looked worse. Worn loafers on his feet. Maybe fifteen pounds more on him than last time she saw him.

The bullet had traveled through the man before he fell, shattering the mirror in the dressing area of the dated bath.

"Q? You okay?"

"Yeah, I'm good," she said softly, remembering Vic with a thick head of hair and clean shaven ... laughing. She tossed the memories, or tried to, in exchange for thoughts on why he called. Professional or personal? Staring at the blood, so much blood, she guessed the former.

Vic, this isn't like you to get caught flat-footed.

She chose to wait to inform Ty she knew the body, wanting his take on the scene first.

Tyson Jackson gave her a long hard study then went back to taking in the body, the setting, eyes moving slowly over details. Having graduated from high school with Quinn, both leaped at the chance to chase bad guys under the tutelage of her uncle, to put their barefoot, childhood sleuthing to work.

However, after a year of working for Larry, doing what Graham Sterling called a farce, Graham ordered his daughter to attend college while Ty stayed on with the department. Quinn was as loyal to her father as Ty was to his mother, though at the time she considered her father too stubborn about her future. After coming home for his funeral nine years later, she'd matured enough to better understand. Daddy'd said she couldn't appreciate Sterling Banks Plantation, Craven County, or her heritage without experiencing another life in comparison. The world would make her a richer personality, he'd said.

Richer. A poor choice of words.

In a flip of fate, Ty stood here as the senior officer and lone detective in the sheriff's office at the same ripe old age as Quinn . . . with Quinn only a PI. Ironic. He still donned a uniform most days, though. The department wasn't big enough to exclude him from traffic stops or domestic disputes.

"What do you think?" she asked, scooching around the body to stand between the two double beds.

"Murdered. Shot once center mass." He pointed to a 9mm on the cheap, blond-veneer dresser barely a yard from the body. "Believe he knew the guy since his weapon is still in its holster over there. He didn't even appear to reach for it."

"No defensive wounds?" she asked.

"Not any I can see," he said.

Her gaze scanned the furniture tops, the bed. "ID?"

"Haven't found any out and about. I haven't searched the body."

She eased beside the victim and stooped down. "Then let's do it."

She saw no lumps in his thin cotton shirt which meant most likely in the pants pocket.

Ty moved toward the bathroom mirror. "Coroner won't like us messing with the body before he gets here. Nor your uncle."

"Then don't tell them." She reached in the pocket.

She opened the folded leather, read, and though she'd known his identity, the confirmation still caught a breath.

Ty had his eye on the door, gazing into the parking lot. "Make it quick, Q." Studying Vic's face closer, she felt a sudden urge to tell him she was sorry she hadn't answered his call. But he'd been a fling, then a distant peer. He never took cases outside of Charleston.

She took a picture of his PI license and slid everything neat and tidy back into his pants. Ty stepped into the bathroom area. Seated back on her haunches, Quinn tried to picture how Vic last looked.

He'd bought her a drink at an Atlanta investigator's conference a long three years ago, flirted, then shared pointers, eating up her attention. With ten years on her, he had a store of experience she'd milked slowly, through two drinks and as many hours. The third drink earned him one kiss. The fourth, however, burned through any professional reservation and took them to his room. She hadn't seen him since, but they'd conversed online, by phone, and texts. At first often, then less over time.

She recalled him being way more adept at his job than this.

Which made her worry all the more about who was able to get the drop on him . . . and what Vic had wanted to talk about. Vic hadn't been a close friend, but he'd left a footprint in her life. Seeing him gone like this gave her a brief whiff of mortality.

"Put his ID back?" Ty said, coming back out of the bath.

She shook off her thoughts and rose to her feet. "What ID?"

He gave her his know-better look.

"Coroner's here," warned Mike in a low voice at the door, apparently recovered from his nausea. "And your uncle's right behind him."

Quinn took another panning view of the motel room.

If her uncle's office processed the myriad of prints that came off this room, no telling how many hits he'd get in the system, but it would be a start, she guessed. Assuming he followed through. Better than nothing.

The motel was old, as in metal key old. No auto lock or keyless entry. She wondered where the key was, which raised the issue if Vic was alone. One duffel bag on the floor next to the dresser, and an open one on the bathroom counter. Did he travel heavy, or did he have a roommate? Too late to rifle through the bags.

One bottle of Jim Beam on the bath counter, near the glasses and ice bucket. The items were in disarray, leaving her unable to quickly read if he'd entertained or just been sloppy with his glassware. He'd drunk bourbon during their night years past, too.

Funny, the things you remember.

She felt the shadow filling the doorway before she looked up.

"Girl, you damn well know better."

Though soft in substance, Sheriff Lawrence Sterling still had a commanding presence and few crossed him. He had his ways.

Quinn dusted her hands in symbolic gesture and faced the music. "That's right, Uncle Larry. I do know better than most of these guys out here. And by the way, I know *this* guy. A Charleston private investigator. One of *my* ilk. Bet that makes your day."

She realized once she'd graduated that her father's deep insistence she get a sheepskin and a job was as much to get her away from her black sheep uncle as it was to teach her about the world. After a double major in business and criminal justice, an honor internship, twenty weeks of Quantico training, and three years of FBI experience, she cleaned up crime like she'd pretended as a kid with Ty. A dream come true.

But the FBI hadn't understood her extended absence after her father's murder, the importance of the Sterling legacy, and the weight of preserving a three-hundred-year-old plantation and all that came with that history. They held little compassion for the crater in her heart or the fire in her belly to straighten out what her uncle had botched, so they'd denied her request for an unpaid leave of absence and given her a return-to-work date. Then let her resign in lieu of firing her when she couldn't return.

Which cut her almost as badly as losing her father.

With a gravelly clearing of his throat, Sheriff Sterling brought her attention back around. "Any idea why he's here?"

She shrugged. "Haven't seen him in years, and we don't travel the same circles." Her history with Victor, however tenuous, was still a connection, though, and she felt an obligation to do right by him. A thought Uncle need not hear.

She'd protect another serious thought as well. The coincidence was too convenient to have Catherine Renault travel all the way to Craven County from Charleston to say she'd lost a PI, and in the same day they find the body of one.

If she told anyone, it'd be Ty. Later.

"Dust the bathroom, too," she said, trying to leave. "Not quite sure he was alone, but he let in the person who shot him, so I'm guessing he was familiar."

Sheriff Sterling wasn't anywhere near obese, just middle-aged pudgy, but like all Sterling men, he stood tall and broad, the height gene likewise making Quinn five foot ten. He shifted slightly to hinder her exit. "Stick to the farm, Quinn."

Then just like that, all she could think of was her daddy's cold case. Sheriff Sterling had already proven he couldn't solve a murder if his life depended on it, and ordering her back to Sterling Banks irritated the piss out of her.

She stretched her backbone long and rigid in a futile attempt to reach his height then leaned into him. "I seem to remember a certain uncle teaching me how to ask questions and not allowing myself to be intimidated," she informed him softly, fully aware that embarrassing him aloud would only make him worse.

"There's a difference between arrogance and courage, little girl." He moved a few inches to make room for her exit. "Stay out of my crime scene. I imagine Jule wants you back at home."

Indeed Jule did. Sterling Banks's foreman, or rather forewoman, was familiar with Quinn's childhood thirst for mysteries, and she wasn't keen on her PI job. They also had both loved Graham Sterling dearly . . . and would forever, privately, hold her daddy's brother accountable for not solving the biggest unsolved crime in four coastal counties.

He turned his back to his niece. "Tyson? Fill me in."

She left, the knowing glances from deputies relaying sympathy, if not empathy, and each smiled or slightly shrugged as she bid them adieu and veered to the motel's front office where she'd parked.

In her beeline to her truck, however, she quickly sidestepped inside that office. She had ten or fifteen minutes, she guessed.

She almost knocked Wynn Ferguson down with the door.

The tiny, dark, squirrelly man scurried back behind his counter. "What's happening, Quinn?"

His daddy built the Jacksonian, capitalizing on his wife's maiden name of Jackson to remind people of tradition, location, and coincidentally, or not—taking advantage of an established brand. After high school, Young Ferg hadn't the gumption to leave town, so he'd worked cleaning rooms until two days after he turned twenty-one when old man Ferguson stroked out cleaning the motel pool. Young Ferg took what little life insurance money he inherited, filled in the offending pool, planted crape myrtles, and staked a memorial sign—custom done at Steedley's Memorials in Walterboro per the inscription. Then he took over running the family business.

Family businesses were common in these parts.

"Tell me about room twelve," Quinn said, keeping one eye on the busy-ness at that end of the complex.

Ferg pursed his lips. "Not sure I'm supposed to."

"I'm on the case," she lied. Everyone understood she held some sort of license on the side and had once been FBI, and with her conduit to the sheriff, most considered her fully legit, authorized, and badged. She never explained otherwise.

"Oh," he said. "Okay." He clicked on his computer and turned the screen around for her to see. "Stephen Smith." He looked pleased with himself, though still a little twitchy. "From Savannah."

Of course Vic used an alias. Probably had the fake driver's license to go with it in one of his bags. "Alone or with a companion?"

"Alone."

"Say why he's here?"

"He said I had to remain quiet about that." He pondered a moment. "Now that he's dead, it doesn't matter, right?"

She congratulated him. "Very good, Ferg. Where'd you learn that?"

With a half-smile he divulged his source. "TV. He was meeting someone, though, and he didn't want his wife to learn about it."

She raised a brow. "Did you see the woman he was supposed to meet?" No way Catherine could get away with incognito, not with her needing a driver. Not with that dog.

Leaning over the wooden counter, he whispered, "Not a woman. It was a guy. I think they were . . . gay."

"Seriously?" Vic was anything but gay, but not a bad cover story.

She studied the screen, the information posted on an ancient point-of-sale program. Vic checked in eight days ago. Paid cash up front for five days, then added two days more like he'd reassessed how long he needed to complete his business . . . until someone completed it for him. "How many times did his . . . friend . . . visit?"

Ferg engaged his memory, his forehead furrowed at the effort. "Three, no, four," he finally said.

"When's the last time?" she asked.

"Two days ago," he replied. "Guy left in a huff."

"Stephen Smith or the visitor?"

"The visitor," he said. "Slammed his car door and everything."

"Describe him," she said.

"Average height. White guy. More your age. Dark hair. Jeans. Nice suede jacket, though. Oh . . . and a cowboy hat." He gave this snarky grimace, not unlike a cartoon character smelling trash. "Who wears those? Like, he could be from Texas. You think?"

"Good clue. See him up close?"

He beamed at the compliment. "Nope. Guy was being rather clandestine. That's the word, right?"

"Sure is." Stepping back to the window, she peered toward the crowd. Ty and her uncle had moved outside the room. Someone pointed her way.

"Three more quick things, Ferg."

"Sure. Glad to help the law."

She'd have to send a gift to him after all this. A fifty-dollar gift card at the Pick-N-Pig would do.

"Any surveillance?" she asked.

"Only in this office area," he said. "And sometimes I forget to do it right and it loops over itself. That's one question." He held up a finger. After all, she'd said three.

The two men still conversed, Ty most likely stalling the sheriff, seeing her truck still parked. "When's the last time housekeeping was in room twelve?" she asked.

Ferg shook his head. "Hasn't been. Guy asked if he could just pick up towels as he needed them." Second finger up. "One more," he said, like he would be rewarded for paying attention.

"Any deliveries to the room?"

"Nope."

"Did anyone call for him on your main line?" With landlines disappearing in a world of cell phones, a novice might not think of that question, but landlines were still mandatory in motels, and if a PI didn't want to release his personal number—

"Wait, that's four questions," Ferg said.

Quinn sighed, acting caught. "Sorry, lost count. Can you grant me one more? About anyone calling? I'll owe you."

"All right," he said, pleased at the upper hand. "As a matter of fact, a guy called daily," he said. "Started the day after Mr. Smith checked in, wanting to know which room he was in. I assume it was the gay guy."

"And you gave the number to him?"

He reared back. "Of course not, Quinn. We protect people's privacy here, and don't you be telling anyone different. I just forward calls to the room."

"When was that last call?" she asked.

"About nine in the morning day before yesterday," he said.

She slapped her card on the counter. "You've got caller ID on this phone, right?" She already moved toward the exit.

"Yeah."

"Text me that guy's phone number, okay? There's something in it for you if you do."

"Wait," Ferg shouted. "Who's paying for the day he didn't pay for? Who's cleaning up that room?"

21

She skirted out, shouting, "I will. Send me the bill," before the door shut behind her. A moment later, via her rearview mirror, she caught her uncle staring at her tailgate, Ty still fighting for his attention.

The game was afoot.

She texted as usual. *Tag, Ty. You're it.*

But this wasn't nearly as fun as their childhood adventures. There was a bitterness involved.

Chapter 3

INSTEAD OF DIVING into the investigation and in lieu of calling back Catherine Renault, Quinn drove the few miles home one-handed, elbow out the truck window, relaxed to anyone who passed by and waved. But in the floorboard, her left boot beat a nervous tap. Her mind churned through the facts before her, and she was overly eager to pick Ty's brain when he got off duty.

Seventy degrees was spring weather which jumpstarted most farms, and the pecan orchards on Sterling Banks had exploded with their catkin tassels. With ample rain of late, the trees stood lush, green, and gorgeous, but Vic kept interrupting her appreciation of it all.

Might as well return to Jule's goats and llamas, her forewoman's side business that Quinn had abandoned in a hurry that morning. At least until Ty got free.

The truck knew the roads, and she'd mindlessly turned through the brick and iron entrance, the crape myrtles still barren and waiting for the heat to stick. The narcissus were up, though, and redbuds filled the woods' fringe, the tiny pink a contrast to budding oaks and hickories. She inhaled deeply, tasting the pollen—thick and exploding from the buds—on the back of her tongue.

With Jonah on a day trip to pick up new brood stock for his mother's goat herd, Jule had been left on her own managing the three dozen hands, most farm-labor related, a couple coordinating product sales. Now was considered a lull in their production year, but key in setting up bulk sales for the fall. When Quinn wasn't on a case, she worked *the farm*, as she preferred to call it. Or *the Banks*. While it still cropped up, mostly out of legacy, sometimes out of habit, the term *plantation* was used sparingly, regardless of what the legal papers said.

The asphalt drive took her a half mile off the highway to the sprawling brick manor, which she passed by, to drive a quarter mile to Jule's house. Quinn parked, looking toward the barn off to the south of the cottage Jule had occupied since Quinn was four years old. Shutting the truck off, she listened.

That's how anyone found Aimee Jule Proveaux, half Cajun by her own account. Found her by homing in on her humming, usually some New Orleans hymn, or jazz if she was feeling spunky. Goats and llamas pricked ears up for their alpha, listening for those tunes.

Quinn located the familiar, short, overall-clad woman by sound scarcely a second before spotting gray hair braided in a banana-colored paisley rag atop her head. A blue one peeked from the back pocket of her denim. A splash of color could be found on her whether she fed livestock, hoed her garden, or attended church on Sundays. One never went wrong with a bandana gift to Jule.

Leaning on her pitchfork, Jule watched the animals outside in the big pen, no doubt released there to give the new llama baby and mother quiet time inside the barn. Baby goats bounced and tippy-toed helter-skelter, spring-boarding on and off anything in their way, including each other. The new arrival was their third baby in two days, making it eight in two weeks.

"Named him yet?" Quinn asked as she popped herself atop a fence rail, never tiring of livestock scent. Feed, hair, down to the droppings on the ground, the combination said *home*. With the summer would come more human odor—sweat—prompted by Carolina Lowcountry humidity. Thank God for the off-setting sweet aroma of hay.

Jule rested her pitchfork against the fence, pulled out the back pocket bandana, and rubbed her face. "Bruiser."

"Awww," Quinn said, looking pained. "He had such a hard time, and you stick him with that?"

"He fought to get into this world, so I reckon he's earned it."

Quinn slung her long legs over the rail and dropped into the confine, walking over to reach inside the barn for two handfuls of feed. Thirty goats. Tentative at the newcomer, the kids skirted back to their mothers, but when Quinn sat on a box, they eyed her closely as she reached out.

Ewes immediately pushed against her, bumping her closed fists. Quinn slowly let the feed be discovered, one morsel at a time until a baby dared to follow. Then two. She caught one and drew it to her lap and lightly rubbed a hand through the soft coat, scratching fingers through the hair. She loved the baby hair.

She couldn't pass a goat without petting, even loving the pregnant moms, all bumps and angles with babies active and eager to get out. Babies so cuddly the first day or two, then finding their legs, ejected pure energy into their bounces.

Jule usually denied she named each goat. She raised them, milked them, sold them, insisting no point in anyone getting attached. But every once in a while Quinn would find a kid inside the cottage in a dog bed, babied and bottle fed when a momma wouldn't cooperate. Aphrodite was the last. Premature, legs like pencils, fed with a dropper. Wore a washcloth with holes cut in it for a blanket.

Yeah, all the goats had names.

Quinn put the kid down and wandered into the barn. Jule followed and met her at the llama pen where they watched Bruiser suckling.

"Jonah back yet?" Quinn asked, not having seen his truck, but he could also be out and about on the farm.

"Nope, the boy's probably sightseeing, glad to get off this damn place for a change. Speaking of running off, where you been?"

"Thought I had a case," she replied, itching to hug Bruiser but knowing better. Mom eyeballed them, wary and protective.

Jule chewed the inside of her mouth, wrinkling up one side of her deep tanned face . . . avoiding judgment.

Still agile and hardworking, Jule had lost some of her sprightly spirit the night Graham Sterling died . . . when she'd also been found unconscious in the manor's entry hall. Her sixty-year-old wisdom ranged from goat breeding to slipping Quinn ginger tea for menstrual cramps, and she could still build a deer stand in a day. By any standard she was an intelligent practical woman, but she somewhat blamed herself for the death of Graham Sterling for reasons strictly kept to herself.

"Say it," Quinn said down at the hard-thinking, five-foot-nothing woman with nary an extra pound on her.

"You got a responsibility here. And there's no danger."

"I can handle myself, if that's what you're worried about," she replied. "We've talked about this."

"Just 'cause you're tree-top tall doesn't mean you can't get in trouble." With that, she walked off. Quinn followed.

Jule had tensed when Quinn left in a rush earlier to meet Catherine. She started to tell Jule that she'd turned down the case, but from their past discussions, the less said the better when it came to law enforcement, which Jule considered PI work to be a part of. Since Graham's demise, Jule had no use for that world, and she had disciplinary one-liners from here to forever and claimed the last word as her right in any conversation about the subject.

Graham—the tie that both bound them and alienated them.

But they both agreed wholeheartedly about Larry.

"Anyway," Quinn said as they exited, "you need me to help you here? Got a few hours to give you."

Without hesitation, Jule started pointing, delivering orders. If there was one thing that woman could do better than farm and ranch, it was manage a work crew, the reason Quinn's daddy had slowly converted her from housekeeper for his young family to backup overseer those thirty years ago.

They wormed some of the goats, repaired one side of the corral, and in between the common chatter about livestock and the overabundance of pecan tasseling this year, Quinn analyzed the Jacksonian motel room in her head.

Tree shadows began to spread up the barn wall. Quinn'd told herself earlier if Tyson didn't arrive at her house by seven, she'd head over to Jackson Hole. The diner would morph into a bar about that time, a sports bar feel without the sports but with all the noise that came with drinking. Tyson helped his mother a couple evenings a week, and Tuesday nights were usually light. Quinn was still hoping he could come to her.

Finally checking the time on her phone, five after seven, Quinn fussed under her breath. She was still covered in muck and hungry to her core.

Accepting a bowl of leftover chili from Jule, Quinn wolfed down the venison and beans and headed home to shower. Freshened, she took one last glance in the kitchen's hallway mirror and decided to tie her hair back and dab on a hint of lip color in case she ran into folks. Then she climbed in her truck, disappointed the deputy hadn't sought her out.

Red-headed and fair, she stood a stark contrast to her buddy's darkness but met him eye-to-eye in height. Their fathers introduced them about the time they entered kindergarten when Mr. Jackson asked if the boy could tag along in the orchards, learning how things were run. Quinn and Ty had been inseparable ever since . . . except when she went off to college then the FBI.

The Sterlings might be white and the Jacksons mostly black, but both helped found the county. Originally a Native American settlement called Pon Pon, the town of Jacksonboro had been founded by John Jackson along the Edisto River around 1700. But the family did what many families did over the decades, and that was sell off pieces of land as marriages diluted blood lines. Black Jacksons could be traced back to the white Jacksons, but the former had remained rooted and multiplied while the others scattered. Tyson's lineage was as long as Quinn's, making their friendship respected even to the most ignorant of Craven residents.

As children, the two had swapped clothes, taken naps on the manor's back porch entwined on a rattan daybed under the ceiling fan, and chased feral cats in the barn loft. Cooled off in the Edisto River. She'd even used the goat shears to cut her hair short one summer to look more like her pal. Jule had salvaged the rag-tag cut, the two dads fighting hard not to laugh at Jule's scolding.

Their high school years led to snared kisses behind the widest pecan trees, and they'd hugged, held hands, and joked openly at school, with only one lone boy ridiculing their mixed-race friendship before Tyson made him a believer in respect . . . or at least in silence. Went without saying you didn't mock either Quinn or Tyson, not without facing the other.

Once Quinn entered Quantico, Ty chose to marry a girl who looked more like him, gave her a child, then gave her the divorce she asked for when Quinn returned. Quinn had done nothing other than grow up with the man, but the ex-wife got drunk and slung the Sterling name around the bar like a wet towel one night. She left embarrassed and moved across the line to live in Walterboro. Not far, just not in Craven County.

Ten assorted vehicles, including a patrol car, hugged the bar when she arrived around eight. Uncle Larry usually let his senior officer take a cruiser home at night, and Tyson often parked it at the bar as a tranquilizer to potential trouble.

Quinn strode in to John Lee Hooker's *One Bourbon, One Scotch, One Beer* on the jukebox. A middle-of-the-week mellow night. Just her style.

In jeans and a simple navy t-shirt stretched at the sleeve from arms pumped by the weights kept at his house, his badge most assuredly in his pocket, Tyson worked the bar, doing more reading on his phone than hustling up drinks. A slow night meant people nursed drinks longer, too.

Quinn parked herself on a stool near the register and three seats from the nearest customer. "Beer, sir. And none of that craft shit, either."

He poured her a Yuengling in a chilled glass, like she liked, and set it before her. "What're you doing here?"

"Hunting you down, Deputy, 'cause you didn't come to my house. Don't act all surprised." She took a long draw on the beer. "Fill me in, please."

The song played out, and Tyson waited until a new tune kicked in. Still bluesy, but the bass rhythm would keep ears from tuning in to their low-key conversation.

"Victor Whitmarsh, private investigator, address North Charleston off Rivers Avenue," he said.

Not the worst but not the best neighborhood. One that had gone through a lot of ups and downs over the last twenty years, mostly downs.

"License active per SLED," he said. "Residence is in his office. Unsure of next of kin. Plan on going to his place tomorrow." He leaned closer. "How well do you know this dude?"

"Been three years since I last saw him," she said.

"Saw?"

"You're making me uncomfortable with your line of inquiry, Deputy."

He smirked. "Any carnal knowledge?"

"Once, at a conference. Not important. Don't tell Uncle Larry."

He shook his head. "Is that how you gather intel?"

"You calling me loose?"

He stood back straight. "Nope, not in the least. Though I do recall you being the one always wanting to skinny dip in the river."

The comment made her hunt around for Lenore . . . or any nosy newts who'd take the visual wrong. "We never went past our underwear, and you know it."

Despite the rumors and his ex's accusations, they hadn't slept together. She didn't even allow herself to think about it. To think about it would raise the question why not, and she was confused as to why she was too afraid to cross that line of friendship. As well-known as she was, she held few friends close. He happened to be the closest. Jonah came a near second. At least right now. Some days they switched places. She didn't want to mess up any of that.

She emptied the mug. "You know that client I met earlier?"

A customer strode up. "Draft, please."

"Yes, sir." The deputy handled the purchase and let the man shuffle on to a booth with his friends, then Ty swiftly replaced Quinn's empty with a fresh one. "Thought you decided she wasn't a client."

"I did," she said. "But she wanted to hire me because she lost her other PI."

His look queried her deep. "Lost him?"

"He hadn't reported in. Gone long enough for her to need another PI, apparently."

"Odd. So why you?"

She bumped him with her beer, sloshing a few drops. "We talked about that at lunch. Don't you listen? Anyway, I'm going with you in the morning. Just make sure you leave alone so nobody tattles. Find anything else in the room? Or on Vic?"

"Found a phone, but it's locked."

"I know a guy," she said.

He smiled at another patron walking by. "Another Vic guy?"

"Jealous?"

"No."

She shrugged. "I still know people. Knox Kendrick in the Charleston

FBI office. Maybe I can call in a favor."

The two guys at the other end of the bar left, and Tyson slid down to remove their mugs and scoop up the tip. He came back. "You worked three years, Q. How's that long enough to earn favors?"

"I did leg work for the guy, and did it well." She stretched out her long legs. "Look at these gams. Best leg work in the state."

He laughed, and she repositioned herself on the stool. "Seriously, though. Let's drop the phone off with Knox, then go through Vic's place."

"Not sure what the high sheriff will say," he said.

She waggled her brows. "Screw him. You know you want me to."

He winked. "You know I want you to . . . what? Skinny dip again?"

She drained her second beer. "Quit changing the subject. Pick me up at nine."

"You drive me nuts. Why not earlier? Some of us actually have a reporting time."

"To avoid that Charleston rush-hour mess. Sleep in," she added. "If you go to the office, you might run into Uncle Larry and have to lie about me."

"You're gonna get me fired."

She put bills on the counter, to include a healthy tip she knew Tyson would pass on to his momma. "You can't get fired," she said, pulling keys out a snug jean pocket. "I got an inside track with the sheriff."

"Humph." He stared, the humor not reaching his eyes any longer. "And one day that relation ain't gonna hold up."

"Humph," she mocked back at him and left, knowing how right he might be.

In her pickup, she fixated through her windshield on a flickering neon beer sign in one of the windows, reminding herself to tell Lenore about the bulb.

Ty liked working alongside her, and she alongside him. Uncle understood that they shared intel, and she represented one less uniform he had to hire. Most days anyway. Or so she kept telling herself.

Her mental checklist amounted to little more than finding Vic's client list and letting Ty scout the rest of the place. If Catherine Renault was the PI's client, and his investigation brought him to someone in Craven, something weird was going on. Not that Quinn had her finger on the pulse of everything in the county, but she thought she had a fairly good handle on what went on. When she learned she didn't, she felt naked, and this was one of those times.

She might just call Catherine back for the hell of it and take her boyfriend case. After the search, though. The more Quinn learned ahead of time the better.

She started the truck, her headlights bouncing off the police cruiser as she headed to the highway. Ty was correct in that she pushed the envelope with her uncle, but Uncle Larry would think awful hard before taking any action against her.

As the last Sterling heir, and with no heirs of her own yet, she was bound by will and ages-old tradition to leave the farm to any living Sterling, meaning Archie or Larry. And Larry wanted it the most.

Chapter 4

AT HER SEVEN-THIRTY alarm, a cricket noise specifically chosen to wake her slowly, Quinn slid her daddy's bathrobe over a tank top and sateen pajama shorts. She shuffled downstairs to the kitchen, following the waft of coffee set to a timer.

She'd drunk strong coffee since adolescence thanks to Jule inserting her Cajun ways into the Sterlings. Out and about, Quinn drank it unadulterated and black, but at home, she took it with goat's milk as thick as the memories that came with it.

Quinn had awoken melancholy, anxious. Due to Vic's death, most likely. Coffee in hand, she left the kitchen, went down the hall, and hesitated at the door of the master. Even as mistress of the manor, Quinn held no desire to sleep there. Her children, assuming she ever had any, ought to be able to walk into that room and sense their grandparents as they were when living, as close to meeting them as possible. Her father had kept it preserved that way after her mother died. Now Quinn did so for both.

She pushed off the doorway and entered the walk-in closet. Margaret Kennedy O'Quinn's things remained where she'd kept them so Quinn could borrow something, like a mother would want her daughter to do. Today she needed something to go with jeans.

Rows of scarves greeted her—silk, chiffon, and of course mohair in honor of Jule's goats. Heavy wool and one soft white alpaca. Delicates, fringes, cotton to fit the days when nothing else would do. Sliding hands through the sensory ocean, Quinn chose a thin, loosely woven indigo and slid it into the robe's pocket.

Quinn barely recalled her mother's Irish brogue anymore. "Quinn means intelligent, daughter-of-mine," she'd say, combing out her daughter's tangled curls after a bath. "You're more than a name." Then she'd tug a lock. "You're half Irish, in spite of all that Sterling in ya'."

Graham struggled to honor his Irish wife accordingly after she left them, imprinting the Irish mother in the child's psyche like ABCs while likewise embedding his own ancestral history. "You're like her," he'd always say, touching her hair. "Said she gave you and your brother her maiden name to dilute the Sterling Britishness." Not that they spoke with a British accent. That accent had been replaced with Lowcountry Southern well over a hundred years ago.

Her twin, Quincy, died of heart failure at age one.

Maggie succumbed to breast cancer at age thirty-three . . . Quinn's age minus one.

And Quinn had assumed after that Graham would be around forever.

She pulled the door closed.

Making her way to a recliner in the cavernous family room lined with glass doors facing an unending sea of pecan trees out back, she sank into the cushion, pulling the robe close around her, and sipped her coffee. Rising early didn't mean rising fast.

Bam!

She jerked, opening eyes she hadn't realized had closed, coffee sloshing across her lap.

Ty stood at the middle of the three sets of sliding glass doors that opened across a flagstone patio toward the trees. "Wake up, Morning Glory. Thought you said nine?"

Leaping to her feet, she studied the damage to her robe, the wet seeping through her shorts. "What the hell time is it?" The clock on the mantel read eight thirty.

She slid open the door. "You're early."

"And you'd be late if I wasn't. Sheriff told me to get back soon as I could." He pointed at her, head to toe. "You gotta wash all that or can you throw something on so we can get gone?"

"Butthead. Give me fifteen." Scurrying to the stairs, she hollered over her shoulder, "Coffee's in the kitchen."

Keeping her word, she returned quickly, soft-footing her way to her good boots parked beside her muddy ones, at a carved bench parked outside the kitchen. She slid into the ankle boots, adjusted her indigo scarf, and met Ty staring out across the patio.

The view of what made Sterling Banks famous was irresistible, the house strategically built to appreciate the orchard after the old plantation home burned at the turn of the last century, and the other one burned by Sherman at the tail-end of the Civil War.

Tyson finished his coffee. "Trees looking mighty good this year. Jonah's doing awesome work."

She took the cup from him. "Give me some credit. I grew up out here, too, you know."

"So did I, but he's got the thumb, and Jule's genes."

With a pretend sneer, she slid arms into a lightweight windbreaker. "Thought you were in a hurry, detective."

"If I was, I'd already be in Charleston, gumshoe."

Not many PIs could ride in a police car, but Quinn and her uncle had come to an unspoken arrangement. If Uncle Larry could cart his buddies to barbecues and turkey shoots, she could ride with Tyson from time to time.

Only forty miles to the Rivers Avenue address, but Charleston traffic, regardless of the time of day, meant over an hour drive. They quickly reached the ACE Basin Parkway, and Tyson hit the speed limit and coasted the long stretch of road.

"Calder say anything yet?" she asked, twisting for a comfortable spot after pushing the seat all the way back. "Or is our coroner *ill* again?"

"Still working on the body."

"Man hasn't been sober in ten years."

Ty scowled. "Be nice. He's qualified."

"He's elected."

Frank Calder replaced the seventy-five-year-old gentleman who'd handled her daddy's murder. The previous coroner had been called from a dinner party to pronounce her daddy dead. Old guy died the following year not remembering who his wife was.

Quinn had second-guessed every move of everybody on that case. Those involved dodged her for years, except for Uncle Larry. *You're too close to be impartial,* he said. *You're blinded by guilt.* Said that and more so often that she could recite his lines. In her opinion, he hadn't been close enough to care enough to get the job done.

She was dwelling on Graham, something she struggled not to do. One would think after six years she'd have tempered her frustration.

Nice fencerow, she thought as they flew past a farm. For twenty minutes she watched Lowcountry properties flash by, studying farm fencing on the larger places. She appreciated quality work, having performed every task required for the second largest pecan orchard in the state.

"I'm so grateful not to be so close to Charleston, you know that?" she said. "Have you paid attention to the sprawl?" They passed the 174 turnoff toward Edisto Beach. The Edisto River leading to that same beach area bordered Sterling Banks at its southern end.

Charles Sterling had married Anna Banks, against the better judgment of either father who were agricultural rivals. When Anna died giving Charles a male heir, after he inherited the farm, he added her name to the title. Every farm held some similar wedge of history, but nobody seemed to care much about the past anymore. Sprawl was so . . . impersonal.

"Damn developers are losing their fool heads building crap all over the place," Quinn said. "Every friggin' magazine touting Charleston number one in *The Best Of* whatever can draw tourism these days. And you know what?"

"What?" Tyson replied, accommodating.

"They better not come to Craven. They'd love to tear up the wetlands, but they'd have to plow through me and the Banks to get there."

He gave her a sideways glance. "What's wrong with you this morning?"

Nothing, almost fell out of her mouth. "I don't know . . .," she finally said. What *was* wrong with her?

"Jule have any new babies in her herd?"

"Don't try to distract me with goats, Ty."

He turned serious. "Fine, then want to hear what I think your problem is?"

"You're the seasoned detective. Enlighten me."

Not often, but in their moments of dissension, she played that card. Him being in law enforcement and her not. Forget that she made the decision which cost her the career at the FBI. She still missed that life. Still thought of her top-notch training going to waste. Still got cranky because Ty could put his training to use while she had to wait for stupid cases of marital difficulties and people skipping out on child support. To give her a bit of perspective, Ty would compare his days of speeding tickets, irritated neighbors, and dog control. *Didn't help.*

"Victor Whitmarsh is your problem," he said.

She held the scowl until he looked over and caught it before she asked, "How's that?"

"You knew him, and a murder being local has to dredge up memories. Your uncle, a coroner, uniforms . . . me. Just the fact you were familiar may have stirred things in your head. What do you think?"

She hated him for his insight, for talking bluntly like this. Hated the drumming in her chest which signaled his words meant something. "You're reaching."

"Think what you will," he said. "Don't bottle that shit up, Q. It's not like the people around you don't understand about your daddy."

She turned away. Those people didn't understand fully, though, and without sounding selfish or conceited, she couldn't explain.

She'd been a natural at the FBI. The Banks was supposed to be her second act after twenty or so years with the Bureau, once Graham Sterling retired to sit on that massive flagstone porch in a rocker telling tales to his grandchildren, watching *her* manage the pecans.

A murderer not only stole her last parent but also robbed her of a career that fit her like the boots on her feet, short-circuiting her future. She couldn't say out loud that she was stuck at Sterling Banks, because she indeed loved the place, but she was.

"You're festering, Q."

Of course she was. Why not when the man who shot your daddy ran free as a bird while you lost the FBI career that could've been used to find him?

Halfway there, they turned onto the interstate, getting off on

Dorchester Road, traveling a few blocks to the FBI office. Not large compared to the headquarters in Columbia, but large enough. Charleston's steady activity as a port justified the satellite office and its two dozen staff. The patrol car got them in the gate quickly. After a call to the agent and a couple of checkpoints, they waited in a lobby.

Knox's heels relayed an urgency coming down the hall. Brown hair, an unbuttoned suit jacket as if thrown on, he outstretched his arms which Quinn eagerly fell into.

"Quinn! Girl, haven't seen you in ages." He hugged her, then hugged her hard again. "How're you doing?"

"You missed me," she said, poking him in the shoulder.

"Still do," he replied while stretching a hand out to Tyson. "Senior Special Agent Knox Kendrick."

"Detective Tyson Jackson, Craven County Sheriff's Office. Hoping you might do us a favor." He handed over Victor's phone in an evidence bag. "Can you access this? It's an open homicide investigation. A PI was murdered in a motel out our way."

Knox turned to Quinn. "You know the guy? You still doing PI work, I take it?"

He danced around the unsaid—that PI work was a waste of a good agent. Knox hadn't fully understood why she'd had to leave.

"Yeah," she said. "No longer one of you arrogant types. Nobody compares to a feeb, right? Cream of the crop. Untouchable."

Knox held up a finger, but Quinn matched him word for word in unison. "The Untouchables were never FBI."

They laughed at the old joke.

Tyson grinned cynically.

"So, can you do your phone magic for us?" Quinn asked. "We believe he was on a case of his own, and his target might've done him in. Those calls and texts might shortcut this investigation for us."

"Us? You're working with the SO?"

"You don't remember?" she said. "My uncle's the sheriff."

Knox's brow went up. "Convenient."

"It works," she said.

He bounced the bag in his hand. "Call me later today. I'll see what I can talk someone into doing." He signed a chain of custody document Ty brought with him.

Quinn reached arms out, and he leaned in for another hug. "Thanks, Knox."

Tyson shook hands again, and the agent escorted them back out.

"Never saw you as much of a hugger," Tyson said, buckling his seat belt, watching Knox wave once before returning inside.

"He's the hugger," she said. "And I forgot how awfully good he was at it. But forget Knox. Let's go break into an office."

THEY EXITED ON Aviation Avenue, following GPS to Hawthorne Drive. There, behind a Burger King, stretched two strip units of offices. On the end, a brass sign reading *Private Discovery Agency* hung on the brick next to a door labeled only by "Unit D."

"This looks like it." Tyson put the cruiser into park and studied the outside. "Not sure I should laugh at that title."

"All the good names must've been taken," she said, getting out. "Come on. I assume you have a key?"

The door had a standard lock and deadbolt, and after trial and error with the ring of keys, they entered.

She smelled vacancy and dust, saw the latter on a gray Naugahyde sofa, matching chair, and plastic ficus in the corner. A glass window in the wall had an opening at counter level.

Quinn wrote her initial across the counter, leaving a trail. "Either he hasn't used this place in a while, or his clients are few and far between."

"Got it," Ty said, fumbling the keys at another access at the end of a short hall.

In the inner office, an array of cabinetry spread across one wall, upper and lower with a DIY desk and two chairs for clients. She peered through another threshold to find what used to be a storage room and bath . . . previous living quarters for Vic Whitmarsh. Double locks on that door.

She thumbed inside to the makeshift bedroom. "You can handle the personal stuff in there. Not sure I want to go through a guy's sheets.

I'm hunting for the client list in his desk."

A laser jet printer sat on the cabinet's counter along with a portable scanner which she hoped didn't mean he'd gone all electronic with his records. A mini-library of reference books. *Human Error* and *Ten Case Studies About Human Error*, and two others capitalizing on the word. She laughed once, wondering if he really read those things.

Now, the books on investigating fires, workmen's comp, and so on . . . those she could see. They looked read, tabbed with sticky notes. Quinn was surprised he didn't have a better office, but then she operated out of a bar, her computer in the corner of her den.

"Relied on a laptop," she said, noting no wiring or ethernet line to the desk. "You didn't find his laptop at the motel did you?" she shouted.

"Nope, woulda told you," he shouted back.

"Wonder why he even paid the rent on this place?" she mumbled, opening a box labeled *Personal.* A stack of contracts, billings. "Oh," she said. "Ty, he owns this strip mall."

"Guess he had a back-up plan to private investigations," Tyson said, returning to the office. "Frugal as hell back there."

"Wouldn't be surprised to find a decent bank account someplace," she said.

Didn't take her long to find the current client stash in Vic's lower right hand drawer. Ty started pulling the closed boxes out of the cabinets.

Names she didn't recognize. Marital, marital, marital, background, disability fraud. "Here we go." She lifted out a folder labeled *C. Renault* and laid it on the desk. Ty moved over to see.

"God, look at the handwriting," he said. "Can you read that?"

"Some," she uttered, scanning the first page of scribbled notes. She flipped a page, then two, gleaning every other sentence. Mickey was spelled out once, then the initial used thereafter.

Quinn skipped to the back, to four photographs clipped together. She freed them and dealt them out like cards across the desk, hesitating at the second, then quickly positioning the rest.

"Ty, look."

"I *am* looking," he said.

"Am I seeing right?" she asked.

"Yeah, girl. I believe you are. What are the chances?"

The photos showed a man about thirty. Twice wearing a cowboy hat. Twice with Catherine, one hugging, one laughing.

"It's Mitchell Raines," she said, a bit breathless, then snapped her head around toward her friend. "Mickey Raines! The guy y'all investigated about Daddy."

Ty kept quiet, letting Quinn take it in at her speed.

She lifted one without the hat, with the best close-up. "Son of a bitch, Ty. The guy who might've killed Victor Whitmarsh is the guy who found Daddy dead."

Chapter 5

HEART BEATING double-time, Quinn let Tyson canvas the rest of Vic's office while she remained at the desk, browsing files and searching on her phone for Mickey Raines, Mitchell Raines, Mick Raines in any of a dozen locations. In seconds, she found a website where he touted his phone apps, a Facebook page, Instagram, comments on a Reddit group, and mentions on minor tech pages that probably struggled for brand more than he did.

Where he lived, however, remained vague. South Carolina at best, with some mentions of Georgia. His professional head shot still looked young . . . babyish even. Nothing posted online in four weeks. The same time period Catherine Renault hadn't received a call.

Yesterday, Ferg had followed through from the Jacksonian Motel, texting her the number that called Vic's motel room several times. The same number as on Mickey's website. She'd dialed it with no luck. She dialed it again. Mailbox still full.

Quinn started with what she knew. Three years younger than she, Mickey had been a freshman in the same high school where she'd been a senior. Different social groups, but still, someone she'd met. His family farmed on the other side of the county. Vegetable crops, mainly, meaning hard, back-breaking work hauling produce to grocers and farmer's markets. She admired the profession but wasn't familiar enough about the Raines family to have a clue of Mickey's ways, desires, or dislikes.

The Banks relied heavily on seasonal help. Mickey had worked for her father during the summers, but she'd never known until after the fact. Jule and a couple others ran the show back when Quinn was FBI, and prior to that she was away at school or interning. Jule's son Jonah had been off doing his own thing with an upstate commercial farm back then. Tyson worked full-time with the sheriff's office.

The authorities hadn't inquired why Mickey wasn't working his own family's farm instead of someone else's. Officially he was just the seasonal hand who found Graham's body. Unofficially, the rumor mill suspected him of the deed.

He didn't attend the funeral, and when Quinn visited his family to get the answers Uncle Larry hadn't, the parents said Mickey'd taken a job in Georgia and wished to be left alone. They acted almost fearful of her. After all, a member of the local "royalty" was dead, and the princess had become queen and wanted answers.

Chances were—given her shock and grief—she hadn't been overly pleasant. They'd quit taking her calls.

Quinn tapped Vic's file papers on the desk and replaced them in their folders. Later at home she'd dig into her purchased database services used readily by private investigators and cops alike. She really didn't want to visit the Raines farm, but she saw the need coming. She might take a gift. But she might not call ahead.

"When we return, you dive into Mickey Raines," she said to Ty, spinning around in the chair. "Check every damn source you have that I don't."

"I figured that out already, Miss Q," he replied. "I'm done here. Grab that—"

"File. It and all the open files." She held folders to her chest, snatching an empty banker's box to drop them in. Opening one cabinet again, then another, she pointed. "Throw the most recent closed case file boxes in your back seat and trunk, just in case."

She didn't stop at two or three, either. Ty gave her a second once-over, recognizing the ignition of her impatience, and without conversation soon loaded eight boxes in the cruiser. All the car could hold. A dozen other boxes were left behind, but they'd recover those if the need arose. Quinn was almost electric to reach home and get to work.

She plopped into the car's front seat. "I'm calling Knox on the outside chance he got that phone open."

But no such luck. More urgent cases had pushed the favor to the back burner for at least a day, likely two. She thanked the agent nicely but hung up sighing. "Head on home," she said.

But Tyson held off cranking the engine and reached across the back of the seat, not touching her shoulder, but showing her he could if it got to that. "Breathe, Q. Get a grip."

She almost snapped at him, but she wasn't breathing. So she did. Several times.

"Don't let this be about your daddy," he added, his gaze soft, patting the seat like it was her. "Focus." He started the cruiser. "And quit shouting orders at me."

He read her well, damn him.

As many times as they'd seen each other in their worst light, this slip from professionalism still embarrassed her. "You're right, old man," she said, then added a smirk to her occasional nickname for the mature-for-his-age reputation he'd worn since high school.

Contented, he left the parking lot and took the couple of streets that put them on the interstate—the traffic thicker than before. He remained silent, appearing to recognize the need for his friend to dwell.

She took a long fifteen minutes dwelling. Blindsided by Vic's loose association to her daddy, her thoughts weren't gelling as they should. Not after being coincidentally asked to hunt for Mickey Raines. Not with the PI hired to look for him being found dead . . . the same one who'd tried to call her. The last twenty-four hours swirled around her in so many pieces.

"Calling your lady client after finding all this?" Tyson asked finally.

"No," she said. "I want all the information you and I can dig up on Mickey first."

He nodded in agreement.

"I don't believe in coincidences," she said as much to herself as him.

He nodded again. No cop did.

Traffic slowed at the turn off 526. She unhooked her seat belt, leaned over the back, and retrieved the file on top, plopping the Renault folder open in her lap.

"Buckle up," he said.

Still reading, she reached for the strap, only to knock the papers into the floor. "Damn it!"

She leaned down, the papers askew, the photos sliding in the floorboard. After scooping them, she rebuckled and began the effort of reorganizing in chronological order, glancing at each item as she did.

"This is odd," she said, studying one page.

Ty just waited.

"Catherine Renault didn't hire Vic once Mickey went missing, like she told me at your momma's place. Catherine hired him months ago. There's all sorts of intel in here about Mickey." She fingered through the pages. "There's supposed to be a credit report . . . yeah, here it is." She held up a stapled stack of pages. "She researched Mickey from day one, from when they met. Hell, from *before* they met."

The credit report gave his address as his parents' farm. God, she didn't want to go out there.

"I realize your lady's rich, Q," Tyson said, "and your rich ass might answer this better than I can, but does someone at her level immediately hire a PI when finding someone they may like?"

"Possibly," she muttered, reading, letting the old worn insult blow by. "Some do that. There's stuff about his past apps, his family. Who he banked with." Turning to her friend, she frowned, weighing the conversation she'd had in the bar with this woman. "It's like she went after him first. Maybe they met about the apps then she fell for him. Maybe he pitched her somehow? Maybe his ideas were that good?"

"Maybe their relationship's legit," Tyson said. "But I agree, don't call her yet."

"Nope, I'm not. More to learn about before I throw a contract under her nose. She needs to think she's in charge, and I need to be able to forecast what she's going to ask before she asks it."

He grinned. "Aren't you the savvy sleuth when you put that temper behind you?"

"Knox told you I had skills, old man." She hit him in the arm. "And I'll forget I heard that temper remark."

AFTER AN HOUR at the Banks for Quinn to scan the Renault files into her computer, Tyson returned to work with the originals, vowing to let her in on anything he found. She left it up to him to analyze the closed files. Her microwave read ten after two, so Quinn made a PBJ sandwich with some of Jule's wild plum jelly before opening shop at her desk in the den. If she didn't eat now, she'd forget to.

Her desk angled neatly into the corner abutted by two pecan-paneled and windowed walls—custom built to fit the room. The pecan tree vista welcomed to her left, ever waiting for when she lifted her head and needed a break. Typing one-handed, eating with the other, she worked, no sounds other than paper shuffles and her great-grandmother's Ansonia glass-domed clock ticking gently over the fireplace.

She created a file on Mickey, inserted the scans, and noted facts into her system for ready reference before securing copies in her safe down the hall. Then she opened TLO, the database she commenced a case with to research both clients and investigative targets alike.

Sandwich and milk consumed, she went at the keyboard full force. Databases never replaced experience, talent, and instinct, but decent PIs appreciated the leads these databases provided. A licensed investigator with a permissible purpose could access sensitive information unavailable to the public.

She subscribed to five such databases, driven to be sure of all available facts before relaying details to a client . . . or accepting a client before they were fully checked out.

Mitchell Raines, aka Mickey, established an LLC for his apps. Undergrad degree from the College of Charleston and master's degree in IT development from some college she never heard of. His mediocre education had led to a comfortable living off his techs-pertise, hovering just over a hundred K. The dirt farmer's son had evolved.

Vic's paperwork correlated with the intel from Quinn's sites. Mickey's finances were managed through an online banking site, nothing brick and mortar, which matched his techie profile. Seeing his bank statements would be nice, but that wasn't going to happen. Legally, anyway.

Registered to vote . . . in Craven County. Not a property owner. No apartment. Car, a 2015 white Lexus, registered in Craven County. His address had danced around over the years with the most recent being a UPS Store mailbox in Charleston. She bet if she asked UPS for Mickey's residence—and they were willing to reveal any information—they'd direct her to the same Craven County address known as Mickey's parents. No telling where he actually lived before shacking up with Catherine. Maybe some other girl. Maybe bunking with friends was how the kid saved some of his money.

Vic's personal notes made no deductions. They just recorded facts, keeping suspicions to himself or logged into notes on the missing laptop she never expected to recover. Regardless, she assumed he'd uncovered something serious enough to be killed for it. And that discovery carried him to Craven County.

So no defining direction on why Mickey remained elusive. She would guess he wasn't dead yet.

He did okay for himself. His living habits smelled scammy, but he had no criminal record, no traffic violations. You had to work hard to stay off the public record radar like this.

Rearing back in her chair, she spun by habit to watch the trees, thinking.

Too early to contact the family or they'd tell Mickey. If he didn't want to be found, he'd scatter. If he was kidnapped, as Catherine insinuated, the family would be distraught and already beating on the sheriff's door. They would've reported him missing, unless they were estranged. So either he didn't stay in touch with them or they knew where he was.

She started a timeline. Catherine hired Vic at least four months ago per the files here, but the Jackson Hole conversation with her indicated something shorter. Quinn leaned back in her chair again, reading Vic's documents, trying to understand why Catherine lied, wondering if there were other files.

She managed to translate more of Vic's scribblings, noting references to other times he'd worked for Catherine as indicated by generalizations about *last time* and *last year* and what Catherine wanted *differently this time*. Standard opening comments taken down when the client hires the PI and defines the task.

Quinn had scanned everything written or typed into her system, which included the folder and its tab. She flipped to that tab. The number 2 was written small to the far right of the active case folder.

Quinn would bet half a year's crop on a guess that Catherine utilized PI services more often than she admitted. And file number one represented a closed file with Catherine as the client.

Someone of Miss Renault's means often hired investigators to scout out scammers asking for investment, examine potential friends, and especially check out romantic interests. All of which would allow her to make decisions without having to rely on her father, his opinions, or involve him in her business. All legit. So why lie about it?

Quinn went to the kitchen and refilled her milk glass, half and half with the goat's milk. Leaning her backside against the counter, she took a sip and licked the thickness off her upper lip, wondering something else. The updates in Vic's files stopped one week before Craven SO found his body. Catherine said she'd quit hearing from the PI a week before. Two days dead seemed the preliminary estimate per Ferg's accounting of facts at the motel. So what happened in between his last week-old report and the day he died? Why the silence?

Vic had found the elusive Mickey. After all, how many people wore cowboy hats in Craven County? And the Mickey-looking guy had made an appearance on the day of Vic's death and called on a regular basis.

Either Mickey killed Vic, the most obvious, or maybe Mickey operated under duress, possibly coerced by some unknown entity to set Vic up. However, someone from Vic's past could've tracked him down, too. Catherine's deception likewise made her a suspect, though Quinn would be disappointed in Vic if he'd let a blind girl take him out. However, the blind girl came with a driver.

The motel footage showed neither, however, if you considered Ferg's security reliable.

She returned to the family room and texted Ty. *Need all files from his office not just what we brought.*

He quickly replied. *Already have the North Charleston locals picking them up in the morning.*

Of course he had, and she kicked herself for giving him orders again. The guy was too damn nice to her, and sometimes he even told her so. She'd behaved nothing like this while under the FBI umbrella, but then, no supervisory agent would've tolerated the first smidgeon of attitude. Out here, untethered in the wild, she had no bridle. Sometimes good, but more often to her chagrin.

Shame Ty hadn't had the chance to go to college. He would've been scooped up by Quantico in a heartbeat. From behind a grin, she wondered how that would've played out . . . if they could've landed similar assignments. The two kids grown into special agents, like the crusaders they pretended to be in their mystery creations across the woods, fields, and rivers of Sterling Banks. Minus the burlap-sack capes and dime-store binoculars.

Knuckles rapped on the glass doors barely a second before one slid open. "You okay for company?" Jonah said, hesitating as she rounded the corner to meet him.

She waved him in, sighing. "Thinking hard. What time is it?"

"Five," he said, passing her to head straight to the kitchen where she'd just come from. He returned with a ginger ale, from a stash Quinn kept supplied just for him. She returned to her desk, whirling her chair around to see him.

Plopping his long, lanky self in a swivel leather recliner, he propped one work boot over the opposite knee and unscrewed the drink top, tucking the bottle cap in his shirt pocket.

Jule, his mother, and de facto mother to all on Sterling Banks, disallowed cans and plastic for environmental reasons, and if they couldn't abstain from carbonated drinks, then make it something decaffeinated with some semblance of beneficial value . . . but always in glass.

Tyson, Jonah, and Quinn. They'd always be children in Jonah's mother's eyes . . . and friends in each other's.

"Heard about the body at the motel," he said, raking through long auburn hair, getting it out of his face. "Who was it?"

Shaking her head, Quinn pivoted her desk chair slowly side to side. "Nobody you know."

He chugged the soft drink a second time, then propped it on his knee as if finally sated. "But you do?"

"From a long time ago," she replied. "Bring home the new goats?"

"Yeah." He rocked the chair, clearly recognizing the change in subject. "Cashmere. One buck and two nannies."

48

A grin and image of Jule took her mind off the case. "Aww, she's been wanting cashmeres. That was good of you to fetch them for her. Any of them bred?"

"One, yeah."

"Hmm," she said. "Think she'll cross the buck this fall with the other breeds?" Bucks mated better in the fall, higher libido and sperm count.

He laid his head back and continued to rock. "She hasn't said."

Both hushed for a few seconds, the house feeling immense in the silence, the two so natural where they sat. When she looked back, figuring goats the safest subject, he beat her to the punch. "So this means you're doing your PI thing again."

She popped forward, both feet flat on the floor, her gaze softened by a friendly scold. "So what if I am?"

Jonah arrived on the Banks at age four when Jule was hired to assist Graham and Maggie in handling their newborn twins. Jonah and his mother had lived in the manor for their first couple of years on the farmstead, at first for Jule to assist in the late-night feedings. After Quincy died three weeks past his first birthday, Jule tended as much to the grieving mother as Jonah, age five, gravitated to Quinn. He'd been her big brother her entire life.

And he had never acclimated to her law enforcement tendencies.

"Had just hoped you'd gotten that out of your system, Quinn. It's been a couple months since that straying husband thing you had in Walterboro."

"*Out of my system?*" she mocked. "It's part of my system, you clod."

"You should be paying more attention to Sterling Banks," he said. "While I'm honored to be working this place, your daddy would want you—"

She pointed at him. He hushed, but he'd endured her lectures before. This was their perpetual crossroad. "Don't lecture me, Jonah," she said. "Besides, you only came by to learn who the body was."

"No." He polished off the ginger ale. "Just confirming if you'd be involved and how much time you'd ignore the trees."

"You've always hated me being in law enforcement," she said.

49

"But you're not in—"

She jabbed the air with that still pointed finger. "Not joking with you about that, Jonah. Don't tell me what I'm not. If you can't function without me present—"

"Simmer down, Princess." His mouth flattened, and he quit rocking. "Jesus, you're sensitive today."

"Then shut up about the arrangement," she said, rising from her chair. "Sometimes you treat me like a brat."

"Only when you act like it."

She growled under her breath at his calm. "Be back in a second. I've got to go pee."

In the hall bath, she did her business but paused before going back out. Jonah did this every single time she took a case. Even on the occasional, boring infidelity case, he turned all brotherly on her, chastising her for *choosing danger*, he called it. Always emphasizing why be a PI when God had gifted her with this wonderful other life.

She loved the boy, well, the man. No doubt he wanted the best for her. But he clearly attributed anything law enforcement as potential for harm. He couldn't give her abilities credit for protecting herself.

She turned on the faucet and vehemently scrubbed her hands. But how dare he, in his entitled sort of way, rub her nose in Sterling Banks. Yes, she adored the place, and she understood damn good and well her fortunate circumstances, but screw him. That didn't mean she couldn't have other interests. Just like he could have other interests.

Hers was being a PI. His was . . . goats. And Jule.

Okay, not his life's choice either, and any decent operation anywhere in the state—the Southeast even—would be grateful to hire him. Sometimes she fathomed he stayed for her, but logic told her he stayed for Jule. At least he had a parent.

And Ty had Lenore.

She turned the water off, dried her hands. With a hard exhale, she leaned stiff-armed on the pedestal sink and dropped her chin to her chest.

God, she could be an ungrateful bitch at times.

She took a few breaths and straightened the towel. It wasn't that

Jonah criticized as much as he fought to protect her. Like he'd done since before she could walk. He couldn't stand to see her hurt.

And damned if she didn't run to him when she was.

After Graham's death, Jonah returned to Sterling Banks and stuck around as both caretaker of the farm and caregiver to Jule, who'd been clobbered by Graham's murderer. Quinn had mourned her father deeply, too. Very deeply, and Jonah tended her as well, regulating the booze, not letting her sleep for days on end when depression struck her. For months they coexisted as a makeshift family.

He'd seen the worst of her.

Then he never left.

She and Jonah were bound by a similar fate, having given up the career each thought they'd done all the right things to achieve. Him managing a commercial agricultural genetics program in the upstate, and her chasing bad guys. Both rising stars in their chosen professions.

Tyson, too, for that matter. Even if he could've afforded college, he'd have never left Lenore, the mother who opened a diner when her husband died of leukemia. They'd all three been saddled with an unspoken, unintentional responsibility bestowed upon them by parents . . . with each of the trio holding onto a small resentment that went unsaid.

Their unrequited destinies filled the spaces between them, conjoining them in a natural camaraderie. Though hinted at like Jonah had just done . . . they never expressed in clear sentences how their beloved parents had unintentionally harnessed them to a different future. So they spoke of other things, changing topics, leaving the scab unscratched.

Their lives could be much, much worse, though.

Guilty for making him wait, fully expecting to find Jonah napping in the recliner, Quinn was eager to make amends. She halted entering the family room, not surprised at how fate had punished her poor behavior.

Jonah was gone, and Uncle Larry sat in his place.

Chapter 6

"BROUGHT US PLATES of chicken, beans, and slaw from Lenore's place," her uncle said, stiffly pushing himself to the edge of the same recliner that had just held Jonah. "Thought we could talk."

"Where's Jonah?" Quinn asked.

"He said something about chores and his momma when I invited him to stay. That's a damn fine boy, you know it?"

She agreed, but she'd scold him for leaving her alone with her uncle.

After pouring two glasses of tea, she opened bags and set out plates in the dining room, per the sheriff's choice. She recognized her uncle's message coming long before he put the napkin in his lap.

No, sir. This meal wasn't going to stay down easy.

Both Quinn and her uncle bore the height and slender genetics of the family. The average person walking into the dining room would see an uncle and his niece breaking bread by the dimmed light of the chandelier. Relatives relating. Maybe a bit opulently since they were seated at the end of a long, highly buffed mahogany table built for twelve, silver candlesticks dating pre-Civil War honored on a table runner of Irish linen. She never lit the candles for him, though.

Those closest to Quinn would recognize the awkwardness of two relations who rarely spoke to each other without keeping score.

Their game ran deep and often cut meat. Her Uncle Larry grew up in the manor with his older brother Graham and younger brother Archie. Graham loved the land more than the other two, falling naturally into place when their father groomed his sons to take the reins. Archie rebelled after college, joined an architecture firm in San Francisco, and moved off with his life partner.

Larry married, became sheriff of Craven County, and at thirty-nine broke up with a mistress in Beaufort who got even by telling his wife . . . who went after what would hurt him most. To keep Sterling Banks from landing in the hands of an angry woman, Graham bought her out once the divorce settlement was reached and sent her happily off to Charlotte.

And his death moved Quinn to the pinnacle of the Sterling hierarchy.

Her uncle still owned three hundred acres of the historic three thousand, much of it in marshy bottom land, the rest along one end of an orchard that Quinn managed, with her keeping the pecans as payment.

Burgers, fried chicken, pimento cheese sandwiches. Didn't matter. Dining at the mahogany table was his way of reminding Quinn he still belonged there. They both knew she ran things now, no matter how much he wanted to believe differently.

She hadn't asked for his key to the house, though. While she'd had the locks changed after Graham's death, in a moment of weakness she'd given her uncle one of the new keys . . . before she realized how much he had botched the investigation. Asking for it back seemed . . . wrong. Therefore, occasionally, he showed up uninvited.

The reason she kept a lot of things in her safe, like case files.

Jackson Hole diner bags spread across the table between them. Larry made it through half his coleslaw and a chicken thigh, lifted the breast to start in on it, then changed his mind and wiped his hands. "We need to talk."

"They make phones for that," she said, wolfing down a forkful of beans, rushing the meal.

He gave a long stare. "Your mother would be shocked at the things you say, you know it?"

"And yours wouldn't?" she blurted back, a clear memory of a grandmother who took no prisoners when faced with insolence or forgotten manners.

His eyes narrowed, then as if catching himself, he played like her bite had fallen short by groping for a biscuit in a bag. "Can we be civil tonight?"

Like I started this? After washing down a bite, she set her tea glass on the placemat. "*We* can try. You didn't come over here for my company, Uncle."

"You seem to think I never *want* your company, Niece."

"That's because you always arrive with an ulterior motive."

He sat back. "All right then, I'll get to it. Steer clear of this murder. Don't make me lean on Tyson."

She pushed her half-finished meal aside. The fight was on.

"Has Ty fully filled you in?" she asked.

"He has," he replied, the face-off stoic, daring . . . with her expecting his half-truths.

"You could use my help on this one," she added, then inserted the taunt that always irked him. "Unless you're calling in SLED." The State Law Enforcement Division in South Carolina had the forensics and stood ever willing and able to assist any local law enforcement entity when a case was beyond their expertise or manpower. Larry hadn't let SLED enter his county for his entire reign as sheriff.

"I'm not calling SLED."

"Okay then."

His brows went down, mashed over his eyes. "Okay then, what?"

She could spot all stages of his annoyance . . . knew every button to push. "Okay, then you need my help."

"I'll deputize you so you work for me."

Pausing, she threw him her sideways glance. "I will not work *for* you, Uncle Larry."

Thus far, the conversation was a canned version of past confrontations. Alone, the two of them could speak their minds without witnesses. But this new murder and her potential involvement had all the makings of being the worst clash of their roles since her daddy's . . . his brother's . . . death.

Her uncle's stubbornness had stood hard and fast back then, his grief not strong enough to override it and allow SLED into his territory. While the entire force was put on the case, none of the deputies had ever worked a murder. Traffic stops, marital disputes . . . all took a back seat to interviewing half the residents of Craven County, ticking off the same boxes. Did you know Graham? (Most did.) Were you aware of any issues on Sterling Banks to warrant the murder? (None did.) Do you know who did it? (Nobody did.) Did you do it? (None of them would consider such a thing.)

A haphazard, non-directional, half-assed investigation that allowed the murderer to escape, the clues growing stone cold. Deputies awaited direction until the sheriff had no more direction to give.

Quinn often envisioned the murderer residing in the county, watching, more and more secure in the hope of continuing a life in peace— unlikely to be caught by these county cops. She never believed, as Sheriff Sterling swore, that the killing was likely some seasonal farm worker who came and went, never to return. *Probably across the border by now . . .* he said for months after.

Mickey Raines had found the body and discovered Jule unconscious in the hallway. The boy was queried that night, per the sheriff, but then he left to parts unknown. Nobody Quinn knew had seen him since.

"You're not booting me off this murder," she said.

"Do you know the dead man?" Larry asked.

"I do. A PI friend of mine."

"Do you know the man he was hunting for?" he asked.

She paused at that. He would've used Mickey's name if he'd known it. Tyson had not fully enlightened the sheriff.

"I might," she answered trying not to let her gaze wander the room, a sign of untruth she easily spotted in others. Larry Sterling might not be Dick Tracy, but he was nobody's fool.

His mouth flattened at the *maybe.* "Does this involve one of your clients, Quinn? Because I cannot have you running over my work while you're chasing somebody's errant spouse."

"And I cannot discuss my client's business with you," she said.

He worked his mouth a bit, as if finding a stray piece of coleslaw. "If you want my office to cooperate with you, then you best return the favor, little girl."

She read between those words easily enough. If she wanted access to Ty, and all that came with the sheriff's office, she'd best cooperate.

The condescending way he said *little girl* irritated the crap out of her. Always had. But she'd been raised better than to call him *old man,* and besides, that was Ty's nickname. "The dead man was hunting for Mickey Raines," she finally said.

His forehead furrowed. "Did Tyson know this?"

She stood and snatched the empty take-out bowls and food bags off the table. "Damn it, Uncle Larry, focus. Focus! This isn't about Ty. My client wanted me to look for a business acquaintance, who I just realized this morning was the same Mickey Raines who found Daddy. There, you got your information."

"Give me your client's name."

"Uncle, you know better. Go do your job, and you'll get your answers." There. If he did his police work well, he'd figure it out. And if he'd sat down with Ty instead of expecting investigations to solve themselves, he'd learn the name Catherine Renault.

Frustrated he'd gotten under her skin again, she left for the kitchen, put the remaining biscuits in Tupperware and the two pieces of chicken in another. The coleslaw and beans were gone. Uncle Larry remained at the table, turning his glass to watch the overhead light reflection. She handed him the two containers. "Here's your lunch for tomorrow. Thanks for dinner."

"I wanted to talk," he said.

"Gotta work the books for the farm and do some research on a couple of my cases." She'd given him enough intel, which he'd confirm once he left here, if he had enough incentive in his bones.

Vic was a nobody in Craven County. Her uncle would ordinarily lose no sleep finding the culprit who'd murdered a nobody. Not unless he saw some sort of personal value in the solution. Someone transient, he'd believe. *Probably across the border by now.* But this time his niece was too curious, and she hadn't been able to hide that. Plus, Mickey was involved. He knew she wasn't walking away easily.

"You're booting me out, huh?" he stated.

"I said—"

"I heard what you said. It's what you're not saying that interests me. You're up to something. Mickey Raines used to eat at you like a cancer, and I had hoped you were done with that. The poor kid simply found your daddy and your caretaker. The murder was random. Make peace with it, girl."

Temper rose into her face, and she was well aware her cheeks blushed loud and clear when she was peeved. She was just as aware she hadn't always hated her uncle.

In fact, the notification call came to her in Atlanta from Uncle Larry. He'd been gentle. Graham had died the late afternoon of June 8, discovered by a twenty-four-year-old Mickey after he couldn't raise his employer on a short-range walkie-talkie. The kitchen door usually stayed unlocked during the work day, and Mickey had walked in at six fifteen.

Graham lay sprawled on his belly, skull cracked open with a heavy object they never found. Killed instantly. The assumption was that Jule had been in the kitchen, heard Graham give an exclamation of surprise and hit the floor. Hearing her come running, the killer hid, let her run past, hit her as well, but for some reason, maybe in the terror of seeing what he'd already done, had not quite landed his aim. She survived, but her injuries had robbed her of details.

Mickey had called 911.

"I have work to do," Quinn repeated.

Larry rose from the table with his leftovers and went to the patio doors, the canopy of freshly leafed pecan trees making the evening seem darker than it was. "If you see Mickey, tell me." He spoke like she was a child. "I'm not so sure he did this killing, either, but the facts will tell. Kid didn't seem the type. I know his family."

She bet he did. Part of why they never set foot on her side of the county. The man had no business being in law enforcement. "Good night, Uncle."

Once he exited, far enough away to no longer hear, she locked the doors. One day he'd push her to the point of locking him out. One day.

But not today. Not if she wanted in on this case.

She probably had more experience in violent crimes in her three years with the FBI than Larry Sterling had in his twenty plus with the Craven County Sheriff's Office. Her training alone better equipped her for a case such as Vic's . . . such as her father's. However, she wasn't so naïve to not see she represented a professional challenge to Larry. She should focus on solving the crime, though, not running over the sheriff and making a display of his ineptitude. Not unless she had to.

What she wouldn't give to be dealing with her other uncle, because Uncle Archie found his niece fascinating, loved her adventurous side, and sympathized with the heavy weight of history and the Sterling name on her young back. He'd be the one to have the serious drink with. But he craved urban and preferred people with diverse, more global thoughts than those carried around in the brains of the average Craven citizen. He preferred people not entrenched into the ways *things have always been done*. He'd sold his acreage to Graham after their father died, to be shed of that burden. At least he knew how to go after what he wanted in life.

Shaking herself away from thoughts of her faraway uncle, she lifted her phone and dialed, recorder on and notepad at the ready. After telling Uncle she had a client affiliated with the murder, she better get one. "Catherine? This is Quinn Sterling. Is this a good time?"

"Um, yes. I guess. Surprised you're calling. Thought you'd pretty much dumped me yesterday."

"My apologies," Quinn replied, willing herself to conform. "My first impression isn't always my best. I've had time to think, but first, are you seated?"

The "Yes" was delivered hesitantly, with a small question on the end.

"Was your private investigator Victor Whitmarsh?"

Silence.

"Catherine?"

"Not sure I'm supposed to tell you who he is. Do you ask your clients to let others know that you're in their employ?"

While she was correct, this was not the time. And Vic was no longer employed.

"Vic Whitmarsh is dead, Catherine. Killed in a motel in my county. He was already dead when you and I met, so trust me, you're not betraying a confidence."

The gasp was loud enough to grab someone's attention in the background. Catherine's voice faded as she pulled the phone away and told the person she was fine. While Quinn hadn't thought about it,

Catherine might have live-in help with her means, her blindness, and her boyfriend missing.

"How do you know he was my PI?" Catherine asked.

"His office file."

"Oh."

"And your friend's full name is Mitchell Raines. He grew up in Craven County, and his parents are Chester and Vicky Raines. He's slippery about his address, graduated from some obscure school in Florida, and developed a handful of semi-successful phone apps over five years. Keeps private. Hasn't posted to social media in the four weeks he's been gone. Am I getting warm?"

"Yes, you are. So what are you saying?"

"I'm saying I'll take your case."

"Not sure I still want you," Catherine said. "My word wasn't good enough? Did I not present my situation convincingly?"

Truth was, without the missing guy being Mickey and the dead guy being Vic, Quinn wouldn't care about the case. Taking it had not a thing to do with Catherine or her word. "The death of Vic Whitmarsh told me this could be quite serious," Quinn replied. "And your boyfriend might not have just walked off. Nothing to do with you. So is your offer still on the table?"

"Yes," Catherine said without a second's breath.

"Thanks for trusting in me. I'll email the contract. Meet me tomorrow at Jackson Hole again, only at eight a.m. No reason to have half the county know your business."

"Will the place be open?"

"It will be for me."

Quinn hung up. With ample hours left before bed, she'd do a little background work on her new client. They never told you everything, and she found it best to uncover what she could on a client before ink went on the paper.

But something else dangled undone this evening. She hadn't finished her conversation with Jonah. He would've met up with his mom, and they would've discussed Quinn working another case. Jule might harp anew on Quinn for dabbling in her silly PI work.

Trouble was, the involvement of Mickey Raines opened doubt about that June 8 night. And that drew in Jule.

Just what did Jule see that night? While she'd had a head injury and memory issues of the incident, Quinn caught too many faraway stares on days someone mentioned how Graham did things, or what a good guy he was. Maybe Jule couldn't recall clearly, but maybe more bits and pieces of memory had drifted back and she didn't want to say. Out of courtesy, nobody asked her anymore.

Quinn adored the woman who'd all but raised her, as much as Quinn loved Jonah like a brother, but that fateful night might come back to light, because if Quinn found Mickey, she'd ask him details about more than Catherine. She might finally get to talk to the person who might have seen her father die.

Chapter 7

AS QUINN REQUESTED, Lenore opened Jackson Hole early, but instead of waiting inside, Quinn parked behind the place and watched for the BMW. The driver led Catherine and her black shepherd to the door where Lenore escorted the guest inside.

Quinn waited at the car.

"I'm the new PI," she said. "Quinn Sterling. Wanted to make your acquaintance since you're the eyes and ears for Ms. Renault."

Wide in the shoulder, but not as thin in the waist as she imagined he once was in his younger years, the man remained fit, in brown dress slacks, a button-up shirt without the tie. A lightweight leather jacket hanging long and open. No jewelry. His dark hair cut crisp and tight with silver around the temple, olive complexion, and heavy brow hinting at a Latin background. Only a smidge taller than Quinn, he honored the shake. "Chevy Castellanos." He shook with strength in lieu of formality, his hand warm.

"A professional driver named Chevy. Easy to lock that in. You worked for Ms. Renault long?"

"A few years."

"Great. Any suggestions for me before I walk in there and interrogate her?"

His expression clouded. "Interrogate?"

Palms up, Quinn tucked her head in apology. "My bad. Loose terminology. Habit of the profession. We're just meeting to talk about what direction she wants to point me in and to sign a contract. Did you ever meet this guy she's hunting for?"

"I meet everyone," he said.

"Including her PIs?"

He just stared.

Leaning on his car, one boot across the other, she took him in. Attractive. Twelve or so years older than she. "Did Mickey seem genuinely interested in her or did you smell a con? Surely she uses you as a barometer, especially now that she's sight-impaired."

The man had the expression of a statue. "Kid seemed all right."

"What do you think happened to him?" She reached up as if to pick a piece of lint from one of his leather shoulders. Lint that wasn't there.

He tensed ready to respond if necessary but let her flick the spot. "Not my place to say."

With a doubtful scowl, she played on. "But I beg to differ, Chevy. You appear to be more than a driver. Your typical guy who lives behind the wheel would spread a little wider, if you get my meaning." She glanced around in attempt to see how his backside filled his slacks. "You're no stranger to a gym, so I view you as more of a protector." Letting her gaze come slowly back to his eyes, she added, "Maybe even a bodyguard, in which case you carefully vet her friends. Even follow her friends. Maybe even me."

"Maybe."

"So let's try this again. What do you think happened to Mickey Raines?"

"He took off," he said.

"Why?" she asked.

"Ms. Renault doesn't like to be kept waiting, Ms. Sterling. You can ask her. She's the one hiring you."

Quinn studied him over once again. "Thanks, Chevy. I'm sure we'll speak again."

He gave her the last word and got in the car. She tapped once on the glass, mouthed *thanks* and went inside.

For all she knew, ol' Chevy himself scared Mickey off, the driver seeing *the kid* as too socially inept or financially hungry. He could've even chased him off at the request of Catherine's father.

Mini breakfast biscuits sat on a plate at the table, a suggestion by Lenore last night when Quinn relayed the plan. Egg and cheese on one side. Ham on the other. Catherine already held a coffee. By the time

Quinn slid into the booth, Lenore met her with her own mug, gave an edgy undesirous glance down at Nero, and left the two alone.

"Let's get this straight up front," Catherine began, quite firm. "I'm not entirely comfortable with hiring another PI, but I can't see my way around it."

"And I'm leery of rich women with big black dogs," Quinn replied, accepting the challenge. Sometimes clients displayed vulnerability. Sometimes they preferred to show control. Regardless, the personality clashes needed addressing before they could dive into the business. They were both Type A women. Quinn got that. "Lenore orient you to the biscuits in front of you?"

"Yes."

"Good, then I can eat. I'm starved." She put two of each kind on her plate and quickly set her phone on record in the mixture of noises and movements. Clients rarely spilled easily at first and often distorted what they did. She preferred to have a baseline reference and facts to fall back on when clients turned sour after an investigation that went unexpectedly sideways.

Quinn opened the talk with something benign, segueing into Catherine's world. "Poor Nero, having to smell all this good food and pretend he isn't drooling for a taste."

"He doesn't drool. He's highly trained and didn't come cheap."

"Guard dog?" Quinn asked.

"Guide dog," Catherine corrected. "I chose a shepherd so that he'd just look mean like a guard dog. Had to go to Europe to find him."

Quinn peered at Nero, wondering if he received any loving at all.

Catherine's hands lingered on her cup before she used one to lift a biscuit, taking a hesitating nibble before deeming it edible. "This is really good."

Quinn bit into the egg one, her preference, itching to slip one to the dog. "Of course it is. Lenore's the best cook in three counties, but then I'm biased. She halfway raised me here in this diner." Two biscuits down. What was it about tiny food items that made them taste better?

"She sounds black," Catherine said. "You're obviously not. How did that work?"

Instinctively hunting for Lenore, Quinn heard her in the kitchen. Lenore would've rolled with the remark, but Quinn didn't want her to have to. "Through love and respect, honey," she said. "Love and respect." She took a swig of coffee to close the door on ignorance and change the subject. "How many PIs have you dealt with to hold such a dim view of our profession? Some of us have a lot to offer."

Catherine gave a small head toss. "Plenty. And I've read up a lot about private investigators. None of it good."

"I see," Quinn said, noting she was eating her fifth mini-biscuit. She dusted off her hands, wiped her mouth, and started to push the platter aside before realizing Catherine might want one, and she'd reach for where it was. "Have you ever thought that we might be the saviors for a lot of people in their hour of need? When the cops won't bother? When no one believes them?"

Sure enough, Catherine took another biscuit. "You make it sound like you're heroes."

"While you make us sound opportunistic," Quinn replied. "So now that we've peed in each other's sandbox and gotten it out of our systems, can we get down to business?" She laid out the papers. "It's a standard contract. A five thousand dollar retainer. Once it's depleted, I bill you weekly. Probably not much different than Victor Whitmarsh. Want me to pull Chevy in here to validate what you're signing?"

Catherine hesitated. Most likely at Quinn knowing the driver's name. Possibly at her abilities being doubted. "No," she said, wiping her mouth. She reached for Quinn to put the pen in her hand. "I know where you live."

Touché.

"You're shaking your head," Catherine told her newly hired employee even as the PI positioned the papers for a proper signature.

Quinn smirked, almost admiring the woman. "I didn't, but good guess. I thought about it."

Pulling out her checkbook, Catherine ripped off the already completed slip and handed it to Quinn, surprisingly for the right amount. Catherine had a good feel for things, apparently. No doubt if the dollar figure had been different, Catherine would've negotiated until it fit. "So what're you going to do first?" the new client asked.

"Find Mickey," Quinn replied. "And whoever murdered Victor Whitmarsh."

Wrinkles formed over Catherine's glasses. "I'm not hiring you to solve Victor's murder."

Quinn leaned forward to avoid being heard in the kitchen. With the place empty and jukebox off, their voices carried. "Mickey's disappearance and Vic's death are most likely linked. Any info learned about the one helps solve the other."

"You called him Vic."

"I did," Quinn said. "Most of the PIs in this state have heard of each other. Been a while, but we'd met."

"And you think Mickey killed Victor?"

"Not what I said." Quinn almost shook her head for emphasis. "But I need you to answer a few questions before I buckle down and start earning my money."

Catherine sighed as if put out by the request. "Ask away."

"Why was Vic killed?"

"How would I know? Find Mickey," she said. "Just find Mickey. He's my concern." Her voice waivered. "He's my world."

"Vic could've died *because* of Mickey. You thought about that? His murder wasn't a random act of violence." As much as her uncle might think it. "Who do you think could've done it?"

One sniffle. Jury was still out on the legitimacy of her emotional displays, subtle though they might be.

Lenore pushed through the swinging door from the kitchen and started prepping the bar. Peering over at the table, she waited for Quinn to nod back things were okay. She did.

"Go ahead," Quinn said to her client. "The owner can't hear us. Just don't get emotional or she'll feel she has to mother-hen you. Who do you think did it?"

"Not Mickey," Catherine said. "He's too sweet. Too focused on his future to mess it up."

"What if Vic discovered Mickey's past, in essence *jeopardizing* his future. If Mickey was on the brink of losing all he'd worked for, would he turn feral?"

"Mickey turn wild? Not a chance," Catherine said, without a beat.

Quinn popped right back. "What would *you* think about him if he lost everything? If he turned into nothing more than a kid with a dream that fell flat."

Catherine's voice softened. "I'd think no differently. Like I told you before, I love him. He's real. I don't find that often in my world." She hid behind her cup a while.

Lenore appeared, set a thermal coffee pot between them, and left, taking the platter with two cold egg biscuits with her. Quinn refilled her cup then hovered the pot. "Let me refill that for you." Catherine let her.

The air in Jackson Hole had begun filling with aromas in preparation for lunch. Onions grilling, mainly. Lenore stepped behind the bar, leaned down and put on background music. Folksy ballads. Volume subdued.

The early customers, those who started their manual labor close to dawn, would arrive around eleven, famished. The rest would steadily file in and out until two after which Lenore would start her transformation of diner to bar. Drinkers strolled in around four thirty, and during the week she shut down at eleven. Long days. The reason Quinn rarely made these early morning requests.

Time for more questions, before Chevy got impatient and Catherine tired of the *interrogation*. "What did Vic say in his last report to you, and when was it? Was it oral or written?"

"He called a week ago," Catherine said, back to her matter-of-fact self. Nero shifted under the table, his tag jingling until he laid his head down. "Said he had a solid lead about Mickey, and if things went well, he'd have positive news in a few days. And before you ask, he wouldn't elaborate, because I asked."

Quinn could understand that. "You've used Vic before, right?"

"On and off for a few years."

Now she tells the truth, and clearly didn't care she'd lied before. And the files didn't cover their entire timeline. "What kind of work? Backgrounds on boyfriends? Details on someone threatening to blackmail you? Simple business checks?"

"Why does it matter if I've used any PI before, for any reason?"

"Whoa, girlfriend. I'm checking off the necessary boxes, but it seems I struck a nerve which makes for more concerns on my part."

Catherine smacked the table, drawing Nero out from underneath. Standing on alert, he peered over the top at his handler first, then Quinn . . . holding the stare on Quinn.

"All. I. Want. Is. Mickey," Catherine said, her jaw tight. Maybe a few tears. Hard to tell behind the glasses.

Nero's whine for direction drew her hand to him.

Quinn kept still. "If you care to find another PI, feel free, but every question helps. Every honest answer helps more. The more you don't answer is more research I do and the more of your retainer I eat up doing it."

"I can afford it," she said.

"Not the point," Quinn replied, reaching for the folded contract papers. "The more time this takes, the less likely we find Mickey. Drag your feet and the further he gets from us . . . or the colder his body gets." She crinkled papers. "Want me to tear this up?"

"No." Catherine sulked. Nero must've been through this sort of behavior before, because he lost interest and lay back down.

"Let's run through this list and get you out of here then," Quinn said. "Nero's tiring of the drama."

"Nero—"

"First, did you and Mickey have a fight before he disappeared?"

"No."

"All was perfect on the home front?"

"Yes."

This was better. "Be aware that in absence of other information, until cops decide otherwise, your boyfriend is lead suspect for killing Victor Whitmarsh. Where do you think he is?"

"Um, his mother's place? His old apartment he once shared with a friend in Savannah?" Her gaze, if you could call it that, wandered left, as if she hunted for the right something to say.

Quinn recalled the Savannah address from the file . . . and of course she already knew the parents' address. "Did you ever go to his parents' house? Ever meet them?"

Again a negative reply.

Quinn opened the notes feature on her phone. "Give me his number," she asked, already having noted the number Vic had on file for the guy. "What happens when you call Mickey?"

"Mailbox is full. I've called him a hundred times. At least." As if realizing how that sounded, she lowered her chin. "That sounds rather desperate, doesn't it?"

She gave Quinn the same number she and Ty already knew. A hundred times? No wonder the mailbox was full. "You hired Vic earlier than you told me. Like months before, and that doesn't count the other times you hired him. He ran Mickey's credit and background. Why'd you lie about that last time?"

Big inhale from across the table. "So you wouldn't think I couldn't function on my own."

Maybe they had more in common than Quinn thought.

At a fast clip, Quinn hit the last routine items. Who were his relatives and friends? Had Catherine met any of them? Had he been previously employed outside of his independent phone app business? Former girlfriends? Where did Mickey grow up? Some subjects thrown out to gather intel. Some as tests.

"You know damn good and well where Mickey grew up, Quinn." Catherine's stern about-face cut the momentum. "Why do you think I ran you down all the way over here in this sad-sack county?" She removed her glasses and delivered more of that seeing but not-seeing stare of hers. "He's from Craven County. He used to work for your father. He called the authorities when Graham Sterling was murdered."

Touché again, Catherine. "I'm listening," Quinn said, admittedly knocked on her back foot.

"He wanted to avoid you as much or more than you probably wanted to find him," Catherine said, no sneer, no laughter, just elemental fact. "Once my go-to PI went silent, I figured the next best person to hire was Quinn Sterling. Who else would be interested enough to go after this particular boyfriend?" Catherine lifted her purse and retrieved a lip gloss. "So, Miss Hot Shot, think I'm more than a daddy's girl now?"

Nope, not so much. And kudos to the blind girl on her delivery.

Quinn glanced at her phone, to ensure it still recorded. "Did he kill my father?"

"We never talked about it."

"You knew about the incident and didn't ask?" The question had instantly flipped their roles, and Quinn regretted asking as soon as it fell out.

"Frankly, I just didn't care," Catherine said . . . and smiled.

Chapter 8

CATHERINE RENAULT left Jackson Hole properly chauffeured in the back of the BMW, leaving with the upper hand Quinn never saw coming. It was ten a.m., too early for lunch, yet she remained seated, simmering until she finished the last drop in the thermal coffee pot. Jazz still played in the background and in an hour might change to soft country when the first customers moseyed in.

"Staying for lunch?" Lenore asked. "I got some chicken-fried steak prepping back there."

"No, ma'am." Quinn looked up at the bar owner and longtime conscience mender. "Sometimes I hate my job."

Lenore mashed her lips in a half-smile and slid into Catherine's spot. "She bested you, huh? So quit messing around with this stupid, silly-assed job. It's not like you don't have a farm to run."

Quinn's heart fell a little. "I can't believe you said that."

But the woman's expression was more compassionate than critical. Lenore was the balance for Jule's tough love. People with real mothers should be so lucky.

"Sometimes your name gets the better of you, Quinn. You're so used to having an advantage around here that you aren't used to someone else winning."

Quinn squinted, trying to read the woman's eyes, hearing what sounded like a repeat of what Jonah said last night. "You calling me spoiled?" She started to say she had nobody to spoil her anymore but caught herself. Lenore was ever there when Quinn needed her, as were Ty, Jonah, and Jule.

Lenore squinted her eyes a tad. "A bit spoiled, yes. Not all of it your fault, though. You couldn't help being born with that name. You didn't cause the tragedies that made you grow up wary." She reached over and rubbed Quinn's hand holding the empty cup. "And you didn't ask for that farm to tear you away from what you wanted to do."

Quinn didn't cry in front of people. Hadn't since Maggie O'Quinn Sterling died from breast cancer when Quinn was a kid too young to lose a mother. Dry-eyed even at her daddy's funeral, she found weakness in publicly displaying her feelings. Lenore had tapped a raw spot, but Quinn shoved it back down, way down.

"You got nothing to prove," Lenore said. "But if you believe you need to do this PI business to make you whole, then accept it, girl. The bad comes with the good, and nothing's worth doing that isn't a challenge. You can pick and choose life only so far and so many times, but the best character comes from when it picks you, roughs you up, and forces you to wade through it."

Lenore ought to know after picking up the pieces when her husband died of a heart attack at age forty-two, when Quinn and Ty were fifteen. Her hardworking Mr. Jackson had fostered a solid work ethic in the entire family, and Lenore had approached Graham for his opinion on a plan to help her continue that ethic for Ty. Ty's daddy had left them enough insurance to put a down payment on an empty store outside town, and if they buried the father frugally, had enough to outfit most of a restaurant. That and a small loan put Jackson Hole on the map.

"Yes, ma'am," Quinn said, ever willing to listen to this woman who was the epitome of goodness, hard work, and sound living. "I hear you. Suck it up."

"Right, girl. Now, you need some okra?"

With a weak smile, Quinn answered, "No, ma'am. I kinda overdid your biscuits. My client only ate two of those, you know. The others are piled deep in *my* gut."

"Hunh." Lenore stood and smiled. "You'll be hungry by two. Think about it. Won't take me a minute to pop those things in some grease." Another pat on the arm, and she was gone.

That woman was a saint.

Truth was Quinn admonished herself for not thinking that Catherine would've researched her. She hired PIs like hairdressers, for God's sake.

Who's to say she hadn't employed more than one? She'd probably had Vic checked out before she hired him.

The Charleston blue-blood lady didn't care how involved Mickey was in Graham Sterling's murder. She hadn't asked her pillow partner about his past, and once she learned of it, hadn't delved deeper. Even if she didn't give a rat's ass about the Sterlings . . . she wasn't concerned how such a traumatic experience had impacted her boyfriend's life?

Quinn had misread Catherine. Hell, the woman might not even be blind.

Who said Mickey wasn't hiding from her?

Quinn typed on her phone. *Can you come to the house?* Then tacked on, *Don't tell the sheriff.*

He's in his office and watching, Ty texted back.

Come after work?

See you around five.

"Miss Lenore?" she hollered. "I got time for one cup of okra, please."

By the time she finished eating, lunchtime would be here, drawing hands out of the Lowcountry fields. This was the time of day when most climbed off the tractor, kicked off the boots, and came inside to grab a bite to eat.

The perfect time to visit Chester and Vicky Raines.

QUINN HADN'T BEEN to this side of the county in a while . . . maybe years . . . maybe since the last time she visited the Raines family six years ago.

The Raineses didn't have much more than seventy acres, but in vegetable crop language, that was a sizeable spread. Truck crops, as they were called, took considerable hands-on labor once the ground was tilled and bugs sprayed. With this being April, Chester, maybe even Vicky, would be planting their fool heads off. April Fool's Day meant the end of any frost hazard, and that had been a week ago. Some even dared to plant the third or fourth week of March this close to the ocean since warm currents kept things balmy . . . at least until it turned jungle-sweltering hot in June.

Lunch was the best time to catch them.

No GPS needed; she remembered the location. The long, three-hundred-yard dirt road took her truck through the middle of tilled fields which had already been planted. Looked like melons breaking ground on the left . . . tomatoes planted as seedlings on the right, expecting stakes in another week. Both would ripen in ninety-five degrees and eighty percent humidity, with the only way to harvest by hand. Yeah, she preferred pecans. Always in the shade.

Closer to the residence, trees grew thicker, encroaching as if protective of the dirt-farming family. With underbrush assistance, the dense forest turned black barely ten feet in from the mowed surroundings, with poison ivy as thick as your arm snaking fifty feet up to disappear into the canopy.

The small brick house stood boxy in shape, maybe eighteen-hundred square feet tops, at the base of all that growth. The barn in back dwarfed the house, but then the barn was what housed the operation. That and an open pole barn beside it.

The residence had been freshly painted, though, and the mature shrubs showed pride of ownership, pruned into tall, rounded domes on three sides of the house. In the yard, monster George Tabor azaleas in eight-foot clumps bloomed powder pink with purple throats.

Quinn parked her upscale rust-red pickup behind another Ford fifteen models older and ten shades duller. A federal-blue Toyota sat nearby, old enough to have crossed the hundred-thousand-mile mark and then some. She waited a few seconds, watching for anyone moving around . . . for anyone to come to the door. When nobody did, she studied the windows for blinds to crease or curtains to flutter back into place.

Her truck didn't say Sterling, but even if they didn't recognize her vehicle, her red hair was a dead giveaway. When she wanted more anonymity, she drove a nondescript gray sedan and wet her red hair to slick it into a ponytail that could be coiled up under a hat.

But here, with these people, she needed to be open with no clandestine air of any kind. The only way to build trust was head-on . . . especially with people who'd already painted the Sterlings as untrustworthy.

She studied her surroundings. The equipment under the pole barn ranged from decades in age to much newer purchases. A few farm hands—some dark-skinned from the sun, others darker by heritage—huddled near two old trucks with wooden sides, used to haul produce when the time came, and whatever else before. A light layer of dust touched it all.

She'd timed her arrival just right. Workers glanced up but quickly turned back to their lunch and conversation. She stepped onto the abbreviated porch too small for a rocker and rang a doorbell she couldn't hear . . . then knocked.

Quinn breathed deep, held it, and let it loose when the door opened behind the screen.

In work clothes showing sign of wear and dirt, Chester Raines displayed no emotion. "What can I do for you, Ms. Sterling?"

Home-cooking aromas filtered through the screen, reminding her of Lenore. Quinn mustered a soft smile. "Sorry to bother you, Mr. Raines, but I wondered if we could talk. I figured you'd be at lunch about now, so if we could chat while you took your meal, I'd be grateful."

He moved nary a muscle. "Tell me why I should."

She'd played these excuses in her head on the way over. Should she offer to bury the hatchet? There really wasn't much of a hatchet, though. Their son had found her daddy dead, called 911, then left town. She'd approached them a week later, on this same stoop, seeking Mickey.

It hadn't been her finest moment.

"Mr. Raines, I want to apologize for . . . that evening I was last here."

He remained frozen, no doubt recalling the details.

"I made demands I had no right to make," she said. "But I'd lost Daddy, and I just wasn't thinking straight."

"Chester," came a voice from within the house. "Let her in. Your lunch is getting cold."

He opened the door and held it for her. Quinn nodded, said "Thanks," and entered.

Though she hadn't taken stock of the décor last time, she noted a sense of familiarity. Dated furniture, crocheted protectors on the sofa and end tables. Homey mixed with antiques and thrift store.

In the kitchen, a coat rack hung on the wall leading to the back door, through which she could see the barns. On the rack hung two jackets, one a lined flannel, the other a Carhartt, with several agriculturally branded ball caps, smudged and well-used. Totally unlike the clean high school and college caps on the hall tree she passed on the way in.

Souvenirs from the days Mickey lived there, maybe. Mickey's old phase, before he considered himself more of a Stetson cowboy kind of guy.

Chester led them to the Formica table for four where a half-eaten plate of ham, potato salad, and field peas sat waiting. Quinn figured the peas were from the previous summer's crop, put up and frozen to last through the winter and spring. The smell would've enticed her if her belly weren't so full of Lenore's biscuits and okra.

Mr. Raines sat and resumed eating. Vicky Raines had aged, her shoulder-length brown bob now long, pinned on the sides, riddled with gray. "Can I fix you a plate?" she asked.

"No, ma'am," Quinn replied.

"Then what do you need?" Having shown enough manners to get by, the wife's brusque tone made it clear they cared little for small talk.

Quinn sat proper, feet on the floor, hands on the table. "I'm trying to locate Mickey," she said.

Chester forced down a forkful of peas to grab his voice. "What the hell for?"

"A close friend of his came to me, knowing we were from the same county, and asked if I'd help find him. He quit communicating with her a month ago, and she's beside herself."

"She?" Vicky asked. "What's her name?"

Quinn expected this. "Afraid I can't reveal that."

Dropping his fork on the plate, Chester scowled. "Then get the hell out."

"I'm sorry," Quinn said, leaning on the table, hands out in a plea. "But she's worried sick that something's happened to him, and she hired me to find him."

Vicky absentmindedly folded a dishtowel. "Is it true that you're some kind of law?"

"Used to be FBI," Quinn said, only because she hoped the acronym and agency reputation would carry weight and reassure them she was more than just a Sterling and all that implied.

"Used to be?" Chester asked.

"Yes, sir. Came back to Craven County to run the farm after Daddy died, but I'm also a private investigator. Our ethics don't allow us to reveal our clients, so my apologies about that."

Vicky glanced at her husband, then back at Quinn. "Mickey in any trouble?"

"Not that I'm aware," Quinn said. "Has he been in touch with you?"

Again with the look exchange.

"No," Chester said, and picked up his fork to polish off his last bites.

"Mrs. Raines?" Quinn asked.

She shook her head.

They weren't budging off whatever stance they'd decided on. "I have noted that Mickey uses your address to register everything in his life," Quinn said. "His vehicle, voting, even a tractor purchase. Make and model like the Massey Ferguson parked out there under the shed. He must have been in touch in recent months, right? Can you please just tell me that he's local and not hurt?"

Vicky rose and cleared the plates, putting her back to the table. "Haven't heard from him in three months."

Quinn stood and carried a dirty glass to the sink. "Is that different than his usual routine?"

The wife glanced over. "Mickey has no routine, Ms. Sterling."

"Maybe he's been in touch with other relatives. Other friends? Maybe he found another girl. At least that would be closure."

"For Catherine, you mean," Vicky said.

Chester snapped to attention. "Shut up, Vicky. Our son's personal business isn't open to the public, especially the Sterlings."

"Have you met Catherine?" Quinn continued, drawing upon the mother figure. "Were they serious? A mother can tell, you know. They can read it in their child's eyes."

76

"We haven't met her," Vicky said.

Scraping the chair's stoppered metal legs across the linoleum floor, Chester'd had enough and rose. "Vicky," he said more forcefully, "I said quit talking." Then in a harsher stare, he threw orders to Quinn. "You can leave my house. My family's business is none of yours. We gave you some benefit of the doubt the last time 'cause you were in mourning. But now you have no damn excuse other than to snoop for some passing girlfriend of Mickey's who happens to have more money than sense. Her money doesn't work here, and neither does yours."

Time to excuse herself. "Thanks, and here's my card in case you hear from him. We're only worried about his wellbeing. Again, I'm sorry about my behavior from before." She went to leave and paused in the foyer. "Just like Daddy did, I respect every farmer in this county. If there's anything I can do for you, please call. And you're welcome to come by any time." She let herself out without hearing the response. Small farms had a lot of pride.

She directed her pickup back up the dirt road from whence she came, Quinn knowing full well that they needed to get back to work. On the highway, however, she traveled a couple hundred yards to a chained-off path of a hunting cabin and pulled in, shutting off the engine.

The bug she'd planted under the kitchen table wasn't crystal, and most certainly wasn't legal, but it was doing its job.

"How much damn trouble are you in, boy?" Chester scolded.

The mom and dad had phoned their son demanding explanation, putting the call on speaker for both to hear.

The responding voice came across distant, but Quinn recalled Mickey well enough to bet a thousand on it being his. "Why do you think I'm in trouble?"

"Quinn Sterling was in our house just now asking, that's why," fussed the mom. "Is this old trouble or new trouble?"

"Not for you to worry, Mom."

"Damn it, Son, you don't need a Sterling on your ass. She noted the Massey tractor you bought us, so she smells you. What's going on?"

"She holds a grudge," Mickey said. "Do not get involved."

Quinn blinked hard. No, no damn way. She'd never threatened Mickey. *Tell him the message I gave you, Vicky.*

"We'll help," his mom pleaded. "Call the authorities."

Mickey scoffed. "What, her uncle?"

"The FBI, then," she said. "They won't like her acting this way."

"Like she still doesn't have ties there?" the son argued, his fluster at his parents' ignorance almost rude. "You can't get involved," he said. "This is between me and Quinn."

Quinn stared off into the trees, stymied, having no idea what the heck he was talking about.

Some of the county stigmatized him for disappearing while Larry quickly blew him off. While Quinn wanted to talk to Mickey, she didn't hate him. Didn't blame him. She had pursued him early on solely for closure. Pursued him now because of Catherine.

Quinn and Mickey had no vendetta. They had no feud.

But this behavior sure made him look guilty when it came to Vic.

Chapter 9

THE WEIGHT OF being a pariah in the Raines household pressed heavier than Quinn expected, one she wasn't quite sure she merited. Her last visit to the farm went rudely, but damn. Mickey downright lied to his parents on that call. She didn't blame him for her father's death . . . and she had no mission to *get even.*

Should she?

Or was Mickey diverting his parents' attention from the real problem that had chased him underground? Something to do with Catherine, or more seriously, Vic.

At least Mickey wasn't dead.

Yet she was beginning to feel that Catherine wasn't worried he was.

A patrol car rolled by, and she exchanged a wave with the driver. Harrison, she thought. Ty wasn't due at Sterling Banks until after his afternoon shift, another three hours or so away. Patience wasn't her best virtue, and she yearned doing something in the interim to expedite this case . . . something like clarifying the unexpected twist she'd just overheard. A twist well worth the cost of the bug she'd planted under that kitchen table.

But like everyone reminded her, she also had a farm to run, and visiting the Raineses had reminded her why she ought to be grateful she managed pecans instead of vegetables. The sun beamed exceptionally bright in a cloudless sky, and she donned shades from the center console, giving the spring flora a popping green on her way home to tend to her agricultural responsibilities.

Once on the grounds, she chose to cruise the side roads around the orchards, noting the cleanliness of the grounds beneath the trees. The trees shed limbs naturally, and while it wasn't critical that they be gathered the day they hit the ground, it was important that they be disposed of in a somewhat timely manner. Squirrels helped shed the smaller limbs, and the older trees shed more than the younger as their widespread canopies vied for the full sun that prompted more excellent production. She waved at a couple hands tossing branches in a farm truck bed. All seemed good. Thus far, fingers crossed, she and Jonah had seen enough signs to dare hope for a remarkable yield. A lot still depended on the rain throughout the summer . . . and no fall hurricanes, ever the coastal Carolina worry.

Jonah waved her down on the southwest quadrant. "Climb out of that truck, and I'll put you to work," he said. "Got guys spreading fertilizer in the southeast. Was about to go check on them. If I find time, I plan to grab a cherry picker to thin out some upper branches in Heritage."

The oldest orchard nearest the house.

"Dang, Jonah. You need to tell your boss to cut you some slack." Quinn slid the glasses atop her head, shoving red curls back with them. "Let me change clothes, and I'll go get the picker for you." Short of gathering pecans, the picker was her favorite task. That lift could carry a man thirty feet into the branches, and she'd loved that chore since her daddy had first let her take a ride, a makeshift harness in the bucket designed just for her.

"Bring an extra saw with you," he said, and she nodded and drove off, eager to get her hands dirty and brow sweaty for the rest of the afternoon.

Took her ten or twelve minutes to reach the house where she parked in the garage, going in through the kitchen door.

Silence greeted her and it washed over her as it did sometimes. Scarlet alone in Tara . . . without all the suitors. She remembered her daddy's presence, shoes in the mud room, dishes in the sink . . . his scent in the coolness of air-conditioning. The washer running when she hadn't started it. Dinner in the oven on the days he chose to cook.

Now nothing happened without her doing it . . . with nobody around to share it with.

Didn't take long, after grabbing a pair of cargos and a tee, to escape her melancholy and leave her almost giddy at rolling out the cherry picker. She fished a long-sleeved shirt out of the dryer, worn to avoid scratches amongst the limbs.

She glanced at the alarm screen out of habit. The devices hung in four strategic spots on the first floor, installed when she'd gone off to college, and while she rarely activated the system, she did check it for malfunction. A message flashed about the front door being ajar.

Odd. Everyone close to her entered through the kitchen or via the back porch. The front door was reserved for the unfamiliar, the salesman, or, in her mind, a con casing to see if anyone was home.

Shimmying into her second sleeve, she cut through the kitchen into the hallway, but one foot into the foyer drew her up short, the sight stealing the breath from her body.

Exactly where Graham Sterling had fallen before, spread an eighteen-inch puddle of maroon.

In her mind her first instinct would be to touch it, see how warm it was, but training threw herself against the wall instead. She snatched glimpses to all sides. Nobody at the exit, the entry way to the living room, or either side of her in the hall. No noise. No breathing . . . other than hers that she fought to quiet in order to hear.

With a swift ricochet to the past, she was standing there years ago, the coppery odor of her father's life filling her nose though she hadn't arrived home until fifteen hours later. Back against the same wall, she was unable to peel her gaze off the same type of stain.

Her mind launched back to her painful pleas for details from Tyson, her uncle, various other deputies . . . everyone but the killer and the man who discovered the body.

One of those last two could have recreated this scene for her. Had to be someone who'd been here before.

The front door remained open a few inches, but that could be a deception. Someone could be in her house, watching how this prank played out. Or outside waiting for her to scout the front.

No way to get past the spot without exposing her to whoever could be waiting in the two adjoining rooms . . . or in the yard.

Quinn backtracked her way to the family room and her desk,

hugging the wall, the furniture, the corners and doors, instincts activated before she thought to use them. From the upper right drawer, the nine mil filled her hand first, her phone second . . . speed dial straight to Ty to get his ass there.

A 911 call wouldn't dispatch anyone nearly as fast.

Then a text to Jonah to come quickly, keep it stealth, and be careful. She didn't have the time to say why, and he'd come with his handgun.

Set on mute, she tucked the cell in her shirt pocket and swept the house, praying to God she found the son of a bitch. For the first time since she could remember, she welcomed being related to the sheriff, because if she found this bastard, he was going down . . . and the story could be sorted later by Uncle Larry.

Blood throbbed up her neck. Room to room, from the den through the kitchen, into the side room off the hall, she cleared one space at a time, knowing full well someone could be mocking her by staying one room ahead . . . or behind.

She finally made it to the porch, touching nothing except with the toe of her shoe or elbow. House clear, she decided. She hoped.

No vehicle waited to give a perp an escape, nothing in disarray. With weapon still in hand, she came out, around from the kitchen side to protect the scene, and she sat on the front top step, leaning a shoulder against the river rock wall, waiting for her support team to arrive.

Enough time to let her pulse lessen, her temper quell, her mind wrap itself around the what-ifs and whys of this makeshift déjà-vu.

The sirens sounded in the distance well before she saw the first blue light, Ty leading . . . the sheriff driven by a deputy right behind. A third cruiser with two other deputies bringing up the tail.

No screeching tires or fishtailed arrival. No rubber streaks or ruts in the manor's lawn, but they piled out like ants, weapons drawn, tensed and fanning out until Quinn stood and approached. "No one's here unless they disappeared into the orchards. Feel free to cover the grounds, but I'd prefer you cover the house area first."

Ty holstered his weapon and, hands on both her shoulders, he gripped hard. "Are you alright?"

To assuage his concern, she draped a limp wrist across one of his arms, her firearm at her side. "Don't I look all right?"

He drew her to him so others couldn't hear. "You didn't sound a hundred percent on the phone."

"I didn't panic either, did I?" She pulled away as her uncle strode up. "Hey, Uncle Larry."

"See the guy?" he asked.

"Yes, I'm good, Sheriff. Not injured at all. Thanks for asking."

With a discreet growl for only her ears, he blew out hard. "Quinn . . ."

She waved toward the front door. "I believe by the time I came on the scene, he was gone. Blood's already congealing. Noted no strange vehicle when I drove by the house to check the orchards, and none when I returned to the house." She avoided saying *her* home, or *her* entryway. Not to Larry Sterling.

"If you called in SLED, their forensics might help you ID the blood faster," she added.

Jonah ran up breathless, his .38 drawn. "What happened?"

"A lot of good you are," the sheriff said, giving him a once-over, turning back to his niece. "You and I need to talk, you hear me? Once we're done here, meet me in the—"

"Already obligated," Quinn said, capturing Ty with a glance to let him know they were still on for later. No way she wanted to miss the scheduled powwow with him now.

"Tonight then," the sheriff said.

"I'll give you a half hour tonight and then I'll come in tomorrow," she countered.

Her uncle homed a stare on her, then accompanied his deputies inside the house.

"Never liked that man," Jonah said under his breath before turning to her. "What the hell, Quinn?"

"Someone left me a sick present on the hall floor," she said. "Would like to say they broke in, but you know how that goes. A lot of folks have access to this house."

Ty gave her forearm a gentle shake. "I'm headed inside. You sure you're okay?"

With a smile she said, "Go be a cop, Ty." And he left.

Jonah pulled her to the rockers on the porch, apart from the others, and slid his chair around to halfway face her. "What've you gotten yourself into?"

"Jonah, don't rail on me about the PI business."

He sighed. "Just tell me what happened."

She gave him a brief recap about being on a case and, without naming Catherine or Vic, how Quinn thought the person she was seeking was someone she knew. How she came home and found blood in her house in a copycat mode. At the end, she gave up the name Mickey Raines.

Jonah rested a gaze on her and let it sit there. "Your case has not only crossed your life, but also ours."

"May not be because of my case."

"Stop. You're hunting for Mickey Raines. How is this not personal? You accepted it because it *involved* Mickey Raines, didn't you?"

When she didn't answer, he stared down at his feet, their toes inches apart. "I oversee this farm, and my momma does not need this . . . again. Whether you admit it or not, we're affected."

The unexpected response hurt, like she'd do anything to harm Jule. "What, you think I baited this guy? You dare to insinuate I asked for this?"

"No, I mean . . ."

She stood. "You don't know what the hell you mean, but now isn't the time. *Jacket* meeting when they get done in there. Say, seven?"

He paused at the old code word. "Haven't heard that in, what, fifteen years? Where, in the family room?"

The meeting wasn't for reminiscing. "I said *Jacket* meeting, Jonah. Someone's made himself at home where I eat and sleep. We meet at Windsor." She took out her phone and sent a text to Ty. "There, the three of us. If those guys take longer handling the crime scene, I'll text you with a new time, but if the past is any indication, they'll be done pretty quickly."

He slowly nodded, accepting the invitation. "I'll bring sandwiches or something," he said. "You can't do much in there," he nodded toward the manor, "and no point Ty going all the way to Jackson Hole to bug his momma. Might even thrill Jule to pack a picnic lunch like the old days. She needs something to occupy her mind right now."

Quinn hesitated at that last sentence. "Why? What's wrong?"

"I'll tell you later. Windsor at seven."

"Good," Quinn said, grateful he'd fallen into the old rule without argument.

Only the most critical of issues merited the utterance of a *Jacket* meeting. A takeoff of their initials, J, Q, and T, the clandestine summits had gone on for a dozen years, continuing until the eve of Quinn and Ty's high school graduation, long after they'd outgrown the commemorative matching windbreakers Jule had ordered them when Quinn was nine.

Jonah trotted down the front steps. "Let me tell Jule," he said with some exasperation. "See you there."

She watched him leave, trying to recall how he looked the last time they'd held a meeting, all long and lean, almost too lean, having just come home from college to honor Quinn and Tyson's high school hurrah. The physical work on Sterling Banks kept him fit, but he was thicker and more mature now. She was surprised he'd not found a girl, but the thought of sharing him made her glad he hadn't.

His big brother behavior proved he absolutely hated when she acquired her PI license. He couldn't keep her safe in that world like he had throughout their childhood. He'd taken his responsibility to heart when the adults explained he had to help Quinn overcome the loss of her brother, then later her mother, and when he returned after Graham's death, he fell right back into that role. A natural protector and caregiver. Trouble was, Quinn wasn't so easily harnessed.

Sometimes he turned grumpy, if not adversarial, when a case came along, like tonight. He'd get worse if any of this involved his mother.

Quinn studied him until he disappeared around the corner.

Jonah and Tyson were the brothers who'd replaced the one she'd lost. While they weren't her twin, they were every bit as related. They knew her quirks and driven spirit better than anyone sharing her DNA.

Jule loved her. Lenore loved her. Hell, even on some level Uncle

Larry loved her, but these two guys were blood brothers. For the most part . . . during the times she didn't let her thoughts misstep to them being otherwise. A line she was afraid to cross for fear of ruining what they had.

It had been forever since the three of them had gathered at Windsor, the secret locale in an oak tree overhanging a secluded bend in the Edisto River, but the place made an odd, perfect sense. A childhood loyalty pledge that still mattered. That and the fact that there was no telling if a bug might've been planted in her place. If she could slip a bug anywhere she chose, so could someone else.

Chapter 10

IT WAS 6:30 IN the evening, and Quinn stood at the drive like any good hostess seeing her guests off. These just happened to be in uniform. However, she accompanied her uncle to the door of his cruiser—just being the proper thing to do. "Thanks, Uncle Larry."

"Quit leaving those damn doors unlocked," he said, backing into the car and falling in the seat.

"Yes, sir," she replied, pacifying him so he'd not hang around to scold.

He pointed at the house. "You said you saw and heard nothing, but these things can come back to you later. Give it some thought. But little girl—" and he mashed his lips tight, lasering her with a stare. "If I don't see you by close of business tomorrow to discuss names and how tonight might cross into your cases, I'll find you and you *will* talk to me. You will *not* skirt the issue. This incident wasn't an accident or random or anything other than a repercussion for whatever you're doing."

"Yes, sir," she obliged again. "Let me dwell on it. I'll see you tomorrow. Promise."

Then as the cars circled around to leave, Tyson made sure he drew up the rear, with a gesture noting he'd be back, and he disappeared toward the highway.

Yet again, the sheriff denied the assistance of SLED, but his people dusted for prints throughout the downstairs rooms and agreed to send the blood off to Charleston's forensics lab and the Colleton hospital, the latter in hope for a more immediate response as to the blood's classification.

One of the most incompetent sheriffs she'd ever met, but he was hers by birthright.

The devil you know . . . and all that.

In his shoes, Quinn would've called in the state's forensics team, but admittedly, calling them in might make someone wonder why they hadn't been called for Graham's murder. No way to avoid disclosing that with this incident being so copycat in nature. And with their involvement, no telling how out of hand the investigation would get . . . meaning the sheriff's hands.

As she returned inside, even steeling herself, she seized up at the now-smeared, half-dried blood. Nobody'd even tried to clean it up. Not that law enforcement did that, but this was family. *Thanks, Uncle Larry.*

The metallic odor she expected. Print dust everywhere. Footprints on her carpet and hardwood floors. Around the corner, drink bottles lay scattered on her kitchen counter where they'd helped themselves to the refrigerator, probably at her uncle's invitation.

She took stock of what was missing in the fridge, then pulled out a six-pack. Retrieving a small cooler out of the garage, she iced them down for the meeting.

At a quarter to seven already. Ty might struggle making the appointed time, but he'd get there soon enough. Jonah would likely be waiting on her. That's how he rolled, as if he still set the example for the two younger members of their trio.

She started to drive out to Windsor instead of walking the half mile, but she wanted to remember the path and the innumerable times she'd taken it . . . and all the silly and serious reasons why. The others may not have been out to their hideaway in fifteen years, but she had.

Several times a year, actually, though nobody was the wiser.

The most memorable being the day after Graham's funeral. Alone. Jonah tended to an injured Jule, and the sheriff had Ty working traffic for the funeral and catering to dignitaries. There'd been no time for the three to console each other.

Once everyone had left the wake, the house's silence oppressing, she'd run into the night, into the orchard. Subconsciously she wound up on the path to the treehouse that had dearly served her all her years, and that's where she'd slept. Jonah fetched her home the next day, having checked on her during the night.

Tonight the walk seemed to take no time. She rounded the last curve, nobody in sight, and she shot up a thank-you for the small temporary gift of solitude.

The massive live oak stood its reliable vigil. Upon reaching the five-foot-wide trunk, she rested palms on the bark then leaned into it for a hug, accepting the healing power.

Thank God for Graham Sterling recognizing that a little girl losing her mother needed a getaway haven. Unable to fill Maggie's shoes for his tormented daughter, he built his baby girl a retreat, resting it in the broad, welcoming arms of a live oak as ancient as the plantation itself, with branches dipping gnarled and bent over the dark, black waters of the Edisto River.

This tree house meant more to her than the manor. No one understood that more than the two friends about to meet her there. One of whom was arriving from the sound of a truck engine rebounding off the wild, natural jungle-like woods that buffered the treehouse from the pecan orchard a couple hundred yards away.

As if in reverence, Jonah parked on the outskirts of the tree's reach then got out, picnic basket in hand. "Wow, cannot believe I haven't been out here in so long," he said, his head tilted back. "Still looks good." His gaze traveled down to her. "Why aren't you up inside?"

Quinn continued rubbing the bark and murmured. "Didn't really want to break the spell until you two got here."

He sat on the ground next to a large, knobby root, and she slid down beside him, leaning her head over on his shoulder as if they hadn't just fussed on her front porch. Windsor allowed a different time and place away from the real world. "I miss the old days," she said.

"Yeah." He didn't have to elaborate on what the old days meant. Their memories were both unique and conjoined, neither needing explanation.

She jerked her head up and grinned in his face. "Remember when I first kissed you by surprise out here?"

His laughter came easy, captured under the low leaning branches strewn with Spanish moss. "Yeah, you scared me shitless. I was eighteen and you were, what, fourteen?"

She chuckled back at him.

He nudged her. "I must've lost a week's sleep worrying what your daddy'd do to me." He nudged her harder a second time. "For all I knew you told him I did more than kiss you."

She patted his chest once and removed herself, wedging back up against the tree . . . maybe putting a little distance between them. "No, you were too much of a gentleman, Jonah, and I trusted you to remain so. Daddy did, too."

He laid his head back against the ragged bark. "Until you turned eighteen."

"That was so unfair to you," she said, picking at the bark of the gnarled root beside her. "I'd dreamed about losing my virginity to you since puberty. Built it up to this whole Snow White affair. You were safe . . . and older . . . and you'd know what to do. I'd decided it would be your graduation present to me."

"That was wrong in so many ways." He ended the remark on a short, uncomfortable laugh, then snatched a glance. "Tell me you never told Ty."

"I never told Ty," she said.

He shut his eyes, head laid back. "Worried my ass off. Kept waiting for you to say you were pregnant . . . or for your daddy to rip me out of my bed."

"Wasn't bad for a virgin, though, huh?"

"Jesus Christ, Quinn," Jonah said, then added, "Changing the subject, once Ty gets here, I need to tell y'all something."

Another vehicle was making its way through the woods. Tyson arrived in his personal Jeep, no doubt to remain under the radar.

"Look at this place," he said, getting out in jeans, a cooler of his own in hand. "What's it been . . ."

"Years," Jonah inserted, and Quinn warmed at watching her two guys, seeing the history playing out in all their minds.

"Well, come on," she exclaimed, breaking the spell, hopping up to lead them to the stairs.

What had been a ladder in her elementary days had been replaced with risers and railings in her teens. Graham Sterling understood Quinn needed her buddies, and he'd remodeled it as they aged, probably never envisioning its use into adulthood. The house measured eight-by-ten, originally with half-wall sides to keep kids from toppling over, but after a few snakes, raccoons, and squirrels took their toll taking up residence, Windsor earned full walls and enough electricity in a double outlet to offer light and a boom box. Three real windows with latching shutters. A screen door allowed the breeze off the river into the room while excluding mosquitoes.

A bent, metal trunk in the back, covered with an old tablecloth robbed from someone's mother, served as a table sometimes, a footstool others, but inside held more than cherished childhood possessions. Once Graham was killed, Quinn tucked away a handgun in a tea towel. Her father would've approved.

The place had become a class act of a treehouse. Thus earning the name, Windsor.

Quinn had spent entire nights in the room, and each visit had brought some new decoration. The boys had donated their own memorabilia from Jonah's rattlesnake tail to Ty's perfect attendance certificate earned the year his father died, which hung in Windsor out of respect for the man.

Windsor was where frustrations were vented, wrongs righted, and hormones tested, but this rendezvous was about more than memories. Recent events touched them all, and before she took a step further, she needed their input . . . and their perspective. This case was deeper than a girl hunting her boy, and Quinn suspected Catherine had found Quinn for more reasons than finding Mickey.

"What'd you bring in there?" Jonah asked, kneeing Ty's cooler on the way up.

"Soft drinks . . . and a little vodka," he said, as he let Quinn pass him to climb up the stairs.

"And to think I only brought beer," she said, opening the door.

Jonah trailed in. "Jule sent two bottles of muscadine wine."

Ty grimaced. "What, is this high school? Any and all alcohol is fair game?"

Quinn laughed big. "Sounds like we're drinking dinner."

"Nope, Jule made me bring sandwiches, too," Jonah said.

"No surprise there," she said.

The banter resumed as if the years hadn't passed. Quinn snared the rocker, Ty claiming a straight-backed chair donated by someone they couldn't remember, leaving Jonah with the bean bag that could entrap you after one too many beers. Ty pulled out the trunk to lay out the bar.

"You still got that gun in there?" he asked.

"Sure do," she replied, helping position bottles and glasses atop the tablecloth.

"When's the last time you checked, much less cleaned it?"

"Often enough," she said, not really liking to talk about it since its presence reminded her of why she hid it up there to begin with. "Dang, look at this spread. Like we planned for a party."

It was as if they'd forgotten the afternoon's event at the manor, and they allowed themselves the luxury until the sandwiches were gone and they'd moved on to their second beers.

"So," Quinn said, thumbnail popping the tab of her beer can. "Let's bring this meeting of the *Jacket* league to order."

As old as they were, no one chuckled at her words because there were meetings . . . and there were *Jacket* meetings. This one being called on the heels of a threat to Quinn gave them nothing to smile about.

"What do you think is going on, Q?" Ty said. "Not sure what Jonah knows, but maybe it's time to enlighten us fully. To hell with your client confidentiality shit. You called us here for a reason, and we expect the full story to give you decent feedback."

Polishing off her second beer, she threw the empty into the open cooler. "I was hired by Catherine Renault of Charleston to find her boyfriend Mickey Raines, who we all know and who has been missing for a month. Or so she says. The day she met me, another PI, Victor Whitmarsh, was found dead at the motel. Turns out he worked for her at the time. Ferg at the motel saw a guy repeatedly visit with a cowboy hat, and from pictures Ty and I saw in Vic's file, his visitor was probably Mickey. Earlier today, I visited the Raines farm. They claim not to know where he is, but I overheard them phone him after I left." She motioned for Ty to bring out the vodka.

"Not asking how you heard that phone call, but okay," he said, handing her a plastic cup with ice. As she held it, he poured ginger ale over a finger of vodka.

"What's my uncle doing about Vic?" she asked, taking a sip then licking the sweetness off her lips.

"Rounding up the usual suspects," he said. "Until he can corner you. He has concerns, and frankly, so do I. The first being how well did you know this Vic character?"

She shook her head. "Mostly professional. One time social. He had a respectable reputation, though, Ty. He was a solid investigator with decent ethics when I knew him."

"Private investigators have ethics?" he asked with a snort.

Jonah listened, attempting to put pieces together without half the story the others already knew. "Explain to me why this Vic guy hunted for Mickey again?"

Quinn covered the gist of the reason Catherine hired her, down to the details of Nero the dog and Chevy the bodyguard/driver.

"You believe her?" he asked. "I'm having trouble accepting that someone like her would give a damn about someone like Mickey. I just don't recall him being particularly . . . appealing, not that I'm saying I can read that sort of thing."

Quinn shook her head. "I agree with you, plus I'm not believing anybody at this point," she said. "Especially after what happened at the house this afternoon."

"Well, that's sort of what I wanted to tell you," Jonah said, and hesitated long enough to polish his beer and launch into the vodka like the others.

Quinn's heavy inhale took in the aroma of the river and the dampness in the tree. She thought she read his mind and leaned her rocker forward, hovering above him as he burrowed in the bean bag. "You haven't told Jule about the blood, have you? Don't," she said. "Your mother doesn't need to be dragged into this if we can help it, Jonah. She went through enough the first time."

With his foot, he pushed her chair back to right. "She already has been. Jule found one of her nannies dead earlier today. Neck slit, the body left outside the barn on a stump."

For a second, all three let that image sink in.

"Son of a bitch," Quinn grumbled under her breath. "He didn't just violate my sanctity, but he violated hers." She sank the remnants of her drink in a swallow and held the glass out for more.

"Might go easy on that," Ty said.

Hammering the bottom of the cup on the arm of her rocker, she demanded a refill. "Fortification. Pour."

But as Ty did, she homed in on Jonah. "Why didn't you tell the sheriff about this while he was here? I know you're not a cop, but damn, Jonah."

"It's why I was late getting there, Quinn, and I wanted to find a good way to get you aside and tell you first," he said. "You aren't exactly open with your uncle, and I figured you'd rather know before he did. Tell me I'm wrong."

He had her there. "Then I'll tell him tomorrow. Did you take pictures of the scene or anything? What was the weapon he used?"

"Nothing had blood on it, if that's what you're asking," he said. "I looked."

"And where's the goat?" she asked.

"In the freezer. In case you needed to see it."

She might have a buzz going on, but she saw that Jonah had tried to read her mind and act accordingly. He still should've told Uncle Larry, but the trio's allegiance to each other had won the day. How could she argue with that?

"Jonah . . . tomorrow ask every single worker if they saw a stranger or a strange vehicle. All of them, you hear?"

Her voice rose at the last, then silence filled the treehouse.

"Sorry," she finally said. "I'm shouting orders. You aren't my flunky. Can we pretend the vodka made me do it?"

He gave a long slow exhale. "We get it, Princess. Just don't beat us up with the tiara."

"Yep, you've had enough," Ty said, reaching for her glass, but she pulled back.

"Nope, let's continue," she said. "And let's start listing what we know and the what-ifs. I realize this isn't Jonah's area of expertise, but this shit has decided to roost where we sleep, and I felt he deserved a voice. So . . . start throwing out possibilities."

Ty started. "You mean besides the blood on your floor being from Jule's goat?"

"Mickey's on the run and scared of something," Jonah said. "He could have killed your Vic guy."

"Or knows who did," added Ty.

"Sounds silly, but I'm not seeing him kill the goat to rub my nose in anything," she said. "Not after laying low for all these years." Sucking in a piece of ice, she moved it around while thinking, then crunched it away. "No doubt Catherine ran me down for a particular purpose rather than hire some bigwig PI firm out of Charleston," Quinn said. "She told me it was because Mickey was from my county, but I sensed more then and feel even stronger now about a lot of unspoken crap. What if Mickey ran from *her*? And what if Vic learned enough about Catherine Renault to *warn* Mickey?"

Again, she recalled the guy who got his face bashed in early in her career because she thought the client was always on the up and up.

"Warn him about what?" Jonah asked. "Like what would she want Mickey for? She has all the money she could ever spend, so some silly phone apps don't mean a thing to her."

"Bingo," she said.

Jonah was good at asking the obvious, and he was eager to help. Another brain couldn't hurt, especially one which hadn't already thought it through too hard like hers and Ty's. Jonah'd hit on an important point—Mickey didn't appear to have anything Catherine would need to chase him down for.

"Plus, your client doesn't seem too keen on contacting the police," Ty said. "Let me attempt to get Mickey's recent phone and text activity. Might as well try for Vic's as well, since your hugging FBI dude isn't finding time for us."

Quinn threw him a look about the hugging, the room taking a tilt as she did. "And I'll dig into Vic, Catherine, and maybe her trusty sidekick Chevy."

Ty threw his own stare back. "What, not the dog?"

She laughed. "Of course you check out the dog, dude. Goes without saying."

They sat around and finished one last drink. They didn't have to say what Jonah would do. He might not be LEO, but he was protector of Sterling Banks, keen with a firearm, and possessed a sufficient skillset to take down any farm trespasser. Nobody was killing another of his mother's precious goats, much less get at Jule.

Chapter 11

HER HANGOVER didn't set a record by any means, but the dry mouth and dull headache necessitated a tall glass of water and three aspirin before Quinn tackled coffee. Yoga pants with a run in them and an oversized t-shirt, oil-stained from shelling pecans, matched her mood for this morning's first duty. Just a quick brush of her teeth first.

In an hour, she would plant herself in front of the computer, read more of Vic's files, and hunt details on Mickey. The rich lady hadn't been too forthcoming about anything, telling Quinn only the meagerest of details, so Quinn would branch into Catherine Renault's past.

First, however, she cleaned up blood.

Last night she'd only thrown two old towels over the spot, eager to get to the boys at Windsor and too drunk to tackle the spot afterwards.

As Quinn scrubbed the flagstone foyer with bleach water, she pondered the details of her assignment to keep her mind off the red mess muddying the water in the bucket, staining the towels.

Why booger things up with too many facts, right? Catherine's order was elementary . . . find Mickey, a singular goal. Find him, get paid, and leave the boyfriend in the arms of his wealthy girl who'd make him incredibly wealthy with his phone apps.

Bullshit. Quinn was being sucked into something she couldn't make sense of, and her biggest fear was that *something* would be up her back and all over her before she saw it coming. Even if she found Mickey, what did Catherine have in store for him? He'd sounded healthy enough when talking to his parents, meaning he could reassure Catherine if he wanted to.

What the hell had Vic paid such a morbid price for? Had he found

Mickey then let him go? Or been killed by him? One or the other. Maybe both.

Her knees soaked red, her shirt splattered with pink splashes, she rose, pushing hair out of her face with the back of her left hand. Crap, this would take more than one bucket. She rinsed it out in the kitchen and refilled it with fresh bleach water, grabbing three more old, ripped towels from the laundry room . . . towels only worth tossing once she was done.

Again, back stooped in the entryway, scrubbing at pink now.

Was Quinn a rook or a pawn on this chessboard? Catherine had certainly had Quinn checked out by a man who could easily do it, but why would she since she didn't need Quinn until Vic was dead? Had she planned on confronting Quinn all along?

In the back of Quinn's mind danced the thought that Vic was disposed of for knowing too much. The hairs on her neck kept warning her of something out of sync. An invisible intent.

Last night, she, Ty, and Jonah had established their marching orders, not leaving until almost midnight. What they discussed and agreed to in Windsor stayed in Windsor. They shared concepts and dared to talk about the darkness in humans, placing blame on anybody and everybody just to walk through the what-ifs until they dead-ended. And while they had a lot of dead-ends, they still set paths to follow.

Without a doubt, the main goal was locating Mickey. He was who she'd been hired to find, but there were many other reasons to find him. Graham, Vic, Catherine, and now the blood on the floor were linked to Mickey. Maybe he had reasons to go underground.

Quinn held no idea as to any of them.

From the sound of Mickey on the phone with his parents, however, he didn't want to be found.

She and Ty didn't see Mickey as a prankster or threat who'd leave blood in the manor. Jonah, as the Banks's foreman, was promptly assigned the duty of installing security cameras on the house exits, at the pecan barn, on the goat barn, and on Jule's house. Quinn kicked herself for not having upgraded the system after Graham's death, but she hadn't been thinking too clearly during those days . . . weeks . . . months . . .

until there seemed no need.

Ty would stay atop the BOLO on Mickey and work the NCIC database, and Quinn would sift through Accurint, TLO, PACER, and others, letting those databases steer her to whichever other databases she needed. Some investigators hated the tech searches. She and Ty enjoyed them, having races at who could drill down to the best intel first.

Of course, she would deal with Catherine.

Finally, she rose, using her last towel to dry off the surface water on the floor. The grout still showed moisture, and squinting, she tried to imagine the spot, wondering if she'd studied it too long to really tell if she got all the red out.

They hadn't bothered scrubbing the last time blood was spilled in this entry. Instead she'd replaced the hall's floor. Big difference between goat blood and human blood. Quinn had wanted as little to do with the repairs after the murder as possible and wrote the check for the stone floor without inspecting the finished job. She didn't enter that hall until she could weather a day without her heart seizing too tight, suffocating. Took a while.

She tossed her brush and wet towels in the bucket and went outside to lay the contents across the wood pile to dry. Later she'd burn them with the other trash. She hated plastic and landfills with a passion.

After a quick shower, she slid into jeans and her mother's Eric Clapton tee, clamping damp hair back in clips. Sometimes curls were a blessing, but mostly a curse. A curse she didn't feel like fooling with today.

A half hour into her database searches, in the midst of trying to understand how and why Mickey had designed and reorganized his business three times, her phone rang, caller ID Lenore Jackson.

She leaned back in her chair, bare feet up on her desk. "Hey, Lenore. What's up?"

Jazz riffs sounded faintly in the background. "There's a lady here for you. A real estate lady asking directions to your place," she said.

Not again. A week didn't go by without someone asking if Sterling Banks was available. What part of *no* didn't they understand? "So why is she there?" Quinn asked, slowly taking her feet down. "Why not just come out here? Or better yet, call, which is the mannerly thing to do. Who can't remember 1-800-NUTLOVE?"

Lenore snickered. "Honey, whoever thought of that was the nut. Do I send her there, are you coming here, or do I tell her to disappear?"

Instead Quinn replied, "Put her on the phone, please."

The phone's static indicated exchanging hands. "Yes?" said a middle-aged-sounding female, voice dripping with Charleston authority. "Is this Quinn Sterling?"

"Yes, ma'am, and you have me at a disadvantage. May I ask who you are and what sent you to Craven County without advanced notice? It's not like Sterling Banks isn't on the map."

"My apologies, Ms. Sterling, but my offer is unique enough not to discuss over the phone, and frankly, I didn't want to just show up. I heard you often v this diner. May I come out to the property, please?"

And she probably thought she was original in coming all impromptu like this.

And *the property*. Sterling Banks wasn't in any way, shape, or form addressed as simply *the property*. Sterling Banks Plantation was as close to a living, breathing being as a piece of dirt could get. Over a hundred of Quinn's relatives had walked across that acreage, drawn water from the Edisto River, and planted all those stunning, dignified nut trees for generations to come. To call it a piece of property was like calling Princess Diana just another Brit.

The woman still hadn't identified herself; plus, she'd used Lenore to reach Quinn.

"No, ma'am. I'll come to you," Quinn said. "Give me twenty minutes."

"Well, I was hoping—"

"Or we can just not meet, if twenty minutes is too inconvenient for you."

The woman paused. "I look forward to meeting you."

Damn straight she did.

Quinn jumped up and ran to throw jeans and a collared shirt on. Her black leather jacket and favorite matching boots with an outback hat. Hair down, big and in charge, with strands pinned with a turquoise barrette at the lower back of her head. She knew how to dress like money that didn't have to dress like money.

This woman had started off on the wrong foot and had attempted to shove Quinn on her back one, off balance. These real estate agents of late acted like Sterling Banks was already listed on MLS. Once upon a time they got the message. *Not for sale* meant *not for sale*. Graham had hammered it home, and it didn't take long for agents to realize the daughter was just like the dad. Quinn wouldn't go out and see this one except she already promised to see her uncle after last night. Going to him would keep him from interrogating her over another drawn-out takeout dinner.

Once in the truck, Quinn texted Jonah where she'd be. Then the closer she got to Jackson Hole, the more she wondered what the heck was driving these realtors. The average agent didn't represent clients wealthy enough to place an offer on an estate. Especially this one. Sterling Banks was an anomaly . . . a ridiculously large number of acres that would never go up for sale. Totally unlike the ones sold out of old Southern families into the hands of corporate outsiders because the grandkids no longer felt the history.

Just after eleven, with the early diners straggling in, Quinn lucked up on a parking space just outside the door. As she walked in, Lenore motioned to her back booth. Something tomatoey cooked in the kitchen.

Fluffy was the first description that came to Quinn's mind as she strode up and reached for a greeting. "Quinn Sterling. And you are . . .?"

"Halley Manson." The grip was brief and jingled her bracelets. She quickly retracted her hand to place her business card on the table before Quinn had a chance to sit. "I'm with The Manson and Stafford Agency. You can call me Halley."

Lenore spirited herself in to refill Ms. Manson's cup and set an iced tea before Quinn along with a plate of four brownies in the middle. She disappeared without word or look.

The agent's gaze followed Lenore to her place behind the bar. "She didn't even ask what we wanted."

"She reads minds. Especially mine," Quinn said, grateful Lenore had read her correctly on the phone. This was not a conversation that would lag into lunch, nor was Halley a client to be courted. Quinn took a sip from her tea. "Now, what's this about you having an offer for my . . . *property?*"

"Yes," Halley said, her ample bosom heaving once beneath the cropped jacket. "My client told me to approach you and ask that you entertain their offer."

"Who's the client?"

Halley sipped and watched over her cup. "I've been asked to maintain anonymity at this stage of the negotiation, but they are highly motivated, trust me."

Quinn chuckled. "They are, huh? Not just *very* motivated but *highly* motivated. Why that makes such a difference." She snagged a brownie and took her time chewing as the agent struggled to readjust.

The value of Sterling Banks didn't merit discussion, not at this point. That much acreage, an hour between both Charleston and Savannah, would hold ample promise for developers. Most realties had given up approaching Graham once he'd made his decision known to fifteen or twenty of them . . . at least until he died, and then they'd turned on Quinn, pestering her as soon as five days after the funeral. Halley Manson and her firm, however, didn't ring a bell. Maybe it was time she heard the same speech Quinn gave the others. "I'll be elementary about this," she started.

Halley lifted her chin. "My client is willing to offer ten percent above appraised value."

"And what do you feel that value is?"

"A reasonable eight figures."

Nothing Quinn didn't already know, but eight figures covered a wide spectrum. And at that level, that was so much money that ten percent didn't matter. "With a Land Trust easement on eighteen hundred acres of it?" Quinn said.

Meaning that land could not be developed with the only exception being family building a house or two on it.

But that left almost a thousand acres without an easement, and nobody wanted that much land without busting it up, developing it, destroying several hundred acres of pecan trees. Not to mention walling in the Sterling graveyard so that it didn't disturb the high-brow folks with enough wealth to forgo a daily commute to a city. Maybe part of the plantation would be used as a tourism attraction, the river frontage sold to high-end enterprises.

"Only so many people have that level of investment," Quinn said. "I've spoken with the land trust about entering five hundred more acres, by the way." She hadn't, but she might now if interest was stirring back up.

But Halley didn't move. "We're aware of the possibility. We'd hope you wouldn't."

"So give me the name."

Halley shook her head in a subtle genteel manner. "Sorry."

Motioning with the last bite of her brownie, Quinn's jaw tightened. "If you and your client know so much, then you also are aware that my family founded this county, and in many ways helped found this damn state. I have twelve generations buried on that *property*, as you called it, and it'll take some mighty creative negotiating to budge me off it. So far you've fallen way short, Ms. Manson, like oh-so-many of your predecessors. The answer is no."

Halley smiled as though having forecasted the reply. "That's a lot of money to decline, Ms. Sterling."

"And someone went through a lot of effort finding someone misinformed enough to approach me with it," Quinn replied.

The agent braced a bit, then tried to hide doing so. "This is purely business, Ms. Sterling. Nothing personal. Maybe I did catch you too off guard. Let me talk to my client and see if we can arrange a meeting."

Quinn scoffed. "Halley, I have to admit that I only came here to see who you were and to see if you'd drop a name. Now we've met, and kudos to you for protecting your client's privacy, but if you'd done your homework, you'd have known that I've been approached before. Don't bother asking your guy to meet with me."

Smiling, the woman seemed not to grasp the message. "Well, he's incredibly busy, but for a property like this—that can mean millions and a remarkable future for all involved. I'm sure he'd be happy to set aside a day for you . . . maybe on his boat. I'm sure you're familiar with the Yacht Club?"

So the buyer was indeed male and most likely Charlestonian.

Quinn grew weary of this back and forth. "The answer is still no. Now eat a brownie before you go. You don't want to hurt Lenore's feelings."

When the agent showed no interest in a snack, Quinn stood. "Have a safe trip back to the city. I've work to do back on the *property*."

When Quinn didn't leave, Halley slid out of the booth, tugging on a too high skirt to keep it from riding up to expose legs unfamiliar with walking farther than a parking lot. "I'll be in touch, Ms. Sterling."

Quinn just smiled. She wasn't playing the having-the-last-word game. No was still no.

Once Halley Manson left the building, Quinn returned to her booth. Lenore showed up with her bowl of fried okra and a piece of cornbread. "Lunch time."

"You do read my mind, Miss Lenore."

"Don't take a mind reader to see you riled up. Eat, now," she said, wiping hands on her red apron. "Settle down before you head back to the Banks. You seeing Tyson later?"

Quinn blew on one of the okra morsels, still hot from the kitchen. "Might."

"You two are up to something," Lenore said. "Just stay out of trouble."

"Yes, ma'am."

Ty's mother called okra Quinn's brain food, not for the nutritional value of the green pod, which was sort of negated by the deep fat way of serving it, but because Quinn took her time eating it. One by one she'd empty the bowl, staring off in thought, or using the okra as a prop to drag out a conversation with a client like Catherine.

"Wave if you need a second bowl." That's how Lenore left Quinn . . . lost in her okra.

Not two bites into the pile, Quinn concluded somebody was putting out feelers. Feelers coincidentally coming the day after Quinn and Jule were warned with a puddle of blood and a dead goat.

All this kept cycling back to Quinn, or maybe to Sterling Banks . . . and since it involved Mickey, maybe back to Graham Sterling's murder.

Mickey wasn't that savvy, if she recalled properly, and he wasn't that bold. Maybe he'd changed. Maybe she was wrong about the timing of Catherine hiring her, though she doubted it. Maybe she overthought Halley Manson arriving unannounced. Lots of loose threads, but Quinn couldn't discard the sense they might be woven in the same cloth. She might not be FBI any longer, but the instincts remained intact.

Chapter 12

QUINN LEFT JACKSON Hole as the place began thrumming with diners. Lenore could better use the booth to make a dollar, and Quinn owed her uncle a visit.

In town, she parked in front of the Craven County Law Enforcement Center, an oversized spit-and-polished, blond-brick affair with a silver metal hip roof. A simple large box structure with square, paned aluminum windows across the front, surrounded with shrubbery not a year old. Ten-foot chain-link fencing protected the back and glistened in the midday sun. One of the perks about a poor county was the abundant availability of grants, including the huge community facility pot of money Uncle Larry acquired from the U.S. Department of Agriculture to build the place.

The center was quite the contrast to the eighty-year-old, flat, tar-roofed concrete block building across the street—the hand-painted sign over the door stating *Sheriff's Annex*. Rusted razor wire remained atop its old fence since the ancient jail had been prone to escapes. Today they, whoever *they* were, deemed the structure *historic*. Quinn, however, knew the County Council held its off-book, secret meetings there, as well as the sheriff when he needed a private spot for his assorted consultations.

As twelve-year-old scalawags, she and Ty spent one afternoon locked up in a corner cell when they'd grabbed a watermelon off old man Yancy's produce table at the farmer's market. She'd not spoken to her uncle for two weeks after that. Any other kid in town would have gotten off with a lecture.

A lot deeper water ran under that bridge now.

Inside the contemporary building, Quinn strode through the lobby and up to a woman with a whale spout of a ponytail atop her head.

Frosted. Per her stories, she owned the eighties in high school and intended on carrying the decade straight through to her grave.

"Hey, Carla," Quinn said, noting the light flitting off the woman's huge gold hoops. "Liking the earrings."

A hand to an ear, the receptionist greeted her warmly. "Thanks. Can you believe I saved these before my mother threw them out?"

"Vintage, if you ask me."

"Exactly. By the way, your uncle's *in a meeting.*" A hard roll of her eyes toward the hallway to Sheriff Sterling's office. The following telltale wink belied the meeting as *fictitious.*

Without a word, Quinn marched past.

"Still wish I had your hair," Carla shouted.

"Trust me, you don't," Quinn said over her shoulder.

She tapped on the closed door, then without waiting for an answer, entered. Her uncle straightened with a snap from where he'd been looking over the shoulder of a visitor in his guest chair.

A woman in her early forties, dressed for the office in a neat shift and low heels, pivoted in her seat. Quinn recognized her as the new administrative assistant in the Civil Process and Warrants Division. The only person in that division. And she would be required to do way more than type warrants. The department didn't need that many warrants.

Hand outstretched, Quinn greeted her. "Quinn Sterling. Niece to this gentleman. I hear you're the latest hire around here. Welcome to the Sheriff's Office."

With his characteristic growl dialed to low, Sheriff Sterling made his way back around the desk where Quinn thought he should've been to start with. "Wasn't expecting you," he said, his backside dropping the last few inches into his chair.

Quinn peered over to see what they'd been discussing. A firearms catalog. "Oh my goodness. You shoot?" she asked the guest. "The sheriff knows his weapons, honey. He can give you some great advice on what to purchase, though I'd suggest you fire a few before settling on one."

Blushing, the lady rose. "I don't shoot, but Larry was just convincing me how a single woman ought to learn. He was showing me my options. It's fascinating."

Motioning back to the door, Quinn stepped once toward it. "Oh, then, sorry I interrupted. I can always come back later."

The lady shook her head. "No, no. I need to get back to work. I can see the sheriff any day and do this sort of thing. You probably have business with him. Nice to meet you, Ms. Sterling. I've heard so much about you."

Quinn beamed and reached out to shake a hand in passing. "Nice to meet you as well, and I'm sure I'll be hearing great things about you. They only hire good folks in here."

They exchanged light chuckles again. Then once alone with her uncle, Quinn closed the door.

"What are you doing here?" the sheriff asked.

She plopped in the still-warm guest chair. "You told me to get in touch today. In no uncertain terms, I might add, so here I am."

"Figured I'd stop by tonight," he said.

"I know you did, but we already had one of those evenings this week. Wasn't up to another." Propping a boot atop the opposite knee, she relaxed as best she could in the stiff chair. She was surprised the sheriff hadn't moved a softer seat in here to flirt with the woman from warrants. "A Charleston real estate agent just tried to convince me to sell."

"Must be new," he said. "Thought we made the message pretty damn clear some time ago. Who was she?"

Quinn noted the plural pronoun, like he had a voice in the say-so, and she fished the card from her pocket, slapping it on his desk. "She wasn't novice, but I sent her packing."

He studied it, then tucked it in his middle drawer.

"So," she said, "I'm here. What do you want from me?"

"Yes, let's jump right in," he said, leaning over his desk as if speaking to a perp. "Who would break into the manor and dump blood? I want all the possible suspects."

"No longer worried about whose it was, huh? That much blood would make most cops concerned about where the corpse was. Was it goat's blood, by any chance?"

The obvious short-circuited him only a hair of a second. "Yes, it was. Now you get to explain that, too."

She softened having to talk about the animal. "One of Jule's nannies was killed yesterday morning sometime. Left on a stump for her to find."

In a frown, his brows almost met above his nose. "Why didn't you tell me yesterday?"

"Because Jonah told me after you left last night."

The brows touched now. "Why didn't *he* tell me then."

"He wanted to tell me first."

The sheriff physically waved that argument aside, obviously seeing no reason to take up that particular fight. "The point is what prompted the prank?"

She uncrossed her leg. "So you've reduced it to a prank?"

"Girl . . .," he sighed before continuing. "You left the house open and the blood was animal, not human. Unless we can relate it to something you're working on, or someone with a grudge against you or Jule or whomever, it's just that, a prank. So . . . do you care to share your case with me so I can determine if it is a threat?"

"It was also burglary, but I'm confident my client was not involved in the goat incident," she said.

"But the case links to Mickey Raines," he countered.

"Yes, and my assignment is to find him."

"And who was this Vic Whitmarsh guy in relation to all this?"

Her uncle might've been sheriff since Quinn lost her first baby tooth, but he wasn't a fan of PIs. "My PI predecessor on this case," she said, "who also hunted for Mickey."

Her uncle sat back and weighed all that. "You think Mickey killed him?"

She sucked the inside of her cheek. Though her uncle wasn't Mike Hammer by a long shot, a murder occurred in his county, and as long as she kept Catherine's identity secret, Quinn could share. As long as he shared back.

"I'm not convinced Mickey's the killer," she said, "but I believe he's tangled up in knots with it. He's been in the area, and I'm putting out feelers to locate him. First, to fulfill my obligation to my client, but second, because I think he may know the killer . . . who might be after him."

"He's been seen?"

"Not yet." She stopped short of telling him about the Raineses, their son keeping in touch, and her planting the device. She planned another trip back in the very near future, at which time she'd weigh whether to remove that bug. It was too weak to listen to this far anyway.

"Back to the blood," he said. "I still don't rule out a prank, but regardless, it appears personal. And you're too smart not to believe this can't be tied to Mickey. Blood in the hallway, Quinn. That blood stain, in that particular spot, in that amount."

"A suspect list that consists of only Mickey thus far," she said.

"Mickey didn't kill Graham."

Good, he'd said it first. Their gazes met. "So you say," she said. "I never got a chance to interview him."

"You didn't need to."

Both got rigid.

Then she crossed the line she crossed so many times in her head. "Didn't have to be me to interview Mickey, but someone who knew what they were doing sure needed to."

"Three years in the FBI doesn't make you Eliot Ness, Niece."

And to that she had to bitterly laugh, not believing she got to say this twice in one week. "Actually, Eliot Ness wasn't in the FBI. And between the internship, cooping, the Academy and three years in the field, I brushed against the criminal element more than you have in your twenty years plus as sheriff in this county."

She wasn't bashing Craven County. It was part of her bones. Its river borders ran through her veins. But crime amounted to little more than domestic spats, poaching, and break-ins into residences containing a modicum of monetary value. While Sheriff Larry Sterling claimed all the credit for the limited crime, this area had little to burgle and generations of families who policed themselves. A benefit of living in an area where progress hadn't devastated tradition. So unlike Charleston, having lost its Southern-ness in its quest to be the queen of tourism.

Her claim to better crime-solving skills didn't bait him, though. Maybe because he'd sparred with his niece more than enough times over the subject to have worn it thin. Or he didn't care. God, the Sterlings were not stupid people. They'd thrived through famine, pestilence, war, and politics, but Uncle Larry seemed more complacent than those before him. In other words, he preferred reputation over accomplishment.

In those seconds of worn-out analysis, she tired, disappointed at the same old conversation that tasted more bitter each time said. "Then think of it this way, Uncle. You don't believe Mickey killed Daddy. He's now a person of interest in a new murder, and someone attempted to pull a repeat performance of the blood scene. Maybe someone who appears to have risen up from six years ago."

"Copycat, maybe," he added.

She nodded.

"But I get the point being made," he said. "And you do too." His chair creaked in his coming forward. "Give up your PI case, Niece."

She leaned back at him, hands on her knees. "My client's interest is important. Vic's murder is important. They're intertwined, and I have an obligation."

They stared.

"Still not seeing why either matters," he finally said.

Her reaction was instinctive, just slightly delayed at the incredulity of what her uncle had just said. Heat rose under her shirt and across her collarbone, and she could feel it. He would see the red blotches. The plight of being a redhead. "I knew Victor Whitmarsh. Goddamnit, Uncle Larry, this is Daddy's case all over again. You're afraid to turn over rocks for fear you'll find the killer."

He remained unstung. "Not so, little girl. It's called triage. You were federal. United States attorneys do it all the time just like the state attorney general. They determine which cases merit the resources."

Enforcement did pick and choose, but not as flippantly and dismissively as this. Overloaded dockets, budget cuts. Neither applied here. Hell, she was even glad to assist the small county sheriff's office . . . pro bono. She'd done so before.

"Why the hell are you even in law enforcement?" she asked. "I'm serious. Give it to someone who gives a damn."

"But you're wrong," he said. "I keep this place safe."

Unbelievable. "And you say that with a straight face. Tell that to Vic's family, or have you tried running them down?"

"He doesn't seem to have any."

"No family means no investigation? That helps make your decision sound?" After realizing she held her breath waiting for a response she wasn't getting, she stood to leave.

"Sit down," the sheriff said, trying to sound parental. "I'm saying this murder was personal, and we don't need it to become personal for the Sterlings, or the Jacksons, or for any other Craven County family, and that stunt at the manor was a clear warning. Heed it."

What little patience she'd gathered for this meeting dissipated. A lump formed in her throat she couldn't swallow. "Daddy had family, Uncle Larry. How's that work into your half-baked reasoning?"

His jowls softened, and God help her, she saw a glimpse of her father. "I'm afraid for you, Quinn," he said. "You live alone in that big house with a dated security system you don't use."

"It's being used, and Jonah is updating it. At Jule's place, too."

"Maybe I ought to come stay at the manor a while. Just in case."

She smacked her hands on the desk and remained stiff-armed. "I don't need a babysitter, and I sure as hell don't need you breathing down my neck. Focus on your job, Uncle. Try that for a change."

He leaned a forearm on his desk and sighed. "Don't start."

"How do you even look in the mirror in the morning?" Tears threatened, making her angrier. "How do you call yourself a Sterling?"

He first appeared unphased as he stood, but his coloring began to change. "I could ask you the same thing, Quinn. You're the last heir of this family, and you damn sure haven't done anything to continue its legacy. We're it, sweetheart. You, me, and Archie. I'm too old and your uncle's gay. I'm not just trying to save your neck . . . I'm trying to perpetuate a history that men and women died for, while all you can do is play cop and spew righteous indignations that don't mean a damn in the grand scheme of Craven County." Red-faced as well, he motioned at her. "Now go on back to the farm and be responsible. And damnit . . . grow up."

She spun and exited, trying to sling the door against the wall . . . failing as it hit a rubber stopper. She strode past Carla, past a half dozen other employees who knew her on sight and read her face well enough to get out of her way. Outside, she leaped into her truck and sat there, mentally repeating the zipping, popping exchange of angry words.

Then she cranked up the truck. The old and new cases were conjoined, and if she couldn't find Mickey, she'd go to the next best witness she had, and she wasn't taking no for an answer. Jule needed to start remembering what happened that day.

And Jonah wasn't invited.

Chapter 13

WINDOW DOWN, Quinn drove through the brick and wrought-iron gate toward home, hardly remembering holding the steering wheel. She studied the dark gray clouds overhead before she disappeared amongst trees too thick to see through other than straight up. Having just been fertilized, the pecans could use the rain.

Through a smattering of light drops, she passed the manor and Jonah's farm truck in the drive and continued along the asphalt back to Jule's place. Her stomach clinched at the realization a stranger had taken this same route, killed a goat, and escaped unseen. In spite of the farm being so spread out, few people entered the property without notice, and this guy had done so in such a slick, covert manner . . . with Jonah, Jule, and her on the place and oblivious.

After the *Jacket* meeting, the trio got busy. Jonah had gone to Charleston for security equipment first thing and was apparently back and working on the manor's system. Still not seeing Jule, Quinn parked near the goat barn, but before she slid out of the truck, she shot a text to Ty.

Anything on the BOLO for Mickey?

Ty didn't respond, and she pocketed her phone, hoping he had his hands full on some traffic stop and that the sheriff hadn't shifted from his meeting with her over to Ty in an attempt to get him to talk her out of the case. Ty would talk a good line, make assurances, and then rat on her uncle to her. Not a more loyal friend in the state. She just hated he dealt with so many obstacles with her name on them.

The ground was barely damp when Quinn left the truck. The rain had stopped, and she was unable to walk past the corral without visiting. She reached over the railing and petted the nearest goat. Blizzard—snow white when he hadn't kicked up or rolled in the dirt. He'd been born during a rare bout of two-inch January snow. Older than most, he still served as stud.

"Where were you yesterday, fella? When everything went down. Gotta protect your ladies," she said, scratching him between the horns, him pressing obsessively for more. "Wish you could tell me what you saw."

Hesitantly she scanned the herd, seeking which goat was missing. Her hopes fell when Bonnie Blue didn't appear for a rub on the head. A small, two-year-old gray and white female. One of the more docile girls . . . one of the easiest to catch.

Instead of being angered, Quinn wilted at the loss. Not wanting to stand there wondering if the herd missed their sister, Quinn left in search for the goats' shepherd. In and around the barn, then to the house which she gratefully found locked up. The farm had left all its doors open for years, for friends, family, and hands to more easily find each other. Damn she hated how this one low-life reprobate was forcing the Banks to change its personality, and she wanted him more than ever now.

Jule didn't reply to knocks on the house door.

"Jule?" Quinn hollered, then headed toward the production building, which sat beside the nut storage structure. The rain held off, but small gusts of spring wind played tag between trees, reminding her summer still hadn't set up camp quite yet.

A one-level, sprawling building off to the south of Jule's place housed the assembly of internet and statewide-sold pecan products. The bagged nuts, shelled and not, the gift baskets, the candied items. Their inventory wasn't all that diverse because Sterling Banks netted most of its profit from commercial and bulk sales of pecans that barely touched floor in the nut house before being shipped. The most efficient way to handle an orchard of this size.

Come mid- to late-summer, however, this building would fill with temporary hires and crank up, using county residents who loved the seasonal work and the holiday money, to prep for the fall and Christmas demand. Jule enjoyed overseeing the baking, roasting, and coating the nuts, and once she orchestrated staff into their daily routines, she experimented on recipes with Quinn often stopping by to sample.

Other than the goat barn, the production building was Jule's favorite place on the farm. Quinn unsurprisingly found the woman toasting nuts in a cast-iron skillet, spices of all types scattered across the chopping block counter to her right. The air hung rich with the scent of toasted pecans.

Over Jule's denim overalls draped an apron with the farm's logo, a pecan silhouette in dark brown ink on a beige background, inside a square with *Sterling Banks* in an old-fashioned script pretty enough to go on a liquor bottle. The logo was older than Quinn's great-grandfather, too deeply rooted to ever change.

One of Jule's signature bandanas restrained her hair, tied in the back under a long braid. A pink one today. One hand on her hip, she aimlessly stirred in a slow circular motion in the wide skillet with a flat-edged wooden spoon.

Quinn sniffed at the hint of scorch in the air. "Jule? Aren't those ready to come off the heat?"

"Yes, I believe you're right," the older woman replied, using the spoon to shove the skillet onto a cool burner.

"Better dump those out of there," Quinn said, hurrying to hand over a pot holder.

The nuts weren't inedible, but they weren't the quality to fill an order with, and Jule dumped them onto a paper plate and shut off the stovetop. "I'll try that recipe again later. Not sure it was fit to eat anyway." She untied her apron as Quinn picked up a nut and blew repeatedly on it to cool, testing the new recipe per their routine. Jule, however, placed the apron on its customary wall hook and made for the door.

"Jule? What the hell?" Quinn said. "I came looking for you."

"Got work to do," she said over her shoulder, not making eye contact as she headed out.

Quinn caught up and took Jule's arm. "No, ma'am. Whenever you thought I needed an ear, you wouldn't let me draw up inside myself, and I'm not letting you go off alone either. We're talking."

She planted Jule at a long, rustic pecan-wood table for twelve, if you put that many seats around it. Stained a rich medium brown to accent the natural grain, when things got hopping, it managed people, taste testing, and designing gift baskets. Right now, however, it was only meant for the two of them.

Seated on the end, Jule to her right, Quinn rubbed her arm. "I'm sorry about Bonnie Blue."

Jule stared down the table past a wooden bowl full of unshelled pecans, a couple of handheld nutcrackers jammed in the nuts . . . a furrow deep in her forehead. "Just a damn goat. Not like we don't have enough of 'em out here. With the cost of feed, we're probably better off." She slid her arm out of Quinn's reach and tucked both of them in her lap.

Quinn rose and went to put on a short pot of coffee. "You found her, I hear." From the corner of her eye, she watched Jule nod. "Tell me about it."

"No need."

"Yes, ma'am, there is indeed a need." The coffee began to drip as Quinn retrieved a small pitcher of goat's milk from the refrigerator and poured a finger's worth in each cup. "Did Jonah tell you what happened at the house?"

"Some," she said.

"Then you understand the importance of us establishing a timeline as to what happened. You know your goats. When did you last see her alive? When did you find her? Think about it a moment."

After allowing time for the coffee to finish, Quinn took a beige logo coaster from a stack on the table and set the hot coffee before Jule. Then she sat with her own cup and waited for the not-very-forthcoming answers.

"When did you call Jonah?" Quinn asked.

"They did it behind the barn," Jule replied, choosing to replay the day instead of answer . . . suddenly a steel in her voice. "Didn't find her till I was counting heads in the afternoon. You know goats." Finally she looked Quinn in the eye. "They're curious, always getting into trouble. I just thought she was occupied, snooping into something, but she didn't

117

come when I threw out snacks. Then I thought she might've gotten herself stuck or pent up someplace . . . but she didn't call for me to come get her."

"So you went looking for her," Quinn finished gently.

Jule loved her animals more than most people. This woman would've slit the throat of the human responsible if she'd caught him in the act of doing the same to her nanny. Quinn was so glad she hadn't seen the culprit. "So you last saw Bonnie Blue when?"

"Around lunch," she said.

"And you found her when?"

"Around three."

Meaning the son of a bitch did this while Quinn was on the property, while she drove around inspecting trees. She'd been a considerable ways from the barn when Bonnie met her demise, and Quinn wondered where the killer had hidden, watching to judge when to complete his task. He noted Jonah's absence. The hands would've been occupied in various orchards.

Thank God Jule didn't walk up on him.

"Show me where you found her," Quinn said once Jule's coffee had gone cold. Out of courtesy she grabbed a heavy handful of Jule's overcooked pecan halves before they left.

The barn took a few minutes to walk to. "When did Jonah tell you about what happened in the manor?" Quinn offered a nut to Jule who shook her head.

"Early this morning."

Made sense. They'd stayed at Windsor late. "Thanks for the wine, by the way. Haven't drunk muscadine in a long time." Nor would she drink it atop liquor again for an even longer while.

Seeing the woman caught up in an internal war with herself, Quinn held out a hand to stop their walking and shifted in front of her. "Are you okay, Jule? I mean, to relive this?"

Though her eyes were red-rimmed, the older woman's ire punched through the sorrow. "Hell, yeah, I'm okay. I want you to catch this sick bastard, Quinn. You and Tyson. Maybe even that uncle of yours. But this killer . . . this sick bastard came for more than my goat. Why did he have to stir shit up and recreate your daddy's scene with my baby's blood?"

Jonah had indeed gone into all the detail with her. "That's what we're trying to find out," Quinn said.

But when she tried to draw the short woman to her, Jule pushed back. "Come on. I'll show you where I found Bonnie."

The next several dozen yards consisted of Jule's grumblings and threats to cut off his balls or gut him and throw him to the gators in the river, so that by the time they reached the back of the barn, she was teeth-gritting fuming. "There." She pointed to an ancient oak stump three feet wide and two feet tall, the darkness of the blood-letting still evident across its surface. It would serve as a reminder for months to come, too, having soaked into the irregular chops in the wood.

Quinn looked closely across the stump then fanned out her scrutiny, seeking footprints and dried blood elsewhere. He probably did it with gloves, but regardless, no real place to leave fingerprints. Even if they'd had cameras on Jule's cottage or the barn, she doubted they'd have had one back here. They would now. Jonah had two jobs today: install cams and interrogate workers about sighting any strange faces yesterday . . . before . . . ever. "Find the weapon he used?"

"No, and I looked hard for it, too. Must've taken it with him."

Walking the area, Quinn tried to reconstruct what happened, but there wasn't a lick of evidence to go on. The killer left no trace on dry ground now moist and littered with leaves and hay.

Jule moved toward the goat barn. "If you want to see Bonnie, come inside. Jonah bagged her and set her in the chest freezer. Not sure how much you can tell—"

Quinn's pulse did a sudden gallop at the thought of laying eyes on the carcass of that sweet animal. "Um, no need, Jule. Let Jonah go ahead and bury her." She paused a second. "You see any strange vehicles yesterday?"

Jule shook her head.

Any unfamiliar truck should've caught someone's eye. A fit person could've tucked a vehicle back in the woods on the highway and walked in. He had walked to the barn from wherever he hid it, though, because

Jule was way too observant to let a vehicle go unnoticed.

But Quinn considered herself fairly observant, too, and she'd not noticed anyone different. This was a far cry from a prank like her uncle said. This was planned, with a mission to leave a message that someone watched and waited to see how Quinn handled the results. She also expected him to watch to see where she'd take things from here. Frankly, she expected a second chapter.

Three anomalies. First, Mickey Raines . . . second, a realtor dropping in from nowhere to buy Sterling Banks. The connections were tenuous but connections, nonetheless. Vic's murder fell in there somewhere because he had hunted Mickey and most likely died for the effort. Everything remained as clear as the black water in the Edisto River.

Quinn gave up analyzing the crime scene and moved around the barn, Jule following. Back at the pen, she leaned over the railing again, and scratched a different billy between his horns. "I need you to come up to the house, Jule. You got a moment?"

"Why?"

"Trust me."

Jule hooked a finger into Quinn's belt loop and yanked. "Did I say I didn't trust you? You talk plain with me, girl. The question was *why*."

Maybe the timing was wrong. Jule was tied up in knots. Or maybe that's what made the timing perfectly right.

Bonnie's killer was far from her primary reason to get Jule to the house, and the woman who'd been caretaker of both Quinn and Sterling Banks for three decades knew it. She didn't venture often into the manor since that horrible evening except to maybe stock something special in the fridge or leave a casserole on the counter when she worried Quinn hadn't been eating right. She always entered through the sliding doors, like most everyone else, but Quinn understood the real reason she remained toward the back of the house. Maybe it was time Jule entered the manor through the front.

Quinn touched the pink bandana, letting her fingers slide along the woman's cheek until she looped fingers under Jule's overall strap. She lightly tugged once. "I need you to walk me through that day."

Jule pulled loose. "Like I keep telling all y'all, I don't remember."

She started back toward the barn, to her beloved goats that had been her unblemished haven until yesterday.

"No, ma'am," Quinn said, reaching to grab a sleeve. "I need your help."

God, she loved this hard-headed woman, but Jule couldn't forever stick her head in the sand. Six years was long enough. "Because you were the only witness to what happened to Daddy, if we are to believe Uncle Larry. And all this shit . . . Bonnie Blue, a new realtor, the blood on the floor . . . Mickey Raines. It all means something, and until I find Mickey, you're the only person who can help me figure this out."

She hated doing this, but Jule knew more than she spoke of. Quinn was sure of it. Everyone let her keep her thoughts private, giving her her wall of protection, but this was about all of them now. More than just Jule, though it still cut into Quinn for having to open that wound. "Surely after all this time you could try to remember something. You can't tell me you don't remember anything. That's . . ."

Hands tight on her hips, Quinn huffed hard for control and turned away, ashamed to show an emotion she reserved for the privacy of her bedroom or the hideaway of Windsor.

A touch brushed Quinn's cheek. Quinn turned to look down at the strongest woman she'd ever known, expecting a firm refusal, only to see Jule's tears riding old creases to her chin.

"All right," Jule said. "Let's go to the manor."

Chapter 14

THE SKY REMAINED drab, matching Quinn's frame of mind as she drove Jule back to the manor. She started to take Jule in through the back sliding door until Quinn remembered the newly instituted lockdown mode, so instead she used a key to enter via the side door into the kitchen. The next best way Jule and everyone else used to routinely enter before the additional security had robbed them of their sense of security. Funny how that worked.

The manor served as a community center during busy times. Folks knocked and wandered in from eight in the morning to about six in the evening. Graham Sterling had established that lifestyle, feeling community bred loyalty. Quinn grew up with overseers, family, and friends coming and going, the refrigerator filled with drinks for all. A framed note at the kitchen and back doors instructed that muddy boots were to be left on the rug provided. Hand towels had been stacked at the entrances for the sweatier souls.

Once Quinn lived there alone, the courtesy of an open house shifted without much discussion, extended to only the closest of friends . . . Jonah, Tyson, Jule . . . and Uncle Larry.

Even they would have to use their key now.

From routine, Jule kicked off her boots in the mudroom and followed Quinn inside as if all they planned was fixing dinner. The interior held an unusual, tombed sensation that Quinn attributed to nothing but her imagination. She reached behind them and locked the door.

Sock-footed, the short woman padded into the kitchen near the sink. "What do you want me to do?"

Quinn pointed to the family room. "Sit in the recliner. Want something to drink?" She opened the refrigerator not waiting for an answer, unaccustomed to telling Jule what to do, uncomfortable at having to expose this woman to such dark memories. Made her feel mean. So she fixed both of them a juice glass full of milk to cozy the mood.

"I need to walk you through some thoughts, first," Quinn said, debating whether to sit back or lean forward. She chose the latter. "Can you think of any events or anomalies that led up to that night?"

Jule laid elbows on the rests, glass in her fingers, focused anywhere but on Quinn. She seemed childlike in the oversized chair, milk in both hands, waiting for guidance. "What do you mean?"

"Was Daddy upset about anything?"

Jule shook her head and waited for the next question.

"Were any workers giving him a hard time?"

"No worker problems because your daddy nipped issues in the bud rather quickly around here," Jule replied, a bit of pride in the memory. "He was the best employer in the county, and those people didn't want to mess up a good thing."

That he was, and Quinn allowed herself a smile. But while Graham had been a stellar employer, he could be a task master, too, and he'd fired his share of slackers with minimal discussion in the process. Just said, *You did this, this, and this.* (Counting on his fingers.) *We can't have this, this, and this. Follow me to the house for your last check.* He handled them alone unless they kicked up a fuss, in which case he'd point to two other workers to escort the guy not only to the house but off the farm. Didn't happen often, but it made enough impression such that he didn't have to do it again for months.

"Had he fired anyone that week?" she asked. "That day even, since it was a Friday."

Jule shook her head. "Not that I was aware of, and I was in the manor that evening, readying for dinner, if you recall."

"Had anyone unusual made a delivery?" Quinn asked.

A shrug and another denial. Jule sipped her milk.

"Had my crazy uncle been by?" Quinn threw that easy one in to give Jule a break.

But the snicker came out bitter. "Larry?" She laid her head back into the recliner's tufted cushion. "Larry did come by earlier that day, but he was his usual self. Sarcastic, prideful, you know. The same as always."

Jule had never liked Larry Sterling, going back to when he almost lost his share of the farm in the divorce. But Quinn already knew Larry had come and gone hours before the incident. Larry called it a drop-in while in the area. Quinn wished she'd been around to hear what was really said. The brothers weren't terribly close, with Larry resentful of how their lives had spun out. Graham had bailed out his brother too many times to listen to his unsolicited advice about pecans.

"What about threats? Not that day but anywhere around that time," Quinn asked.

Jule slid back even more, almost swallowed up in the chair, and she shrugged. "A nut buyer fussing about price here and there. A handful of realtors asking if he was interested in selling. He didn't talk to you about any of this? God, he was forever saying he had to call you, what, once a day?"

Quinn pursed her lips. "Maybe every other day, but nope. He always tried to talk about me and what I was doing." And like the oblivious twenty-something she was, she took advantage and bent his ear. "But this is about you and what you know, okay?"

Another shrug, ensuring compliance, but a shadow of worry laced her mouth.

"Let's go back to the realtors," Quinn said. "More than usual? Nastier than usual? More persistent than usual? Any certain one?"

But Jule didn't allow the conversation to detour about realtors. Not at first. She shimmied to the front of the chair, so that her feet were planted firmly on the rug. "First, there was sugar in the tanks of three tractors."

"What?" Nobody told Quinn about that.

"Random," Jule replied. "Some scorned worker, he guessed."

"Not if there was a string of incidents. What else?"

"No wolves at the door," Jule said, "but he grumbled about developers *all the time*. Personally, I believe someone was making a concerted effort to acquire Sterling Banks. And he pondered whether the trees were being sabotaged."

"The fire in the pine thicket on the east side?" Quinn asked.

Jule scrunched her nose. "He said that was nothing but workers cooking lunch on a campfire and letting it get away from them, but the patch of pecan trees drilled and salted is what I'm talking about."

Quinn took note. Losing a dozen nut trees in their prime was egregious. Graham had informed his daughter of that one, only he had given the credit to a disgruntled worker cut loose months before the discovery. It just took all those months for the trees to react for the deed to become known, he'd said.

"He told me there was no way to point to that hired hand because of the time that had passed," Quinn said, though Uncle Larry might've broken at least a little sweat to run the culprit down.

With a parental dismissive look, Jule eyed Quinn as if she were twelve. "He didn't actually think that was a worker, Q, and maybe he didn't want to upset you. He blamed that on a peeved developer after a string of verbal altercations. And that's when he went back to using that old security system . . . at night anyway."

"Which developer?"

"Spartacus."

From Charleston. Major developer, but he hadn't approached Quinn since she'd taken over. Surely if he were that malicious, he would've tested the daughter.

But this was new to her. Damn, why hadn't she queried Jule sooner? *Because she hadn't thought she had to.* She assumed the woman would tell her everything. Ty wouldn't have known unless Graham had notified the sheriff's department, and Jonah didn't live there during that time. How many of Graham's thoughts were taken to the grave? How many behind a wall in Jule's mind?

Quinn rose from the sofa and strode to the glass doors facing the trees. She spun around. "You wait all these years to tell me this? I deserved to know that there had been threats."

"I didn't think," was the only response for a minute. "Then you lost your job and moved back here. I felt that you'd learn one way or the other. Through Larry maybe?"

Quinn fumed at the stilted, disjointed remarks that fell way short of decent justification. "Son of a bitch, Jule."

Jule spoke softly. "The timing wasn't right, Quinn. Just never seemed right." She emptied the last of the milk. "You had enough on your plate with the farm."

Red hair slapped her across the eyes as Quinn held her temper and escaped to the kitchen. She opened the refrigerator and stuck her head in, breathing the cold.

Damn it. She'd have pursued people with a vengeance back then. Realtors, contractors with the pecans, hired hands, everybody, and anybody, but today this trail was as cold as a Canadian glacier. She yanked out a bottle. "You want a beer?" she called to the family room.

"No," Jule called back.

Quinn screwed off the top and chugged half the bottle until she had to take a breath. Guess she knew more now than when she started today. *Look at it that way.* She returned and sat. "Daddy only told me about the pine tree fire."

"Yeah, I know," Jule said.

"So . . .," Quinn started.

"So," Jule repeated, brow raised.

Get to the murder. Get to Daddy. "Was . . . the security alarm on that night?"

"No. It wasn't the end of the day yet. People still coming in and out."

Noted. "Any threatening mail?" Quinn asked.

"No, but Graham wouldn't have said if there was."

The way Jule said *Graham* had a calming effect. Almost instant, the sensitive, melodic way Jule said *Graham* reminded Quinn of when there was a Graham.

Just a couple years apart in age, Jule and Graham had become what everyone assumed was brother-and-sister close. Maggie's death only made the remaining two adults tighter in their need to share grief . . . and raise Quinn. As a high school teen, Quinn often wondered if her father and his caretaker had crossed the line and done the deed. Later, however, Quinn began to see them as more like herself and Ty. But then, they'd almost taken things past the fraternal level, too. Where she *had* taken things with Jonah the night of high school graduation.

Friendship, love, and attraction had a way of becoming complicated between the sexes.

Quinn stood. "You were in the kitchen that night?"

Jule stiffened. "Yes, I'd started supper. It was just him and me." She paused at the memory. "It usually was only him and me in those days."

"What were you cooking?" Quinn asked, reaching to help the woman up.

"It was a Friday." Jule strolled to the stove. "Fried chicken night. Collards. Mashed potatoes and gravy, but we . . ." She trailed off, her palm running across the glass stovetop. "We never got to the gravy."

Quinn relaxed her tone. "Where was Daddy?"

Glancing over to the sink, Jule seemed to be remembering, maybe seeing the dirty dishes in the sink, the skillet on the stove. Her lips barely lifted in the slightest of smiles.

"I was frying," she replied. "He was draining the potatoes for mashing. There came a knock on the door. I kept cooking."

Quinn didn't interrupt.

"He called, 'Who's there,' thinking it was a worker. Some asked for advances on Fridays. Others might give notice." She cut a glance at Quinn. "You know how it was."

Quinn indeed knew.

Jule continued. "The vent was on over the stove, so we couldn't rightly hear. He wiped his hands on a dishtowel and went to see who it was." She gazed at some unseen distance.

Quinn caught herself trying to hear what Jule did.

"When he didn't come back, I called his name. When he didn't reply, I turned down the vent, still hearing nothing. So I poked my head around the door, you know?" Her eyes pleaded with Quinn to see it all like she did, so she didn't have to explain it too much.

"Yeah," Quinn said. "Come show me."

Hesitantly, Jule walked around the corner toward the entryway. "It all goes dark right here."

As difficult and scary as facing this moment must be for Jule, Quinn saw the woman doing this for her. Quinn wanted to hug her so hard, but this wasn't over. "This is where you dropped?"

The woman had moved her focus to the slate floor ahead, to the spot Quinn was sure she'd scrubbed layers off the grout and stone to be rid of the red. The area had dried, but between old memory and new stain, the slightest, vaguest hint of pink remained if they looked hard enough.

And how could they not?

Jule remained fixated on the slate. "It went quiet, too, when I was hit. You know you don't just snap and wake up when you're unconscious."

"What do you mean?" Quinn asked.

"Smells came to me first."

"Like what?"

Inhaling, Jule released the breath. "Burning grease mostly. The chicken on the stove."

Made sense.

"Men's voices," she continued. "The way men smell. Took until someone laid a cold rag on my head for me to open my eyes and figure out who. I drifted in and out. At first just Mickey, then later Mickey and two strangers."

Quinn had figured her uncle to be there next. "Strangers?"

"EMS," Jule said.

"So Mickey called 911?"

"Who else could have?"

The guy who clobbered the two of them, that's who. Could've come in for Graham, not expecting Jule. The surprise could've thrown off his blow enough to keep her alive . . . or his blow was off because he had no intention of killing her to begin with.

But Uncle Larry had told Quinn that they'd confirmed Mickey called 911.

"When did Uncle Larry get there?"

Jule repositioned her bandana, as if a sensation of her head had returned. "When EMS was working on me. Tyson came soon after with a couple others. Couldn't tell you which ones, but Larry interrogated the hell out of Mickey before they all arrived. I recall wanting to shove my fist down his throat, for him to lay off the kid. How could Mickey know what happened? Poor guy just came in the house looking for your dad."

Jule was reaching inward and doing well, but right there she'd assumed Mickey had innocently walked in instead of doing the crime. "Before Tyson and the others got there, what did Uncle Larry ask Mickey, and what did he say in return?" God, she wanted to add, *Think, Jule. This is so damned important*, but too much pressure could shut her down.

For too many reasons to count, Quinn never believed her uncle's accountings.

"Mickey said he saw someone leave," Jule said, now homed in on the front door. "Someone dark. Maybe he said more. I don't remember."

"Describe *dark*."

Fussy, Jule let a little spark fly. "Ask *him* to describe dark. He said it, not me."

"Okay. Sorry. Keep going," Quinn said.

Acting like she fought a headache, the little lady lowered her chin, eyes closed. "Larry was intense. Maybe because of your daddy . . . because of me . . . but he was crazy mad."

Quinn almost whispered, starving for anything other than her uncle's storyline. "What did he say?"

"Get . . . something. Get . . . home. Get . . . out of the way." Jule seemed dissatisfied with the guesses.

Quinn waited, breath held.

"Get *gone*," Jule said, heavy accent on the *gone*. "Get the *hell out of Dodge*."

"Which was it?"

"Both," Jule exclaimed. "He said both to Mickey."

"What did Mickey say to that?"

But Jule couldn't recall.

Uncle Larry had chased Mickey off, and Mickey hadn't been seen since. He'd taken *get gone* to heart.

Who told someone to leave a crime scene if they'd been involved?

Quinn's ire built at the fresh addition to the sheriff's old, worn-out version he told the world. "Okay, I'm seeing it. You're doing great." Then she had to ask something more, that she maybe had no right to ask, but she wanted, needed to know even though the answer had nothing to do with the case. "Did you . . . see Daddy?"

Jule gently shook her head as if it still hurt to move. "Larry barked at those EMS guys about your father, though. Raging mad. Asked if there was another ambulance coming, and they said no, just the coroner. He went ballistic for them saying that in front of me." She teared just a bit, and for the first time slid her stare to Quinn, as though coming back around from a trance. "That was how I learned he was dead, honey. That's how I learned he was dead."

Unable to restrain herself any longer, Quinn wrapped arms around the woman, her chin on the gray-haired head. "And I'm so sorry you had to be there, Jule. There was nothing you could've done. I'm happy Daddy wasn't alone, and that his last hours were with you. Especially you."

For the longest minutes they rocked in the entryway, Jule reliving those horrible moments . . . Quinn silently vowing to find Mickey.

She'd deal with Sheriff Sterling in due time.

"Quinn?" came a voice from the back of the house.

"Front hall," she hollered, still hugging the small momma figure.

Jonah strode in and halted, almost dropping his bags to the floor in an effort to reach the two. Laying a hand on his mother's back, he gave a harried look to Quinn then back to Jule. "What's wrong? Momma? What happened?"

"She . . . was remembering," Quinn said, laying her cheek on the woman's hair again. "She did good."

"You mean she did what you made her do." He reached in and eased his mother away from the hug. "How dare you, Quinn."

"No, Son, I offered," Jule said, as she slid off one to the other.

But Jonah clearly wasn't convinced. "This was not the plan. This was not in our discussion last night."

Quinn tried to show empathy. "It might help us, Jonah."

"Help *you*," he replied, jaw taut.

Which tensed her up. "What affects Sterling Banks affects us all."

Jonah's face only darkened. "Says the queen to the pawns." He moved his mother closer, and one arm around her, picked up his bags.

"Security is up on your house, Your Highness. It goes up on *her* house next."

As he turned, Quinn raised her voice. "Put one behind the barn, where Bonnie was killed."

He didn't reply.

"Lock your doors," Jule said before they disappeared through the kitchen.

Then they were gone. Leaving Quinn empty, in a huge empty house, on a huge plantation of a farm that she liked—apparently naively—to think belonged to them all.

Because she had nobody else, and all this was too much for one.

She didn't move until the kitchen door shut, and even then she waited to see if they'd come back in. Jonah's attitude stung, but he protected his mother. The night Graham was murdered had embedded that trait. His mother almost died, and he came home to stay, to see it didn't happen again. He had little patience for violence, which spilled into his intolerance for Quinn being a PI.

After Graham, she left her dream job with the FBI like he'd left his with that huge upstate agriculture operation. To him, her rebounding into private investigations only kept her tied to crime and tragedy, which they'd had enough of for all their lifetimes.

He'd have relocated his mother years ago if she weren't so concerned for Quinn. Jule couldn't stomach abandoning someone she'd practically raised. Nothing would piss off Jonah more than for Quinn to take advantage of that relationship.

But she wasn't trying to do that.

Jonah just didn't understand the criminal element. Law enforcement fit Ty and Quinn with Jonah the odd man out. It had taken a *Jacket* call to order, a dead goat, and a bloody stain on the floor to get him involved.

Quinn grabbed a Diet Coke, the image of fried chicken still vivid as she passed the stove. To keep from thinking about Jonah, she lit up her computer, with plans to dig deep into the night. If she couldn't find Mickey online by morning, she'd confront his parents again, and she wasn't leaving easy this time.

Mickey Raines was crucial whether he killed Vic or not, whether he killed Graham or not, whether he was Catherine's lover or not. Catherine didn't have nearly the desire nor passion to find this guy that Quinn did. Nowhere near close. Especially since someone had violated Sterling Banks.

Her phone rang. Expecting it to be Jonah or Ty, she accepted the call a split second before registering caller ID.

Catherine.

Chapter 15

QUINN WILLED HER nerves to still, her emotions ordered back in the closet to make room for the nothing-phases-me persona required for PI work. She switched hands on her phone. "What can I do for you, Catherine?"

"It's been two days. I need a status report."

"You hired me yesterday, Cat."

A pause. "I didn't say you could call me that. The name is Catherine. No nicknames. No baby names. No abbreviations or initials. Is that clear?"

"Catherine." Quinn said the word long and stretched. "Again, you hired me yesterday. That was a Thursday."

"I spoke to you Tuesday."

"You signed the contract Thursday, but regardless, I haven't found Mickey. I'll let you know when I do. Anything else?"

Quinn heard the aristocrat inhale all the way from Charleston. "You don't dismiss me," she said. "I decide when to hang up."

"Fine. So do I," and Quinn hung up.

But before Quinn could open a file, Catherine called again. "I said I need an update! Who have you spoken with?"

Quinn could vacate the contract and continue investigating on her own. She'd already been accused of flying solo anyway, but she had concerns about Catherine and her relationships with Mickey and Vic. Mickey dating Catherine was akin to a mixed breed rescue dating a fifth generation kennel show winner. Not that it couldn't happen, but it probably wouldn't. A lot of missing motive here.

So she played along. "Who have I spoken with? Let's see . . . the Craven County sheriff, a Craven County deputy, Mickey's parents, and some county residents who knew Mickey in the past."

"Oh," Catherine said.

"Nobody's seen him," Quinn said, "but he's not far. It's not like he's gone to Hong Kong or anything, and word has it he's pretty local."

Quinn could picture Catherine's mouth gaping. "Oooh, that's good. How local?"

"Like within a couple hours' drive local. Close enough to get here in the same afternoon if asked to do so. But that's all I've got. You have to give me rein here, Catherine. Let me run at my own pace."

"Hmmm. I'm accustomed to regular updates."

"I call weekly and when important information comes to light. That's pretty standard."

"Daily?" Catherine asked after a silence.

"When I have something, or at least every other day," Quinn countered. "Plus a thorough weekly report you can show your father."

"Oh, no," Catherine said. "No, no. Nothing to my father."

They had agreed on that, but Quinn wanted to test her again. Despite Catherine's heated love for Mickey, in spite of her first PI dying in the midst of his work, she nevertheless wanted to keep dear old daddy out of the loop even when his reach could most definitely aid in finding the beau if not the killer.

As in most of Quinn's cases, the issue was as much about the client as the person being pursued.

"Yes, sorry," Quinn said. "You are absolutely right. You are the client, Catherine, so everything I do, I do for you. How about we meet tomorrow for brunch? I'll come to you. What's your address, and I'll pick you up."

The *uh* and *um* from the socially poised blue-blooded Charlestonian told Quinn she'd caught that woman so off guard she'd lost her entire vocabulary.

Catherine came off pompous, which had turned Quinn adversarial in the beginning because she wasn't sure she wanted the case. The attitude had nixed the deal. This woman lied, but she was the closest link to Mickey . . . and Vic . . . that Quinn had. In the mire of Catherine's aristocratic bullshit floated truths and clues that Quinn needed, and if stroking Ms. Renault was the cost for that information, then Quinn would stroke away.

"Unless you have something eating at you now," Quinn continued, "in which case I can book it right over there to you. Dinner is doable. Keep it informal, if you don't mind since it'll be late by the time I arrive."

"I just want you to find Mickey," Catherine said. "Coming to me will accomplish nothing."

"Oh," Quinn said. "I beg to differ. Plus, like you said, you need a thorough update. Tomorrow at nine a.m. or lunch at noon. Text me the place."

Breakfast it was, and Quinn hung up, ruing the early hour, but grateful for the opportunity.

She stayed busy, trying not to think about Jule or Jonah, so she called Ty. He'd been awful quiet today.

"Was about to ring you," he said. "Had supper?"

"What time is it?" she asked, turning in her desk chair to check her computer screen, her afternoon with Jule having stolen her sense of the hour.

"Six thirty, give or take. Momma got a good deal on catfish today, and she's willing to fry us up some."

"Depends. You got news for me?" she asked, teasing.

"Yup. Finished scouring Vic's files."

She'd already moved toward the door, keys in hand. "For that I'll come."

Actually, Ty had her at fried catfish, but without a doubt, that *whatever* he'd discovered could affect her meeting and agenda with Catherine in the morning.

Twenty minutes later, she sat in her booth, waiting for Lenore to fry up the fish, which from the heavy lemon-pepper, cornbread scent in the air, had been ordered and cooked up repeatedly since Jackson Hole's door opened for the evening crowd. All the lights were on. None of the low-key, dusky, jazz environment of the other night. Pop country played loudly.

She took a moment to enjoy the atmosphere and aromas. Sometimes grease could smell so damn good.

"She's frying you up some pickles, too," Ty said, handing her a folder of copies. But Quinn tucked them out of sight beside her on the cushioned bench, wanting some social time with her buddy. The room hummed as endless plates of catfish exited the kitchen.

"Shouldn't we be helping your momma?" she asked, watching the staff sling plates on tables.

"Already gave her one hour this evening, and after dinner, promised to help her to close."

"I can stick around and help close up, too," she said, a strong whiff of two plates going by their table making her all the more hungry.

They spoke of folks in the room, Ty's day, as if they avoided talking about the case at hand until she finally itched too hard to not ask. "Can't stand it," she said. "Brief me."

"Vic might've been hunting Mickey, but he was also looking at Sterling Banks," he said.

The hushpuppy never made it to her mouth. Not answering Vic's voice mail had left her with the haunting *what-if* by not calling him back.

Ty pretended not to notice the hesitancy and nodded toward where the folder hid on the seat. "In looking at Mickey, Vic ran across the story about your daddy. As you'd expect, the murder piqued his interest."

"And my name popped up," she said, hardly tasting the fried cornbread ball. She wished to God a thousand times over she'd returned that call now. "I need a beer."

"Yeah, I imagine you do." He left the booth to help himself behind the bar for the both of them.

Unable to resist, Quinn opened the folder then shut it. Here was not the place to spread out papers, but the curiosity almost made her forgo the meal and get to the real meat of her existence of late.

She tried to call Knox instead, for the status of Vic's phone. No answer, so she left him a message.

Ty returned, two filled, iced mugs in his big hands. Quinn sucked down a healthy swig, welcoming the ice shards before they disappeared to room temperature. Ty dove into his own then came up for air, a lick over his lips to remove the foam. "You sure you haven't talked to Vic or Mickey in recent months? You've been known to hold back stuff."

"Wish I had," she said. "Vic tried to call, though."

His forehead deepened with an all-knowing look. "Like I said . . . you've been known to hold back."

"Just a message asking me to call him," she said, trailing off, totally guilty of his accusation. "Sad thing is I might've intervened if I'd called him back."

"Or you could've been taken down like he was," Ty said, sitting back as a young girl slid platters of hot crispy fish before them along with a fresh basket of hushpuppies and fried dill pickles.

When the girl left, he unfolded a napkin. "What else might be on Vic's phone, or have you checked back with your FBI buddy?"

She lifted three of the fish onto her plate. "Just left him a message. With him doing this as a favor, he can't exactly push us ahead of their own work." She pulled out the top fin, stripping most of the bones from the first fish, opening it up to that luscious white meat. "I wish she'd fix these more often," she mumbled into her first bite. Two bites later, she lifted her head. "Tell her she doesn't charge enough. Look at all the people in this place. She could add on."

Ty was already on his third fish, a pro at dissecting the delicacy. "She's the size she wants to be. Doesn't want to be anything high and mighty."

Kudos to Lenore for doing what she wanted, in the manner in which she wanted to do it.

Quinn could use a lesson from her on that. "Heard about any sightings of Mickey?"

Shaking his head, Ty swallowed a mouthful. "Not a thing, but if he was involved with your PI buddy can you blame him for going dark? He's a strong person of interest until he proves otherwise."

She disagreed. "He stayed out of sight for years, so his absence isn't what makes him a suspect. It's his ties to Vic and Catherine."

"He ought to be coming forward."

"Maybe he doesn't know about Vic," she countered, but frankly, she believed he did.

A scream erupted from the kitchen. Ty leaped out of the booth before someone managed to yell *fire*, his napkin fluttering across the floor. An alarm rose to pitch and jolted everyone in the room. Only then did the savory grease smell turn burnt.

The room of patrons sat up to take notice, as if needing to see flames before believing the threat . . . waiting for direction.

Quinn bounded from her seat. "Everyone stand and leave the building. No running."

"What the hell?" bellowed an older gentleman who seemed to have grown roots to his chair. Mr. Padget, a man she recognized from the Fourth of July barbecues at the Banks, going back to when Graham had started them twenty-odd years ago. Whoever he'd been eating with, however, had gone, but Mr. Padget;s girth indicated he wasn't a man of much action.

She rushed to him, but not before repeating her directive to each table in passing, touching elbows, helping to scoot out chairs. "Outside, please. Orderly and no running. Please be careful and don't trip. Sorry for the inconvenience."

Finally reaching her father's old friend who showed no intention of leaving a hot catfish dinner, she laid a hand on his back. "Sorry, Mr. Padget. Better safe than sorry. Let's go."

"Like I told my two buddies, I'm an old man, Quinn. No wasted energy. They'll put it out anyway." He reached for another fingerling.

She snatched the fish out of his hand, then with an effort due to his wide spread and established belt size, she dragged the chair away from the table, its feet protesting on the cement floor. "I said leave, Mr. Padget." Lifting him to his feet, she pivoted him toward the door and gave him a light push. "Don't stop until you're at your car."

He blustered with grumbles after a slight double-step, but she had no time for apologies. Not with plumes of smoke boiling around the seams of the swinging kitchen door.

Half the place had emptied, but the other half remained stunned, curious, doing anything but leaving. One table shouted she needed a to-go box for her meal.

Enough. "Get the hell out of here!" she shouted over everyone's heads, then she chose individuals and pointed. "You with the red shirt, get up. And you, next to him. Now!" Moving quickly amongst tables, she handed women their purses, pulled out chairs, and ordered folks to evacuate, good manners no part of the hurrying-up process, her force prompting others to come out of their daze. "For God's sake, people, the place is on fire!"

With the last person gone, she took a deep breath to last her and bolted toward the kitchen. Ty had gone in for his mother and not come out.

Arms in front of her face, she opened the door, immediately confronted with a wall of haze. Through watering eyes, she smelled grease and something chemical, and caught sight of a thicker cloud of gray smoke over the fryer. Loud sizzles kept popping, refusing to give up, or getting started, she couldn't tell. A thinner cloud hovered everywhere else. Unable to be sure of what she saw, she dropped to her knees in the doorway, where the air was cleaner, hoping to find people from the new vantage, see feet behind equipment and tables, or folks on the floor, but she saw no one.

She had to gasp at that point, but the fumes, though way less dense, still served to choke her, and instinct wouldn't let her take another inhale for fear of suffocating. Going in was not possible.

Her eyes stung and watered. Crab walking, she scanned behind the bar for anyone else, then she remembered the file still in the booth.

The electrical had gone out leaving the room black, and her sense of direction was all out of sorts. Her chest burned, her throat raw and dying to cough. The moment she inhaled once there'd be no second. Not with this smoke.

Then light appeared. Had to be the main entrance . . . and what looked like flashlights.

Hands took hold of her as she reached the opening. Tight grips practically dragged her off her feet to her truck, and by the time they planted her butt on the tailgate, she hacked coughs so deep her belt cut into her middle. Someone handed her a bottle of water, and unable to stop coughing, she instead tilted back and poured it in her eyes to stop the burn.

"You all right?" came at her from all sides, but she hadn't the air to answer. People spoke near her, yards away, all around, the sea of bodies unidentifiable. Weren't they too close to the restaurant? What if the place exploded?

"We've got to get away," she croaked, trying to stand blind.

Not seeing orange and yellow flames, for a moment, she worried she'd done more damage to her vision than her lungs and poured more water in her eyes, her shirt soaked. More blinking. Couldn't take in enough clean air without her lungs hacking it out.

"Ty?" she finally yelled. Two short gasps. "Ty?"

Soon came the reply. "I'm here, Q." Her friend touched her face with the palm of one hand.

She blinked some more and pulled back, his image taking shape, a herd of people milling around the two of them. Another grouping twenty yards to her right. A siren sounded in the distance, then another.

"We're too close," she managed to say. "The fire . . . grease, gas . . ."

"It's okay. It's okay," Ty kept saying before she realized he thought she was crying. "The fire's out."

"You sure?" Blinking, blinking. "My eyes won't stop stinging." She doused her eyes again. "Where's Lenore?"

"She's over there with the staff. She's fine. Got her out the back door with the others."

Quinn made out his face and touched his sweaty cheeks. "What about you?"

With a sad grin he held up a hand. "This hurts like hell, but otherwise I'm good."

She winced at the red on his palm . . . red meat. Missing skin. "Oh dear Jesus. What the hell happened?"

He let her cradle the back of his hand in both of hers. "I shoved Momma out of the way then touched something I shouldn't have, groping for the extinguisher," he said.

"Oh, Ty."

This man was her strength, and out of their trio, he was the last person she expected to take a hit. He was too savvy and common sense solid.

Poor Lenore. She loved Jackson Hole almost as much as her son. "You sure your mother's not hurt?"

"Positive," he said.

The fire department arrived along with most of the on-duty Craven County deputies, and upon examination of Tyson's injury, the fire captain asked one of his men for the ambulance's ETA.

"An ambulance?" Tyson disliked the attention, typical of a first responder thrust into the victim role. "I can drive myself to the ER."

"No," said the captain. "That's serious."

"I'll see he gets attention, Captain Lawson," Quinn said, and the captain left to tend to his people.

Together they sat there on that tailgate, watching Lenore smothered with attention at the end of the parking lot nearer the kitchen entrance. Uniforms came and went, taking notes, photographs, interviewing people.

The ambulance arrived, and as a medic tended Tyson, Jonah came running, breathless and pale, a bag in his grip. "Someone called Jule and she called me out of the orchard. Damn, y'all," was all he could say.

"We're fine," Quinn said, leaning against the ambulance door, hating the nasty, greasy way her arms and neck felt, a bitter taste in her mouth from the odor she couldn't wash out. "What's in the bag?"

"A cold six-pack and a couple of my t-shirts. The beer was my idea. The shirts were hers."

Jonah unscrewed the bottle and placed it in Tyson's good hand, the medic reluctantly declining the offer to join them.

The beer did a much better job of expunging the smoky taste and easing the last little jumping jolts of adrenaline that had kept Quinn's arms and hands twitching. Gently applying the last piece of tape, the medic told Ty to get to the hospital if he wasn't riding in the van, and not to delay.

"Can he finish his beer?" Quinn asked, raising her bottle and giving the medic a laugh.

"Just one," he said. "I'll see you guys another time."

"I sincerely hope not," Quinn replied.

The trio strolled back to Quinn's pickup. The two helped Tyson change into one of the t-shirts then sit on the tailgate. Quinn exchanged her beer for the second shirt. "Keep anyone from coming over, if you don't mind."

She went to the side of the truck and stripped herself of the damp, stained, sticky shirt, took a whiff of her bra and quickly whipped it off, too, deftly slipping the new shirt on. Her two friends gave strict attention to the restaurant.

Tugging the shirt down, she came back and hopped up beside Ty, laying his incapacitated hand back in her lap before reclaiming her beer. "What about the file?" she asked him. "It's still in the booth."

"Smoked up but shouldn't have caught on fire," he said.

"Anything we ought to worry about if someone else read it?"

He took a swig and thought. "Only if they knew Victor Whitmarsh. Good thing, though. Out of commission like this gives me time to work with you without the sheriff in the way, if you think about it."

But he wouldn't be traipsing around with her for a few days, she imagined. "What caused the fire?" she asked, low enough for only the three of them.

"I'm thinking something got tossed into the fryer," Ty said. "And I'm not ruling out on purpose."

"Maybe the grease vent overhead?" Jonah said, not wanting to head down more degenerate paths than they already were. "I hear a lot of commercial fires start that way."

Ty finished the one bottle, and Jonah passed over another. "Not in this kitchen. I cleaned that hood myself not two weeks ago. What bothers me is that when I pulled the handle for the fire suppression system, it didn't want to work. It just spit instead of smothering the fire." He aimed his bottle at Quinn. "Your daddy made Momma put that system in. Said it would pay for itself with one small fire. Glad we had an old-fashioned extinguisher as backup."

For a moment, they watched the comings and goings of others . . . dwelling on the situation.

Jonah studied the diminishing number of firefighters. "You think those guys are shrewd enough to identify the cause?"

Nobody answered, not sure.

"Is that system you're talking about inspected?" Quinn asked.

"Just two days ago," Ty said, eyes narrow and staring harder at his mother's pride and joy diner. "Momma mentioned it."

"Get me their address and phone number," Quinn said, just as Jonah blurted, "Who are they?"

"Don't worry about it," Ty replied.

Quinn nudged his shoulder. "Gotta be from Charleston, and I'm headed there early tomorrow, so let me take lead on this."

"You're not a cop," he said.

"Ouch, Ty, but I'll give you that under the circumstances. Truth is neither are you for a day or two since you'll be on sick leave. And Jonah's too nice."

Jonah leaned in her face. "I wasn't too nice earlier this afternoon."

"Humph," she said, dropping her empty into Jonah's paper bag. "Your mad ain't got nothing on mine."

True in fact, but it didn't matter. What bothered Quinn more was that a perfectly good, recently inspected system had failed on the heels of so much else happening in Craven County, with Catherine and the realtor having sat inside the place. Who couldn't help noting Quinn's relationship with Lenore and the diner? Vic had died, and Mickey had gone into hiding due to their affiliation with Catherine, she was sure. And a realtor out of the blue, representing a big name and a lot of dollars, had taken issue with Sterling Banks not being available.

Big money in both cases, and big money didn't like not getting what it wanted.

No, Quinn doubted the inspection company had been to Jackson Hole at all.

Chapter 16

CATHERINE'S TEXT dinged through just before midnight, saying to meet her at *Toast!* at ten, an hour later than decided and at a restaurant Quinn hadn't been to in ages. All she did was reply with a thumbs-up, giving the woman the uncontested say-so because the meeting place really didn't matter.

While the restaurant's signature cinnamon apple-stuffed French toast religiously appealed to her breakfast appetite, Quinn had other plans. She rose early after checking with Lenore on Ty, both at Lenore's home for a few days as the police, fire marshal, and insurance people did their jobs. Then she struck out for Charleston, but her first stop wouldn't be *Toast!*

Arriving at the originally scheduled nine, Quinn had no expectations of being allowed into the highly secured, five-story complex in the heart of Charleston with its wrought-iron protection and cobblestoned entrance.

She parked a half block down on a meter. Soon she waited, seated on a decorative brick planter exploding with fresh plantings of sweet potato vines, vincas, and lantana. The day was bright, the air balmy, and the morning temp in the seventies. Added to the atmosphere of the historic city, and all Quinn needed was a cup of goat-milk-laced, dark roast coffee to pleasantly bide her time. She settled for Starbucks.

At nine thirty, a gate opened, and the BMW appeared, Chevy at the wheel. Quinn stood, waved, and waited to see what they'd do. The driver made a right and kept driving, but Quinn's phone rang pretty damn quick.

"Our meeting was at the restaurant," Catherine said.

"Figured the rules were negotiable," she replied. "Pull over and let me in your car."

Soon the vehicle appeared from Quinn's left, and when the gated access to parking opened, Quinn took the hint and walked through. Chevy drove in and parked in a bottom floor spot in the back right corner of the low-ceilinged garage.

Quinn caught up about the time the driver exited the vehicle. "Hey, Chevy. Mind waiting outside while we hold our meeting?" She didn't wait for an answer, however, instead peering in at Catherine in the back seat. She entered.

Nero sat in the front.

"Well?" Catherine asked.

Quinn reached once over the seat to pet the huge black dog. He made no move to stop her.

"Most people don't dare try that," Catherine continued, a hint of surprise in her expression when Quinn sat back.

"You take direction from their eyes," Quinn said. *No different than people, and apparently you're not as blind as you lead on.*

Catherine stared through Quinn this time. "My time is precious, Ms. Sterling. Admittedly I'm glad we didn't waste it over the formalities of a meal. You called for us to meet, yet you said you had nothing new on Mickey. What has changed?"

Testing, Quinn reached over to pet Nero again and Catherine seemed not to notice.

"You mean, what's the point?" Quinn asked. "Maybe I wanted to meet face-to-face. Maybe I needed to hear the truth as to why you have an interest in Mickey Raines." Catherine seemed to tightly leash any sort of reaction.

But Catherine thought quickly. "Oh dear Lord, Ms. Sterling, we've been over that. You want something more tawdry? We fucked in back seats or slipped away to moldy motels so I couldn't be recognized?"

Quinn had to admit the woman wasn't very flappable. "Not really, but thanks for the images."

Catherine delivered a breathy sigh of impatience. "I was exaggerating."

"No doubt," Quinn said. "But let me run something by you, then you tell me how close I am to hitting the mark."

A slight up-tick of Catherine's chin.

"You and Mickey didn't happen to meet in Marion Square." No change yet. "You hunted him down once your personal PI connected him with Sterling Banks Plantation."

No explosive denial.

Quinn had spent a couple hours sitting with Ty in the ER last night, going over the smoky-scented papers a fireman managed to salvage. She'd promised a firefighter an invitation to the next Banks Christmas regalia in order to retrieve them once Jackson Hole was cordoned off.

"You needed someone to research more than a title chain about Sterling Banks, but nobody could be bought. At least anyone knowledgeable of anything."

Just a slight eye twitch.

Quinn continued. "Vic wouldn't have told you he knew me. Not with his reputation in the business, and definitely not about me in particular. That he knew me was just a coincidence, but you had him research me and my place. Tell me I'm wrong so I can read your expression." *And half blind or not, read your eyes.*

"You were friends with him?"

Quinn gave a hard grin. "Guess he didn't tell you?"

"Did he tell you I was researching Sterling Banks?" Catherine asked, not overly disturbed.

"He called," Quinn replied, not releasing the fact she hadn't phoned him back. "Like most clients to PIs, you haven't been exactly forthright with the facts, so I'm entitled to hold onto a few trump cards as well."

"But you work for me."

"I can easily *not* work for you, too. Plus, you hiring me doesn't give you carte blanche to anything I find outside of your orders. And if I decline to work for you, tell me how efficient any other PI would be trying to check me and mine out without me being aware. Spill what you're doing, or I end your contract. What's your interest in my family's land?"

Catherine came from money, and with money came a certain resilience to pressure. But Quinn had been called *Princess* by more than

146

Jonah and more than a few times in the profession. She had no problem wearing the crown. She had the means to continue this case without compensation from Catherine.

She did PI work to exercise her law enforcement training to whatever degree she could. Without the PI license, she had no way to dally in law enforcement *and* run Sterling Banks. *With* the license, law enforcement professionals gave her half a glance versus none. Add her family name, and therefore her uncle's name, and she trespassed across more regulatory lines than the norm.

And *because* of her name, few people saw her coming. Why would a Sterling do PI grunt work? But she didn't take the grunt work cases. She carefully chose her cases. They had to make a difference, challenge her, and convince her they merited taking her away for a little while from the farm.

The only reason she took Catherine's was to find Mickey. However, she hadn't expected Mickey being the bait dangled as a means to get to her.

She was a dog with a bone now.

But why Mickey? How did the correlation to Graham Sterling matter? Mickey would have so few insights into her life, the farm . . .

"We keep our wagons circled pretty tight at the plantation," Quinn said, using the word. "But then you'd know that if you felt Mickey had any sort of in-road to me. You wasted your time with a realtor yet?"

"No," came the curt response.

"This is your lone opportunity to 'fess up."

Catherine stayed quiet.

"Oh, and Sterling Banks never goes up for sale. At least not in my lifetime."

"You have no heirs, Ms. Sterling," she said through soft laughter. "Your plantation's days are numbered."

Uncle Larry's similar words drew Quinn up short. Her biological clock was as big a threat to Sterling Banks as any fire to her trees. The farm was to be left to the bloodline . . . something Graham and his father and grandfather before him had been eager to maintain. Everyone in Charleston knew the old families and their lineage. Everyone considered the old families part of the area's history, which made it their business.

Those in real estate especially.

The Sterling family tree was rapidly thinning out.

Catherine stared at Quinn in her half-gaze manner. "Everyone has a price, Ms. Sterling."

"And you just raised mine to triple the market value. You can't buy legacy, Ms. Renault."

"You can't either," the socialite scoffed. "What happened to Catherine?"

"She went away with the contract," Quinn said. "Which you can consider null and void."

But Catherine only chuckled. "I apparently no longer need Mickey to delve into your secrets, anyway, so your services are no longer needed. I've learned more about you without him."

Like when they first met at Jackson Hole, Quinn gave the woman the last word. Last words were overrated. Instead, she opened the car door to leave in silence, a satisfaction she'd learned to relish a long time ago.

Inside, however, she seethed.

"Oh, one more thing," Catherine said, leaning a hand on the middle of the seat toward the open door. "Tell Lenore that I'm sorry about her place. Jackson something, right?" Her smile crept eerily to her eyes. "Glad nobody was seriously hurt."

Quinn froze then leaned back into the car, reaching Catherine's face before she had a chance to sense the movement. "I can get to you," Quinn whispered. "And it won't be with goat's blood."

Catherine flinched, head bumping against the tufted leather headrest.

Quinn left the BMW, bumping back into Chevy whose approach indicated he'd noted the oddities in the women's parting exchange. She patted him on his leather-jacketed shoulder. "I didn't bite too hard."

At which he hesitated before turning attentive to his charge in the car.

Quinn left . . . amazed she'd given herself the last word after all.

But she still had no concrete idea why Catherine elected Mickey as her pawn to start with. He was a weak conduit to the farm and herself.

A thread was missing, and she pondered whether she prematurely cut Catherine loose. Catherine had been shrewd enough to remain mute about her intentions and had cast Mickey aside like he was nothing.

Worry niggled her as she reached her truck and cranked the engine, sitting there letting the last half hour sink into her system. Did Catherine still have a plan? Quinn's gut said yes, but what . . . and why?

After she succinctly and decisively declined any sale of the farm, there shouldn't be a plan for Catherine to pursue, so why did the tender part on the back of her neck sense crosshairs?

Here she was, back at square one . . . needing Mickey, only this time for his insight into Catherine.

She felt sure Vic had discovered something amiss. His job had been hers . . . find Mickey. He had, yet kept it from Catherine. Now he was dead for his trouble. Mickey could've taken him out, but Quinn wasn't sold on that. Mickey had no record. He'd come out of hiding to meet with Vic, several times. A deep gut sense told her that whatever trouble Mickey'd stayed ahead of for those years had taken out Vic for discovering Mickey's whereabouts.

What had he learned that sent him running from Catherine? And with Vic's death Mickey was probably scared shitless all over again.

By the time she crossed the Ashley River Bridge, she vowed hard to find this guy.

Funny, but her last visual of him was as a high school freshman. Thin, vulnerable, and clueless in jeans that barely held up on his hips. Worlds far apart back then, but today entwined. She had no idea why or how, but she took up his case as her own. And she needed to act fast.

Vic's killer hadn't banked on his actions setting Quinn's festering vengeance anew.

She formed a semblance of a plan, and once she got home, she'd flesh it out and run it by Ty. Her only reservation was how she'd protect the Banks and her people from this crap. She couldn't be in all places at all times. Jonah had assumed the role of security, but he was one man over three thousand acres. Ty was limited by his injury. Lenore's livelihood was damaged and Jule's environment violated.

An icy trickle of fear followed her spine. She had no idea what was going on, but lives were at stake. Lives who'd brushed against her and were paying a price for it . . . lives she loved. Whoever this culprit was stayed not one but two steps ahead. And whomever *he* worked for coasted even further out of reach. Probably feeling mighty sure of him or herself.

Last night she'd slept with her old service weapon. She'd advise her buddies to start doing the same.

God, this smacked too much of six years ago. At least then she had Jonah sleeping in a guest room watching over his mom and her, standing guard. She wished she had him there again, but no way would she ask.

With events targeted at her, she felt even lonelier in that empty manor.

If wishes were horses, beggars would ride. Her daddy taught her that during some ages ago bedtime lesson, and up until middle school she pictured wishes turning into horses so everyone could have one. She understood it when she couldn't get what she wanted during one particular teenage tantrum. You had to work for things in life. They weren't granted by wishing for them.

If wishes were horses. . . . No point *wishing* all of this would go away. The onus was on her, and she would start by interrogating the company who failed to manage Jackson Hole's fire protection needs.

Chapter 17

FIRE GUARD SYSTEM Provider flashed a motto across their website as *Lowcountry's most cost-effective fire safety solutions*. When Quinn arrived at the brick-and-mortar sales showroom in West Ashley, the same words made the same promise across their storefront window, in letters that morphed from red to a soft blue. Guess that meant they put out fires. Quinn parked her pickup, gave herself a last touch of lip gloss before going inside to ask why they hadn't held up their end of the bargain at the Jackson Hole diner.

A wide variety of contraptions hugged the walls, from simple fire extinguishers on her left to aggressive special hazard systems with knobs, tanks, tubing, and cages. A crisp-looking gentleman approached her when she reached the commercial fire suppression part of the display. "May I help you?"

She handed him her PI card. "Yes, I have some questions."

Reading the card, his own fire cooled as his jovial expression shifted to not so welcoming, though he attempted to throw a smile back up. Private investigators probably didn't fall into his brand of customer. The smile seemed pasted now.

"You installed a fire suppression system at a restaurant called Jackson Hole in Craven County," she began. "You may have heard about their fire?" The fire marshal would've been in touch ASAP. The issue was only whether this particular guy got the word.

"And may I ask who you represent?" he asked.

Truth be told, she officially represented nobody. "The owner Lenore Jackson. My father, Graham Sterling, backed that establishment, and frankly, he pushed her to install your system. It failed to function."

He paled a shade or two. "I heard nobody was hurt. That true?"

Liability obviously his first and foremost thought, passed off as concern.

"A deputy, the owner's son, received pretty nasty burns on his hand trying to unsuccessfully activate your system. He put out the grease fire with the backup fire extinguisher while I emptied the place of customers."

"Oh," he said, uncomfortable. "You were there."

"Yes, I was there."

He dipped his head in acknowledgement. "My apologies, but I'll tell you what I told the Craven County fire marshal late yesterday. We didn't do it."

"Do what? Install the system? Records show—"

He was shaking his head. "No, no, sorry. What I meant to say is that we didn't inspect the system."

Wait, wasn't that as bad or worse? "Come again?" she asked. "You are required to inspect—"

He was waving his hands now. "Please, let me start over and explain. Yes, we installed the system. Yes, we are the ones who do the inspections. But no, we didn't recently inspect that property. It wasn't due for another month."

Quinn started to say *well, someone inspected it*, but didn't. He had no need to know. "We'll need a copy of your records showing the inspection schedule, if you don't mind." Something to show the prior inspection routine, something to compare this new inspection against.

"Already sent to the fire marshal. If the business's security system captured this individual on camera, we agreed to look at it and confirm it wasn't our man."

"I'll see what I can round up." She hoped the security system was as state-of-the-art as the suppression system was supposed to have been . . . and worked better.

"Any chance you can elaborate on what might've gone wrong?" she asked. "What's something simple and discreet someone could do to disable it?"

He motioned for her to turn and face a particular system to her left. "This isn't the exact model, but take a look. A saboteur has multiple options."

Cut a tube, shut off a value. Puncture any of several assorted places. Indeed they had options.

She left the man with his perfunctory apology, his business card, and a brochure of the current model of Lenore's system in hand. Once on the road, she cleared the more choking traffic on US Highway 17 before ordering her truck's Bluetooth system to call Ty.

Last night Quinn had escorted him to the ER in Walterboro after the fire and waited for him for the several hours necessary for treatment. Second-degree burns on a third of his right palm and undersides of two fingers. Thank goodness nothing third degree. On the way home, they joked about him having to learn to use his service weapon left-handed and that he might have white scars on those dark hands, but by the time he made it to Lenore's, he was popping pain pills. His momma didn't want him staying alone at his place. Lenore needed something to do while they worked on the restaurant, and Ty needed tending.

"How's the hand?" she asked first thing when he answered.

"Hurts like a bitch," he said. "Don't know how the heck I'm supposed to function if this mess takes three or four weeks to heal. Can't go to work for three days, minimum, and even then on limited duty. A lot depends on what the doctor says at my next appointment and the appointment after that."

"I'm sorry, Ty. I'm still glad it wasn't worse."

"So Momma keeps saying. Something tells me this doting thing is going to wear on my nerves, though. She acts like I hung the moon, the sun, and all the planets."

"You do," Quinn said, laughing.

His voice sobered. "So glad you cleared out the place for us, Q. She really appreciates you saving anyone else from getting hurt. She also says while she's home she wants to cook dinner for us every night. That includes you. Says she doesn't want you alone in that big house."

Sounded like Jule. Quinn loved Lenore, but . . . every night? "Kind of busy today."

"I'm supposed to call you every day to ask. I'll put you down for a no . . . tonight."

"Oh," she said, forecasting how the well-intended attention could cramp a schedule. She only ate when she got hungry, but neither she nor Ty would dare hurt the woman's feelings. "Guess we need to make sure that restaurant gets up and running as quickly as possible, huh?"

"You read my mind," he said. "So what are you up to?"

"I'm headed to talk to my uncle. Nobody from Fire Guard inspected your momma's suppression system, by the way."

"Can't be," he said. "Momma said someone—"

"Someone might've come, Ty, but it wasn't from Fire Guard. They swear whoever did it wasn't from their staff."

Some silence stretched between them. "Deliberate, then."

"There's no two ways about it. Somebody targeted us."

"Define *us*, Q."

"Maybe me," she said.

"That's more like it," he replied. "The rest of us are collateral damage."

Wow, that was blunt. She'd thought it, but to hear someone hammer it home sort of stung. "Of course I'm worried it's because of me, and I believe it's from taking Catherine Renault's case. Whose contract I terminated, by the way."

"I'm glad, but that doesn't make me feel much better," he said. "If anything, things might escalate. So now what?"

She'd reached the county line. "I head over to see the high sheriff," she said. "Without confidentiality, and with Catherine having misled me, I see no need to hide what I've been doing from him anymore. Not after what's happened to Jule, to you, to your momma."

"And you."

Yes, her, but that's not what stoked her fire. She feared more for those around her. Quinn would now spill to Uncle Larry the pieces of her investigation that he'd been denied, so he could do his thing. However, she'd continue doing hers. If she hadn't known Mickey and Vic, if she hadn't taken Catherine's case, how much of this wouldn't have happened in the first place? She was the binding thread in this whole damn situation, and the only person to bring it to a conclusion.

She let Ty go, and started to call Uncle Larry, then stopped.

It was Saturday; dang how the week had passed. She'd lost count of days. Uncle Larry wasn't in his office. He was a nine-to-five, Monday-through-Friday kind of guy, and rarely did enough crime happen in the county to warrant him changing that schedule, unless an event like a Chamber dinner could get his picture in the local news.

Off duty meant she'd have to meet him in person at his place . . . or hers. Unfortunately, she felt the obligation to invite him over since the meeting was her call. Since invitations from her were rare as hen's teeth, his curiosity would pique and he'd show. With Jackson Hole out of commission, he wouldn't be able to bring something that wasn't from a drive-through window, anyway. Guess she'd even have to cook.

Almost two in the afternoon, she dialed his cell. He picked up after two rings.

"What's up, little girl?"

Talking heads barked news in the background. From the sound of the chaos, Uncle Larry's dog Pickle—a rat terrier as wide as he was tall, yapped close by.

"Um, would you like to come to dinner?" she asked.

He didn't act surprised. He didn't even ask why. All he said was, "Do I dress?" which threw her aback.

"It's just meatloaf," she said. "Just you and me. Come as you are."

Which drew a laugh. "Don't believe you want to see this." More laughs. "Let me scrub up, but casual it is. Time?"

"Five thirty," she said, lightly stunned at the congeniality. Late enough to allow her to get home and thaw some ground venison, and early enough to get the evening over quickly.

Almost made her feel like she'd never given him much chance to behave like a real uncle; however, she had enough experience to not totally cave in to the guilt.

SHE ANSWERED THE door when the bell rang. The sheriff arrived ten minutes early in khakis, white sneakers, a soft green Columbia fishing shirt rolled up at the sleeves . . . and a bottle of Zinfandel in a gold cloth wine bag. His hair could use a trim, but he pulled off the extra waves well. The Sterlings always had good hair. Hers just had more personality than the rest.

"Here," he said, passing the bag.

She widened the door to let him in, suddenly realizing he hadn't let himself in with his key. *Nice touch, Uncle.*

"The meatloaf has ten minutes left," she said, leading him to the living room. The mashed potatoes were done and staying warm in the pot, green beans from Jule's garden cooked up in a cast-iron skillet with bacon and onion, lid over them. Crescent rolls just put in the bottom oven, out of a can she'd picked up last minute at the Jacksonboro Bi-Lo on the way.

She went ahead and opened the wine, feeling they'd need it. At least she sure as hell did. She'd had quick takeout meals with her uncle before, but this felt different. An intense effort at civility she really hadn't expected.

He accepted the wine glass without reservation and without complaining that he preferred beer, and he took the sofa rather than the recliner. His comportment alien, she couldn't help but see his manners as a precursor to something else, which ought to be absurd since she called *him*, not vice versa.

The dining room set, she'd finished one glass of wine by the time the meal was ready. He'd barely sipped his, setting it at his place to free up his hands and help. Soon a platter, two serving bowls, and a bread basket awaited them, and she patted herself on the back for timing all items properly. They sat.

"So, what's up?" he asked after they used up a considerable amount of overtly polite chatter.

She was grateful he'd broken the ice. Quinn motioned to the meal. "We can talk and eat. Don't let it get cold."

He did as told, offering her the proper accolades about the taste and presentation, but the oddity of the evening still left them eating in silence, the huge dining room resembling an auditorium with the occasional echo clink of silver on china. Yeah, she'd used china, for a reason she couldn't recall now.

"I'm eating," he said, breaking the quiet. "When's the talking?"

"Wanted to tell you I fired my client," she said, "Thought it safe to tell you more about her. Name's Catherine Renault."

Even in the dark wood room, in spite of the candles she lit this time, she swore she saw her uncle pale, taking a double-take at her like she'd spoken something foreign.

Pushing down his last forkful of meatloaf, he said, "Is she trying to buy the place?"

"Why would she hire me as a PI to try and buy Sterling Banks?" Quinn asked. "That other realtor tried, like I told you, but nothing I've seen says they're connected. Catherine asked me to find Mickey Raines, but she had me researched as well. By Vic, the dead guy at the motel."

"And?" He waited like she'd stopped mid-sentence.

"And what?"

"Why was she hunting Mickey?"

"He was her boyfriend. She thought he took the money she loaned him, but also thought he might be hunted down by some nefarious party. He's local again, I heard. His parents have been in touch with him. I was hoping to meet him to learn what the deal was about Catherine, while finally getting my chance to talk to him about . . . Daddy."

He looked torn as his amiable facade threatened to crumble.

She continued, watching him closely. "You were pretty adamant about learning who my client was. Now you know. What do you think?"

His plate pushed back, he rested elbows on the table, chin on crossed fingers, then changed his mind and refilled his wine glass . . . heartily. "Why'd you fire her?" he asked.

"She lied to me," Quinn said. "I got the feeling Mickey's not the whole reason she hired me. And I believe Vic Whitmarsh died because he uncovered something he didn't want to tell her, yet maybe wanted to tell me. He didn't file reports for several days before he died, though he met with Mickey, who's on the run again. Something in all of this . . ." she waved her hand in a circle, "caused him to scramble back underground."

Uncle was tense, and his old self peeked through the good uncle pretense. "I'm not hearing much proof here. A lot of feeling and supposition." The wine was almost gone.

"You're blowing off these details rather flippantly, aren't you?"

Quinn asked, sensing the meatloaf dinner now taking on the feel of one of their takeout interrogations.

"Details, yes. Facts, no." He wiped his mouth.

She began down the path she'd rehearsed throughout meal prep. "By the way, Jule came in here . . . and talked." His eyes darted at her, then back to his glass as she continued, "I asked her to relive the night Daddy died. Spent over an hour discussing what she remembered and what she didn't."

His jaw appeared to work at a piece of something left in his mouth, his gaze on the green bean casserole dish, his fingers gripping the wine stem.

She gave him the chance to ask what Jule said, but he clearly wasn't willing to give his niece the pleasure of knowing she'd struck a chord . . . like she couldn't tell, when in fact she'd reeled him in like a fish by having this dinner.

"Why did you tell Mickey Raines to *Get gone* the night Daddy died?" she asked. "Why did you tell him to *Get the hell out of Dodge* before the authorities arrived?"

"I *was* the authority," he replied.

"He was your only witness," she said.

"He told me all he knew, which was nothing," he countered, though . . . forced.

"He must've known more than you're saying the way he *got gone*. If he was innocent, if he'd seen nothing, he'd have stuck around. You'd have wanted him to stick around." She bent over the table. "What's up, Uncle? What aren't you telling me?"

"None of your concern," he replied, monotone.

"But it *is* my concern," she said, with just as hard a tone.

"The case is over."

Her fist banged on the substantial table, muscles taut all the way up to her shoulder. "This case is over when someone is held accountable."

"Not all cases are solved, little girl."

"Damn it, this was my daddy, your brother, this county's beloved Graham Manigault Sterling, and you let him die without closure. A random illegal immigrant? Really? Round up the usual suspects while the real one gets away?" She rose, the table hitting her hips as she straightened. Her fist hit the table again, beside his plate. "Who owns you, Uncle? Who the hell could convince you to disrespect your own brother?"

"That's enough," he yelled in her face.

She winced then steadied.

Staring, he released a hard breath. "Sit your ass back down."

But she didn't. "You've been saying we need to talk. This is me doing it. Where's your contribution?"

"Sit, I said!"

She did, letting him see her breathe.

"All I've ever thought about after Graham died was protecting you and Sterling Banks."

She waited, but he didn't seem to have much more to say. Not good enough. "And?"

"Leave that day alone," he said, firm but weary. "Take care of Sterling Banks. Find someone and have an heir. All of that three-hundred-year history is on us."

"On *us*?" She hit that last word hard, remembering her father's arguments with his brother over the divorce which threatened to divide the farm in two, because Larry had almost let his share slip away.

"On you, then," he corrected, clearly hurt at having to. "There's enough on your shoulders, Quinn. He died, the killer got away, and I have to live with that."

"You didn't do enough to find the killer, Uncle Larry! How the hell can you live with yourself giving up like that? You ordered a key witness to disappear . . . over what? Why?"

He pushed his chair back, palms against the table's rim, and blew hard through his nose. Then he finished standing. "To save lives, little girl. To save history. To protect a legacy. To prove that two wrongs don't make a right. A myriad of reasons. But that was then."

He lifted his plate to take it to the kitchen, walking like a man older than his years.

Confused, feeling cut off and short-changed, she hollered at his back. "There's dessert." The words fell out of her mouth in a too demanding way, so she lowered her voice. "You don't have to leave."

He put his dishes in the sink and turned toward the kitchen door.

In a whirlwind of feelings, she realized he wasn't coming back, and she scurried to catch him. For the first time in her life, he'd given her a glimpse into his soul, but it was darker than she expected. He walked like someone unforgiven, having done something that couldn't be forgiven, but she just wasn't seeing the sacrifice.

But she had to. All of this wasn't up to him. He didn't have the right to take secrets about this family to the grave.

"I said you don't have to go," she said, moving to stand in his way. "We aren't done."

With disappointment in his expression, he simply let his niece study him, take him in and make whatever determination about him she wished.

When he tried to take another step to leave, she stopped him yet again. "You know who did it, don't you?"

He pulled himself loose. "Thanks for the dinner, little girl. You went to too damn much trouble."

Then he left.

Chapter 18

QUINN'S EYES OPENED, sluggishly, peering through her hair. She took in the way the sun made long, thin triangles across her mother's antique dressing table. Chilled, she shut her eyes and blindly reached for her covers, finding her gray sheets tangled, tossed, and out of reach after a long, unrestful night.

It was Sunday morning, not too long after dawn, and way earlier than her customary waking from the weight of her bones. She dragged her grandmother's block quilt up to her chin and attempted to burrow back into the bed.

But last night began replaying, and she told herself the mental hang-over from the argument with Uncle Larry wasn't about her. She'd told herself the same last night, too, repeatedly, as she crawled into bed. Figures she woke up still thinking the words.

Her mind had engaged. She was awake now.

Wait. No coffee smell. How damn early was it?

Her phone rang. Guess she was really up now. She grappled for the phone off the nightstand, caller ID reading Goat Lady, and put it to her ear not in the pillow. "Hey, Jule."

"You up?" she asked, sounding like she'd been up for hours. "Getting dressed yet?"

"For what?"

"Easter service, girl. You know you're expected. Pick you up in an hour."

Quinn hung up, releasing a huge sigh ending with *damn*. She'd let recent happenings consume her to the point she didn't know what day of the week it was, much less remember a holiday. She had planned to visit the Raines farm again . . . unannounced again.

Another *damn*. Another sigh.

The Sterlings didn't miss holidays in Craven County. At least not the top four.

The family had traditionally honored the Fourth of July and Christmas on farm grounds, ever ending with her admitting they were worth the trouble of the planning. Quinn's worst inconvenience was keeping folks on the ten acres of open ground and out of the groves. Craven County people considered Sterling Banks as much a part of their heritage as hers, using the two events to admire what put their county on the map.

Two other events commanded her presence without any sort of planning. The late October Jacksonboro Pecan Festival and Easter at the Pon Pon Episcopal Church.

Her daddy's robe around her, she plodded downstairs and punched the button on the coffee pot to override the timer, leaned against the kitchen counter arms crossed, and closed her eyes to wait.

Easter wasn't on her mind.

Though she should hold no remorse about the confrontation with her uncle, she couldn't explain the bruised feeling from the encounter. What pained her, however, was her uncle's lack of desire for revenge. No . . . the biggest hurt was him keeping a secret he still refused to share.

There were three Sterlings left after all these generations, and the men had all but walked away from the ticking clock of the family's demise.

Her father and uncle hadn't been the closest of brothers, but Sterling blood was supposed to run thick. Either her uncle was too cowardly to face the killer, or he didn't care to take up the challenge. Too gutless or too lazy. How were either of those choices taking care of her or the family name, like he'd adamantly proclaimed at the dinner table?

Finally, the coffee sputtered to a finish. In went the goat milk, which immediately cooled it enough to drink outright. After a long sip of caffeine, she headed to find a dress.

As promised, an hour later, Jonah poked his head in the kitchen door and shouted, "You ready, Quinn?"

Never one to preen, she'd been waiting in the kitchen. "No need to yell."

Her front tresses twisted and pulled over her ears to a clip behind her head, the dynamic pushed the curly-q tresses to fall down her back. Not having thought ahead enough to remember Easter, she pulled a dress out of the back of her closet. Bought to attend someone's wedding at least five years earlier, a yellow, floral, spring number with a fitted bodice accented her long thin waist, the skirt full and flowing coming right to her knees. A thin shawl from her mother's closet. Her go-to pearl droplet necklace Graham gave her when she graduated high school.

Jonah stood motionless, taking her in.

"What?" Quinn asked, like she didn't know.

"I'm just not used to seeing you without boots and jeans," he said. "Sort of forgot you were a girl."

She swatted him, grateful he'd foregone his anger with her, and passed through to the driveway, letting him lock the door . . . allowing herself the enjoyment of knowing he watched her from behind.

Jonah was so easy to mess with.

She rode in the front, Jule in the back. "You okay?" Quinn asked, peering between the seats, wondering how many demons Graham's death had caused in Jule's dreams last night.

Jule reached up and patted her shoulder. "I'm fine."

A spat with Jonah she could get over. Jule, however, never. She was precious.

Jonah got in the driver's side.

As they made their way the ten miles to the church, Quinn rethought her plans about canceling the Raines farm. Easter didn't have to postpone it. Not really. Church over at noon. An hour to chat with churchgoers in the aisles, outside in the parking lot, then home to eat the ham and potato salad dinner that Jule always fixed with deviled eggs. What time would that be over, say three?

She could still make it to the farm, on a day the couple wouldn't be in the field. Better yet, Mickey might respect his parents enough to make it home for Easter dinner, thinking everyone else was too busy to give him a second thought.

THE SERVICE WAS beautiful, but the sermon was the same one the minister had trotted out last year. Sitting still, only one ear on the minister's words, her mind drifted. She wondered how to approach the Raines couple and not appear too terribly rude. She rubbed her hand down the delicate material of her dress. She'd have to change to be taken seriously.

Benediction. Finally. She gathered her purse, painted on the smile, and addressed those around her in the pews.

"Aren't you just the loveliest thing!"

The elderly women made a point to compliment Quinn, half of them naming off grandsons and nephews still single, good looking, and available. The elder men asked her about this year's crop potential, winking at Jonah as they did and showing they truly understood who ran the place. Then in an afterthought, thinking she was out of earshot, someone inevitably asked him why he hadn't put a ring on Quinn's hand.

God, they hadn't kissed since that graduation night. Heaven help Jonah.

The farm's status quo was a habit now of the three of them being the Sterling team, having evolved from the integration of the Proveauxs and the Sterlings into a strong unit with over thirty years of them each tending the other. Quinn, Jonah, and Jule.

God Almighty but folks everywhere seemed to be hammering her about procreating. How selfish was it of her to have no such immediate plans? Hell, in any of her plans? But sure as heck, the community would hold it against her if she didn't continue the Sterling line. Wasn't fair for three hundred plus years to boil down to her ovaries. Hers and hers alone.

Unless one of her almost-sixty uncles knocked up somebody.

That was a creepy thought.

Damn Catherine for referencing the same when it was none of her frickin' business, but she only said what real estate folks thought . . . when Quinn was gone, Sterling Banks might become fair game.

Jonah, Jule, and Quinn came back together, after having made the rounds of the family pews, and greeted their way to the parking lot. They navigated chit chats and hugs in their steady march toward the truck. Quinn checked her phone for the time, the socializing taking longer than expected.

Jonah's height made him taller than most around, and Quinn watched him protect his mother an arm's length in front of him. Quinn thought how dependent she was upon Jonah and Jule to revolve their lives around Sterling Banks. Her retirement plan was the farm. Theirs was . . . what? Her?

Of course she'd take care of them to the end of their days, but what if she was gone? What if one of her own clients pulled a Vic Whitmarsh on her?

Another hug interrupted her thought. Another compliment on the dress. Yet another wish they'd been born with her hair, which they'd rethink if they had to corral it every day. The truck still sat a dozen parking places away. She fought to keep a smile on her face when people slyly wondered when she was going to settle down, in spite of her three-inch white strappy heels mashing her little toes.

Across the parking lot, the sheriff made his own rounds with a different strata of folks. From the looks of things, he had no particular interest in seeking her out. He usually said Happy Easter, and sometimes Jule invited him over.

She waved in his direction, when she thought he looked her way. For a change, she had more interest in him than the other way around, because they needed to finish their meatloaf discussion, but he turned to shake another hand. Intentional, maybe. Maybe not.

"Uncle Larry!" she shouted and waved again, this time catching his eye. Catching it long enough for him to give her the long, staring, unspoken message, it wasn't happening today.

Well, all right then. She still had plans, and if they ripened into more intel as she hoped, he'd be begging *her* for supper.

A hug came from nowhere. Her high school English teacher, who wasn't a small person. The tackle almost pushed her into her seventy-year-old childhood Sunday School teacher.

God help her, excuse the blaspheme on the most holiest of holy days, but Easter obligations were getting in the way, and she had to get out of here.

Her phone showed almost one, later than she'd planned to leave. "Let's go, Jonah," she hollered over the heads of three other retired teachers whom she'd already properly greeted. Jonah nodded, redirected his mother, and Quinn beelined as well, meeting them at the truck.

She waited until they turned through the front gate to ask, and at her request, Jonah agreed to drop her off at the manor. She said she'd pop over in no time.

"Dinner just needs warming. It'll be on the table in minutes," Jule said. "Can't you just come with us like normal?"

Of course dinner was ready. Jule was never late. And past Easters had been about the three of them, sometimes four with Uncle Larry, lolling around with heels kicked off, ties discarded, and a game of Spades around the table as they nibbled on one dessert, then another. Jule always made more than one. A favorite for each in attendance.

"I'll be right there. Promise," Quinn said, running inside, cursing when she had to unlock the kitchen door.

Kicking off heels and tossing the dress on her unmade bed, she grabbed jeans and . . . stopped. *It's Easter, Quinn.*

She regrouped and took out slacks and a white collared shirt, warning herself that she better not drip anything on it before deciding to snare a scarf to run under the collar. She sorted the ends in a knot on her chest. She put on her good boots then ran out the door to Jule's.

Jule and Jonah still wore their church garb, per unspoken tradition, and said nothing about Quinn's wardrobe change. Throughout the meal, they also never scolded Quinn for cutting her replies short, though Jonah gave her a few hard glares at opportune moments.

However, when she avoided seconds and asked what was for dessert, Jonah had to ask. "Where are you going when you get done here? You obviously have bigger plans than us."

"To see Mickey's parents," she replied, hating how discourteous she appeared.

"On Easter?" he replied, ripe with disgust.

Even Jule gave her a tsk, then a look, and made for the kitchen with plates in hand.

Jonah let his mother get completely out of the room. "Quinn, stop obsessing."

"I'm following through, not obsessing," she said. "Vic died, and someone else violated this farm, to include your own mother's sanctity. Uncle Larry stonewalled me last night, not telling me what he knows about Daddy. I'm sure of a correlation now, and I'm worried. No, I'm terrified that if there isn't some sort of conclusion brought to all of this, the danger will accelerate. I feel responsible. You and Ty both said so."

His eyes narrowed. "Not sure we meant it like that."

"Yes, you did. You said my meddling caused the incident with Bonnie Blue. Ty labeled everyone hurt as *collateral damage*."

He bounced his fist on his chin, trying to find new words. "I think what we're saying is that you accelerate the danger by messing with it all, Quinn. You're damn stupid if you can't see that."

Lowering the dishes in her hands back to the table, Quinn's expression fell, hurt. "Don't say that, Jonah."

He scoffed. "I watched you all morning in a hurry to get through church and past all the people. Even your uncle wouldn't take time away to address you."

"Like I said," she added. "He got upset I backed him in a corner last night."

Jonah shook his head then waved his arms as if addressing an entire room. "You could stop this right now. Don't worry about Mickey. Don't seek revenge for your father. Don't pursue who killed the goat. Don't dig up whatever it is you think your client did behind your back. Because all of these things . . ." A broad sweep of his hand. "All of them . . . are hurting us, the farm, and most importantly, you. You . . . the person who can't seem to get on with her life, only weighing her life on what she's lost, not what she has."

"Jonah," Jule said low in the doorway.

"No, Mom, I won't hush. You've devoted your life to Quinn and this place. I won't say I gave up my life for her, because I chose to come back since I was raised here. I also did it for you and Sterling Banks. I'd like to say for Quinn, too . . ." His words went up on the end, a pause in

167

the air. "But I'm not so sure she'd notice. She's on this . . . trip to God knows where because she isn't sure she wants to be a Sterling married to this land anymore."

Balling up a fist, Quinn pointed a finger at him. "You have no right."

"Ha," he said, tensed, a hand going to his waist, the other in her face. "I have every right, and you lie to yourself to say otherwise. Could you even run this place without me? Without my mother?"

"Jonah, that's enough," Jule said firmly. "It's the Lord's day, for Christ's sake."

"Tell *her* that," he shouted back.

Heartbeat racing, Quinn caught the tremor in Jonah's shoulders, a vein in his neck distended that she'd never spotted before. She started to speak then stopped. Started to yell, then didn't. "Nobody," she started . . . then continued, ensuring that her retort fell on him and him alone. "Nobody asked me to step into this investigation, and at first I didn't. But someone I knew was killed." Was that how she wanted to start this? She wasn't so sure she shouldn't just leave.

Jule stood aside and back from her son, clutching a dishtowel. Her eyes sagged more than her sixty-two years meant them to.

"The best years of my life were on this farm," Quinn continued. "Bucolic, you might say, in spite of losing my brother, my mother, then later Daddy. But truthfully? I don't remember Quincy, and barely remember Mom, so I cannot say my life was permanently damaged by their deaths."

Neither of the others wanted to touch the mention of Maggie and Quincy.

"Which meant all of who I am is credited to my father, to Ty's family . . . and to you two. But I've been told so many times that I ought to be exorbitantly grateful for being heiress to this estate." Arms out, she gave a gentle turn to her left, then her right. "I was born into this world and expected to die in this world; however, nobody seems to feel I ought to be anything but queen of Sterling Banks." She pointed at Jonah. "How many times have you called me *princess*? How many times have you told me not to tell you what to do just because I own this place? I didn't ask to own this place, yet I'm expected to run it. Condemned for wanting anything more."

Her ears were ringing, her jaws sore from angry pressure.

"Baby, sit," Jule said, coming around to pull out a chair.

"No, Jule. I will not sit." She took a deep, deep breath, but released it long and slow, staring at Jonah through it. "Someone I knew just died, maybe because he knew me. Mickey Raines is running scared for something he might be blaming me for. Then to scare me, they infiltrate my world." She stomped once on the floor. "This world. This very place that you just accused me of not wanting to protect. How could I not take action?"

But Jonah didn't back down. "Would any of this have happened if you hadn't been in law enforcement?"

The icy smack of the question stole her fire.

If she hadn't been a PI and met Vic. If she hadn't been off working for the FBI when her father was murdered. If she hadn't become a deputy for her uncle right out of high school, pushing Graham to send her off to college . . . her defying him using her business studies to entice an internship with the FBI.

She had no comeback for Jonah's remark. "I think it best I leave now," was all she could bring herself to say.

"Honey," Jule started, reaching for Quinn.

Quinn gave the short woman a proper hug. "Thanks, Jule. Dinner was superb as always." Then she left to retrieve her truck at the manor.

Jonah's words had plunged through her like a saber, but to give up the chase now would leave a hole in her so wide she'd never recover.

Their differences would remain a wall between them. Jonah wouldn't respect her if she quit, regardless of what he said. And even though he might not respect her if she did solve these crimes, she'd take that chance.

The least she could do was respect herself, and she knew no other way to do it than pursue whoever had opened old wounds on Sterling Banks Plantation, at the same time protecting those she loved.

Chapter 19

DRIVING ACROSS THE county to the Raineses' neck of the woods, on two lanes named by the families living on them, Quinn tried Mickey's number again, just in case. Mailbox still full. Quinn bet Vic had an alternate number for him.

Mickey's disappearance had revealed itself as an active choice now. No kidnapping.

With everyone home for Easter dinner, the roads were bare. Quinn had been in a hurry to leave, but she took her time en route to let her temper chill and let the wounds on her heart scab over. Jonah's admonishments always hurt more than Ty's. Jonah's dressing down did little to prepare her for the task ahead, though, and she pushed him to the back of her thoughts.

Window down, she practiced what to ask the Raineses, assuming she overcame the challenge of getting past the door. They'd be resistant from the get-go, maybe crazy demanding that she leave. Even more insistent if Mickey was there.

She'd been a horse's ass the first time those years ago, and she hadn't exactly won them over the other day. Every angle she rehearsed resulted in expectation of orders to leave their house.

There were times she wished she could pull a Mickey, become a nobody so that people didn't see her coming, particularly in this county. Like that small red-brick box house that rushed by. She peered at it in her rearview mirror until she reached a curve in the road. She bet they weren't noticed on a town street. Simple people with simple goals and a simple lifestyle.

Jonah would ream her for such thoughts. *Be grateful*, he'd say, ending it with a sarcastic dose of *Princess*. Damn it, he'd crawled right back in her head.

This Easter weighed on her like a boulder. She hadn't exactly honored the day and hadn't respected Jule's dinner prepared in honor of it. Truth was, Quinn hated holidays. The days when she had to be more Sterling-ish and make appearances.

These were the thoughts that Jonah referenced, that made her sound selfish and spoiled. Maybe she was. Maybe that was her nature. Why wasn't she entitled to be who she was?

She turned on the highway leading to the farm, almost cursing the soft sunshine bathing everything, a contrast to her need to mope.

Damn, she wished she had somebody in her life that allowed her to be herself without a scolding reminder that she wasn't performing properly for the name she hadn't asked for. Ty could almost do it. Lenore sometimes. Jonah, though. Damn Jonah.

Turning onto the farm road, the mailbox rusted in its seams on a wooden post grayed and rotted at the ground, she drove past planted fields again, the tomatoes on one side and the watermelons on the other.

She slowly took the road toward the conservative Raines home, partly from nerves, partly from the funk she'd sunk herself into. Then the color caught her eye.

Azaleas never disappointed in the South, and those in the Raineses' front yard had half opened in the short time since her last visit. These were old varieties the Lowcountry was renowned for instead of city hybrids. George Tabor pale pink. Deep-purple Formosas. A couple of Snows, which usually bloomed earlier and died quicker than the rest.

Vehicles were peppered with a dull yellow coating until flora quit spewing pollen over everything and rain washed it off, but the beauty made up for the bother. You didn't smell Carolina pollen. You tasted and ate it, but the visual made it all worthwhile.

She arrived in slightly better spirit and shut off the truck, sitting a moment to survey the immediate area.

She spotted no unusual vehicles in the front than the ones from before, a couple less with workers not around. Maybe she'd been wrong assuming Mickey would appear. Maybe he had better sense than she gave him credit for.

The blinds gave a small shimmy like from someone behind them, but when Quinn knocked on the door, nobody answered. She attempted a second round of taps, not hard, envisioning the worn farming couple gathered in front of their own Easter ham on that Formica table, ignoring her once they recognized her truck.

But then the wooden door flew open, the screen shoved at her. Luckily the latter hit against her boot, a couple inches short of her nose, which brought Mr. Raines right in her face. "How disrespectful can a person be?"

"I, um, I know it seems that way, Mr. Raines." It was that way, but murder trumped etiquette.

Ham and coffee on his breath, his mouth was not a foot distant from her. "There ain't no *seems* about it, Ms. Sterling. You damn well interrupted not only the Sabbath, but the day most holy. Bet you didn't even go to church, did you?" Then before Quinn could reply, he did. "Wait, you'd have to go to church. Heaven help the community if a Sterling didn't appear front and center in the family pew on one of two holidays a church is packed."

"Mr. Raines," she started, catching herself avoiding his eyes, which made her notice his black spit-shined dress shoes, Sunday slacks, and white starched shirt, collar open, his dress honoring the day until it ended. "I'm so sorry to come at such a time. I'd hoped you'd be done with dinner."

A voice came from behind the husband. "And you hoped Mickey would be here so you'd catch him." Mrs. Raines reached for her man's arm and slid him to the side. "But he's not here, Quinn." The first name was delivered to equal the ground.

"I can wait out here if you like," Quinn said. "So you can finish your meal."

Mr. Raines pushed the screen open more, making Quinn take a half step back. "Or you can get your ass out of here," he said.

"I wouldn't be here if it wasn't important. Didn't want to interrupt your work day, not at this time of year."

There must've been something about the religious sense of the day,

172

the gentleness of the one time of year when everyone was to be forgiven that gave the Raineses pause. Again, Mrs. Raines moved before her husband, widened the door, and with a nod motioned for Quinn to come inside.

She eased in, trying not to brush them and insult them in some other way.

This time, however, they took her to the living room, where Quinn was told to sit in a floral, upholstered recliner easily older than she. The couple disappeared, leaving Quinn to examine the room for signs of Mickey. No hat, no jacket, no forgotten phone or wallet. Everything in its place, lemon-Pledge dusted and vacuumed. Pictures of Mickey and a girl who had to be his sister on the mantle. Quinn recalled a younger sister, who would've been in middle school when she graduated high school.

Quinn bet the mother had cleaned house for somebody other than her husband, though.

Mrs. Raines appeared first with two coffees served in proper cups on saucers, resting on a small tray with sugar packets and a cup of milk. Mr. Raines followed in tow with two small plates of lemon cream pie slices. With the dishes properly set before Quinn on the coffee table, the husband left . . . presumably, she thought, to retrieve the third of everything. Only he never came back in.

Guess he'd been told to leave the chat to the women.

"Didn't need Chester's fuss," was all the wife said, before she motioned for Quinn to fix her coffee as she liked. Etiquette first, which urged the partakers to maintain a sense of manners. *Nice touch, Mrs. Raines.*

Finally the processes of stirring sweetener and admiring the first bite of confection were done, and with coffee in one hand, saucer in the other, Quinn opened with, "Did you ever get the chance to serve Catherine Renault like this?"

Mannerly or not, she wasn't being turned from her purpose.

Not what Mrs. Raines expected, the rise of cup to her mouth halted, then ending on a sip. "No, never had the opportunity."

Quinn took a second decent-sized bite of the pie, then a third, then returned plate and fork to the coffee table, knowing she'd never finish it.

"I'm not working for Catherine any longer," she said. "I'm here on my own."

"Oh?" came from behind the cup.

"I fired her," Quinn said, then did a short butt scoot forward in her chair. "She wasn't being honest."

"Then why are you here?" asked Mrs. Raines. "I mean, exactly."

"Because I need Mickey," she replied. "There's a strong chance he's still in danger. The last private investigator Catherine hired was murdered in the Jacksonboro motel a few days ago."

The word murder always gave people pause, and Quinn had used it on purpose for effect. Mrs. Raines put down the saucer and placed both hands around the warm cup, resting them on her Easter blue, skirt-covered knees, occupying hands and avoiding the ability to be read.

Quinn continued. "And we believe he was killed because he contacted Mickey."

Mrs. Raines acted like she had to take that in, when Quinn suspected she already knew.

"Based on recent activities, I sense that Mickey's connection with Sterling Banks from years ago is wrapped around his involvement with Catherine. All of which has made me reinvestigate my father's death."

Mrs. Raines traded her coffee for her pie, like she listened to no more than a commentator on television.

At least Quinn wasn't being ejected. "During that night . . . I mean, I've learned from talking to others about that night, Mickey was advised to leave the farm before the police arrived, and to stay hidden indefinitely." Quinn set dishes aside. "Listen, I was no party to any of that, which is why I kept trying to find Mickey after the funeral. I needed to hear directly from him what happened. Not the second-hand version from a deputy, or the official version from my uncle, but the real-time facts from Mickey himself. Can you see where I'm coming from?"

Quinn hoped the same mature, mothering instinct used to protect Mickey would help Mrs. Raines understand Quinn's plea as a daughter just looking for closure.

The coffees got cold.

"Why did he leave Sterling Banks that night, Vicky?" This time

Quinn used the first-name tactic.

"Thought you wanted to speak to him about Catherine?" Defensiveness rose in her voice.

"I do," Quinn said. "So let's talk about her. Was he really involved with her? I just have her word. You have Mickey's."

"He no longer tells us the details of his life, Ms. Sterling." Back to formality. Her voice had acquired a sharpness. "He makes slight advances in his life, the benefits of which he shares with us, like that tractor out back you noticed before. Then events kick him in the teeth, and he retreats. Those are the times we only hear that he's *dealing with a setback*." She'd been talking louder, escalating, until she ended with, "God help us how many times we've heard that phrase."

"And Catherine? Any insight on that *setback*?"

"A girlfriend with money who turned out to only want him for a business venture. Why someone of her caliber would want phone programs is beyond me, but the moment he felt used he left. Trouble was, she has influence, so he said he had to revert to *dealing with a setback* again until she lost interest. Trouble was, she wasn't going away very quickly."

Embarrassed, nervous, worried about—like Mrs. Raines said—Catherine's *influence*, Quinn believed Mickey spoke only in generalities to his parents.

Before Quinn could ask more, Mrs. Raines made hard eye contact. "None of this, none of Mickey's insecurity, would have happened if not for the Sterlings. You tore that boy down, and whenever he regains his footing, the past reminds him he isn't worthy."

Wait, what? "I thought he was successful in his work. Two college degrees, and from what I've gleaned, he's managed to—"

"Success isn't just about money, Ms. Sterling, or is that your only measure?"

Quinn took a deep inhale, uncertain how to handle this. "I'm not a demon, ma'am. I'm nobody your son should fear. Unless he killed my daddy, which I doubt, I'm here to help him. Without his first-hand facts, I can't."

Chester Raines strode into the room from where Quinn suspected was just around the corner in the hall, and impatience flashed across Mrs. Raines's vision. "Chester, don't."

"I sure as hell have the right to have my say, Vicky." He turned to Quinn, cheeks already flushed from the holding back. "You people run this county. Your uncle . . . your goddamn uncle . . ."

"What about my uncle?" Quinn was dying to hear the rest of that thought. She'd already heard from Jule and hoped to hear more from Mickey. She could be open to Chester, too. "Listen, I am not in lock-step with Larry Sterling. I need you to see that Mickey's in danger and my desire is to help, not do him any harm. That murdered man in Jacksonboro was a friend, so he's my second loss, and since Mickey—"

Chester came across the room toward her, and Quinn leaped to her feet, matching him in height.

He stopped with a lurch, like at the front door, barely a foot from her. An angry fisted hand pointed at her chest, and Quinn tensed, preparing to put him face-down on the braided rug. She had to remind herself she was in his house, the guest trying not to be an adversary.

"With a second person in your circle killed," he shouted, "that means you're after Mickey even more. Boy's afraid for his life now, and why would I tell you a damn thing about his whereabouts or what he thinks? Too many damn years of hell you put him through."

"Chester!" yelled Vicky. "Must you be so outlandishly disagreeable?"

But Chester rolled with her verbal punch, yelling, "How the hell am I supposed to be agreeable with the likes of her?"

"She's been civil. Back your ass down."

Vicky's tone ruled.

But they weren't about to give Mickey up.

"I know you don't trust me," Quinn tried again. "My family hasn't given you much *reason* to trust me, but the next time you speak with Mickey, please tell him that I wish to chat. I can use tools at my disposal to help him."

"Help your uncle arrest him for killing this dead guy, you mean," Chester said, again with a snap of his head at her.

Quinn wasn't making headway. If the parents weren't protecting Mickey enough before Vic's death, they damn sure were now. Then the mention of her uncle . . .

"Has my uncle been by here lately?" she asked.

The couple looked at each other, trying to read whether to answer. Which basically answered the question.

"Did he say he suspected Mickey for the motel murder?" Quinn asked when they didn't reply.

She got a nod from Vicky.

Son of a bitch. Uncle Larry didn't give a damn about Vic Whitmarsh. He didn't even care if Mickey killed Vic. After last night's meatloaf dinner, she saw that the sheriff wanted to make sure Mickey Raines remained hidden. Made Quinn wonder even more what Mickey might have to say.

"When?" she asked.

"Early yesterday," Vicky said.

Before last night's supper.

"Then I'm terribly sorry," Quinn replied. Having exhausted her stay, she slid around Chester Raines to let herself out. Vicky made no moves to request she stay.

But the bug remained behind, hopefully still anchored beneath the kitchen table. No telling when Quinn would retrieve it now. She'd have to eventually.

God, no telling when that opportunity would happen.

She drove off like before, then repeated her actions from the last visit. Back on the two-lane, Quinn took herself to the same spot off the road and listened. A lot of movement, scrubbing, and mumbling as before, they returned to the table.

"I don't trust her," said Chester, his fork clinking, making what sounded like intense stabs at the food on his plate. Probably the dessert he'd missed while eavesdropping.

"We should call Mickey," answered the wife.

"It's what she wants us to do," he replied, clearly something in his mouth.

"Whether she wants us to or not, he needs to know what happened. You don't think he'd want to hear?"

Wasn't a full minute before they placed a call, again on speaker so both could listen.

"She just left," the mother said, like Mickey would automatically know who the *she* was.

"I know, Mom," their son said. "I saw her leave."

Chapter 20

QUINN UNDID HER seat belt and twisted around, scouring the nearby woods, the road ahead of her . . . the road behind. Where the heck could he be?

Mickey said he'd seen her leave his parents' farm, but from what vantage? She couldn't just take off in search of him. She might chase him away or drive in the opposite direction. No telling what he drove.

She kept listening to the Raineses relay their visit with her, the details embellished by the father, abbreviated by the mom. The dad wanting to blast the messenger. The mom in protective mode for her son.

"That damn sheriff said for you to never set foot in Craven County again," said Chester. "Look what's happened, boy. Can't you listen?"

"They can't prove I did anything." Mickey tried to sound assertive yet not quite pulling it off. Clearly he believed the authorities would pin a murder, either murder, on him if they could lay hands on him.

"Don't come back," his mother said, a tired gloom in her delivery. "Things are too stirred up, enough to prompt that Sterling woman to come by on Easter."

"She wanted me to contact her?" he asked. "What's her number?"

Chester remained in a huff. "Don't tell him."

Vicky read off the number.

Some silence played out between them like they waited for him to write it down.

"I won't be back, Mom. Not until all of this is over."

Quinn thought she caught a hitch in the mother's voice. "And if it doesn't blow over?"

"Try not to think that way. Love you, Mom. Take care, Dad." Then he hung up.

Quinn sat there in her own silence, accepting her role as catalyst but not as easily carrying the guilt. She didn't have important pieces of the puzzle, but all indications were the Sterlings *had* screwed up this family's life. Maybe not with intent but long-term damage done just the same. At least the Raineses had relayed her request and her number. Thank goodness for small blessings. She'd take all she could get these days.

What now? Window down, she listened, only taking in birdsong, the occasional car in the distance. No point leaving. Mickey might drive by. She couldn't call him, that's for sure, and she couldn't go back onto his family's farm without re-sparking trouble. She chastised herself for two short seconds for not asking for Mickey's new number, but they wouldn't have given it to her anyway.

Half of the PI job was waiting, so she might as well relax and do it and give things an hour to play out, as slim as those odds were. She didn't dare get her hopes up, but this was as close to hope as she'd ever really had. He watched her. He thought about her. Maybe . . . hopefully . . . he'd consider coming to her. All she could do was sit and play target. Avoid the urge to pass time on her phone for fear she'd miss him drive by. She laid the phone on the seat, face up.

Ten minutes later, the screen lit up and a text came through. Jonah. *Jule says there's still dessert.*

She didn't answer. This was Jonah's way of making amends. That man never could stay mad. One of his finer points. She'd given him ample enough reasons to stay mad, that's for sure.

Frankly . . . selfishly . . . she was almost more eager to go by Lenore's and see Ty, so she'd have someone to talk the case with. Cases, rather.

Her phone rang on the seat, and she glanced over expecting Jonah, only the ID said Unknown Caller. She snatched it up. "Quinn Sterling."

"If you move from where you're parked, I'm gone," said the voice.

"Mickey?" He sounded older than the Mickey speaking to his parents.

"I hear you want to talk," he said, very noirish.

"Where are you?"

"Where I can see you," he said. "Where you can't see me. Where I can tell if you've called for backup."

She had to hold him, keep him thinking he held the advantage, preserve the engagement. "Let's talk, then," she said. "I promise I've called nobody."

"You have five minutes, tops. Why are you hunting me? The short version."

More mature than she remembered, too. "I don't think you killed my dad, but you know more about what happened than anyone else. Somebody is going out of their way to make it appear you not only killed Dad but also Victor Whitmarsh."

"I'm listening."

"You've become somewhat of a folklore perpetrator, Mickey, and I'm the supposed vindictive daughter of Graham Sterling. Exaggerations and myths. I believe all you want is your life back. All I want is to know who killed my father. And who killed Vic."

Her gaze hunted through oaks, pines, and gums on both sides of the road, forward and behind her truck. She couldn't imagine Mickey seeing her unless he had technological assistance. That was entirely believable given his talent for developing phone apps could easily have introduced him to other tech skills and equipment. She peered up, wondering how high a drone could be and see her, without her seeing it. She heard no road noise in the background through the phone, so he didn't seem to be moving; however, when the occasional vehicle whizzed by, she scrutinized the driver hard.

"I feel like I'm being followed," he said.

"Um, I hear you on that." But her humor fell short.

He continued, his words picking up speed. "At first I thought it was because I was dating somebody rich, like the chauffeur could be tailing me. Even confronted Catherine after I thought I saw Chevy some place he never would be. She denied it, called me silly, assured me he was driving her to an appointment at that time. That was the first lie."

Quinn hushed, more than willing to be his confessional.

"Catherine was like assertive, all over me to meet these investors for my apps. Kept me running to Atlanta, Savannah, all over Charleston. We even met my folks at a restaurant in Charleston once, at her request, a quadrant of Magnolia's roped off only for us. You have any idea how much that cost?"

Yep, she did. That's why she held as many meetings at the manor as possible, her turf or Lenore's . . . assuming she couldn't do Meetup, Zoom or Facetime.

"I just kept feeling followed. So I tried to slow our relationship down," he said. "But it was like I was in freefall. Along came more opportunities, and before long I was dependent upon her for my finances. Took me cornering one guy in Savannah to learn he was more interested in being in Catherine's circle than mine. Using me to get to her."

Poor guy. This sounded more like the boy from high school.

"I'm so sorry, Mickey." And she meant it. She knew what it felt like to think you were building a career then have it yanked out from under you.

"Yeah."

"What about Vic Whitmarsh, though? All signs point to you." Then she quickly added, "Not that I'm a fan of that theory."

A truck came by, and while the driver didn't slow, he glanced over to see why someone would be parked on the side of the road outside of hunting season. It's what she'd wonder. The aroma of burning oil told her he'd better get that dated rattle-trap to the shop.

"I trust you more than Catherine," she said.

A quick harsh clip of a laugh. "Surely you understand why I struggle trusting a Sterling, Quinn. Your uncle swings a pretty heavy club in Craven County, and what you believe doesn't mean shit when he makes up his mind. Your family wields power." Another laugh. "I've kinda had my fill of that sort."

"I can see why you'd think that."

The sigh came through without reservation. Him debating, she guessed. Weighing whether to hang up or see if there was any way on God's green earth that anyone could believe him.

"I was an FBI agent," she continued, wondering whether she was stupid saying so.

"I know," he said.

"We're trained to look at evidence, not make assumptions before having the facts. I like to think I still operate that way as a private investigator. Everything I've heard about my father was hearsay, in my opinion. All I've learned about Vic only makes me wonder what is missing. I'm still seeking facts, Mickey. And you can lead me to them better than anyone."

She had no recorder. He'd provided no proof. This was no more than a reach out, each testing the other. They had to meet to make this work, or she'd never get real answers. He'd never be truly cleared, and he could stay on the run for years to come.

"I'm moving, Quinn," he said, the use of her name a plus. He was seeking an ally. "Six years wasn't enough, apparently, and with Vic, I just added a decade more. I'll be an old man before this is over."

"Meet me," she said.

"There's no place we *can* meet."

Like talking someone off a building, she held the tiniest sense he might be backing off the ledge.

"Mickey, listen. Half the world's looking for you. My uncle doing so because of Vic. Catherine for whatever reason I haven't sorted yet, and no telling what depth of resources she has at her disposal."

He gave a sour laugh. "And everybody thinks you win the lottery dating someone rich."

She gave him that. Money had highs and lows that changed people, or in Catherine's case, trained her from birth to be a manipulative bitch.

"I can think of a place nobody would dream of looking," she said. Silence. "Mickey, you still there?"

"You're insane if you think I'll ever set foot there again."

He'd picked right up.

"No, no, let's think about this," she coaxed. "Who would hunt for you at Sterling Banks?"

"Your uncle."

Damn if she didn't tire of people fearing that man, which constantly fueled his reputation. "It's my home, not his. Even he wouldn't look there for you."

She'd had Jonah put cams everywhere, and now she wished they'd changed the locks so Larry had no key. But still, they weren't talking much these days. He wouldn't drop in.

Another sigh from Mickey. He sounded weary. "Why are you doing this?"

In front of her, a car approached, but instead of passing, it slowed. *Son of a bitch. Now of all times.*

"Give me a second, Mickey. Someone's coming up on me."

She lowered the phone out of sight. She couldn't place the vehicle, but she soon recognized the driver. Deputy Harrison, off duty, without his wife.

With no traffic, he pulled alongside her, stopped, and rolled down his window. "Thought that was your truck. What're you doing here? Why aren't you eating deviled eggs and ham back at the farm?"

She leaned elbow out her own window and waved her hand. "Been there, done that. Family spat gave me indigestion, and I wanted to be alone. Been driving roads for two hours."

"You can't get away on all that acreage you got?"

She shrugged. "Sometimes you just don't want to be found, you know?" Of course, he wouldn't think that applied to him. She made an obvious glance over him at the other side of his front seat. "Where's the Missus?" Meaning, the woman he hadn't told Quinn he was marrying when he'd shared Quinn's bed at the manor those years ago, before she learned not to be so needy.

With an uptick of his mouth, he snorted a laugh. "Sort of had a disagreement of my own, and my mother-in-law isn't the most likeable person. You know how the Avants are."

That merited a small grin. She'd heard of them, and there were a lot of them. They were a cliquish lot.

Leaning a little further, he asked, "Since neither of us has plans, want to meet and share family stories? Say, your place?"

She held up her phone. "Some of us are making amends." Then she spoke into the device. "Just one more sec. Promise. I think he's about to leave."

With his proposition overheard, Harrison's embarrassment seeped from his cheeks down into the open collar of his church dress shirt.

"What was that again, Harrison?" she asked. "My place?"

With a shake of his head, he threw up a wave and left.

"Okay, he's gone," she said.

"So how many people get invited to your place?" he asked.

She caught the tongue-in-cheek design of his question and relished the normal banter. They'd connected.

"Trust me, that house echoes like an empty auditorium," she said, then remembered how the manor was when Mickey last saw it. "Just me now, and it's treated like my inner sanctum. Doors aren't left open. There isn't a more private location."

"When?"

"Today's as good a time as ever." She dared feel positive again about the day. "Folks are busy, which includes my uncle who's too pissed at me to want to come over anyway. But we can't drive together, in case anyone recognizes you or me and puts two and two together, so head on. You know the geography of the farm. Hide your car at the rear of the barbecue field. I'll pick you up there. Wait in the trees until I arrive."

He didn't immediately agree. "You never answered me. Why are you doing this?"

She started an exhale but released it easy, not wanting him to hear. She thought she had him. To meet Mickey was huge. She needed him, and the fact he'd stayed on the phone this long said he needed someone, too.

"This may sound nuts, but I'm running with a theory that whoever's responsible for Vic's murder is somehow tied to Daddy's."

"And you don't think it's me?"

"No, I don't. But we might be able to uncover the real culprit. Right now you are everything to me, Mickey. The only link to anything, and I have a feeling I'm the same for you."

"I've got to think on this."

She waited for him to do so, willing to wait however long it took, but the click shocked her. Mickey hadn't said, *Meet you in thirty minutes* or *See you there.* He'd hung up.

Nothing left for Quinn to do but head back home and cruise to the barbecue field. As she pulled onto the road, however, she brooded over what she could've said better . . . and wondered which drive, barn, or little red box house had Mickey been sitting at when he saw her.

Chapter 21

QUINN TOOK HER time reaching Sterling Banks, allowing Mickey to arrive ahead, though she fought doing so. Nervous about this opportunity, she rationalized the entire way. He might have to drive by once or twice if other cars were seen. He might get cold feet and come later. And since he hadn't exactly confirmed their rendezvous, he might not show at all. Two cars and a truck passed, hands thrown up in recognition.

Another text from Jonah. *Dessert?*

Not willing to respond while driving, she let it wait. Once she met up with Mickey, she'd reply. If Mickey didn't show, she'd appear at Jule's, and they'd all pretend nothing happened.

Jonah worried about her safety. Worried way too much about it.

She ought to feel flattered. She owed him too much to so easily discount his feelings.

She often wondered if those feelings ran deeper than just protecttion.

She passed through the brick and iron entrance to Sterling Banks, veered left about a hundred yards in, and took the dirt vehicle path around the north end of the barbecue field. Slowly she traversed the two-wheeled track, the massive field bounded by forest on three sides, a few pecan trees lining the fourth, her truck so comfortable in the ruts that she hardly had to steer. The grass spread over the acreage long, wide, and lime green, not needing the bush hog yet.

Years ago she and the boys and whatever friends they could scrounge had played softball out there in summer, until the white kids were almost as dark as those born that way. Afterwards, tucking the bases in the woods, they'd take their sweaty selves to the river, clothes and all, then come back to the field and sprawl out to dry with a tall thermos of lemonade from Jule, waiting for parents to pick them up.

Mickey had lived too far on the other side of Craven to get invited to those games, his age a bit young. Yet he knew the area from summers working the groves.

A crook in the path took her left toward where the staff parked during events. At least they could tuck their vehicles under the trees and the thick shade, where they wouldn't cook in the July sun.

Mickey had indeed remembered. There in the back, between two hickories, he'd backed his dated black Ford Ranger, barely seen under the thick canopy not long leafed out for spring. In two or three more weeks, the green would darken, the leaves thicken, and the area would almost go pitch.

She pulled her own Ford around to put the passenger side toward him and rolled down that window. "Come on," she said, careful not to holler across the ten-yard span. "Get in."

He got out of his truck, and she took note of his boots first, the denim legs, then a small backpack slung over his shoulder as he closed his door. Accustomed to being transient, it would seem, but all in all not a bad-looking man. Taller than she recalled.

She recognized his walk, nothing special but without any sort of hard purpose, and his eyes held the same ice blue that would pop against a deep summer tan. In some ways, he still resembled the meek lad from high school who got by with a B- average and did what he was told working the pecan orchards. In other ways he seemed weathered, and if she hadn't known his age, she might've perceived him as older than she. Life could indeed weigh heavy on a body.

Mickey slid into the seat, his eyes roaming past her to their surroundings, hunting for adversaries, and when he shut the door, he sank down.

"No staff working today," she said. "Holiday, remember?" She inched the truck forward and began the same, slow cruise back up the rutted two-lane trail.

Once he quit hunting for snipers or black ops teams, he gave her a once-over, from the top down. "You look good, Quinn."

"Was just thinking the same, Mickey."

They rode quietly, a clumsiness between them, him measuring her as she measured him.

"Glad you decided to trust me," she finally said. "I'm serious about being more interested in your knowledge than the half-baked theories of others. I'm especially beholden to you for meeting me like this."

His posture wasn't relaxed, but he wasn't primed for a fight-or-flight response anymore. Quinn took that as a hopeful sign. She also hoped he had no intentions of being adversarial. Hoped that his hard-to-get persona wasn't a ruse.

Once they reached the house, Quinn would slip in the questions she'd held for years, along with those she fabricated now, on the fly. Dozens of them. A hundred, maybe. Her pulse amped at the break sitting to her right. She racked her brain for the order in which to ask, how to gain the most traction . . . to learn whatever she could before he disappeared again for God knew how long.

This opportunity could be everything.

She was even willing to harbor this fugitive, if needed. If he was indeed the fugitive he appeared to be. Larry Sterling would be pissed as a wet setting hen at Quinn finding Mickey without turning him over, but mostly because she landed him before he did.

And from the suspicion burning deep in her soul, also because she might learn details that Sheriff Larry Sterling had done his damnedest to hide in sending Mickey hightailing out of the county.

That part made zero sense to her . . . yet drove her the most.

The manor revealed itself from behind the massive reach of gnarled, spreading, two-hundred-year-old pecan trees, its landscape grove rolling out forever behind it. In front, sunlight filtered down to give enough rays for impatiens beds, and breezes could still weave in and around it all. The old brick and iron railings gave an elderly, distinguished persona to the grand dame, and Quinn still remembered her grandmother gathering nuts each November from those particular old trees in front she claimed held the best flavor.

Wait, movement up the drive. White shirt, dress pants . . .

"Slip down," she said, trying not to look over at Mickey.

"Shit." He laid the seat all the way back, and she whispered a thanks for tinted windows. "What is it?" he hissed.

Quinn slowed normally so not to raise Jonah's interest. Damn. She should've texted him back and nixed all chances for frickin' dessert.

He came walking down the one-lane leading to Jule's place, not fifty yards from the manor and closing. She whipped the truck into the garage, shut it off, and exited, hoping Mickey had enough awareness to stay put.

With long strides, she reached the end of the concrete, where it met the gravel, in time to meet Jonah and stop him short. "Sorry I didn't return your texts. I was driving."

"Those phones make calls, too," he said, no longer mad and no longer wanting to fight. That was who he was. Aggression wasn't in his nature, and regardless of who was to blame, the warfare invariably did more damage to him than the other party, no matter how egregious.

"Sorry," he said.

And he always apologized first.

"No, I deserved it," she said, which often happened between them as well, but this was not the time nor the place. "Had someone to meet, and I still have serious conversations to take care of before day's end. So while I really would like dessert, I mean, who doesn't like Jule's pies, I'm under a crunch to interview someone, Jonah. I'll make apologies to your mom later, but right now—"

"I try to get you, Quinn. I really do."

Oh damn, he was touched, his feelings on his sleeve, and he wanted to talk. She counted herself so lucky to have him in her universe, but the timing. An emotional discussion wasn't on her clock, and the minute he laid eyes on Mickey, he'd flip out.

God love him, and yes, she loved him, but Jonah wasn't a cop. He was loyal, noble, loving, intelligent. He could be protective and, when situations presented themselves, he would take up arms and fight, but he couldn't register the nuances and layers of gray involved with law enforcement.

And unfortunately, right now, Mickey mattered more.

Jonah reached for her. "It's that you're so much more complicated than when we were kids."

"We're adults, Jonah. We're supposed to be complicated. We're—"

"Supposed to be mature," he finished. His hand started to reach for hers, and he drew it back like a fourteen-year-old boy.

Was he . . . hitting on her?

Admittedly, she desired to pursue whatever this was he was trying to say . . . to do . . . to show to her. Suddenly she realized she'd felt this coming for a while, even more so of late.

The *Jacket* meeting. Her hugging his chest for that moment under the ancient oak at Windsor . . . talk of sex. The bloody threat in her entry way. Jesus, she got it. His protectiveness and memories of youth had matured, probably surprising him as much or more than her.

Son of a biscuit, of all the days for their feelings to get in the way. Any other time, they might've wound up back at the treehouse talking, a bottle of Jule's wine between them.

She'd thought of a moment like this for years, confused feelings teetering between Jonah being brother or boyfriend. They were natural together. Did that come from a lifetime together? Shared trauma? Or a sense of a future as a pair?

"We're confused about all this . . . this horrible history that's wedged itself back in our lives," she said. "It's wadded all in my head, Jonah. Listen," and she rubbed his arm. "I just want to go work to my investigation, okay? I'd be horrible company for anyone right now. Tell Jule I'll see her tomorrow, and to save me a piece of the blueberry."

Shadows from the outstretched pecan limbs crossed the east corner of the drive, telling her evening was nigh. If she was to spend enough quality time with Mickey, she had to act. No telling where he wanted to be come nightfall.

"Maybe I can help," Jonah offered.

Oh, Jesus, Jonah, don't make me do something mean. She shook her head. "Nah, it's phone call work." She couldn't say confidential, because she'd already aired most of this case with him and Ty in the treehouse. Plus, she shared with Jonah. Shared with Ty. They protected each other's confidences. They never lied to one another.

"No, I mean it." He tried to turn her and walk her toward the house. A walk that would take them right past the passenger side of her truck. "I feel badly," he said, when she didn't budge. "I—"

She spun on him. "Damn it, Jonah, I want to be left alone." She hurt the moment she spoke. Pain from the pretense that she didn't need him when in reality she'd like nothing more than to disappear down to Windsor overlooking the river.

"Just let me be," she repeated, not as sharp.

Anger filled his eyes, giving her the slightest temptation to bring him in on things. He was safe. He'd always been safe, but he still carried a torch about Jule's injury which might interfere with him seeing Mickey as opportunity for a solution other than payback. Even if she read him in downstream, she needed to do this alone first.

"Okay, then," he said, his final stare holding long enough to add, "Sorry to be so stupid, Quinn."

No, no, not what she wanted. "Jonah," she said, falling short as to what to say next.

But he turned, making his way back to his mother's house, the weight in his feet so abundantly clear.

She felt like shit.

"BEER, WINE, TEA, coffee . . . milk? You remember the goat's milk, right?" Quinn asked, heading straight to the kitchen. "Toss your pack wherever. Sit . . . wherever."

"Beer," he said, tossing his stuff and choosing the sofa.

Needing a moment to collect herself, she wanted to hide her head in the chill air of the refrigerator, struggle to get Jonah out of her mind, but she kept aware, one ear on the living room. She grabbed two bottles and nudged the door closed with a hip.

She handed him his bottle, trying to shake the image of the wilt in Jonah's shoulders, and took a moment of composure to face the span of glass doors, still nixing the residual idea to bring Jonah in on this. "Hate to do this," she said, checking the locks first before drawing the drapes to block the orchard's vista.

Mickey lifted his bottle at her in acknowledgement and took a long swig, fully understanding the need for secrecy. "This is all confidential, and I'm telling you up front I refuse to let you record anything. State law says—"

She turned back to him. "I'm aware of South Carolina law on recordings." Mickey was touchy. If he hadn't said anything, she'd been fully in her right to record their conversation, as long as *she* was party to it. Now that he'd nipped that in the bud, she understood how privileged this conversation had to be.

One piece of her, however, wondered why he didn't want proof he'd been there.

He still seemed like an older version of his younger self, however. Over the years, he'd probably attempted to come to terms with Graham's death and whatever Larry'd done to spook him. Vic's death, and whatever else was affiliated with it, however, had dashed any hope he had of coming back into the open. This guy couldn't see his future more than an hour or two ahead of himself.

She felt some sort of responsibility to save him. At first she wasn't sure why, but she should be smarter than that. He held the potential of saving her from spending the rest of her life in the dark about those days. Regardless his motives, she was still the hungriest of the two.

Peering around the room, his gaze seemed to fall on this thing, then that, none of which had changed since he had last been inside . . . except for the computer and manuals set up in the corner for Quinn's PI work. She stood steadfast in her need to preserve the past, everything in its place from where Graham had put it.

"I miss being a part of this," he said, a slight crease of a smile at the collection of wildlife carvings made from pecan wood. He pointed with his beer hand. "I remember those." More scouting of his surroundings, he relished a better time period. "Your dad was a real nice man, Quinn," he finally said. "You honestly live here alone?"

"Me and the security system. My guns. My bookkeeping." She managed a bittersweet grin. "Not nearly as desirable as it looks, is it?"

Giving him the time he needed to acclimate and recall the past, maybe adjust to why they were there, Quinn kicked off her boots, reared the recliner back, and crossed socked feet. A daring move with her not yet clear on his thoughts, but someone had to chill first. Her gesture must've worked on him, because Mickey leaned his head back against the tufted sofa, as if it were a burden carried too heavy for far too long.

She about spoke up when he beat her to it. "Mr. Sterling or Vic?" he asked, and she read his meaning.

"Daddy," she said, without hesitation. "Might help to start chronologically."

"It'll be the same as I told your uncle," he replied.

She took a draw on her beer, a big one, for fortitude. "Pretend Uncle told me nothing." Her pulse kicked up. She was finally doing this with the only person who could give a true accounting of that infamous night. "Tell me about that whole day. Start with when you came to work." She forced herself to recross her feet and act relaxed when she felt anything but.

Mickey started in on the reply, giving enough detail to tell Quinn that he'd relived Graham's final day more than a few times. He recounted which orchard he'd pruned. Who drove the truck while he used the pole saw. The level of tasseling in one area versus another. The fact the day had bumped an unusually warm ninety degrees, making him shed the extra shirt.

For twenty minutes, he revisited Sterling Banks Plantation. Hour by hour he took her through midday to the afternoon, and she relished listening to the details of the life embedded in her marrow through someone else's eyes. Scheduled to get off at five, he'd stayed late, wanting to delay until after the others went home.

Quinn tried not to show herself taking serious note of that statement. Nobody'd mentioned he'd dragged his feet leaving. No telling how many other details Uncle Larry hadn't been too forthcoming about. "Why were you waiting until everyone else left?" she asked.

His distant stare dissipated. "Not for the reason you may think."

Her hand up, she retracted. "I'm not forecasting, Mickey. Just not letting you skip anything."

"I wanted more hours, was all," he said. "I was hoping to bank extra pay for when I had to leave the end of May and tend to my own parents' place when the tomatoes came in. That's their biggest cash crop, and they needed me back. I was a body they wouldn't have to pay."

A crawly feel traveled up Quinn's neck. "Go ahead," she said, easing her chair upright. "You waited till most others were gone and came to the house. Which door?"

"The kitchen," he said, his eyes moving that direction, like he could see himself coming in. "Through the garage. Ordinarily I came in through the sliding doors."

Yep, like a lot of the hands. Easy for Graham to see them come up on the house, easy for them to see if Graham was even there. Nobody was bold enough to waltz in otherwise. If nobody saw the boss in the family room or the left perimeter of the kitchen, they didn't let themselves in, instead going around to knock on the garage entrance to the kitchen. Jule would've let Mickey in at that time of day, but she'd already said she stood at the stove frying chicken, her head too near the ventilation hood set on high, unable to hear a polite tap at the back. Graham was occupied with her, water running at the sink adding to the noise.

Her mouth dry from anticipation, Quinn needed another beer in the worst way, but she wasn't interrupting. As if Mickey were about to predict the second coming of Christ, she fought the desire to rush him to the reason they were seated in her den sharing what no two other people in Craven County could share.

"Did you see either of them when you knocked on the glass?" she asked. They'd be visible in the kitchen. At least Graham might.

Mickey shook his head. "That's why I went to the garage. The door was ajar like two inches, like it had been opened and pushed too lightly to close all the way, so I came in."

She gave him a slight nod.

"I walked through the mud room into the kitchen, instantly smelling the chicken frying. Remember my stomach growling from it, but with nobody watching frying grease, well, that sort of bothered me. Nobody leaves hot grease popping like that."

Her tongue stuck against the roof of her mouth, smelling the chicken. Seeing the pieces blistering in the skillet.

She sensed Mickey stalling with excessive sensory detail, capturing her with descriptions. She was eager. He was anything but. Still, she didn't want him to fast forward for fear he'd miss a critical detail.

"I saw Jule first," he finally said, looking toward the kitchen but more off in the past.

Chapter 22

WITH A SHAKY sigh from the sofa, Mickey leaned elbows on his knees, empty beer bottle dangled between his fingers, and talked into the carpet. "I remember a snap of a thought about whether to turn off the chicken, and then how my mom would kill me for butting into something that wasn't my business. Then something hit the floor around the corner toward the entry hall."

Quinn leaned in more. "Jesus, you were that close to the killer? Damn, Mickey."

No wonder people thought it could be him.

But he shook his head. "Never crossed my mind someone else might be in the house, Quinn. Just wondered what that sound was, but I didn't exactly run to check it out. When I peered around into the hall, though, I saw Jule's boots first, then immediately assumed the old lady might've had a heart attack or something. I rushed to her and was rolling her over when feet scuffed, shuffled, I don't know, but definitely on the front porch."

Quinn wanted to tell him what he could have . . . should have done, so badly.

"Then they landed on the walk, so I think they leaped off the porch over the steps. When I saw the blood on her head, things kicked, and I realized there'd been an intruder in the house."

Quinn held her breath.

Mickey's pain was so damn apparent in wrinkles around his mouth. "She was breathing, you know? So I jumped up to see who the hell that was, and that's when—" He peered up at her. "That's when I entered the foyer and saw your daddy."

"And then what?" she whispered.

"I, I . . . think I sort of got stuck. Looking back at Jule, then at Mr. Sterling, then something spurred me to chase who might've done it while something else told me to take care of them."

As if afraid of being wrong in Quinn's eyes, he stood. Setting the empty on the end table, he ran a hand through his hair and started toward the kitchen, like he had to see it all over again. Then he stopped, as though he couldn't bear it.

"Mickey, it's all right. You weren't wrong either way," she said to his back, totally believing him. He *was* innocent. No way this was an act.

He spun, shaken, strength drained from his face. "I stopped a few seconds, stunned at your daddy. It was obvious he was . . . so I ran outside. Saw the guy bolt across the front, headed toward the highway. Started to pursue him, but how could I leave Jule and your daddy? I just couldn't."

"That's all right." Her heart was so thick with emotion it about choked her. "Describe the running man."

He seemed to reach within. "I think of him as all black sometimes, but he wore shoes that had to be sneakers, cargo pants, and a hoodie. Never saw his face." He looked at Quinn as if needing prompts.

"Height?" she asked.

"About mine," he said, which Quinn judged an inch or so shy of six feet.

"Hair?"

"Dark, long enough to whip outside his hoodie."

"Build?"

He shrugged. "Medium."

"How close did you get to him?"

He shook his head with little abbreviated motions. "Didn't leave the porch," he said. "Guy disappeared past the trees, up the road. He was in good shape, fast, but any killer would be fast getting away, wouldn't they?"

"Limp?" she asked. "Anything about his gait? Anything in his hands?"

He crossed his arms, with a slight rocking motion. "No limp, but he ran like a cowboy, legs wide . . . not someone real young but without much effort. Could be wrong." More rocking. "His hands, his hands, yes, he carried what could be a handgun. Something just made his arm pumping action different while he ran, just obvious he held what might have been a weapon."

Or car keys, Quinn thought.

Then suddenly, in fast strides, Mickey dashed across the room at Quinn, arms outstretched. She stood with the same urgency to greet him, unsure what he needed, her heart pounding.

"I could have caught him," he said with a thickness in his throat.

"You could've been shot," she whispered back. "Thank you, Mickey. Thanks so very much for doing this. I'm so sorry."

They stood there, an arm's length apart until Quinn had to reach over, draw him in, and give him a hug. He looked so badly like he needed one.

She missed the footsteps through the garage.

"Quinn?"

They jerked and parted quickly.

A dark man in jeans and Clemson tee stood in the den. Quinn sniffled. "Ty? Why are you here?"

"Jonah called me, worried. Jesus, Q," the deputy said. "You found Mickey?"

Then from behind him came Jonah, his mouth open, expression confused, but not so lost as to hide his disappointment. "This is your phone call?"

Mickey whirled for his backpack. "You said nobody'd think to come here." Betrayal in the squint of his eyes, he swooped the bag over a shoulder.

"Wait, no, no, don't go," Quinn said, then to Jonah, "What the hell! He's here to help, and I promised he wouldn't be spotted. What didn't you understand about me wanting to be alone?"

"This isn't alone," Jonah said.

"If I'd told you he was here, you'd have demanded to see him and mess things up." Then she turned to the other. "Ty," Quinn pleaded in her rush across the room, snaring Mickey's backpack in a fisted tug-of-war. "Make Jonah understand." Then to Mickey, "Please, please stay. They won't tell anyone, I totally promise. They're invested in Daddy's death as much as we are."

She glanced back at her two friends. The scramble had her frantic. She needed more details. How Daddy seemed. Was he really dead or had he spoken; please let him have said something. She was so damn close to hearing what really happened.

She stared at the two men while speaking to Mickey. "They would do as I ask. Trust me, for them to tell anyone would be a mortal, unforgivable sin against what we've meant to each other."

Mickey shrugged her loose and looked at the two, his chest heaving at the surprise. "Ty," he greeted first, then, "Jonah."

Ty gave him a nod back.

Jonah not so much. "Where was he when I came by?" he said in lieu of a welcome.

"Not important," she replied. "But this is my investigation."

"Um, it's mine, too," said Ty.

"But it's not Uncle Larry's, you hear me, Ty?"

He hesitated.

Quinn raised her tone with a quick swipe across her damp cheek. "Do you hear me?"

Another subtle nod.

Then she let loose of the knapsack and walked over to Jonah, still stunned and deceived. "Hated lying to you," she said, "but I'd promised Mickey security here. You'll have to get over it or he's compromised." She peered back over at her guest, who now sought an out.

"He stayed gone six goddamn years," Jonah yelled, and pushed past Quinn.

Mickey dropped the sack and met him, bracing, the two men equal in height, weight, and passion to test the other. "What do you want with her?" Jonah said through his teeth. "Do you know what you put everyone through deserting like that? Do you know what you did to her? To my mother?"

Mickey came back with a snarl. "I had no choice."

Ty came between them, shoving Jonah with his good hand, the bandaged one against his stomach. "Both of you idiots rein it in. Let's back away and talk."

Mickey stepped away first. "No problem. I'm done anyway."

No. Quinn wasn't letting him vanish again. Her promises of secrecy weren't working, so she chose another route. "Ty, come over here to the recliner so nobody bumps that hand. Jonah." Anger clouded her about Jonah. She marched to her computer station and rolled out the chair. "You sit here," and she positioned it beside the recliner for Ty's easy reach.

Then to Mickey, she went up to and begged. "Please, what do I have to do to get you to stay? Name it."

"I'll still have to disappear," he said. "They've seen me."

"Then I'll help you disappear," she concluded, too low for the other men to hear. "Again, please?"

He dropped the sack and sat back on the sofa.

Being princess, or queen depending on who you spoke to, came with its privileges. In her house, on her turf, about a case she considered to be deservedly hers, she was calling the shots from here on out. Pointing to each, she asked the same as she'd asked Mickey, with more of a bite on each word. "Beer?"

After equipping each man with a bottle, popping Jonah's in his palm with a smack, she sat on the other end of the sofa from Mickey, motioning at Jonah to aid Ty, who declined and showed he could screw off the top himself.

"You're in *my* house, at *my* invitation," she started, making eye contact with each. "We all have a highly sensitive interest in June 8th. Agreed?"

Nods all around, Jonah peering to the side, still singed from being misled.

"The terms to stay here are you allow frank discussion about what happened, or what we think happened, or what may have happened. Then Mickey walks. Is that clear?"

"I told you what I know, Quinn," Mickey said.

"You may think you have, but we're here to make sure, which could mean going over it a few times." Subconsciously, her thumbnail scratched the bottle's paper wrapper. "You see, we weren't there. The two people who were hurt, his and mine," she said, motioning to Jonah then herself, "aren't able to tell us much. Daddy," and she steeled herself so she could continue, "sacrificed the most."

Nobody argued with her after she played the trump card, silently relinquishing to her

"Going back to before we were interrupted, Mickey, we left off with you on the porch, the culprit running up the drive."

Mickey replayed hearing the noise, running outside only to see a darkly clothed man hightail it up the drive. Horribly torn between the two inside bleeding on the floor and letting the man escape, Mickey chose Jule and Graham.

Tears welled and he quieted. Ty sat solemn, Jonah uncomfortable.

"Who'd you go to first?" Quinn asked.

"Your Daddy," he said. "He had the most . . . blood loss."

"He seemed the most critical," she helped.

She tried to channel through him, struggling to see her father. "Did he . . . talk?" The sheriff hadn't said and wouldn't know. Mickey was alone for a while, waiting for help. But he shook his head, and her hope wilted.

Mickey covered how Jule hadn't fully come around, and how the EMTs had worked on her. How she reacted hearing the sheriff mention the coroner. How the sheriff didn't exactly have his act together.

Quinn's disgust for her uncle only grew. He should've done so many things better. She came forward on the sofa. "About the sheriff. Let's relive that."

Mickey's brow furrowed, probably wondering what merited her request. "He seemed overly anxious." he said, watching her to see if he said what she meant. "But I figured it was because he'd just lost his brother."

Her mouth mashed tight. "Maybe, maybe not."

Not reading her meaning, Mickey gazed across at the other two and saw that Ty and Jonah seemed to hold no reservations about Quinn's line of inquiry, their jaws firm. They just followed her lead.

"You know what I mean," she said. "What did he ask first?"

"How I came to be in the house."

"Next?"

"Did I see the incident."

"And then?"

"Did I see the kill . . . um . . . trespasser."

All per the book. "Were you asked to go to the station and leave a statement?"

"No."

"Why not?"

A shrug. "Don't know. I just wasn't asked to." His eyes moved to Ty, with Ty's on his. A solid locked horns visual.

Ty thought like Quinn did. There should have been a statement, one that Mickey should've signed. Here's where she was headed, though. "Other than you, the sheriff showed up before anyone else?"

"Yes," he said.

"Then the EMTs?"

"I guess. They hadn't arrived by the time I left." Mickey gave another look at Ty as if the deputy were a lie detector, giving Quinn second thoughts about whether she should've shown Ty and Jonah the door. The vibes had changed. Ty silently judged, clearly making Mickey wonder what he might say that would incriminate him.

"So you didn't stick around until the others arrived, right?" she asked.

"Um, no. Your uncle told me to get gone before they did. Said he'd get my statement later. He just never did."

The same words Jule used.

"Why's that?" Ty asked, as if wearing the badge. "Why not have you stick around for questioning? Why not walk you through it once the injured had been taken care of?"

Mickey stared, challenged. "Don't ask me . . . ask him."

Then the room went quiet.

"I sense none of you trust Larry Sterling," Mickey said.

They passed glances.

"What exactly is your goal here?" he asked. "What are you going to do?"

Quinn wished she had an answer.

QUINN'S GRANDMOTHER'S mantel clock chimed nine thirty. Jule had texted Jonah once, and Lenore had texted Ty. Two beers each had become three, except for Ty, and all sat exhausted from the mental challenge of sorting specifics, searching for minutiae, ironing out the particulars of the short timeline that resulted in the same end. Nobody saw the man who killed Graham and injured Jule, and the general consensus was that the sheriff had let the case go cold after inept investigative moves.

They'd mentally exhausted themselves.

"That's enough for tonight," she said.

"Is he coming back?" Jonah asked, as if Mickey weren't in the room.

"Sure," she said, smiling. "Can't wear him out in one swoop; plus, now maybe he'll remember things better since we joggled his memory. A night's sleep might help everyone. I'll set up another meeting, but he has to get home. You're not going to disappear on us, are you Mickey?"

He gave a small hitch of a shoulder. "Got no real place to go."

She suspected otherwise, though. He just wouldn't let his lodgings be known. She just hoped it was in the state. Preferably in the county. And she needed his new phone number.

She wasn't asking any of that in front of the two guys, though.

But Ty wasn't buying the easy finale, and when Mickey reached over to gather his empties, Ty caught Quinn's eye. "That's it?" he mouthed.

"Talk later," she mouthed back.

He tipped his chin and led the way to the garage door, turning back to insure Jonah followed.

Instead, Jonah kept watch on Mickey. "You coming?" he asked the guest.

"I drove him here," Quinn said instead. "I'll get him home." If Jonah knew about the truck in the grove, he'd demand to take him there himself.

And he'd be pissed even more at that deception.

Though not the answer he wanted, Jonah conceded and left with Ty. Once the door shut, Quinn carried bottles to the trash.

"You about ready to head out?" Mickey called to her in the kitchen. "God knows I am."

Quinn wiped her hands on a towel and appeared back in the doorway. "Oh, we're not going anywhere until you tell me about Victor Whitmarsh, Mickey."

Chapter 23

MICKEY REMAINED standing, uncertain about how to leave since Quinn had brought him. Quinn returned to her recliner.

"Tell it on your feet or on your ass, either way, fill me in on how Victor Whitmarsh died," she said. "But not until you repeat exactly what my uncle told you in my entry way the night of June 8. *Get gone*. I heard that. Several times from a couple of people. What else, 'cause I'm not taking you home until you spill."

"I can find my truck," he said, his bag now dangling toward the floor.

"Don't threaten me, Mickey. I'm not who you have to worry about, but I'm not one to blow off, either." She nodded toward the garage. "I got rid of the guys, so let's air this mess. Bourbon work for you?"

He eased back onto the sofa. "Prefer neat," he replied.

"Good man," she said, slapping hands on her knees before heading to the liquor cart. She poured them each a strong two fingers of Blanton's. No ice.

Handing his to him, she took her place on the sofa, two cushions down. "What did my uncle really say to you after Daddy died?"

He paused his glass at his mouth. He sipped then propped it on his knee. "His words were, *You didn't see shit*, and *Get the hell out of Dodge*. Slow, clear, without room for misunderstanding, I assure you. And no, he never called me back to sign a statement nor said he would. However, a few calls and texts reminded me of his order to turn invisible . . . or else. In this county, who goes against the Sterlings, especially when it's hinted the murder will be pinned on you if you don't *get gone*?" He took another drink. "Crushed my mom."

The bourbon was a good idea. Made for a more serious conversation while shaving off the edge. "Understandable why they hate me now," she said.

He bobbled a brow in agreement.

"Why would he tell you to disappear?"

"Have no idea."

She wasn't sure about that. "You are the only witness. He should've kept you close. Hell, should've threatened you if you attempted to *leave* the county."

"Said I don't know."

"Why didn't you find that strange?" she asked.

Irked, he stared down his nose. "I was a kid. I'd just walked up on a murder. Not just any murder, mind you, but the biggest name in the county. When the biggest badge in the county tells me to disappear or else, I do it! Damn, Quinn. At the time I just felt I'd been caught in the wrong place at the wrong time, and couldn't risk getting arrested." His voice rang by the end.

"Did you kill Victor Whitmarsh?"

This one sloshed top shelf drink on his shirt. "Is that what everyone thinks?"

"Uncle's spearheading this case, so it matters more what *he* thinks."

"Listen to me. I did not kill your father, or Vic."

"Who was my friend, by the way."

His head went back. "Oh, Jesus Christ and all the angels," he said under his breath. "Only me. Why do these things happen to me?"

"So you swear you didn't kill Vic."

"No," he said, frustrated. "A thousand times no, I did not kill Victor Whitmarsh."

She accepted that. She never really thought he had. "Who did?"

"No clue. As secretive as we were being, when I couldn't get Vic, I assumed he had his reasons to go quiet. All I know."

"So why were you meeting him? Your cowboy hat was all over the motel camera."

"Yeah," he said. "I learned to stop wearing that thing around here."

He was a hometown boy. People would have recognized him with or without it. The hat just made it quicker. "And you didn't answer my question."

A gale of a sigh came from him. "He was hired to find me. He did."

Quinn watched him for tell expressions, but again saw no need not to believe him. "You must've trusted him to agree to meet," she said.

He shrugged. "Common sense told me he was cool, but I'm not a thousand percent trusting of my instincts these days."

The night wore on, but like finding gold nuggets in a Yukon stream after weeks of nothing, she'd found new commitment to keep working this opportunity. There was a vein of material in here and she was hell-bent on staking the claim and taking it all the way to the bank.

She threw back the rest of her glass and rose for another drink, then without asking, walked back to replenish his. "You got scared of Catherine and vanished. *Got gone*, again," she said, pouring. Then whispering, "God, I'll never hear those words the same, ever."

She stoppered the bottle and returned it to the liquor cart, talking her way back to the sofa. "She hires Vic to find you. Vic calls me and leaves a message, saying he needs to talk about something. Then before I can call him, he's dead in the Jacksonian, and there you are with that hat on the video footage four times during his week-long stay. Catherine says she's worried someone is after you, maybe even trying to kill you, but between the two of us, she lies when the truth would sound better." She plopped down. "That about sum up the backstory?"

"Yeah," he said long and slid out. "Believe so. Kind of unnerving hearing I was caught on video."

She laughed once. "And you being a tech guy."

A mild shrug from him.

"So," she continued, enjoying the mellow seeping into the evening. "You left her because she was smothering you?"

"I left because she was owning me."

"Damn that," she replied, holding up her glass in understanding.

He tipped his head. "I was a means to an end, or so that's what Vic said during our meetings."

"What end was that?" Quinn asked.

He sank half his bourbon, his posture melting into the sofa. "You,

Ms. Sterling. Catherine Renault had designs on *you*, and she was hoping to use me to get to you. I was such a fool thinking she wanted me and my phone apps."

She tried taking that in. "What exactly were you supposed to do in relation to me?"

"Kill you," he said so eerily matter-of-fact.

Say what?

Mickey's nonchalance disappeared at her beaded stare. "What are you thinking, Quinn?"

She sat forward, suddenly regretting the earlier beers and later bourbons. Blindsided, too trusting of even part of Catherine's story . . . too busy assuming Mickey was the victim in all of this . . . she rose, the goal to move toward her desk and the drawer in it that held her Glock.

Of course it was about the land. Land made people do incredibly stupid, dangerous, and daring things. Nobody could see, hear, or read about Quinn Sterling without Sterling Banks making an appearance as well. She was it. It was she. The alpha and the omega.

"Not that I would have done it," he gushed out, uncomfortable with the silence. Sounding like a boy full of excuses. Regret showed all over the man as he then froze, eagerly attempting to read her.

Like she tried reading him.

She moved listlessly to not alert who could easily be an assassin, whom she'd invited in with open arms and poured her best bourbon into. Every neuron inside her willed herself sober as she went toward her defense.

"I told her to go to hell." He accented each word, pushing for Quinn to respond.

When she didn't, he set his glass on the end table and stood. "Don't you dare think I could've done it."

She leaned against the desk, sliding the drawer open to her right. "I assume she didn't take that well."

"You're dancing with me," he said. "And you're upset."

The Glock came out easy enough and rested even easier in her hand. She held it down, in front of her, so he could clearly understand. "No, I'm deciding how to take you down if I have to," she replied, pushing authority hard and deep into her words.

Inside, however, she kicked the hell out of herself. Had she played into their plan? She raked her brain for the missteps, but no way they had forecast her going to the Raines farm not once but twice. Not unless they'd planted a bug of their own in the manor or in her truck, but Jonah did a bug sweep when he upgraded the security. Damn, certainly not in Windsor, but Mickey had worked the farm. He'd be familiar.

"Did you kill our goat?"

Her steely tone made the color drain from his cheeks.

Was he shaking?

He took a hesitant step forward, gaze glued to the firearm. "No! What goat? I wouldn't kill a goat, much less you. Listen, I didn't explain that right. Blame the alcohol. Blame my stupidity. I don't care the reason, but I turned her down, Quinn. Hear that part of what I said. I called her a lunatic and turned her down. Then I did what any sane person would do . . . I ran. I hid. She'd asked me to kill a human being, for Christ's sake. I became an instant threat to her, and she had the money to make me disappear."

Was that panic on his face, or was he that good an actor? The cracked voice that fell out, however, pled awful hard. "Hear me out, please. Let me tell you the whole story . . . and about Vic."

"Sit back down," she ordered. "Keep your hands where I can see them."

His eyes darted from Quinn to the exits . . . the glass doors, the kitchen, the hallway to the front. Instincts were ordering him to seek escape.

"I said sit your ass down," she ordered.

Eyes wide, he obliged.

"I might've led into that conversation a bit differently if I'd been you," she said, maintaining her advantage seated on the corner of the desk, easily able to stand and do whatever needed doing. Serious split seconds ahead of him from his seated position on the sofa. "Now start from the beginning. From the day you met her. And this time, if you leave anything out, I'm cuffing you and turning you over to the sheriff to let you explain how you were asked to kill his niece. If you come at me,

I'll win. Are we clear?"

Mickey started and restarted after Quinn made him fill in the blanks he left in panicky jumps and skips. He and Catherine had met in Charleston, in Marion Square, and Quinn suspected Catherine had initially had him tailed, determining when a time was right to have the *happenstance* meet that would culminate into an orchestrated romance. Mickey, being a nice guy, accepted her offer for dinner when she proved so grateful that he took the time to speak with a lonely blind girl, especially one who came with a designated driver and bottomless pocketbook.

Quinn had witnessed enough of that woman to see her pulling this off.

Catherine had a deep well of evil.

Enamored by her interest in his phone apps, he fell for her and her offer to support him, and especially introduce him to individuals who could take his work from a high-level hobby to a professional brand.

It wasn't until he'd moved in, introduced her to his parents, and thought of how to afford enough of a ring for someone who could buy the jewelry store, did she ask him specifically about Sterling Banks. Which led to him spilling an agonizing recount of Graham Sterling's death and describing the threatening cloud that hung over him based on Uncle Larry's order to disappear.

Some of which Quinn suspected Catherine already knew through Vic's research . . . through Vic's knowledge of Quinn. As Quinn thought . . . mention the person and you soon think of the land. Mickey confirmed enough in some pillow-talk evening.

Vic got uncomfortable enough to call Quinn. Or so she would like to think.

"You ever meet Chevy?" he asked. "The dude was way more than a driver, and I didn't want him getting his hands on me."

"Yes, he's a bodyguard," she confirmed.

He nodded gratefully that they'd agreed on something. "I've slept in a different place every night since then." He gave the half-empty bourbon glass a second glance then abruptly took it, downing the remnants in one huge swallow. "Why does she want you dead, Quinn?"

he said, holding the empty between both hands.

Smart for Catherine not to share with him in return.

When she didn't answer, because she wasn't really sure he needed the answer, he spoke back up. "Part of why I agreed to meet you was to clear the air. That and I couldn't stand having her on one side of me and you on the other. If I had to choose one side to stand on, it was yours." Absentmindedly he tried to drain the already empty glass, then under his breath added, "Goddamn, who can afford to get caught between two rich bitches."

"You haven't covered Vic." Private investigators weren't exactly law enforcement, but they respected the blue line. They had to. So many of them had worn the badge before. Surely he wasn't sure of Catherine's plan. She'd have been a fool to show her hand.

"Okay, this is how he brought me around." Mickey steadied himself, palms on his thighs. "Vic convinced my mother to contact me and have me call him. Took me a week to build up the guts. I mean, who was I to believe? He worked for Catherine."

Understandable.

"I went to the motel, wearing that damned stupid hat, which I've thrown in a dumpster, by the way. He told me he was hired to find me and coax me back into Catherine's arms. She was oh-so distraught over my departure, he said at first, but when I said I was scared of her, he made me say why."

Quinn started to speak, and he interrupted. "I didn't trust him, and he didn't trust me. Again, at first. By the third meeting, our last, he assured me he was on my side. He wanted nothing to do with murder . . . especially having to do with you."

Quinn closed her eyes for a long few seconds, so regretting not returning that call. "And then?" she asked, sad and heavy.

"He told me to vanish. Said I'd know when to resurface. Said either I'd hear something on the news to convince me it was safe, or I'd . . . hear from you."

Which was when Vic had called her and left his message.

Son of a bitch.

Pushing back to conversations in Lenore's diner, interim phone calls, then to the one-on-one in Catherine's car with old Nero at attention in the front seat, all signs pointed at Catherine needing Quinn to find Mickey. She hadn't even wanted Quinn finding Vic's killer which made sense now, since no doubt she'd been the one to take him out. No proof, but Quinn was ninety percent sure.

"Quinn?"

Still too many unknowns. Why kill Quinn? Why choose Mickey to reach Quinn?

"Quinn?" Mickey sat, crossed arms across his midsection. "She had Vic research the plantation first, before I came in the picture, you know. That's what Vic said in the motel. If that helps."

It did and it didn't. Still, why choose Mickey?

"Who understands rich people?" he said. "Your sort operate on a whole different level than the rest of us."

Which flipped Quinn out of her reverie. "I am nothing like that woman."

His eyes widened. "Okay, sorry."

Quinn hadn't seen Catherine coming. Still wasn't sure *why* she was coming. She hadn't shown interest in Sterling Banks. She didn't need Sterling Banks. But she fully believed the woman hadn't been thwarted of her plan yet. There was some deeply rooted mission in that crazy woman's head. The goat's blood in the foyer sort of defined that. And Vic's murder demonstrated that Catherine didn't accept mutiny in her ranks. Mickey was correct in assuming Catherine would see that he met the same demise.

The clock ticked then chimed in that century-old sound that gave Quinn comfort alone in the vast house. Eleven thirty.

"Just stay the night, Mickey," she said, laying the weapon back in the drawer.

"I can't do that," he replied.

"She hasn't said it, but you did . . . she wanted you dead."

He sighed.

She contemplated how to handle things. The night first, of course. Tomorrow might take more thought.

"You've had enough alcohol to blow well over the limit," she said.

"And I'm not about to let my uncle get the best of me with a DUI. There are five bedrooms upstairs, not counting the master on that end of the ground floor." She motioned to the east, to her parents' room, in that moment envisioning Graham watching her, watching how this would all play out.

"But your guy . . ."

She frowned. "My guy?"

"Jonah. I assumed you two were—"

"Not your concern." God, Jonah was the least of both their concerns. "Stay here. We have a lot more talking to do when our heads are clear. Don't know about you but a bed's calling me. Seriously, the last door on the left upstairs ought to accommodate you just fine. Towels in the adjoining bath."

"Can't believe you're letting me stay." He rose to make his way to the stairs. "Staying in this house. Who'd've thought . . . after all I said tonight . . . this is so damn weird."

His overnight stay had way more to do with keeping a finger on him than courtesy. This was bigger than her and her PI business. This bled into Uncle Larry, present and past. And since it did involve him, she would demand that SLED get involved. The stink would spread state-wide. Investigations would crawl into everyone's cracks and crevices. Lawsuits would be filed. There was way too much at stake to allow Mickey to escape. Too many lives in jeopardy to leave Catherine loose and fanatically bent on killing people, and without Mickey, nobody could prove a thing.

Mickey made it to the first landing of the stairs before turning to speak down to her. "By the way, for the record, I only saw Vic three times at the motel, not four. He quit calling me back after that."

"Oh, sorry," she said. "My bad."

His steps took him down the hall, and she went to set the alarm, hoping it still worked the same since Jonah tinkered with it yesterday. "Don't try to sneak out during the night," she shouted, loud enough for him to hear. "Unless you want to trip my security system. I won't take a chance. Don't come out of your room until I knock on your door in the morning. I mean it."

"I run fast," he shouted, attempting humor.

"I shoot faster," she shouted back.

She studied the buttons hard before attempting the keypad. The last thing she needed was to trip the system and have Jonah rushing to her defense, only to shoot Mickey.

God, she was glad Jonah had not been around to hear what Mickey said.

She studied the buttons but stopped a moment, unable to get Mickey's comment out of her head.

I only saw Vic three times at the motel.

The motel camera definitely showed a guy in a cowboy hat go to Vic's room four times . . . not three. She wasn't that drunk.

Were there two guys with cowboy hats or was Mickey unable to count straight tonight?

Once they wrangled what to do about Mickey in the morning, she'd get with Ty and study that motel cam footage more closely. Could be they'd let the hat distract them. Could be Mickey mis-remembered. She'd lock her door and sleep with her Glock under her pillow anyway, regardless how innocent Mickey might be.

She punched the code, ending on a short beep, not the long one activating the service. An error message on the tiny screen flashed about not able to activate. With focus, she slow-motion typed again. Short beep again. Error. Shit, what had Jonah done? If she got this wrong a third time, she might set the damn thing off.

"Everything okay?" Mickey shouted down.

"Yeah, my fingers aren't working right. I'll get it."

Wait, had the guys shut the garage access door all the way?

She gathered their drink glasses, dropped them off in the kitchen sink, and went to the mud room leading to the garage. All seemed good peering out, but she strode out past her pickup to test for sure. Secured. She reentered the house and locked that door behind her.

Unsure about the new security, she started to test each door herself, like she was accustomed to doing, but gave the alarm another go. She failed to activate it again.

Not that she couldn't see, but she blinked, for clarity, and to read the entire error message.

Front door open.

No. That shouldn't be. That door stayed locked. Her blood froze at what that meant.

She went to retrieve the nine mil she'd laid on the desk in her final words with Mickey.

"Don't think so, Ms. Sterling. Leave the gun where it is and turn around."

She did as told and straightened, but Chevy strode over and, reaching around her, confiscated the piece.

While some other guy held his weapon on her.

He was someone she'd never seen before. Medium height, medium build. Charcoal sweatshirt with the hoodie down. Black waves of hair tinged with spits of white, long overdue for a trim over his ears, down his neck, almost across his eyes. She wasn't sure if they were oily or his locks were that deceptively dark. Latin, like Chevy, but at least a decade younger, his skin a shade or two darker. A description she remembered from Mickey.

Mickey. She prayed they hadn't been in here long enough to hear him go upstairs.

Unarmed, best he remain upstairs and uninvited to this party. God, let him be passed out from the stress and drink, behind his shut door as he was told. Without his truck in the drive, nobody would look for him here.

Quinn had to assume only the worst would happen if Mickey happened downstairs to raid the fridge. She'd ordered him, under threat of her Glock, to not open his door until she knocked in the A.M. and hoped he listened.

She took a baby step toward the sliding doors, regretting the drapes over them now.

"Unh unh unh, Miss Sterling. Stay where you are." Chevy spoke in that smooth tone of his, motioning her with her own weapon as he returned to his partner's side.

"Who is he?" she asked, halting.

Chevy's laugh rolled out smooth. "Oh, we break into your home and you want names?"

"You're Chevy Castellanos," she said. "The chauffeur. The body guard. Possibly the man responsible for wet work when asked to do so."

Another laugh, almost beguiling in a deep tone, and if he were in a different setting, say, an upscale bar or fundraiser, he'd be downright charming. "Wet work. Odd choice of words. Who says we don't just wish to converse, Miss Sterling?"

"Because you broke into my house, wearing dark clothing, and didn't attempt to hide your identity," she said. "Who is your friend?"

"*Friend* is good enough," said the other.

She shifted her weight, hoping to be closer to the sliding doors, but the unnamed man recognized her motive. "Move again and you'll be horizontal."

This dude shot straighter than Chevy.

"Horizontal? Wow, how Humphrey Bogart is that?" she said. Nerves and bourbon made her mouth run loose, but as she'd learned at the academy, chattering often made way for opportunity, too.

"What the hell is going on, Chevy?" she asked. "Your boss hires me, I do my job, and I locate Mickey. Was going to call Catherine in the morning and inform her, by the way. For a fee, of course."

"She fired you," he replied, cynical.

She dared to rest a hand on her hip. "Seriously? She said *she* fired *me*? That day in the parking garage? You were there. I told your pissant, two-faced, crazy bitch of an employer to take a hike. I don't take on lying clients, and the minute I can't trust them, they're cut loose, contract terminated." She glowered, though she sensed the anger not carrying its full weight. Hard to do with weapons trained on her, but they hadn't shut her up, and buying time worked in her favor.

"Catherine doesn't like taking crap, does she, Chevy?" she said. "That why you're out here? To intimidate me? To make me crawl under the covers, quake in my boots, run and give up the hunt? To—"

"To kill you, you stupid woman," Chevy said.

Not a surprise. "Like you were supposed to do to Mickey? How'd that turn out for you?"

"Would you both shut up!" screamed the partner. "Goddamnit, we don't need Mickey, you stupid bitch."

Her heart already pumped double-time, yet it still leaped. Then she prayed Mickey had the sense to stay hidden and call somebody. Then she doubled down. No way she'd cower. This was when you poked the bear, so he'd make the first move . . . so your move wasn't wasted.

Thank God for the Blanton's in her blood. "I went to a hell of a lot of trouble to run Mickey down for you not to care. You know, it'd be a lot easier if I had a name to call you." She tilted her head. "Something other than *guy* or *dude* or *hey*." She sneered and held up a finger. "Since we're going all forties here, how about *the Shadow?* As in *who knows what evil lurks in the heart of—*"

The unnamed partner leaped the coffee table at her.

She cut the distance in half by lunging at him.

But she side-stepped and cracked the top of his nose with a chop of her hand. Off-balance, he fell forward, gun flying to the side, with Quinn shoving his weight and momentum toward Chevy. The chauffeur shouted, "Enzo!" before his partner fell to the floor.

Enzo rolled with the fall, coming to his knees scouting for his firearm, way slicker than she expected. Unable to lay eyes on it, he snapped around for Quinn's piece still in Chevy's hand.

Quinn bolted to the sliding doors, threw the drapes up in a floating cloud of concealment, slipped a lock and flew outside. Across the patio, away from the light, in sock feet she ran into the orchard where night turned to black. But light or dark mattered little to a Sterling amongst the pecans.

Two shots sounded in the house, but she didn't dare slow to see why. In fact, she ran faster, pounding the grove floor, praying that Mickey hadn't come downstairs.

Bring it out here, you assholes. Nobody knows these trees better than I do.

Chapter 24

FEET JUST MISSING ancient roots, instinctively sensing where wooden knees curled up through dirt, Quinn stretched her run, slipping to the third row of the grove east from the house to make her pursuer second-guess where she'd gone. Then she slowed to a canter, like a racer pacing herself.

She slipped to the side and backed against a tree down row fifteen and listened, hands flat against the familiar gray bark, fighting to keep her panting quiet. No way he . . . they . . . she wished she knew which, would be covert enough to creep up on her. Not the way her soles knew this ground from a lifetime of doing just this . . . running, hiding, and daring others to find her. Nobody could best her in the groves if she didn't want them to.

She wished she knew who shot whom back there. Did one chase her? Two? She couldn't risk believing that they killed each other, and Mickey called the cavalry.

She needed her pursuers to follow her, though. Losing her, they'd consider alternatives. There were Jule and Jonah to think of.

"You underestimate me, Ms. Sterling," came Enzo's voice from the west, about seven trees over. He had followed. He was fast, too, his compass just not exactly right.

Her heart kicked the back of her ribs. His words came across too clearly for her to reply. She'd rather be a few trees farther before opening up a dialogue.

So, did Chevy peel off from his partner, or was he not coming? She fought to hear harder, note the proximity of movement.

She prayed that Enzo shot Chevy, if not dead, at least too grievously to go after Mickey. But she kept visualizing an image of Mickey bleeding out on her living room floor. Regardless, she couldn't stay put.

Mama Queen, one of their record-producing trees, was ten rows over and a dozen trees south. Quinn took off running again, paused five trees down and held her breath. He'd heard her, and his steps told her he attempted to close in.

With a burst she sprinted off again, sorely missing her orchard boots while grateful for spring versus autumn and its thousands of nuts and husks strewn across the acreage. She issued up a thanks for hired labor who kept the grounds clean of branches.

She was halfway to where she wanted to be. The temp had dropped into the upper fifties, when air normally carried a night chill, but heat built under Quinn's shirt from the chase, the adrenaline, and the overwhelming desire to move and outwit this crazed tool, these crazed henchmen of Catherine Renault.

"I was gonna take out Chevy anyway." Enzo's voice carried, louder than before. The guy had decent ears, too, because he was clearly on her tail. A hunter maybe, baiting her to speak.

And now she knew he was the only pursuer.

What unnerved her most was that Chevy was a scary guy in his own right. Him having succumbed to the wiles of this guy meant he was the lesser skilled of the two.

Focus on the one, Quinn.

She guesstimated Enzo's location down to a handful of trees. Jonah and Ty had played against her like this for days on end, years on end. A sophisticated hide-and-seek type of tag which ultimately gifted them with directional and auditory prowess. Night and low light only heightened their powers.

"Ms. Renault doesn't like two-faced people either," he hollered. "Chevy wasn't supposed to come home. Thanks for making that part easy. Dropping him in your house was decent. Using your gun even better."

A setup to take out both Quinn and Catherine's own bodyguard. A setup that triggered a thought.

If he'd agreed to Catherine's original plan, Mickey would've come to take out Quinn. Catherine hadn't given Quinn much credit. If Mickey killed Quinn, Sterling Banks would go up for sale, but if Quinn killed Mickey, everyone would assume she sought revenge. She'd be arrested, possibly indicted. A win-win situation for anyone wanting Sterling Banks. The media would prosecute Quinn. Catherine would silence Mickey.

The pecan acreage would go up for sale.

Quinn's senses sharpened even more. That bitch wasn't getting her home.

Two-hundred-year-old Mama Queen rose in her regal presence ahead, branches out like palms spread and welcoming, the last of her generation in a quadrant long since replaced with trees now half her age, or less.

On the fly, Quinn reached overhead and gripped the familiar branch. Almost smoothed in places from human hands, she let momentum carry her up, her left heel wedging in a two-branch fork to hoist her atop the limb. Then another branch up and one over. Muscle memory achieving perfect shifts and balance, she located her spot twenty feet up, closed her eyes as she had as a child, froze, and listened.

Nobody'd ever masked their footsteps well enough to outfox her. While it'd been a while, she prayed she'd retained her skills . . . and she analyzed.

No storm expected, no weather fronts, which meant no breeze.

Squirrels slept, but an owl expressed his displeasure a couple hundred yards away. Then in seconds, he relocated his hunting ground. She heard him land in his spot off in another direction.

A shoe—a sneaker? She couldn't remember what he wore on his feet, but he stubbed a root, a small one. There he was. She tilted her head, eyes still shut. Four trees over now. She froze to keep him scouting level instead of hunting above.

If she were escaping the man, she'd remain in place, invisible, the scent of tassels and greenery as soothing as the scruff of a baby goat. The ruts and cavities of the old dame's bark, no longer sloughing in chunks like a young tree, remained familiar under her fingers. She could hole up here until dawn. Had done so before after finding the right combination of fork and limbs to let her drift off to sleep with the hushed blissful white noise of long slender leaves.

Worry was whether Enzo'd feel comfortable leaving once he'd lost the chase. She could identify him and knew his first name, thanks to Chevy before he died. She assumed he died.

No, Enzo wouldn't leave without taking her out, too.

She tensed with Enzo only one tree away. With a slight lean left, she spotted him, visible from the waist up. He attempted to scan the darkness, from trunk to trunk.

Then his voice bellowed, "I know more of this place than you think, Ms. Sterling."

Louder than necessary, he'd lost her and was none too happy about it.

This wasn't his first time here. But how many other times were there? Was this the goat's killer?

Was this Graham's murderer?

"For instance," he shouted, "I can slip maybe a mile to the west and find me some more goats."

He indeed had his bearings. His forecast distance to Jule's goat barn wasn't much off.

"But then," he said, slowly turning in a circle, scanning, never looking up. "Who says I have to stick to goats? I can just cut that ol' bitch's head off, stick it on a pike, and plant that clot-covered skull on the plantation gate. How would that look?" His chuckle held a nastiness. "Or toss it up into one of these trees and let you wait and see where the buzzards swarm before you find it."

The mental visual prompted a shiver, and she steeled herself against more reaction. If the man's depravity enabled him to so easily slit the throat of such a docile creature as Bonnie Blue and collect the blood while watching the poor animal's life drain with it, he could take an elder without hesitation. Jonah could wield a gun, but he had no experience in hand-to-hand. He'd brawl with a crazed intensity, no doubt, but he'd represent no more than a welcome challenge, assuming Enzo didn't stealthily take him out first.

"Come out or that's my next stop," he said. "The goat pen and the goat lady. You hearing me, girl?"

She stiffened even as the soft, tender creep of a beetle made its way across the back of her hand. Right now a snake could slither her head to toe and flicker in her ear, but she'd remain fixated on the man waving her gun twenty-five yards away. The man who no doubt carried the goat-killing knife, too.

"No? Next stop goat city. Imagine how easy'd it'd be to lay out all those baby goats, Ms. Sterling. Good eating, too, or so I've heard. Might take me one home for grillin'. But imagine how that'd sound. One goat down, two goats down. Blood flowing. The others would smell death and scream their heads off, calling for their mamas until I shut them up one by one, slicing one throat after the other. Young ones cut easy, you know. Knife slides clean through the neck bone before you know it. The old woman, however, might take some sawing."

Enzo taunted her, his goal to draw her out to do her in. The last of the breed-able Sterlings killed on the very land that had kept the name going. Sitting in a pecan tree, no less.

Sterling. Splendid quality. She'd even considered keeping the name once married, making her own children don Sterling instead of their father's surname in a proper bow to a three-hundred-year unbroken chain of Sterling surnamed heirs.

Anyone in her head right now would deem her insane and ridiculously foolish sitting on a pecan limb, her life on the line with lineage consuming her thoughts instead of survival. But that lineage was about survival. This land, these trees drew their energy from Sterling blood. A strength in the land supported the Sterlings.

"Goats it is then," Enzo said, walking a few steps then halting. Another couple steps. Scanning. Then in a decision proving he had his bearings, he headed west to Jule's.

The thumping in her ears rose to a thrum. He was doing it. He'd already proven he could kill without hesitation. He would slaughter the Sterling Banks goats before executing their shepherd, or sooner if she got in the way.

And her beloved Jonah would go down fighting because he, because of his virtue, would hesitate and give morality a second thought before taking a life. Which meant in that split second he'd probably forfeit his own.

A coolness traveled through the branches, goosebumps skittering down to her wrists. The moisture from running prickled skin under her clothes.

Enzo couldn't rush in the dark, but once he put two more rows between them, just far enough, Quinn eased to the bottom branch again and, upon spotting him another tree farther, she lowered herself gently to the dirt.

The rules had to change.

This could no longer be a lie-and-wait game. Nothing stood between that man and more bloodshed except her. Enzo couldn't be cued into the change. All rules were off. They were both predators now.

Quinn moved a row and two trees over, hugged the opposing side, and shouted, "You were right on top of me, you idiot. You give up too easily. Bet you wouldn't last an hour on a deer hunt."

Eyes closed, neck craned, she listened hard. He made no advances, presumably doing the same listening for her.

"If we both stay in place, nobody wins," she said.

"Aaah," he replied, and she heard the grin in his voice. "I accept the challenge. Entice me, girl. Make it fun."

She ran a ways farther and stopped. He did the same, just a half second after her. She ran in place, kicked a branch, sticking to the same pecan tree. He ran a few yards and stopped.

"This is where I live," she shouted, then took off, muttering, "And this is where you die."

Her remark surprised herself. Call it a flipped switch. Call it a logical decision. She chose to call it survival . . . for her and everyone who'd come before her, because her death wasted every drop of sweat any of them had ever shed.

She bolted and stopped, listened and judged when to navigate the next row. Where to lead him was becoming her million-dollar question. She wasn't armed. He was. She had trained moves but had no idea of his. She had height, but he had size. This was no longer about whether they'd face each other but about where, when, and a heavy dose of how.

She could zigzag trees forever. 'Till dawn if necessary. She and Ty had done that once, her father thinking they'd slept that summer night on the back porch. Whether that game had been a dare, or a simple what-if, she couldn't remember, but the game had had no winner except exhaustion.

Enzo, however, would tire of the chase long before he lost steam, and he'd redirect to Jule and Jonah. Quinn had to stay just beyond his reach, until . . . until what? She hadn't finalized that part of the plan yet, except that she'd walk away. She couldn't fathom anything but walking away.

Then after an eerie night of stagnant air, an unexpected puff ruffled through, and she rushed behind a tree. Just not in time. Enzo lifted his head, catching her scent on the breeze.

Socks snagging, bits of bark bruising like pebbles, Quinn remained on the balls of her feet, molded against the trunk. She no longer wore thick childhood callouses, but the muscle memory of being barefoot remained. She could ignore the pain.

Continually fighting the sound of her breathing, she couldn't help but wish for blue lights from Jacksonboro about now, but that required Jonah having heard the shots. Or Mickey, unless he took off to preserve himself. Two shots fired thirty minutes ago, she guessed. Hope of backup dwindled with so much time in between, leaving her a decision to make.

Once Enzo had scanned too many directions, proving he'd lost the scent, she pushed off toward a boundary line of the property, a half mile ahead, to the mud and the flora, the embrace of the free-flowing, black-water Edisto River. A place as home to her as the biggest, widest, most accepting of the pecan trees.

She smelled the water before she heard it and could predict the steps it'd take to reach its banks. The competition of the water's trickle, however, the closer she got, began interfering with listening for Enzo.

"Losing you, Enzo," she yelled, to lead him.

She could swim as well as she could run.

Leached tannins from Edisto's forested swamp turned the water the color of tea in some places, coffee in others, but nocturnally the water simply turned black. Rich scents and deep three-dimensional layers of earthy colors by day, but too dark to judge well and be safe by night. Alligators ventured out on occasion, and moccasins. Uncalculatable bottoms that could sink you to your knees and dare you to climb out.

Navigating the bank, Quinn traveled back north, roughly toward the manor. She and Enzo had crissed and crossed sections of orchard for time that could be minutes or as much as an hour, she couldn't tell.

Under limbs harboring sleeping slithery creatures, over arthritic roots that served as sunning beds for turtles during the day, and past the threshold of water and muck, Quinn traversed the river's brink. She understood the dangerous places and hoped that soon behind her she'd hear a scream from Enzo having found one.

Instead he tackled her into the water.

She hadn't caught her breath. He was heavier, had the leverage, and him taking her from the back gave him the advantage.

Quinn couldn't get turned to grab hold of him.

He held the upper body strength to dunk her with him, keeping her from air . . . but he floundered for footing. Instead of easily holding her under, he couldn't find traction to stand.

Diving to the bottom, even as shallow as it was, gave her the instant of distance to turn. Then balling up, she kicked for his groin, the water slowing her delivery but also allowing him to forecast her move. He arced to avoid her foot, totally losing his grip.

With little air to sustain her, she pushed away from him, then down and off a submerged rock toward the middle where a sandbar formed from small boulders. She rose just long enough dive upstream.

She and her childhood brothers had played a lot of tag in the river, too.

Ten or so yards down she came up spitting and turned to judge how close he followed, only to see he hadn't. *Shit.* He got out. On land he would listen for her movements and cut her off at whatever part of the river she decided to exit.

With no sign of help, she could only think of one more option. A do-or-die move that drove her and chilled her all the same. A last ditch choice.

Having exhausted her tricks in the trees and the black Edisto River, she had no choice but to escape to Windsor.

Feeling ahead of her, moving silent, she approached the bank and fumbled across a water-logged branch wedged in a substantial grouping of rocks. She chose a solid rock the size of her palm and cast it farther up the water. Then another, and once the stick came free, she hurled it, too.

Then she took her chances and clambered out, running light and perpendicular to the river and back into the pecans. He'd be at the water.

Three rows in she veered right, still in the direction of Windsor with the river running parallel. She passed him, or so she calculated. He'd likely hear her and give chase. The trick was to reach Windsor first.

He caught on quickly.

"I'm coming, chicky," he yelled.

She had a couple dozen yards on him. She kicked it in and headed to an exact point. He only headed after her. She still had hope to arrive ahead of him.

Windsor lodged in live oak, not pecan branches, the five acres of woods around it preserved intact by a father giving his motherless child a fantasy world. And Graham had built it solid.

She reached the stairs and climbed them two at a leap. The screen door latch wasn't stout enough to resist a teenage boy, much less a grown, vengeful man bound for a trophy, so she didn't latch it. No time to anyway.

Breathing hard, dripping and cold not from the night but from the objective, Quinn bumped aside chairs and makeshift tables to reach the child's trunk in the back corner. She snatched aside the tablecloth designed to give the box a playhouse innocence and extracted a key ripped out of a plastic bag taped on the back.

"You can come down or I can come up," Enzo yelled from below, a heavy foot kicking the bottom step, telling her he meant it.

But then bullets peppered the floor from beneath. He'd shifted his attack.

She cringed against the trunk, pulse pounding in her ears. "No good," she yelled, tossing the empty bag, scrambling to unlock the trunk. "My daddy built this house," she uttered to herself. "It'd take a thirty-ought-six to go through these timbers."

His feet sounded back on the stairs.

She opened the trunk, grabbed what she needed, and returned to the door. Through the screen he aimed. On her belly on the floor, she fired.

Chapter 25

QUINN REMAINED belly down on Windsor's plank floor, quivering . . . listening.

Enzo had proven himself an incredibly defiant adversary. The silence could be a ploy.

A long time she waited, unable to give total credit to her well-honed aim, but God, she swore she put a round through his eye.

However, if she stood, that doorway made the perfect fatal funnel for someone waiting below to place a killing shot.

Rising silently to her knees, gun stiff-armed, she crawled against the wall, beneath one of the shuttered windows. After listening for a response, she dared unlatch the wooden cover and peer down. Dark as tar, but with her familiarity of the picture below her, movement might be detected. *Nothing.*

She crossed to the other window. *Nothing.* The back of Windsor faced the woods, windowless. She crept to the door, her left side against the wall, to sneak a look.

At the bottom of the stairs, she made out two legs, the torso hidden behind them as Enzo lay with his back on the last three steps, curled around the bottom rail like he'd landed there, tried to get up, then gave up the ghost.

"Quinn?" screamed a male voice, ripe with panic, from just outside the woods. "Quinn?" Mickey called again, higher pitched.

"Here," she shouted, gingerly stepping down the risers to the body, stopping three steps up. She hesitated then leaped way over it to the right, fear seizing her that he might reach out and grab.

Mickey ran up. His expression soured at the body he recognized. He lowered his weapon to his side. Quinn took the pistol from him, so foreign-looking in a hand not accustomed to using one.

"There's a dead guy at the house," he mumbled, staring at the other before him. "It's . . . where I got this." He held up the weapon.

"This one shot the other," she said, unburdening him of any guilt. The need to soothe someone else to settle her own nerves helped slide her back from the cliff she'd hung on for God knew how long tonight. That step back brought a hearty sigh. Her strength ebbed, and she tucked Mickey's weapon in her waistband before taking hold of a banister. She was suddenly tired enough to want to drop to her knees.

But she couldn't. Regretfully, she suddenly realized her night was still young.

"Recognize the guy back at the manor?" she asked, needing some confirmation that Mickey had been telling the truth.

"Chevy Castellanos," Mickey finished. "Catherine's driver." His stare remained affixed to the man on the ground.

Chevy did more than drive, but no point upsetting Mickey about that. The driver likely served at Catherine's beck-and-call for whatever she needed, crossing the line in all kinds of ways.

But Mickey's pallor worsened, and Quinn had to call his name twice before he heard.

"I think he's . . . I think this dead guy might be the one from that night," he said.

Quinn's blood turned icy, suspecting but desperately needing him to clarify, fast. "Which night?"

"It was dark, and I caught just a couple glances, but—"

She gripped him with new strength, moving him away from the man who still in death stole Mickey's words. "But what, Mickey?"

He tore his gaze off the corpse to meet Quinn's. "He may be who killed your daddy."

Hearing him say it carved shape to the thought she'd briefly weighed. There had been another party. But the fact he appeared in tandem with Chevy in her house, with her demise their aim, told her one fact louder than any other. Catherine Renault was indeed behind all the shit that had rained upon Sterling Banks, maybe going back to the beginning. More if one had to research what caused Graham Sterling's death that night.

Catherine just took up immediate residence in Quinn's crosshairs.

"You can't be here, Mickey," she said, escorting him back to the entrance to Windsor's woods with a hand full of his sleeve.

He went along until they reached the grove opening then pulled loose. "I can identify him."

"Maybe," she said, "but if you can *now*, you could've *then*, and somebody told you not to."

The truth stopped him cold.

"That someone will be here any moment," she added, pushing him. "You can't be here when he arrives."

His understanding locked in.

"Make yourself scarce," she said. "You *got gone* twice before, so I'm sure you can do it again. Just don't disappear for when I may need you, you hear? I'm not my uncle and I'm not Catherine, but I'm getting to the bottom of all this one way or the other."

He nodded, turned to leave then paused. "I'm sorry all this fell on you, Quinn."

"I'm sorry how it fell on you," she said. "But now's not the time. Go. You know how to get me. Send me your real number."

After a melancholy grin, he scurried off, his past years working for Graham Sterling having educated him on how to clandestinely reach his hidden truck near the front of the farm entrance.

She hadn't reached Enzo's body before a different man shouted her name, close enough to make her wonder whether he saw the other one leaving. She prayed Jonah caught no sight of Mickey slipping off.

"Quinn?" Jonah shouted again, his flashlight appearing before he did, the beam catching her eyes before he lowered it. The light did a side-to-side and rested on Enzo, the body stopping the flashlight's arc, giving color to the bloodied face and neck. His weapon, or rather, her weapon, still remained in the dead man's grip.

Enzo had missed her with his shot, and it couldn't have been by much.

"Jonah, it's okay," was all she could think to say, herself assuming the job of consoler again. The cop in the midst of chaos that witnesses could rarely grasp.

Her heart still beat like a rock concert, though. Half at escaping Enzo. Half at deciding she needed to *get gone* just as quickly as she could. Her night still had a ways to go, but not here dealing with cops and a crime scene. Or rather, two crime scenes.

Jonah slid his .38 in his pocket, swept her up, and crushed her to him.

She held him just as tight, then shifted her head to the side, laying her cheek on his shoulder. One of his hands found its way to the back of her head, and he stiffened at the feel of a weapon . . . then managed to adjust to mold against her.

"I should've listened to you about your investigation stuff," he said. "And I should not have listened when you shooed me away last night. God, Quinn." A deeper hug.

Any other time she might've laughed at the contrasts in what he was saying.

"I—"

His kiss mashed her lips hard, passionate, almost desperate, a hand behind her head so she could not pull away. A long kiss. Not as a brother, not as a friend. Not even as the teenage boy who'd taken her virginity. This was . . . a kiss she'd never had before.

Finally he let loose of her, speaking with only his eyes. He was seriously scared.

"Um, I led him out here," she tried to explain, thoughts scattered. "Away from—" and she stopped herself from saying Mickey. "Away from Jule, the goats . . . and you."

He held her back, the flashlight dangling on a loop between them, and he examined her making sure she was really safe. "I saw lights on at the house and . . . took a chance you might be up. But when I got there, the doors were open, that body . . . that's when I heard shots out here. Are you sure you're okay?"

She gave him a light shake. "Yes, I'm fine." She lifted a foot, and he instinctively dropped the light to see. Ripped socks, a few cuts from the dark streaks. "Haven't run shoeless since I was fourteen."

He shoved his weapon in the back of his belt and snatched her close again, minus the laugh that usually came so easily for him. "Do you have any idea how afraid I was?"

She could imagine. She had been equally afraid of losing him.

Sirens sounded in the distance.

"You called Ty?" she asked, pulling back.

"Yeah, but he was already on his way. Anonymous caller."

Jonah didn't speak his name, but he knew, and if he'd seen Mickey in passing, he probably wouldn't say.

Mickey might have taken off, but he took care of business before he did. He didn't deserve all this. Didn't deserve the years of grief that the Sterlings had heaped upon him and wouldn't let him shed. Then all that Catherine dumped on him.

She heard where the car was long before the blue lights appeared. Car, as in one. Ty.

Their eyes had grown accustomed to the darkness, and the bright light harshly intruded. Ty drove up the one-lane path through the grove and parked where he had the other evening when they'd held their *Jacket* meeting in the treehouse. In jeans, sneakers, and sweatshirt, he ran to his friends.

Jonah pointed to Enzo, like someone had to, and Ty went to give him a quick once-over before returning to Quinn. "You okay?" he asked first, then after she nodded, said, "Are you sure?" He scanned her up, down, peered around to one side.

"Promise. I'm good."

He inhaled. "What the hell have you stirred up now? Your uncle's on the way, so give me your best story and make it quick."

Which she did, concentrated and to the point. He jerked his head up hearing of another body in the house. "*Son of a bitch*, Quinn."

"I didn't kill him." She motioned to Enzo. "That one I did . . . gladly. It was him or me . . . for what seemed forever, through these trees."

Her friends could surely envision that chase, but from their stares, they were envisioning her losing, too.

"We believe Enzo may have killed Daddy," she said.

"Damn! Wait, *we?*" Ty asked, the first to catch the slip. Puzzlement splashed across Jonah's face, then once he got it, he turned serious,

233

looking for explanation. "Where's Mickey?"

"Wait a second," she said.

"Where is he, Quinn?" he said louder.

"He shot nobody and did nothing. Wasn't here, wasn't in the living room."

"Get him here," he countered.

"Ty, I've really got to go!"

Ty's arms went wide. "You and Mickey scatter bodies across the Banks—"

"One body," she said, pushing through the impatience. "This one. And this guy shot the other guy whose name is Chevy. Mickey had nothing to do with any of it, I said."

Ty wasn't happy, the deputy in him trumping the friend. "And there ain't no way you're dumping all this on me to tell your uncle, with me having to explain why I didn't cuff you in the back seat of my cruiser to hold you here."

She patted him on the cheek. "You can handle Uncle. Gotta go see someone."

"Wait," Ty said. "Who else is there? It's three in the morning."

Jonah reached out, his palm running down her dank sleeve. "Stay, Quinn. You almost died going at this guy alone. Please, don't go after anyone else."

The tender worry in his voice filled her heart. A tightness welled inside her, something new about him. Ty was her best friend, but Jonah . . .

Her pulse ran harder at the memory of them on that quilt in Windsor on graduation night, at the power of his anxiousness tonight. She hadn't shed the terror in his eyes when he ran onto the scene. God love him.

She slid from his reach.

But then Ty tried to snag her. "No, Quinn."

Raising her arm to slip loose, she dodged him, too, and then headed toward the woods. "Yes, Ty."

"What do I tell Sheriff Sterling?" he hollered as more sirens howled from the highway.

"You tell him he could've solved this a long time ago," she yelled back, pissed at the reality, hating the words as she said them. She also left, knowing full well her friends respected her and the memory of her daddy too much to keep her from following through with her plan.

Even if they had no idea what that meant.

Jogging toward the manor, she hid as a car parked in the front of the house, another passing by her toward Windsor. She entered through the front door, padded in through the kitchen to the mud room in her ripped socks, then snared boots and keys from the hook, and started to ease back out.

"Quinn," gave her a jolt. Deputy Harrison. "What are you doing? Sheriff told us to not let you leave the scene if we saw you."

In a quick move she put on the boots. "Thought I just saw you on the other side of the county. What are you doing here?"

"Been working nights a lot lately." Then a weak uncertainty crept into his voice. "Did you kill that guy in there?"

"No," she said, zipping up the second boot.

"Then what are you doing?"

"I've been outside in my sock feet, Harrison. Kept stepping on pecan hulls." She stood and shuffled as if adjusting her boots in place. Then she walked past him inside, to the living room, past Chevy lying on the floor as if he were a braided rug.

"You can't go in there," Harrison said.

Quinn made for her desk and retrieved her phone. "Why? It's my house."

Then turning, as if Chevy wasn't sprawled in a puddle of blood already gelling, she stooped and lifted a phone that had skidded against the fireplace mantel. She slipped it in her pocket as if it were hers.

"You're walking all over the crime scene, Quinn."

"I'm being careful," she said, and headed back to the mud room, and subsequently the garage.

"Wait, where are you going?" he said.

"How's your wife, Harrison? Did y'all make up this afternoon?"

He hesitated long enough for her to scamper to her truck. He didn't try hard to stop her. Few other than Ty would.

She took the long drive with lights off. In her rearview mirror, nobody followed, but in short minutes, every deputy in the county would descend upon Sterling Banks.

Past the brick entrance once at the highway, she turned opposite from where she needed to go rather than take a chance on passing her uncle and his crew. She pondered every back road, side road, and shortcut to Charleston.

She needed to confront Catherine, because daylight would give her the chance to either disappear or seek an attorney once she realized Enzo and Chevy hadn't completed their tasks.

Which was why Ty and Jonah couldn't know where she was headed. Both or either would simply follow her and ruin her chance.

Chapter 26

QUINN TURNED HER lights on once she got to the highway, boot pressed harder to the gas. Ordinarily the thick of Charleston took almost an hour to reach, but she'd shave off a quarter, maybe more, her deadline being dawn. She didn't want to meet people up and about, didn't want anyone claiming they saw her, didn't care to explain herself being out when any decent individual would be home in bed. Plus it wouldn't be long before her sheriff uncle came looking for her.

She hit Highway 17 almost due east and let her truck stretch out and run, only a car every mile or so, one eye in her rearview mirror. She didn't have a plan, and the closer she got to the Holy City, the more anxious she grew at not having one.

However, there had been enough blood let over whatever this was, and if Uncle wasn't going to get serious about it, she was.

Catherine was the thread, from then to now. And if Quinn believed Mickey, assuming Mickey believed himself in identifying who killed Graham, Enzo served as another. Then Mickey, who seemed to have been happenstance at the first murder, got swept up in Vic's. She might've thought him involved with Chevy and Enzo to take out her until Enzo shot Chevy with her gun, claiming the scenario similar to the original plan of Mickey killing Quinn. Or vice versa.

So convoluted.

Catherine would be of college age back then. Money enabled folks to take chances, especially those steeped in it since birth, so Quinn didn't put it past Catherine to be that deeply unscrupulous. The big *if* was why so many years passed, and why was Catherine still this passionately driven?

Quinn's speedometer matched the pressure in her chest and the yearning to break open Graham's cold case. She'd never been this close to the potential. At almost ninety, however, she slowed to avoid being the bullet on the road. Plus, she needed time to think. She had no clue what she was about to do other than confront Catherine, ask her to confess, and hold back breaking a blind woman's nose.

Sterling Banks stood front and center in all of this, for sure, but what was so critical for Catherine to kill for it? More wealth? Not likely. Just because she could buy and Quinn wouldn't sell? Could she be that ruthless?

The real estate agent had referenced a male client, if Quinn could trust her.

Quinn also couldn't accept the off chance that Enzo, who was a hired man now, had acted on his own back then. She'd definitely nixed Uncle Larry's summation of Graham dying by random accident by some seasonal hand. She didn't believe a damn thing Uncle claimed anymore. Telling Mickey to disappear was unforgiveable. Him trying to tell her how to manage Sterling Banks when he'd lost his share to stupidity. All her thoughts seemed to dead-end when it came to Larry Sterling having done a damn thing right.

She'd reached the outskirts of West Ashley and slowed more, a fingernail ticking the steering wheel.

The other fly in the ointment was Chevy. Quinn wasn't as shocked to see him break into her house as she was at Enzo killing him, then bragging later that the murder was part of his mission. *Two-faced*, he'd called the driver. However, if Chevy served two masters, then who was the other besides Catherine? And what had Chevy done, or failed to do?

With her henchmen dead, only Catherine held answers. Assuming there wasn't someone bigger and badder than Catherine out there. Maybe the man represented by the real estate agent? Was she attempting to outmaneuver someone?

Speaking of henchmen, who said there weren't more?

Quinn cruised across the Ashley River and wound into metropolitan downtown Charleston. Staff movement created shift change traffic as she passed the Medical University, then farther in, minimal restaurant and hospitality staff personnel went about their pre-dawn tasks, but otherwise, the streets kept a silent vigil awaiting the sun to rise.

She reached the apartment complex, the arm to the parking garage down and nobody guarding the entrance, so she parked on the street. Her clothes still damp from the river, she still could present passably to anyone who didn't look close, smell closer. She finger-raked her overzealous mane back and anchored it in a band before shoving on a ball cap so she didn't look too awry . . . or get identified on a security camera. She glanced in the mirror. Passable for a supplier, she needed a computer notepad to finish the image of fulfilling orders, but having none, she reached behind her seat for a paper version from the pocket.

Eager, almost too eager, she inhaled deeply and fed the meter before striding toward an alley. With space at a premium downtown, back entrances opened to little more than stoops. Nobody stood around the apartment complex's metal back door, but unfortunately it required a keycard. Hoping to follow housekeeping in, she walked a half block toward the public garage, which adjoined a corner for the bus route, but after ten irritating minutes she realized the next bus wouldn't arrive for forty and she returned, passing nary a soul. Early enough for a break-in. Too early to blend in as hired help.

Stepping into an alcove in the alley, she pulled out the foreign phone she'd lifted from her living room floor in the off chance she could access it. She even attempted her own thumb print, and when that wouldn't work, she tried her index finger. The passcode was a full six digits, too. No way to figure that out.

About to slide it back into her side pocket, she jerked at the device lighting up to a text. *How's it going?* typed someone coincidentally labeled CR. The diva was up, and she wanted a status report.

But from which man?

Since both men had sprawled across Quinn's hardwood floor, the device could belong to either. She should've checked Enzo's pockets.

Damn it!

Think, Q, think.

In the dark she couldn't make out details of the flora Charleston flaunted this time of year outside every venue, but the scent of forsythia, azaleas, and the remnants of camellia caught her nose, and she chastised herself for the distraction. Staring in the dark at the grayish flowers, she started over in her thoughts.

Maybe she was thinking too hard.

Resuming her role as just another worker earning her wage, she strode back to the front of the complex, passed the garage, and entered the front door of Vendue Manor as if she'd done so a hundred times before.

Nobody occupied the front desk, but some device must've triggered in the back as a concierge made his appearance. He raised a brow. "Help comes through the back, ma'am."

She reached in the back of her notebook and withdrew a business card, slipping it across the granite top divider. He leaned over and read it, taking in the information before daring to touch. "Private investigator, ma'am?"

Quinn nodded. "Working with Ms. Renault. We've had a breakthrough, along with a mishap actually, and I cannot raise her on her cell. I wouldn't ordinarily come this time of day, or rather, night, but her orders to me are to contact her immediately if this person . . . well, I cannot exactly say. Discretion was promised. Please ring her."

In his navy jacket, white shirt, and tie, he dared lift the card, hold it up, and act like he compared it to the person standing before him. "This is highly irregular."

She leaned over the counter, making him rear back a tad. "Hiring a private investigator is irregular, wouldn't you say?"

Eyes at her, then the card, then back on her, he took a breath. "Very well."

Quinn laid her hand over on his forearm. He stared at it like a homeless junkie had touched him. She gave him his script. "Say, 'Your investigator is here with results. Would you like me to send them up?'"

She could see him replaying the script in his head. "Them," she repeated. "No identity. No gender. No description. You never know who's listening."

Another slow nod. He lifted the phone.

She'd sucked him in.

He performed beautifully. "Yes, ma'am," he replied on the in-house phone. "That's what *they* said." He said the last looking up at Quinn for affirmation, to which she smiled.

He hung up. "Top floor. Turn right. Door's at the end of the hall."

"You're awesome, sir," she said, and made her way to the first of two elevators and entered. Calm. Normal. With Catherine's permission all the way.

A tombed silence greeted her on the heavily carpeted hall as she exited at the penthouse. The carpet was designed to replicate a nineteenth-century, pedigreed south, but when she peered at her reflection in a decorator mirror, it gave her pause.

The stark reality wouldn't let her walk away. This décor, this façade of the old south. All this was history . . . and all this was past. She'd become a shell of that history . . . a Sterling figurehead holding onto genealogy, and had lost track of who Quinn was outside of that name.

This wasn't just about saving Sterling Banks or even the Sterling bloodline. Yes, the Sterlings had dwindled, but she had to remember she still had family, real family, and they would remain in danger if she didn't finish this.

She'd escaped the death that Catherine Renault assumed would come to pass. And she needed to make sure everyone else escaped it as well.

Three yards from the apartment, the door opened. Nero centered himself, all fours like stilts, at attention. Ears up, thank goodness, but a hand reaching from behind the door held his harness. That hand could just as easily let it loose.

His size, breed, and color made him ominous, but he was a guide dog. They didn't attack unless their owner was in danger. Violence was not in their system. No *attack* command in their repertoire. Or not supposed to be.

Nero shifted his weight and the invisible voice said, "Stay." The harness dropped.

For a minute, investigator and canine analyzed each other, the human way stiffer than the dog.

"We can talk in the hall if you like, Catherine," Quinn said, her attention never leaving Nero. She felt sorry for the animal and thought she saw more than duty in his eyes. "I have good news and bad news to deliver, and you may not want the neighbors to hear either one."

"Come" came the command, and Nero disappeared. "You can come inside, too," Catherine said. "Please, close the door behind you, and latching it would be appreciated."

Quinn did a swift pan of the room and the doors and accesses to it. A large apartment. Fourteen hundred square feet give or take a hundred. No rugs, no coffee table. Modern in chrome and lacquer, silvers and grays with splashes of turquoise and rust in floral arrangements and pillows. A huge four-by-six oil painting of St. Michael's Church consumed the living wall. Door to the right led to a bath. Door to the left to one or two bedrooms. The open floor design allowed her to see across the ten-foot granite bar into a chrome kitchen with a walk-in pantry, the dining table clear across the apartment next to a window.

"Close the door, please," Catherine repeated.

Quinn pushed the door slowly and listened for the click. She touched the lock but didn't make it catch.

"The good news is that Enzo killed Chevy," she said. "The bad news is I killed Enzo. Guess we need to talk about that."

Catherine headed toward the kitchen without touching furniture, almost as if fully sighted, and Nero followed stoically with soft footfalls, and without being asked. "Who's Enzo?" she said over her shoulder.

Quinn moved to the end of the long bar, its three wide ornate stools distantly spaced, and watched her hostess pause before the coffee maker. "The man who talked too much before he died," Quinn said, holding her phone beneath the bar to lessen the light. Catherine admitted in Lenore's diner that sometimes she could see shadows, and Quinn wasn't sure what that meant. "The dead man who thought I would be easy. The idiot who underestimated being on someone else's turf. The moron who put your name and number in his phone contacts."

"Hmm," Catherine replied, unrattled, maybe eight feet away. "It's almost five a.m. You want coffee or something stronger? Are you a night owl or an early riser?"

Her phone set to record, Quinn placed it on the bar stool seat beside her. "Coffee."

She couldn't imagine stomaching caffeine right now, but she needed conversation . . . and the game required to keep her people safe. Time to determine where this ordeal was going. Quinn could call her uncle, or even the Charleston PD, and start the ball rolling hauling this bitch away in cuffs, but once uniforms took her and some high-priced attorney took over, information stopped. The Keurig gave a familiar gurgle.

"Enzo came highly recommended," Catherine said, hand atop the machine.

"Well, whatever you paid was apparently too much."

Bad guys talked because they didn't believe their adversary would come out the winner. Catherine was firmly entrenched in the thought she would still win.

Catherine was narcissistic with a deeply rooted sense of entitlement due to her name, power, and money. Bestowed upon her by her father. Quinn could only hope that entitlement made her comfortable saying anything. A Renault could not fail. And a Renault besting a Sterling would only ice her cake.

Trouble was, Quinn wasn't here as a Sterling this time. She was here as a protector. Big difference.

Suddenly she was unable to place the dog. "You realize I have to take you in, right?" she said.

"Not sure how many attorneys Daddy has on retainer these days."

"Speaking of fathers, I gathered that Enzo killed mine."

No emotion, no forecasting, and no response from Catherine. The coffee quit gurgling.

"When you hired him were you aware of his priors?" Quinn asked.

The cool lack of feeling in this conversation was inane in its talk of death, murder, and collusion. Like scriptwriters penning a scene for murderers without the actors involved.

"Did you hire a hit man or were you just throwing scares into people, and the situation got out of hand?"

Still no response.

The lights went out.

Totally, incredibly black.

243

Quinn braced, willing her other senses to ramp up, worried they couldn't fast enough.

She closed her eyes then opened them hoping to see lines and shadows . . . seeing nothing.

She slid silently from the stool, putting her phone in a shirt pocket, the recorder still on.

There were no overheads, lamps, nor nightlight. This was unadulterated darkness without even the temporary, minimal intrusion of street lamps because of the shades drawn on the windows.

A slight miscalculation and a major understatement. A see-in-the-dark dog and a blind girl needed no lights, and without them Quinn stood at their mercy.

Black as soot, Nero's paws would make no noise on carpet letting him move unnoticed. So Quinn moved down the bar and around into the kitchen with its tile floor . . . its walk-in pantry at the end.

Shapes formed around the bigger angles as a minimal level of sight fought to take hold.

She'd heard no new verbal order to Nero.

Catherine wasn't fluffed by Quinn's arrival nor Enzo's failure. Not in the least. A pure sociopath who'd leveled the odds. If Quinn wasn't careful, her adversary, blind though she may be, could kill her.

Seeing Quinn as a dead man walking, Catherine wouldn't envision herself as failing. And Quinn knew too much.

She slid around the end of the bar, willing her ears to listen harder. Catherine's move to terminate her guest would inevitably come as what, a gun? A knife? How adept could she be? Quinn hadn't noted where the light switches were. Who noticed light switches?

Catherine might, however, use one weapon before any other. The dog. Regardless of where he was, he could be sitting like a loaded weapon waiting for a command. Nero would do his job first, if he were trained to attack, so Catherine could do hers.

But was he a weapon?

It was a conflict to train a dog to guide and guard, but Catherine wasn't your normal criminal. And she could buy whatever she wanted.

Quinn had grossly underestimated her opponent.

244

A whistle. The dog moved, his tag giving a jingle.

She reached for the weapon in her waistband, hesitating. Damn it, she didn't want to kill a dog that hadn't chosen his circumstances. He also might react to the pistol.

Catherine spoke a long foreign word from the other side of the bar where Quinn had originally been. Quinn didn't wait to see what the dog did.

She flipped her phone's flashlight on in a direction she hoped mattered. Nero was stealthily parked not three feet from her, but the blinding beam shocked him, his head bowing down then turning to avoid the glare.

He growled a guttural, rumbling snarl.

Bolting left into what she assumed was the pantry, Quinn rammed her hip into a washer, discovering a laundry room instead. With a leap she clamored atop the appliance. Nero caught a piece of her pants, his breath hot, wet, and smelling of kibble. She attempted to shake him off only for him to cinch up, bettering his grasp, and finding meat.

Pain shot into her calf.

In the writhing and kicking, her firearm slipped loose, landing on the metal washer lid with a clang. Quinn grasped for it only for Nero's claws scrabbling for purchase on the washer's rim to slide it off. It clattered to the floor.

He shook, still attached to her pants leg. She used her other leg in attempt to shove him back, recklessly reaching around her for a weapon. Clumsy, she swept a bottle off a shelf to the floor, giving Nero a moment of hesitation. She fumbled for any other item, snared a box, and instead of throwing it at the dog, she flung it across the room. Items—God only knew what in the dark—crashed to the floor, the commotion of metal and plastic near Nero's hind quarters, but he maintained his grip.

Fumbling the wall, Quinn found a small fire extinguisher. She wheeled it around and sprayed, distracting Nero enough for him to let loose and gag.

Quinn leaped over him, toward the door, slamming Nero inside the room.

Pulse frantic, breaths rapid, she peered through the blackness for movement, noting some lines and depth. She reached around, finding the corner of a cabinet, her bearings now correct. She ran her hands along the counter and, thank God, happened upon the Keurig. Yes, she had her bearings. But where was Catherine?

Nero scratched incessantly at the door, his nails mechanically digging into wood, meaning Quinn couldn't hear the subtle movements of her enemy.

Then up next to her chest, her phone rang. Shock took her attention away from scouring her surroundings. Her pulse spiked, she reached in to shut off the device, only to see Catherine's caller ID on her screen.

Quinn didn't register the gunshot until the bullet cut through her arm.

Chapter 27

QUINN COULDN'T exactly place from where the first shot was fired, but she located where by the second. By then she'd gone to the floor, toward the end of the bar, peering into the living room. She hunkered at the boom, but not without noting the flash showing Catherine against the far wall, in front of the St. Michael's painting.

Nero barked and resumed scratching, sometimes thumping his weight against the laundry room door in an earnest attempt to join.

Her firearm in the laundry room, Quinn needed another item to throw. Hopefully before Catherine repositioned.

"Oh, did I wing you by any chance?" Catherine said, clearly seeking where Quinn might be. Had she grunted or winced when struck in the arm? Or was her smell that acute?

Silently she crawled a few feet into the living room. Upon reaching a piece of furniture, she slid a hand up the leg to the flat surface. Fingers snared a large seashell-shaped something. She lifted it soundlessly to bring it to the carpeted floor.

"You didn't fire back, detective. Did you forget to bring your gun to work today?"

Her arm wound hurt like a bitch. Quinn could use the arm, move her fingers, but that was the limit of testing the damage. She made a more conscious effort at silence. She forced slow, deep inhales, enforcing control . . . keeping her location secret.

Nero barked once again, then resumed digging, the sounds different. Like he'd increased in his fervor to break free. Given enough time, that eighty-pound dog possessed the power and concentration to claw through.

Surely someone nearby had to have heard the shots and called the cops. Or at least the front desk.

Quinn's stare still fought to carve through the dark. She couldn't risk Catherine moving first. She eased to her knees, then drew one foot under her. The shell was heavy, painfully heavy, and stretched the muscle in her injured left arm. Her right hand touched the end table for balance.

Quinn shot up and hurled the figurine to the corner of the room. Catherine fired at the noise. Quinn bolted toward the flash.

Catherine whirled but not before Quinn slammed into her, gripping her arm, stopping the gun from aiming at her. It went off again. Deafening. Nero barked at the fight he couldn't get at.

Being against the wall, Quinn thought she had Catherine pinned, but she used the wall as a brace and shoved back, taking them both a few feet into the room. Digging into the carpet, pain shooting through the wounded arm and up her leg, Quinn spun them both back against the painting.

Catherine brought around her gun arm, scrambling to reposition her aim. With both hands on that arm, Quinn fought for control. The diva managed to roll them both back against the wall, doing her damnedest to raise the weapon.

Quinn fought, her worst fear being . . .

Boom.

Quinn felt the jolt, the noise earsplitting. Her knees quivered, nearly giving out.

Still clinging to each other, faces but inches apart, Quinn could swear Catherine's blind eyes widened and looked into her own. Both were frozen, waiting . . . waiting for pain, waiting for nothing to have happened, waiting to tell who won the fight, or whether the bullet missed and the fight wasn't yet over.

For the longest stretch of seconds, they both ceased breathing at all.

Catherine took a gulp of air and crumpled. Quinn went down the wall with her, keeping her from falling forward, letting the gun thump to the carpet before kicking it out of reach.

Even Nero went quiet.

Warmth soaked into Quinn's shirt, the waist area of her pants. She told herself not to panic, that panic heightened blood loss. Just because Catherine went down, nothing said the blood wasn't Quinn's. Shock, adrenaline, denial . . . all could delay the brain's acceptance of injury.

In those ticking seconds, she took stock. She remained strong. Catherine did not.

Catherine hadn't spoken, and Quinn couldn't assess her. She reached in her pocket for the phone, but it had disappeared in the scuffle. No choice, she left Catherine propped against the sofa, a pillow pressed against her midriff at the odd chance it could help, and felt her way along the wall. She found another room before finding a way to slip on that room's lights which illuminated just enough for her to locate the living room's switch.

A table lay toppled where she'd attacked Catherine. No blood spatter. But in rushing back to her opponent's side, Quinn gasped at the immense pool of crimson soaking into the soft gray floor covering. Gray like Catherine's face.

Recognizing no time to waste, Quinn rapidly scoured the room for her phone, finding it beneath the sofa not two feet from where Catherine rested, eyes closed, too weak to move. Quinn pressed fingers to Catherine's neck while attempting to dial 911 one-handed. She misdialed and went to try again but stopped after the nine. She let her phone hand fall against her bloodied khakis.

Catherine was dead.

Staring back at her screen, she saw where her uncle had called eight times since she left the plantation, but his was not the voice she needed. She dialed her friend instead.

"I need you, Ty," she said, pushing down the tremor.

"Are you alright?" he asked, speaking low.

She swallowed, then swallowed again. "She's dead. We grappled over her weapon . . ."

"What happened, Q?"

Quinn told her friend the short version, best she could. The local authorities needed to be notified, and delay only worked against her. "Can you tell Uncle Larry?" she asked.

"Shouldn't you?" he said.

For a change she agreed. A visceral need to connect with a Sterling rose up in her, and he was all she had.

But how many shots had been fired in the apartment? Three? No, four. The dog continued his scratching anew.

Sense kicked in. "Police don't need to come without me having called first, Ty. But can you tell my uncle enough to get him to hightail it over here?" She gave him the address. His badge would get him in the door past the concierge . . . if not by then past the officer guarding those entering the scene.

BY THE TIME Ty and Sheriff Sterling arrived at the apartment, Quinn sat with her good arm cuffed to a dining room chair, a medic treating the gunshot wound above her elbow, having already slit her pants leg to evaluate the dog bite. The large apartment now felt too small to contain the mixed aromas of death.

Forensics hadn't arrived yet, but two medics, a coroner, a detective, and five officers had. Catherine remained in place as notes were taken, photography preserving the scene.

Sheriff Larry Sterling entered and announced to the room, figuring whoever took charge would make themselves known. "That woman belongs to me and my force. What the hell is she doing in cuffs?"

"She killed Catherine Renault," said the plainclothes man, maybe five years old than Quinn. "Until we get this sorted—"

The sheriff interrupted. "Has your chief not called you yet?"

"My captain—"

"The *chief*," Uncle repeated. He pulled out his phone and hit a contact obviously in his frequent dials, watching the detective. "Hey, Martin, this is Larry again. I'm gonna hand the phone to one of your boys in a second, so you can relay what we talked about." He listened. "Yeah, I just want to make sure we're singing from the same sheet of music." He moved off to speak quietly.

He'd given Quinn nary a look since walking in.

Exhaustion weighed her bones. She'd been awake over twenty-four hours, fought two fights for her life, been shot, been bitten, and now treated like a criminal. She'd covered what happened twice thus far, once to the first officer on the scene and second to the detective, and she still considered what they wanted to hear as the abbreviated version. With all these people coming and going with their assigned and specialized tasks, she couldn't dream of making them understand how far back this story stretched. She fully expected to cover events ten times more before the day was through, but she'd give a fortune for a cup of coffee and a patient, intelligent ear who would listen without skepticism to the depth and breadth of this incredulous, six-year tale.

She'd taken the lives of two people in six hours, after a third was murdered in her living room. A pet goat slaughtered, its blood displayed in her house by the man she killed, the same man who had supposedly killed her father. Or so she assumed. *Sure*, they'd say, all dry and disbelieving, *No motive for you there at all.* For all she knew, they'd try to blame Vic Whitmarsh on her, too.

Yet nobody could really say why all these people were focused on Quinn Sterling and Sterling Banks Plantation. A major, major piece of the puzzle was missing with all the culprits too dead to explain.

Though it had thus far gone unsaid, none of this took into account what would surely be Ronald Renault's explosion when he learned his only child was dead. He could spin this any way he liked and buy the headlines and attorneys to support the story.

The forensics were on her side. The politics weren't.

"Your boss wants to talk to you," Uncle said, handing over his phone to the detective, who in turn put his back to the room to take the call in the corner.

"Yes, sir," was all Quinn heard, before Ty slid over another chair and blocked her view.

"They don't know the Craven County side of things, Ty," she said. "And so far they haven't wanted to hear it."

"They will," Ty said, glancing at the medic, keenly aware that anything said would be repeated. "Wish I'd come with you."

"In hindsight maybe, but you and I both know that couldn't happen."

"Debatable," he said and side-eyed a look at the medic. Quinn hushed. Not that she felt like talking anyway.

The detective handed Sheriff Sterling's phone back to him and made a beeline to Quinn, silently releasing the cuffs.

Quinn remained seated, waiting for orders, a choice she might not've so easily made if she weren't so tired.

Her uncle waved at her. "Well, come on, Ms. Sterling."

She rose. The sheriff held out his arm for her to accompany him. She limped over, and once she'd passed her uncle, he gripped the detective's shoulder and made him shake a hand. "Glad to hear we understand each other, young man. You'll soon learn I have three bodies versus this lone one of yours, all related, so it only makes sense to join forces. Now, let's get Ms. Sterling to the station before Mr. Renault brings his hurricane in here. Surely we can agree *that* won't do a damn one of us any good," he said as animal control came in the door.

Chapter 28

A QUARTER TO four in the afternoon, Quinn left the Charleston PD headquarters without her phone, without her firearm, limping between her uncle and Ty, an arm in a sling. She rode behind the cage in the patrol car over to where her truck was parked outside Catherine's apartment building.

Larry Sterling had been all business throughout the day, running interference, bringing in a long-term friend of his as legal counsel, just in case. Charleston needed Craven County's wealth of details about this conjoined mess way more than the other way around, but the potential to charge Quinn remained large. Forensics would be in touch, and there were more interviews to be had.

"We need Mickey," Quinn said as they parked behind her Ford. "He can fill in some of these holes."

Her uncle opened his door to get out to open hers. "I understand you've located him, but let's try not to involve him."

Quinn exited and slammed her door, wincing at the pained effort. "How can we *not* involve him? He's the glue to all of this." She recognized her exhaustion, but also recognized the long-time, irritating habit of the sheriff to dodge anyone connected to the night of Graham's death. "None of this is about you. Don't you dare use this," and she pointed up to the apartments, "to polish your badge. If things hadn't been screwed up with Daddy in the first place, maybe none of this would've happened. Did you think about that?" Her weariness had worn down her patience to tissue-paper thin, but this was kin. He could take it. "Own your mistakes, Uncle Larry. For God's sake, be a man."

"Quinn," shouted Ty over the roof of the vehicle. "He went to bat for you today. Give the man some credit."

Eyes tearing, she replied to her childhood buddy. "Yes, he did. But he is not void of blame, Ty. You and I both know it." Then she just hushed. She couldn't think straight. After thirty-three hours of no sleep, a life-threatening chase through the pecan orchard, and bodies strewn across her path in two counties, she stood on the precipice of losing control. Brushing off an angry tear, she jerked a nod at Ty. Another at her uncle. "It's been a long couple of days."

"Give me your keys," Uncle Larry said, and without argument, she passed them over. "Ty," but he didn't have to finish. Ty watched to make sure the truck started then left for Craven County alone in the sheriff's car.

Quinn would've preferred Ty drove, but she welcomed someone else at the wheel regardless. Thank heaven her uncle had to focus on the road.

She held such mixed feelings about this man. Profound, conflicted feelings that held potential to ban him permanently from her world. She already knew from experience that it took only a couple drinks to make her wish he'd died instead of her father.

She studied the scenery, the boats on the river under the bridge, hunted for a dolphin to arc out of the water below.

Off the peninsula, past the Ashley River, and not until they hit the outskirts of the West Ashley area did Larry Sterling speak. Quinn could've caught some sleep except she sensed this conversation coming, and if it came with rebuke, she'd deliver her own. Untethered, unfettered, and raw, she wouldn't be able to help herself.

Totally his choice how this played out.

"I owe you an apology, Niece," he said, glancing over once to make sure she was awake. She returned his look to assure him she was.

"People have wanted Sterling Banks for as long as I can remember," he started. "Your father was adept at diverting that interest, and for the longest time, parties quit asking. He stood that firm."

She already knew that. Graham Sterling took a stern approach to such inquiries, ensuring those asking left with a solid no and an order not to return. Nobody misunderstood his stance.

While other eighteenth-century families had lost their properties through marriage, agriculture disaster, economic mischance, war, and greed, the Sterlings had stared down fate, not without their share of calamity, but with a bigger purpose in mind. Potential buyers lost interest after hearing that purpose from a Sterling man.

Now the mantel draped heavily on Quinn's shoulders. She'd rather catch a nap than a history lesson, though. "I know, Uncle Larry." *Get to the apology part.*

"Ronald Renault, however, wouldn't take no for an answer," he said.

To that she sat up straight. "Go on."

"The man's wealth gave him a relentless, irritating habit of making offers regardless of what your father said. Renault sent a parade of real estate folk. Savvy ones, stupid ones, and the best Charleston had to offer. They'd appear on the doorstep, find him at Lenore's diner, follow him to church. Even appeared at one of your school events." He glanced over to see if she was still awake.

As much as she hadn't wanted to look at her uncle, she found herself staring now, wondering where he was taking this.

"Your father asked me to intercede. I had to explain to him a TRO wasn't an option."

Quinn appreciated that. A temporary restraining order was designed for danger, threats. Overbearing realtors didn't fall in that category.

Uncle took a long heavy inhale and held it. Quinn caught herself holding one of her own until he released his. She didn't remember the offers getting this bad. "This escalated while I was gone?"

He nodded. "Maybe two months before . . . one evening, your father met with Renault himself and came home believing he'd made his point clear. The next week someone tailed him to Charleston. Then someone approached Jule. As you can guess, that pushed him over the line, so he came to me. I went to Renault, warning him to stay away."

This she'd never heard. She and her father had spoken weekly. "He told me none of this," she said, recalling he'd also not told her of the sabotaged pecan trees, either.

Uncle Larry shook his head. "He wouldn't have told you, Quinn. He was proud of you venturing into the world. He envisioned you retiring to Sterling Banks after your career, not chained to it as you built your life." He blew out on a bittersweet note. "He pulled you off my force and sent you to college. Your mission was to create a world for yourself, then bring all you'd learned home when the time was right." Another humorous snort. "Hopefully, with a family in tow."

"Was that a shot?" she asked. God knew he'd told her to procreate for the cause more than a few times. Not that he hadn't dropped the ball on his end.

"No, ma'am," he said, back to being stern. "Just part of the bigger plan. Don't act so indignant about it either. A simple fact of life, girl."

A tangent she didn't need reminding of. "So, go on, you and Renault . . ."

"I ordered him to lay off. Instead, he offered me a deal if I convinced Graham to sell."

A fire built inside her at this unexpected direction, yet she held her tongue, waiting to see how this played out. Larry Sterling might have three hundred acres, only a tenth of Sterling Banks thanks to his marital misdeeds and divorce, but he held no rights to the business. He might be a Sterling, but he was broke.

"And?" she asked hard. What the hell had he done?

"I asked what kind of deal," he softly said.

She sucked in. "You son of a bitch."

"Your daddy wouldn't even talk to me about it."

"Damn right he wouldn't!"

"I offered Renault my three hundred acres," he said, then added, "Thinking he'd accept and use it as leverage to obtain the remaining twenty-seven hundred."

Mouth agape, she couldn't speak at the audacity of the man.

"Renault wasn't interested," her uncle quickly added. She heard a snag in his speech, but his feelings drew no pity from her today.

"Next thing we know," he said, "Graham's dead and Jule seriously injured."

With clenched teeth she stared at him, never imagining that her scorn for him could slide this easily into hate. They were five miles from the farm entrance, and they rode the rest of the way without words.

At the turn to the gate, Ty waited off to the side.

"Pull over," she ordered.

The sheriff parked behind the patrol car and shut off the engine, the quiet in the cab as thick as mud. He unstrapped his belt and turned to his niece. "Renault swore he had nothing to do with Graham or Jule."

Quinn threw off her belt and met the challenge. "And you believed him? Jesus, Uncle. He killed him hoping you'd inherit and sell. Or make me." Angrily, she shrugged off her disconnected belt, teeth clenched. "What about now? After three deaths? Four counting Catherine? One in my house and two at my hand? The fourth an acquaintance." Tight jawed, she shook her head. "If Renault's appetite was so big then, why not now? Damn you—"

Time her uncle accepted the blistering onslaught.

Her arms shivered, her legs twitching, and as spent as she was, more adrenaline dumped into her system. "His desire and your . . . your . . . whatever the hell you call your participation, spawned so much death." She shouted, "You permanently impacted so many other lives." She counted off fingers. "Jule, Jonah, Mickey Raines." Fingers spread wide, she added, "And me."

Rage peaked, she craved him to grovel, and grovel deep. Nose in-the-dirt despondent type of grovel. "Why did you tell Mickey to leave and pretend he saw nothing? God, the rumors he had to cope with. His poor parents. His career!"

But Larry wasn't the groveling type. "Renault did not send a hit man, girl. With no evidence of who the murderer was, without Mickey clearly seeing the man, I made a choice. Absent proof, I instead pinned Renault to a promise to leave you alone."

No. She wasn't accepting this. It was too pretty an answer.

He saw her disbelief. "Quinn. He let years go by. Do you honestly think he was behind this chaos?" He shook his head. "Sorry, not believing it. His daughter was a piece of shit, and she's the one entwined throughout this mess. Your recording nails her . . . or should."

"They are related!" she yelled. "Can you honestly, a thousand per-cent, state he wasn't behind her?" The red in her neck rose into her cheeks; she felt it. The curse of being a ginger. Her pulse hammered in her ears as her last words reverberated inside the truck.

"Quinn," and he reached over for her, but she recoiled, the pain of her doing so intensely evident in his eyes. "Honey, after that night, I personally went to see Renault. I barged into his office demanding accountability. Told him I'd smear his name to the attorney general and back. State law enforcement, Charleston PD, the papers, everybody. I told him never to set foot in Craven County, much less on Sterling Banks. I couldn't prove this man overstepped his bounds in some sort of scare tactic gone wrong against your father and Jule, which is what I think happened, but I could sure enough make the world think Renault's greed had no bounds."

Quinn's shoulders shivered in fury. It was all she could do to hear the man out, but she had to. This was the secret she'd always felt to her bones existed, but it wasn't the satisfaction she sought.

"I made him promise because of you, girl. Seeing the burden heaped on you, the reluctant princess, so to speak—"

"What about Mickey? Look what you did to that man and his family. You labeled him a pariah instead of claiming responsibility yourself. Instead of letting him say he thought a man meeting Enzo's description did it."

He couldn't look at her.

She couldn't stop staring laser-hot mad at him.

"We still have some hurdles to overcome before we see you clear of this," he said.

Quaking at him, at his news, at the fatigue about to make her collapse, she motioned toward Ty. She no longer wished to talk. She was beyond the forgiveness her uncle seemed to desire. She didn't trust herself not to say something she'd regret, though she couldn't think what that could be.

All she wanted was him out of her sight.

He left the truck. She slid over and took the wheel, one-handedly drove herself home, took a pain pill and a shower, then cried herself to sleep.

Chapter 29

AFTER NIGHTMARES of chases, Quinn opened her eyelids sluggish, attempting to measure the time of day. Seven maybe? She didn't want to move. Not yet. She lay on her back, a position she never preferred, the pain in her arm a reminder why. The full-body ache brought back more reasons, then memories.

She turned her head, pondering the need to get up. On a chintz cushion in a rattan chair Quinn's mother had refurbished, Jonah sat arms propped, head dangling to his left, mouth half open in sleep.

Quinn's heart stirred.

How long had he been there?

She attempted to get up.

Jonah snorted to attention, blinked, then scrambled to his feet. "Quinn. Let me help you. How do you feel?" He assisted her upright then eased down beside her.

"Like a herd of elephants plowed over me," she said, testing neck, shoulders, back, nothing exempt from hurt.

"Let me help you down the stairs," he said.

"Help me pee first," she said, rising, feeling double her age.

His contemplation of that need drew a tired laugh out of her. "I can manage the bathroom. Just give me a sec. All I want is my recliner."

She came out of the bath with robe and slippers on, but Jonah hesitated when she headed to the hall. "Um, your living room might look a little different," he said. "They didn't leave until almost noon yesterday. Mom and I did what we could—"

"Don't care," she said. "As long as there isn't a body."

Regardless of her assurance to Jonah, she crept down the stairs with tentative steps. She took the turn at the landing and, hand on the railing, steeled herself with the expectation of what she remembered from the night before.

The furniture had been rearranged, except the recliner parked where it had always been. The braided rug was missing, blood-soaked, no doubt. One from a spare bedroom had been put in its place. Not exactly the design she would've chosen, but it beat seeing stains in the hardwood floor. The coffee table, fractured when she and Enzo went at each other, no longer there. Everything dusted, polished, and vacuumed. Even her desk had been straightened, its papers having been scattered that night in the melee.

She let him guide her to the recliner, though she had the steam to make it alone. He needed to help. She saw that.

"Where's Jule?" she asked, taking the cup of coffee and goat's milk from him.

He settled on the sofa, at the end closest to her. "She's directing workers today."

"Oh, crap. I'm keeping you from work." She started to inch forward.

He pushed palms down at her. "No, you stay put. It's all taken care of. I asked. Jule agreed. Until you're up and around, I'm here, Quinn."

There he was again . . . the caregiver.

His tenderness touched her, took her back to last night when he'd held her under Windsor differently than he'd held her before. Or maybe it was the first time she'd allowed herself to feel him differently.

"You don't have to tell me about everything if you don't want," Jonah said.

To which she smiled. "Did enough of that yesterday to the police. I'm sure I'll have to repeat the details more than a few times before this tangled heap of trouble is over. Today let's just enjoy sitting here." She turned to the grove. "Let's just relish what we have, Jonah. I'm not into reliving the crap."

"Your wish is my command, Princess."

Which drew a smile from her. Ty used *Q*, and Jonah came up with *Princess* only God knew how long ago.

For a long period they relaxed like an old couple sipping coffee, much as she had imagined her parents doing. She softly sighed at the lushness of that view. So many had walked within these manor walls and across the grounds of the Banks. There was no escaping that history or the sense of obligation, but seated here, where one could take the time to bask in the accomplishments handed over, one could also feel the rich satisfaction of family.

But family was more than legacy. She also had friends and community, and she saw clearly now that family was more than blood. It was what you forged over time, with whomever you loved.

Only she and two uncles remained of the bloodline. One having discarded his legacy. The other having betrayed it. She could name so many others who'd earned a place in her family as much or more than these.

She took another sip of coffee, gaze affixed to the sway of those long leaves on hundred-year-old branches. She heard Jonah's leather cushion give a squeak as he got up for something, but she gave him no mind.

A shadow came from her right, and as she turned, his mouth met hers.

The kiss took her back into the tuft of the chair, full of meaning, full of concern, full of yearning he'd held onto yet held at bay for years.

His hand reached around to the side of her face, and she placed hers over his.

Was this love for him or need for missing affection? Was this loneliness or realization of fate? She didn't know and didn't care at the moment. She needed the kiss. She needed someone who cared.

He pulled back, a hint of pride in his smile at having charmed her. "There, now we can watch the pecan trees," he said, retaking his place, reclaiming his own cup from the end table, and sinking into the sofa's cushion.

She'd give him that satisfaction. Frankly, seeing him happy went a long way in giving her satisfaction. Only time could tell whether this was driven by fear of loss or hope for the future.

In the back of her head, however, came the words she'd heard from Catherine. From her uncle. Without heirs, Sterling Banks had no future.

TWO WEEKS PASSED. Quinn's arm ached but the leg healed quickly. There'd be a scar.

Charleston newspapers savored every step of a favored son's grief, Renault's daughter dying from a gunshot deemed accidental. At least Quinn breathed easy over that.

The part about two rich spoiled women going at each other stung. Some online media bashed them both.

She'd relived that night to the point some sentences came rote to her when interviewed. Mickey came out of hiding and offered what he could offer about Graham's death, but when he admitted to being asked to kill a Sterling for a Renault, social media went wild. Catherine's attempt at colluding to obtain the plantation was absorbed by the media and construed as fact, particularly with Vic's records confirming same. His murder served as a period on the end.

Painfully, Quinn had to accept Vic died by an unknown hand. Most likely Enzo or Chevy, but they'd never know. The mysterious other guy with a cowboy hat on the motel video had tried to mimic Mickey, but in hindsight, walked differently and carried more heft on his bones.

They were ninety percent sure the fire was ordered by Catherine, but Jackson Hole's surveillance caught no clear image of the saboteur. Not Enzo or Chevy, though. Smaller guy.

While some hardliners in the law enforcement mix attempted to unravel facts, in search of felonious intentions on either side, Sheriff Sterling proved correct in the ultimate results. There wasn't enough evidence.

The only living souls with firsthand accountings were Quinn, Mickey, and dear old Uncle himself.

All the others were dead.

Except Ronald Renault who couldn't say much without the risk of incriminating himself.

Finally, dressed in heels to push her past six feet tall, and a fresh pants suit from an upscale King Street shop, Quinn tucked a loose tress of hair behind an ear and accompanied Uncle Larry through a marble lobby into Ronald Renault's brokerage office on Charleston's infamous Broad Street. Uncle wore his best uniform complete with all the appropriate accoutrement. They left the attorneys behind, instead carrying flowers for effect.

This was a one-on-one scenario, private, and they had graciously suggested the meet on Renault's turf as a generous first attempt at a cooperative gesture. Plus, Quinn wasn't letting that son of a bitch set foot on Sterling Banks.

A clerk took the flowers, and with it being ten a.m., an assistant dressed so sharp she could cut glass with a glance, delivered a coffee service with some kind of almond-orange cookies, with a promise to produce hot tea if one was so inclined. She poured and left. The three sat silently until the click of the door closing—she and Larry on a navy leather sofa and Renault in a matching arm chair. They'd agreed on no recordings and no other ears.

Two families accustomed to respect for what they and theirs had accomplished out of life.

"I'm sorry about Catherine," Quinn said, feeling the reach-out more appropriate from her, the one who'd seen her die . . . and had a hand in it.

Renault wasn't a big man in stature, but his dress, his manicure, his fitness and manner presented as a stanchion of power. "You didn't have to kill her," he said, but he said it controlled and direct, the emotion locked in some mental compartment he couldn't afford to open.

"She attempted to kill me, sir. I don't have to rehash the details." Quinn hesitated. "Or play the recording."

He cleared his throat. "No, you don't."

She had to try again. "My uncle explained to me how badly you once wanted Sterling Banks. I presume the real estate agent who approached me recently was yours?"

Renault didn't deny.

"When I refused to entertain an offer by her anonymous client, I coaxed enough to learn he was male, well-established in Charleston, and a member of the yacht club. She wasn't as good as she thought she was."

"Yes, I had someone test the water," he admitted. "Not that it matters."

"Actually, it does matter, sir. I believe that's what forced Catherine to take harsher action. She wanted to best you."

The tension escalated, felt in the air. Larry Sterling stepped in. "We offered to meet in hope we could all negotiate some sense of closure."

"Was she involved with you six years ago?" Quinn asked, the option incredulous but not yet discounted.

He shook his head. "God no. She was twenty-four years old."

"Was Chevy working for you or Catherine?"

"He was assigned to my daughter, but loyal to me."

Thus the two-faced remark by Enzo. "That loyalty cost him his life," she said. "The plan was for Chevy and me to kill each other in an event orchestrated by Enzo, at Catherine's behest. A similar effort she'd planned for Mickey Raines to do but he refused."

Again, Renault shook his head. "I knew nothing of any of that."

Not that he didn't believe his daughter would do such things, but that he was oblivious to plans in play. That said a lot.

"We're sort of taking off on tangents, people." Larry cleared his throat. "The goal was—"

The leather squeaked softly as Renault leaned to the front of his chair. He clearly held no interest in the sheriff. "Ms. Sterling, Catherine only wanted to impress me. Your property was my white whale. I work hard and I might bend rules, but I am no killer, my dear, thus the reason I came to the agreement with your uncle. I believe Catherine wanted to hand me the only deal I never could land. That's all this was, Ms. Sterling. A daughter trying to prove herself to her father. Surely you can understand that."

This was lunacy. Sure, she could understand wanting to impress a father, but Quinn went into law enforcement to make her own mark in the world without seducing innocent kids or hiring hit men.

However, Renault's pact with her uncle had proven the catalyst for the daughter. He'd promised not to go after Quinn and not pursue Sterling Banks any longer in order to save his reputation over a mistaken murder. Renault deserved some layer of blame. So did Larry Sterling. She wasn't making excuses for either of them, and forgiveness was nowhere in sight. Sadly, she'd already decided this meeting was for naught.

She yearned to tell the man his daughter was nothing short of a sociopath, but what was the point. He felt guilty enough about his hand in this history. Or rather, he should, unless he was completely blind to what made Catherine tick. And his attitude told Quinn that no way he'd allow his parenting to be doubted.

Yeah, that apple hadn't fallen too far from the tree.

"Mr. Renault," and she hesitated, yearning for the final say. Points had to be made. New ground rules established.

"Thanks to Graham Sterling's murder, I'm the last heir . . . of the oldest family . . . of the oldest county in the state of South Carolina. To some degree because of your hand. I have been reminded of it often and by many, to include your daughter. I'm sorry for your loss. I'll forever regret mine. Can we end on that note?"

She could see it in his expression. He couldn't. His mind sought to achieve the last word, the last point, the most important thought to have his own last say.

"I will never forgive you, Ms. Sterling."

She was caught off guard but only a second. "Nor I you, Mr. Renault."

"I had no intention for any of this to happen," he said.

"And neither did I," she replied.

If asked, there was one thing on which they could agree. This horrible, twisted course of consequences held no chance for closure.

Quinn would not be surprised if they crossed paths again.

Chapter 30

BACK AT THE MANOR, Quinn shed the suit, the formality, and the intensity of the morning and donned her jeans. A spring gust of weather had whirled through the farm causing trees to shed an overabundance of old limbs. She could think of nothing she'd love more than to clean the grounds.

Alongside three others, she worked until her injured arm almost went numb then offered to drive the truck carting the branches. She inched along, perfectly happy in doing nothing but something for her trees, but the more minutes she clocked, the more her mind wandered away.

It would be a long while before this period in her life took a back seat to enough other things to be a minor thought, or at least forgotten for days at a time. Like a scar, one day it would only be there when she thought to look at it. Or so she hoped.

Quinn would never believe that Ronald Renault wouldn't one day go right back to plans to acquire the title of Sterling Banks, if for no reason other than to avenge his daughter's death. He was a man accustomed to delivering the last word, and hadn't.

But he had to know Quinn would rebuff his efforts. If she were so inclined to dark thoughts, she'd halfway expect a bounty on her head. At a minimum, she'd watch her back and maintain watch on her enemy, maybe pay for her own PI to keep watch periodically, because Renault wouldn't die easy without having bested the Sterling name.

That could mean years.

She still held reservations about her uncle. He'd rallied to her defense in the end, but in a not so tiny way he'd been a part of

Graham Sterling's demise . . . and concealed his involvement from her. How was she to completely forgive that?

A horn sounded behind her. Peering at her side mirror, she spotted Jonah in another Sterling Banks pickup.

She let him come to her, and he hopped up on the running board. "How'd it go this morning in Charleston?"

She shook her head. "Agreed to disagree I guess is about the best way to describe it." The details were unnecessary. Jonah worried way more than the average person, so the less said the better.

He brushed some dirt and bark crumbles off her sleeve. "We're not going to have a problem from Renault are we?"

"I doubt it," she replied, purely for his peace of mind. She'd remain alert.

She heard less noise going in her truck bed, and via the side mirrors spotted smirks from the workers, their attention on Jonah hovering closer than usual to the boss.

She'd accepted Jonah's offer for a date a week ago. It had gone surprisingly well, so they agreed to another. Nothing overnight. But the farm workers seemed to read in their body language that something had changed between them.

Jonah didn't seem to mind. "So we're a hundred percent back in the pecan business, huh? We can use all the hands we can get, including yours." He tapped a finger lightly on her injured arm. "Once you're back up to par."

"You," and she tapped him back, "are supposed to ensure the pecan business always stays a hundred percent in business."

"Yes, ma'am." He started to hop down then pulled back up. "Oh, Jule says she made fried chicken tonight for you."

The fourth time in twice as many days that Jule had finagled Quinn over to the house, and Quinn couldn't say no to the woman. Jule clearly felt safer, her past better put to bed. Quinn enjoyed Jonah's company, always had, and even with this hint of a new level in their relationship, she wasn't deterred. He was coming out with his feelings while holding them in low gear. No demands. What wasn't to like?

"Heard from Samantha yet?" she asked.

"The dog place?"

"What other Samantha is there?" she said, picking at him.

While Quinn wrangled detectives and attorneys, Jonah had rescued Nero from Charleston Animal Control. With Catherine gone, Renault wanted nothing to do with the dog, and Quinn felt to blame for the animal being tossed aside.

He was a beautiful beast, trained as a guide dog, not for attack, but with Quinn having presented to him as an enemy in his owner's apartment, she was told she was not the best home for him. She paid to have him tested and put through his paces. Reprogrammed, so to speak, if needed. Fathom K9, a training facility on Edisto Island, offered to take him and determine where he'd be best placed, with mention of a police department since they had well-trained handlers.

Still, Quinn was saddened by the decision. She'd envisioned herself with a trusted buddy at her side, riding in her pickup, and running through the grove while she worked. Maybe swimming in the river. Plus, the manor got awfully cavernous and lonesome some days.

Jonah must've read her. "He'll be all right, Princess. Samantha said not to worry." He looked back, toward his truck. "Be right back."

He disappeared.

Why Quinn worried so much about a dog, she didn't know. She ought to be more concerned about Jonah's increasing use of that horrendous nickname for her. Better than her old worries, though. Her father could rest easier now. So could she.

Jonah seemed relieved, too. He'd spoken more than a couple times about her being more focused on the pecan enterprise, and nothing would make him happier than for her never to be distracted again with her PI work. However, nothing would deter her from the occasional, intriguing, gumshoe case. Investigations were a part of her being. She'd proven that to Graham Sterling pretty damn well, she thought, and Uncle wouldn't underestimate her quite so easily anymore.

She looked in her mirror to see what called his attention and saw him leaning in the passenger side of his cab. "Quinn?" he called. "Can you come here for a minute?"

She shut off the engine and slid out, wondering what was so important to warrant looking inside his truck. About the time she reached the front grill, he stood . . . his arms full of a fat, somewhat fearful bundle of belly and ears.

Her heart fluttered a bit. It might have even melted. She took the pup from his arms without asking. "Oh, Jonah, he's adorable." She hadn't even looked to see if it was a he or a she. She didn't care.

"He's male," he said, running a hand over the black-faced muzzle, back over his floppy ears. "A black-mouthed cur."

"Aww," she said, bringing the pup up to her face, nuzzling. "Don't pick on him yet."

He laughed. "No, that's his breed. Not easy to find, but I wanted something protective and loyal that would fit in to a farm. He'll attach tight to you, Quinn, if you train him right. Samantha said just let her know when you're ready to start learning."

As if already sensing he belonged, the pup hunkered in Quinn's arms, but not before slathering her face with two quick kisses. She laughed. "What's his name?"

"You get to pick it," he said.

Quinn shifted the baby and reached out to Jonah, pulling him in for a quick kiss of her own. This man . . .

"I think Bogie works," she said. "Not quite as pretentious as, say, Sterling."

With a chuckle, Jonah ran a hand down its back again. "Bogie Sterling. Sounds like some Humphry Bogart detective mystery."

She took in a small, pretending gasp. "Why, yes, it does, doesn't it?" Then smiled.

The End

Acknowledgements

Thanks first and foremost to hubby. Gary asks almost daily, "You need to write?" or "Do you have a chapter you want to read to me?" When I accepted the writing profession, he accepted his assumed role as taskmaster, or as he named himself, my uncompensated, executive, personal assistant.

Thanks to the community of Chapin, South Carolina who have unofficially dubbed me "Chapin's Author." Somehow, during COVID, when all of us were confined to smaller circles, my Chapin circle grew tremendously stronger. That especially includes Jerry Caldwell and his staff at The Coffee Shelf, who touts my books front and center to all the coffee aficionados they serve.

Thanks to Karen Carter and The Edisto Bookstore. During COVID she lost her staff but exploded in sales. Bless her, she's been tested this year, but has risen from the viral ashes successful. She is my mainstay on Edisto, and a staunch supporter I could not do without.

Thanks to SC's Talking Book Services for grooming me these last five years on how to be an audiobook narrator. Through them I've come to appreciate the audiobook in terms of serving the needs of those who cannot read a traditional book, which in turn encouraged me to branch out into audiobooks of my own.

Thanks to my core groups of readers who are so incredibly sweet to me. Some tell me that they feel they know me, and that we are friends. Of course we are friends. As intimately as we've shared stories over the years, how can we not be?

Finally, thanks to my publisher, editor, and partner in all things caregiving. Debra Dixon has shown me that a publisher indeed can have a heart . . . a big one.

About the Author

C. HOPE CLARK has a fascination with the mystery genre and is author of the Carolina Slade Mystery Series as well as the Edisto Island Series, both set in her home state of South Carolina. In her previous federal life, she performed administrative investigations and married the agent she met on a bribery investigation. She enjoys nothing more than editing her books on the back porch with him, overlooking the lake, with bourbons in hand. She can be found either on the banks of Lake Murray or Edisto Beach with one or two dachshunds in her lap. Hope is also editor of the award-winning FundsforWriters.com

C. Hope Clark

Website: chopeclark.com

Twitter: twitter.com/hopeclark

Facebook: facebook.com/chopeclark

Goodreads: goodreads.com/hopeclark

Bookbub: bookbub.com/authors/c-hope-clark

Editor, FundsforWriters: fundsforwriters.com